Crossing the ... ...ng
mount beside Abby's wagon.

"Think you can handle the team, or would you like me to help?"

Abby gave him what she hoped was a haughty look. "I think I can handle my own team."

He touched the rim of his cap and swallowed the smile that threatened. "That's fine, m'am. Just remember I'm right here beside you if you need me."

She had no chance to respond. The mules stepped into the water and the wagon jolted along behind them. As the wheels hit a submerged rock, she was nearly yanked from the seat.

"Hold 'em steady," Rourke shouted above the sound of rushing water.

She drew back on the reins and felt her muscles protest. Several times the wagon pitched and tilted, but she managed to keep the mules from spooking. Then the wheel hit a boulder. Abby pitched sideways and landed with a splash in the water. Rourke jumped down and waded through the water until he came to her. Slipping under the water, she came up coughing and spitting like a wildcat.

Rourke pulled her upright, and hauled her firmly into his arms. His arms held her gently, but she could feel the strength in them.

Feelings she'd never known overpowered her. Through her clothes her skin was hot where he was touching her . . .

Books by Ruth Ryan Langan

Destiny's Daughter
Nevada Nights
Passage West
September's Dream

Published by POCKET BOOKS

Passage West

RUTH RYAN LANGAN

POCKET BOOKS

New York   London   Toronto   Sydney   Tokyo

To the Ryan and Langan families.
Adventurers, dreamers, tinkerers, and builders.
Saints and sinners. Survivors.

Another *Original* publication of POCKET BOOKS

POCKET BOOKS, a division of Simon & Schuster Inc.
1230 Avenue of the Americas, New York, N.Y. 10020

ISBN: 0-671-63980-3

First Pocket Books printing July 1988

10 9 8 7 6 5 4 3 2 1

POCKET and colophon are trademarks of Simon & Schuster Inc.

Printed in the U.S.A.

Author's Note

After thoroughly researching the routes taken across country to California, through scholarly works as well as diaries and personal journals, I came to admire the courage of those who chose this perilous journey. What drove them? Ambition, greed, hunger, despair. And for some, a sense of adventure, an overwhelming desire to reach new horizons.

What really opened up the West was a terrible war that divided a nation and drove men and women to seek a better future.

I grew to love the Market women, and the men who enriched their lives. And when their story finally ended, I was sorry. We had traveled a long road together, and it had become a wonderful adventure. I hope their story touches you in a special way.

Chapter One

Independence, Missouri—1865

THE SETTING SUN had long ago bled into the foothills of the Ozarks. Riding through the muddy streets, he saw them: the drifters, the displaced families, uprooted from their farms and plantations, looking toward the west for another chance, a brighter future. Some looked ravaged, numb with shock from the War Between the States. Others appeared grief-stricken. Still others were angry, striking out blindly at anyone, anything. Almost all of them looked tired.

The saddle-weary man pushed through the swinging doors of the saloon. He paused a moment just inside to allow his gaze to travel slowly over the occupants. No one seemed to take any notice of the tall stranger. His boots were caked with red clay and his shirt bore the sweat of more than thirty miles under a relentless sun. Satisfied that he knew no one, he moved to a corner table and sat with his back to the wall. When the serving girl appeared, he ordered a bottle of whiskey and a plate of stew.

While he ate he watched the participants of a poker game, seeing their greedy eyes shift to the pile of chips in the middle of the table. To the left of the dealer a man with a patch over one eye kept stroking the gun at his waist.

1

"Evening, stranger. Want some company?" The saloon girl sidled over and offered to ease the new-comer's loneliness.

For a moment she nearly distracted him. Then he saw the man's hand grasp the gun butt, saw the flash of light reflecting off silver, and he reacted without thought.

Before the one-eyed man could fire, the gun was shot from his hand. He twisted to face the one who had foiled his plans, his face contorted in pain and rage. His single eye blinked furiously.

Someone from across the room flashed a deputy badge and hauled the wounded gambler from the saloon. The others at the table hurriedly pocketed their winnings and edged toward the bar.

One man, leaning heavily on a cane, limped over and paused beside the corner table. Already, he noted, the gun had been returned to its holster. The man who had fired it went on calmly eating his meal.

"Quick thinking." The voice was strong, with a slight Scottish burr. "I like that in a man. Got a job?"

The gunman paused in his eating, shook his head, and set down his fork.

"Got a wagon train ready to head out to California. Could use a good man."

"Doing what?" The voice was a low growl.

"What you just did here. Keeping trouble away from my train."

The man seated at the table continued looking at him without speaking.

The one with the cane shrugged. "If you're interested, come see me tomorrow noon. Behind Tremaine's Stable." Without another word, he hobbled away.

Behind him, the younger man watched until the swinging doors blocked his view, then picked up his fork and finished his meal. That done, he drained the bottle of whiskey.

* * *

The rider approaching the wagon train was young —no more than his mid-twenties. But his eyes were world-weary. Shaggy black hair in need of a trim and a day's stubble added to his craggy appearance.

As he dismounted, half a dozen pairs of eyes watched him. He had a way of moving, quick, catlike. And a way of looking a man in the eye, studying, taking his measure. He said little, but when he spoke, the others listened.

"Name's Rourke." He shook the dust from a battered Union cap before replacing it. His voice was low, with the tone of one accustomed to having his simplest order obeyed without question.

"This is the fella I told you about," the man with the cane explained to the others. "Welcome, Rourke. Name's Stump. Mordecai Stump." He offered his hand and felt it engulfed in a powerful grip. Nodding toward the men standing in a semicircle, he introduced them. "Brand's my scout."

The scout was as thin as a sapling. His hair, coal black, hung below his shoulders. His eyes were a pale blue; his mouth soft like a woman's. There was some Indian in him, Rourke figured. But not much.

"Parker's the cook. This is his first crossing," Mordecai added.

Rourke nodded toward the balding man whose stomach protruded so far over his belt, his feet had to be a mystery to him.

"Thompson here is my right hand. An order from him is an order from me."

Rourke offered his hand to the tall, gray-haired man with the bearing of a general. Both Stump and Thompson wore buckskins tucked into tall boots.

"Know how to use that thing?" Thompson asked, pointing to the gun at Rourke's waist.

"When I have to."

Not one to brag, Mordecai noted. He liked that in a man and smiled beneath his bristling mustache. He already knew Rourke could handle it just fine.

3

"This is Reverend Coulter," Mordecai said, indicating a hunched man, no more than thirty, with sad, hound-dog eyes. "Six families from his church here in St. Louis have decided to join us on the trek west."

"Reverend." Rourke touched his hand to his cap.

"And this is James Market. He and his family just joined us today. That makes eight wagons plus the chow wagon."

Rourke glanced at the square-jawed man who studied him with open curiosity. More than a little gray glinted in thick, sandy hair. His midsection had gone to paunch, but his arms rippled with muscles. His ruddy countenance was peppered with freckles.

"Farmer?"

James Market gave a curt nod. There was nothing friendly in his look.

Rourke's gaze scanned the circle of activity. "That all the wagons you're taking? Eight?"

"We have four more joining us tonight. We should be on the trail by midmorning."

"Where's his gear?" James Market asked, nodding toward Rourke.

"He has all he needs right there." Mordecai indicated the gun and gave a sly smile.

"You don't know anything about this Rourke." Market was aware of cool gray eyes appraising him as he spoke. They were so cold, so calculating, he felt a shiver of fear along his spine despite the heat. "How can you trust our lives to a man whose only recommendation is that he reacted quickly in a saloon brawl?"

Stump cut the man off with a look. "There is one thing you'd better learn right now, Mr. Market. This is my wagon train. I make the rules. If you dinna' like them, you're free to leave. But if you decide to stay, I willna' tolerate any challenge to my leadership. Do you understand?"

The man's face reddened beneath the freckles. Without another word, he turned and stormed away.

Mordecai watched him with a frown before he returned to the business at hand. "Pay's no better than the army. Twenty dollars a month and all you can eat."

Rourke nodded, apparently satisfied.

Watery blue eyes crinkled into a smile. "Welcome, Rourke. Anytime you get tired of sleeping under the stars, you're free to sleep in the cook wagon."

The newly hired gunman swung into the saddle. "I'll be here in the morning." Wheeling his mount, he headed back toward the saloon.

Behind him, Mordecai Stump watched in silence. There was something about Rourke. He was no hothead, but last night he'd used his gun instinctively. Yet he was slow to anger. When James Market had questioned his ability just now, Rourke hadn't even said a word in his own defense.

As Rourke's horse crested the hill and disappeared from view, Mordecai's eyes narrowed. He'd just hired a loner, who wouldn't mix well with the people on the train. Probably a man with a past he'd just as soon keep secret. But that didn't matter. What did matter was whether or not he would be around when trouble struck. Mordecai was a gambling man. He was betting Rourke would.

Scowling, James Market returned to his wagon, still smarting from the dressing down he'd been given by the wagon master in front of the others. It grated to have to take orders from someone else. But, he reminded himself, it wouldn't be for long. When he reached California, he'd be master of his own fate. He was sick and tired of life beating him down. He'd had enough of a land that took and never gave back. How many years had he hitched a mule and leaned his shoulder into a plow, only to encounter rocks and trees and barren soil? Barren. He thought of his wife, dead of childbirth, carrying his only son who was stillborn. And of the women who cluttered his life.

His dreamy spinster sister, Violet, who lived in a world of pretty pictures and useless songs. She couldn't even cook a man a decent meal.

Carrie. His scowl deepened. A silly, frivolous girl who didn't have a brain in her head. Fifteen, and still listening to her aunt's fairy tales about pretty dresses with matching bonnets and tea in the afternoon.

Then there was Abby. His hand curled into a fist at his side. At seventeen she could already work circles around the other two. Man's work, mostly. She could sit a horse better'n most men. Inside of a day she'd learned to handle the new mule team and wagon. Her meals were fair; not as good as Margaret's had been, but she kept them from starving. But she was ornery and obstinate, and getting harder to handle every day. He saw the look that came into her eyes whenever he confronted her. She tried to hide the anger that simmered just below the surface. She reminded him so much of . . . One of these days he'd have to take a whip to her. He pounded his fist into his palm. By God, if she challenged his authority, he'd do just that. He was the ordained head of his house. And none of them had better ever forget it.

The object of his angry thoughts came into view as he rounded the side of the wagon. She was small and slender, no taller than a ten-year-old boy, with a tiny waist and narrow hips. Since they'd left the farm, she'd taken to wearing a pair of his pants. Her only good dress was saved for Sundays and special occasions. The buttons on her faded shirt strained across softly rounded breasts. She'd tucked her hair up under a wide-brimmed felt hat. Moist tendrils stuck to her forehead and the back of her neck. Stirring something in a pot over the fire, she lifted the wooden spoon, tasted, wrinkled her nose, then added water. It hissed and sizzled, sending up a spray of steam.

"You burned it, didn't you? That rabbit I caught this morning?"

Her head jerked up at his angry accusation, then

she turned away quickly. "It isn't burned. Just a little tough. Needs to simmer longer."

"Then why didn't you start it sooner? A man could starve waiting for his meals around here." He picked up the jug, brought it to his lips, and drank deeply. When he corked the bottle, she could still smell the liquor on the breeze.

"I was tending to the animals and helping Aunt Vi mend the lid on her chest."

"Damned chest," he hissed. "She doesn't need all those ribbons and lace. They're just an extra burden."

Abby lowered her voice, hoping her aunt hadn't heard. She couldn't bear to see the older woman's feelings hurt. "It doesn't take up much room, Pa. And it makes Aunt Vi happy."

He caught her arm, twisting her to face him. "It's obvious her love of those frills hasn't rubbed off on you. Look at you. More boy than woman."

Plain. Abby had heard it all her life. Her mother had been a rare beauty, with hair the color of cornsilk and eyes bluer than a summer sky. Carrie had inherited Margaret's hair and eyes. Even at the tender age of fifteen, her figure had already blossomed into lush curves.

Aunt Vi was like a little China doll, with milky skin and pale, silvery hair. Her voice suited her, so soft it sounded almost like singing. Each day she insisted on wearing a clean gown and bonnet with matching ribbons. She'd never learned a woman's chores, could barely cook and sew. But she was the most cheerful woman Abby had ever known. It would be impossible for Violet Market to say an unkind word about another. Her dreamy smile would brighten anyone's day.

Abby glanced down at her free hand, rough and callused from her labors. Self-consciously she ran it along the slim, boyish figure. She wished she hadn't been born a girl. Life would have been so much simpler if she had been her father's son. Angrily she touched a hand to her hat. She had inherited her father's hair: thick, unruly, the color of carrots. Unbound, it would fall nearly to her waist. Her pale skin had been burned by the sun, despite her constant use of a hat. Her cheeks were tanned to a rich bronze. Thankfully, the Market freckles dotted only her shoulders.

Her nostrils flared as she yanked her arm free. Rubbing the tender spot, she said softly, "I do the best I can, Pa."

"Starting tomorrow, you'll have to do better. I'll need to hunt our food and keep the wagon in repair. If you can't handle the rest of it, you'll just have to teach that lazy sister and useless aunt of yours how to help."

"They do help." She stared at a spot on the ground to hide the anger she felt at his cruel words.

He gave a snort of derision and pushed past her. "The two of them together couldn't do the work of a two-year-old."

When he disappeared inside the wagon, she crouched beside the fire and listlessly stirred the contents of the pot. Carrie was young and scared. In the past month she'd lost her mama, her home, her whole world as she knew it. And Aunt Vi had always lived in a dreamy, happy place in her mind. She was more suited to a parlor, with an organ to play, and jam and tea for lunch. This trek across the west would probably kill her.

Hearing her father's angry voice from inside the wagon, Abby stood wearily. Her aunt and sister counted on her to stand up to James Market whenever his temper rose. As she had so often, Abby wondered just how strong she really was. She hoped she'd never have to be tested.

Chapter Two

Just before dawn ghostly ribbons of mist hovered between ground and trees, silvering the leaves of a clump of poplars. Lanterns bobbed inside wagons as families rolled from their blankets and prepared for the first day of a journey that would take them across the plains, over the Rocky Mountains, and into the untamed west. In the cool morning air, horses blew and sidestepped in their anticipation. Harnesses jingled as men murmured and swore and hitched teams of mules and oxen. Inside the wagons, babies cried, and children giggled, while women scurried about making certain everything was secure.

While they worked, the men argued good-naturedly.

"Oxen make the best team for this kind of journey."

"Mules," another called, hitching the obstinate beasts.

"Oxen. Three to five years old. They're compact. Not too heavy."

"Mules are faster. And if your wagon falls apart, you can pack out on a mule. I'd like to see you try that with an ox."

"If my family is starving, I can eat my oxen."

"Believe me. If I'm starving, I'll even eat a mule."

The arguments were never-ending.

Just outside the circle of light Rourke sat astride his horse watching the flurry of preparations. He felt oddly distanced from these people. This was their train, the business of crossing this vast land theirs. Whatever problems they encountered were their own. The pain and suffering they had yet to endure were no business of his. He had pain enough of his own.

His gaze slowly encompassed the circle of light. The other four wagons had arrived just after dark, bringing the total to twelve as Mordecai had promised.

At the sound of a whip cracking, Rourke turned toward a wagon to his left. He recognized the stocky man. The Market wagon. A mule kicked frantically.

"Goddammit, hold him still or I'll turn this whip on you." James Market's angry voice lifted above the morning sounds.

Rourke watched the small, slender figure struggle with the nervous team while James Market untangled the harness and approached the first mule. It backed away from him and the man swore again.

"So help me, this is your last chance. Hold that animal still until I get him in the harness."

The diminutive silhouette fought the kicking mule. Rourke saw the thin arms tremble under the animal's tremendous strength and felt a surge of pity for the boy. Market wasn't only impatient, he was unreasonable.

When the mule tossed his head in fear, the halter was ripped from the small hand struggling to hold it. Swearing viciously, James Market raised his whip.

With a muttered oath, Rourke began to swing from the saddle. No man, not even the lad's father, had the right to use a whip in that manner.

A firm hand on his shoulder caused Rourke to spin around. Beside him, Mordecai Stump sat astride a chestnut mare.

"Not thinking of meddling, are you, Rourke?" His voice was as soft as the morning mist.

Rourke's body actually flinched as he heard the first crack of the whip. Mordecai could feel the coiled tension in the muscled shoulder beneath his hand.

Rourke's eyes narrowed. "And what if I am?"

"I wouldna'. In my years, I've found it best to let families solve their own problems. You step between those two, you'll have them both scratching at your eyes."

"You'd stand by and let a man whip his own kin?"

Mordecai shrugged and removed his hand from Rourke's shoulder. In his anger, his Scottish burr was even thicker. "I've na use for a man who would do such a thing. But life has a way of evening the score."

"Maybe." Rourke glanced at the Market wagon. His fist clenched and unclenched in impotent fury.

The two men stared at each other for long silent minutes. Mordecai heard the man beside him suck air into his lungs. Slowly Rourke unclenched his fist and clamped his fingers around the horn of the saddle. Almost as if, the Scotsman thought, he was clamping the lid on his own emotions.

As Mordecai's horse moved away through the lifting shadows, Rourke wondered what would have happened if the old man hadn't stopped him. He might have ended up killing Market in front of his kid's eyes. Stump was right. Better to stay out of it. It wasn't his fight.

Gradually the mule settled down, and the team was hitched to the wagon. All the while he worked, James Market unloaded a stream of oaths on the slight figure who worked closely beside him. When they were finished, Market began lashing the last of their belongings to the wagon floor. The youth hurried to the stream with two buckets nearly as big as he was.

Pulling a cigar from his pocket, Rourke bit the end and struck a match. Puffing lightly, he emitted a stream of smoke, blew out the match, and slid from the saddle. He wasn't going to meddle, he promised himself. He was just going to satisfy his curiosity.

As he made his way toward the stream, he glanced at the sky. It was so light now he could make out the faces of the people around him.

The figure was kneeling at the edge of the stream, dipping the first bucket into the icy water. From the back, Rourke could see where the whip had split the shirt neatly open from the top of the shoulder to a spot where it was tucked into the waistband of faded britches. A narrow ribbon of blood trickled, leaving the shirt clinging in sticky red patches.

"Need some help, boy?"

A head swiveled. Two eyes rounded in surprise. Leaning against the trunk of a tree was a tall stranger, with a stream of smoke swirling above his head. His hair was dark and shaggy, curling over the collar of his shirt. His shoulders were broad; the muscles of his arms visible beneath the sleeves of his shirt. He had one booted foot crossed over the other in a careless pose. But there was nothing careless or relaxed about this man. A gun and holster rested against a muscular thigh. Dressed all in black, he looked like the devil himself. The handsomest devil Abby had ever seen. Without blinking, he met her gaze. It was his eyes that held her. Gray, almost silver in the morning mist, they were fixed on her with the most piercing look she'd ever seen.

"Thanks. I can manage."

Rourke nearly swallowed his cigar. The voice was low and husky, but definitely feminine.

The slender figure leaned over, filling the second bucket. Rourke studied the softly rounded hips. When both oaken buckets were brimming, she stood and tugged until she had lifted both to the grass. She turned. Rourke's gaze studied the boyish figure in a man's oversized pants and shirt. She was slim, but had the soft contours of a woman.

He grinned, feeling at once foolish and awkward. "I guess you aren't James Market's son."

She didn't return the smile.

He saw the tremendous effort it cost her to lift both buckets. As she moved past him, head high, arms straining, he saw her eyes. Green. Green as the meadows of his home.

She never paused; never looked back. He watched her until she disappeared behind the wagons.

Tossing the cigar aside, he strode back to his horse. Damn James Market, he thought. And damn his arrogant woman.

A scorching sun burned off the last of the mist and beat mercilessly on man and beast. Dust from the churning wagon wheels swirled in little eddies, rising up to choke the driver of the next wagon. From the front of the train it was impossible to see through the dust cloud to the last wagon in the line.

Aunt Vi had dipped a white lace handkerchief in water and handed it to Abby to tie over her nose and mouth. Still, sand clogged her throat and burned her eyes. Pulling the brim of her hat lower on her forehead, she gritted her teeth and urged the mules on when they fought the reins. Her arms ached from the long hours of driving the wagon. Her cramped muscles protested every rut and hole along the well-worn trail.

In the back of the wagon, Aunt Vi and Carrie lay upon their blankets, holding similarly dampened handkerchiefs to their faces and gagging on the heat and dust. Every other woman and child on the train was out walking beside their wagons. Only these two rode.

"How can Abby stand it?" Carrie moaned.

"I don't know, child. It's been hours since we stopped. She has the endurance of a mule."

"Like Pa."

The older woman leaned up on one elbow. "Don't say that. She isn't like your father."

"Is too," Carrie pouted. "They're two of a kind. All they know is work, work, work. And once they make up their minds, there's no stopping them. How could Abby allow Pa to sell everything we own and head west?"

"Your sister had no choice." Violet dipped her handkerchief into a bucket of water and wrung it out carefully before wiping her forehead. "Your father's running, Carrie. Running from the pain of a dead wife and baby; running from the backbreaking labor of a farm that never yielded anything but failed crops and sickly cattle."

Violet lay back, ready to expound on one of her favorite theories.

"Maybe everyone in this train is running—from a land devastated by war; from shattered dreams. And everyone is expecting to build a better life." She sighed. "But if they bring along all the old hatred, all their cherished prejudices, they'll find themselves with the same old life in a new place."

"What about us, Aunt Vi? What's going to happen to us in the west?"

"I've heard the land is rich and verdant, and the weather quite hospitable."

"And the Indians?" Carrie chuckled at her aunt's sudden grimace. "Maybe I'll marry an Indian chief and live like a princess."

"Don't even think such things, child. I've heard horrible tales about how the Indians treat their captives."

Carrie tossed back her golden curls and noted the soiled smudges on her once-white muslin gown. With a sideways glance, she asked, "Are Indians one of your cherished prejudices, Aunt Vi?"

The older woman's eyes opened wide as she contemplated her niece for long silent moments. Nodding slowly, she said, "Out of the mouths of babes . . . "

"What does that mean?"

Violet touched her handkerchief to her flushed cheek. "It means that I will have to give the matter some thought." In a brighter tone, she added, "We must make dinner tonight for your father and Abby. The poor thing will be too exhausted to cook when we make camp."

"I can bake biscuits," Carrie said, feeling a sudden wave of sympathy for her older sister. What must it be like to sit on that hard seat all day beneath the searing sun and handle an unruly team?

"And I'll make a stew with the last of that venison," Vi said, rummaging through the sack that held dried vegetables.

It was nearly dusk, and Mordecai knew the travelers were exhausted. When the first wagon reached the banks of the swollen river, he decided to get the train across before making camp for the night. That way, the morning could begin with ease. Signaling Thompson, he waited by the water's edge.

"Where's Rourke?" he called as his partner approached.

Thompson pointed to a horse and rider high on a ridge.

"Bring him down," Mordecai ordered. "He can help get the wagons across."

"Maybe we ought to wait until morning to cross."

The old man shook his head. "They may as well learn the rules of the trail. When there's a river to cross, we do it before dark. Besides, I don't like the looks of that weather. I'd like to cross before we get more rain. The water's already deep enough to be a problem."

"These drivers are pretty green," Thompson reminded him.

"I know. And tired. But the sooner we cross this river the better."

Thompson wheeled his horse and urged him into a

gallop toward the far ridge. Half an hour later, Rourke and Thompson joined Mordecai at the river.

Several wagons were halted at the edge, their occupants staring in fright at the rushing water.

There were big, cumbersome Conestoga wagons, their white canvas bleached by the sun. Many of the families had outfitted farm wagons for the trip. They were easier to haul and repair. Several of Reverend Coulter's families had painted their wagon boxes blue, the wheels red, and stretched white canvas over the bent hickory bows. On this, their first day, they looked like a festive parade.

"I'll cross first with the cook wagon," the old Scot said. "Thompson, you tie a lead rope to each team and tow it across to the other side. Parker and I will tie it to that tree over there, so the horses and wagons can't be swept downstream." He jabbed a finger in the air. "Rourke, I want you to ride alongside each wagon as it crosses. If the driver panics, you'll have to take over."

The men nodded at his terse instructions. Climbing from his horse, Mordecai took the reins from his cook and urged the team into the swirling water. While more wagons eased toward the riverbank to watch, the old man firmly guided his team toward the center of the stream. Water reached clear to the floor of the wagon, but the horses never paused or stumbled. With a crack of the whip, the horses strained, making straight toward the opposite bank.

A cheer went up from the crowd as the wagon creaked slowly up the steep embankment and came to rest in the tall grass.

As soon as the cook wagon was clear, Thompson tied a lead rope to the next wagon. While the driver whipped and cursed his team, Rourke rode alongside, offering encouragement. One of the mules stumbled and the wagon tilted dangerously. While the onlookers gasped, the wagon tipped further and flopped onto its side in the water. Children screamed and cried.

Boxes and bundles fell loose and floated downstream. The mules twisted in their harnesses, brayed frantically and churned the water, trying to right themselves.

From her vantage point, Abby watched the scene with a mixture of horror and fascination. They were going to die. That entire family. Swept away in the current. And the same thing would happen to her family when they were forced to cross. She could swim, at least well enough to save her own life. But she couldn't simply save herself and allow her sister and aunt to drown. But if she tried to save them, they would all be lost. Panic-stricken, she looked around for her father. He had left hours ago to search for game, and hadn't returned. As usual, it was going to be up to her to take care of all of them. Silently she watched as Rourke and the others righted the wagon and calmed the terrified team. The children were plucked from the water and handed to their parents. Household goods were retrieved and tossed into a soggy heap. While the family clung to the back of the wagon, Rourke climbed onto the broad seat and took the reins. A few minutes later the wagon emerged on the opposite bank. Its occupants and their worldly goods were thoroughly soaked. But safe.

When Rourke returned for the next crossing, the crowd along the shore was deathly silent. Searching their faces, Rourke could taste their fear. No one would volunteer now. They would have to be bullied.

Spotting Abby, he shouted, "You there. The Market wagon. You're next."

While Thompson tied a rope to the team and took it across the swollen creek, Rourke slowed his dripping mount beside the wagon.

"Think you can handle the team, or would you like me to help?"

She gave him what she hoped was a haughty look. "I can handle my own team."

He touched the rim of his cap and swallowed the smile that threatened. Despite the terror in her eyes,

17

she held herself erect, her hands gripping the reins so tightly he could see the whites of her knuckles.

"That's fine, ma'am. Just remember I'm right here beside you if you need me."

She had no chance to respond. The mules stepped into the water and the wagon jolted along behind them. As the wheels hit a submerged rock, Abby was nearly yanked from the seat. Bracing her feet against the boards, she used every ounce of her strength to tighten the slack reins and keep the mules from bolting.

"Hold 'em steady," Rourke shouted above the sound of rushing water.

She drew back on the reins and felt her muscles protest. The animals nervously tossed their heads, pitting their strength against hers.

"Carrie. Aunt Vi. Get up here and help me," she called frantically.

Two heads poked out beneath the canvas.

"Hurry. I need you," Abby shrieked.

As the two terrified women scrambled to take a seat, she thrust a piece of slippery leather into their hands. "Pull back," she ordered. "Hold tightly, or they're going to run. If they do, we'll tip and lose everything."

While Violet and Carrie held tightly to the right rein, Abby pulled the other, keeping the team on a slow, plodding pace. Several times the wagon pitched and tilted, but they managed to keep the mules from spooking.

Beside them, Rourke marveled at the girl's nerves. He was certain she'd never handled a team before. And especially a frightened team crossing a swollen creek. But she never lost her composure. The worst of the crossing was behind them.

As the team scrambled up the steep bank, Abby gave a triumphant laugh. "We did it. Carrie, Aunt Vi, we did it."

Just then the wheel hit a boulder and the wagon

tipped precariously. Losing her balance, Abby pitched sideways and landed with a splash in the water. In an instant, Rourke leaped from his mount to the wagon seat and grasped the reins from the startled women. When the wagon came to a halt on the bank, he jumped down and waded through the water until he came to a sputtering, gasping Abby.

Her hat had fallen off and floated downstream. Her hair, which she always kept piled up under the hat, now streamed down around her face and shoulders, the ends floating about her on the water. She started to stand, but a wave caught her, knocking her off her feet. Slipping under the water, she came up coughing and spitting like a wildcat.

Catching her hand, Rourke pulled her upright. The weight of the water dragged her clothes downward, plastering them against her figure like a second skin. He felt a moment of surprise at the stunningly beautiful woman facing him: hair the color of fire, falling nearly to her waist; a body that, though slim, was round and soft in all the right places. And those eyes. So green they put the sea of prairie grass to shame.

Another wave engulfed her and she was once more swept down. This time he dragged her upright and hauled her firmly into his arms. Instantly he felt the jolt, and a fist seemed to tighten deep inside him.

With the water threatening to swamp her, she was forced to cling to his waist. His arms held her as gently as if she were a child. But she could feel the strength in them.

Feelings she'd never known nearly overpowered her. Through her clothes her skin was hot where he was touching her. She found it hard to breathe, as if a heavy weight was pressing on her chest. Despite the cold water, her blood heated and she felt her cheeks redden.

"Are you all right, ma'am?"

Embarrassed at her reaction to this man, she quickly covered up her confusion. "I'd be a whole lot better if you'd have come to my rescue right away instead of waiting until I swallowed half the creek."

She pushed herself roughly from his arms and staggered through the water toward the bank. Rourke followed, enjoying the sight of her slender hips swaying as she struggled against the waves.

"If I'd helped you first, your wagon would be floating downstream right now," he said to her back.

She stiffened at the deep voice that did strange things to her nerves.

Struggling up the steep bank, she sank down in the grass, too weary to move. Shielding her eyes, she stared up at him standing above her with his hands on his hips.

"I suppose you expect me to thank you."

"No, ma'am. I was just doing my job. And I don't expect thanks for that, especially from you."

She flinched. Why did this man bring out the worst in her? Forcing herself to stand, she tipped her head back to see his face. Wiping her hand on her dripping pants, she grudgingly held it out to him.

"Forgive my manners, Mr. . . ."

"Rourke."

She swallowed as he took her hand in his. Forcing herself to sound formal, she said, "Thank you, Mr. Rourke. For saving our wagon and my sister and aunt."

"You're welcome, Mrs. Market."

"It's Miss. Abby," she corrected, wishing suddenly that she had a beautiful name. "Abigail Market."

Rourke didn't know why her words should make him so happy. It certainly wasn't the fact that she wasn't Market's wife. "Abigail." The smile was back in his voice. Market's daughter. For long moments he continued holding her hand. So small. So callused.

Feeling suddenly self-conscious, she pulled her hand away and strode toward the wagon.

"Better learn to handle that team quick, Miss Abby

20

Market. You've got a lot of rivers to cross before you reach California."

Her chin lifted defiantly. "Don't worry about me, Mr. Rourke. I can take care of myself."

Behind her, Rourke watched the way she stiffened her spine. Even with water dripping from her ill-fitting, boyish clothes, she carried herself with dignity. While she managed to infuriate him, he felt a grudging admiration for her. Yes, he thought, slapping the sodden hat on his head and swinging into the saddle, from the looks of things, Miss Abby Market could damn well take care of herself.

Chapter Three

IT WAS LONG past dusk before all the wagons crossed the creek and formed a circle for the night. When James Market returned with a sack of game, he found Abby huddled under a blanket while Aunt Vi and Carrie prepared dinner.

"Well, Miss High-and-Mighty, is it nap time?"

Vi cast a gentle look at her sleeping niece. "Leave her be, James. She's put in a hard day."

"And I haven't?" He tossed down a sack and picked up the jug, taking a long pull before corking it. Jabbing a finger at the lumpy sack, he snarled, "That's enough food for two or three days, if you don't get greedy. I scoured miles of this countryside hunting game to fill your lazy stomachs." He swung away, muttering oaths.

"Where are you going?" Vi paused in her stirring.

"To wash in the creek. My dinner had better be ready when I get back, woman. And you," he roared at Abby, who sat up, grinding the heels of her hands over her eyes, "had better see to the team and our horses. They have to be rubbed down and fed before you even think about resting."

Violet watched his retreating back, then wiped the

22

back of her hand across her brow. "He'll be nicer after he gets some food in him."

"Huh." Carrie bit back the hateful things she was thinking and cast an anxious glance at her older sister, who was already climbing wearily from her resting place.

"Come on, Carrie," Abby said. "I'll show you how to tend the team. There may be plenty of nights I won't be able to do everything."

"Can't," the younger girl mumbled, running a finger through a pan of dough. "I promised Aunt Vi I'd help her make dinner."

"Put those over the fire and help your sister," Violet said gently. "I'll watch your biscuits."

Reluctantly Carrie did as she was told. Even back on the farm, tending the animals had been the one chore she hated. Abby had a way with animals. They seemed to listen to her as she cooed and murmured, letting them eat from her hand. Carrie had been more comfortable around her mother and the household chores. From her mother she'd learned to sew and do handwork. Carrie could take a piece of plain cloth and turn it into a work of art, with shirring, embroidery, or smocking. Glancing at her sister as she carried buckets of water and pitched hay into a trough, Carrie thought how beautiful Abby would look in an emerald-green gown with satin roses and velvet bows.

"Doesn't it bother you to dress like a man, Abby?" she asked softly.

Abby turned and tousled her sister's hair. "Why should it? You're the pretty one, Carrie. I'll leave the fancy dresses and lace shawls for you to wear. You're going to break men's hearts, you know. You're as beautiful as Ma was."

Carrie's eyes rounded. It wasn't often the two sisters had time for girl talk. "Don't you know anything, Abby?"

"Know?" Abby pitched the last forkful of hay and rubbed a hand along the mare's velvet nose. Turning, she saw the look of surprise on her little sister's face. "Know what?"

"Abby. You're beautiful." Carrie flushed in embarrassment. She'd never said this before. She'd never thought it necessary. "Haven't you ever looked at yourself? It's true, you don't look like Ma. But with your hair, and skin, and those eyes . . . " She giggled at the look that came into Abby's eyes. "Lord Almighty. You really don't know, do you?"

"If Pa hears you swear, he'll box your ears."

"Pa," Carrie said with venom. "You match him swear word for swear word every time the two of you fight. Pa treats you worse than dirt, and you take it. Someday . . . "

When she stopped, Abby touched her shoulder affectionately. "Someday?"

"I'll be big enough to stand up to Pa the way you do."

"I don't stand up to him," Abby protested softly.

"You know you do. You're the only one who does." Her voice trembled with feeling. "Someday I'll make him do all his own dirty work." She took a deep breath. "And you and I and Aunt Vi will act like la-de-da ladies."

The two girls shared a laugh before returning to the wagon.

With the team taken care of, Abby crawled under the blanket, too tired to change her clothes.

Carrie lifted a pan from the fire and handed her a steaming biscuit. "Try these, Abby. Tell me if they're as good as yours."

Abby was too tired to care, but hoping to reassure the girl, she bit into a biscuit nearly as hard as the boulders they'd encountered in the stream. Forcing herself to swallow, she said, "They're fine, Carrie. Next time, use a little more lard."

"Will Pa eat them?" the girl asked nervously.

"Pa will eat anything after another swig of that whiskey." Abby's lids flickered, then closed.

"Poor thing," Vi muttered, glancing at the huddled form of the young woman. "She's done more than a body should ever have to."

"She ought to eat something. If she isn't careful, I'll soon look like her big sister."

The older woman shook her head and touched a finger to her lips to silence her young niece. "What she needs more than anything is sleep. She can eat later."

Under a canopy of stars Rourke tossed in his bedroll, his body bathed in sweat. In his mind he saw them again. Bodies. The fields and meadows littered. Forests, rivers, swamps, all teeming with the dead. His own body tensed, then relaxed. In his dream, he was heading home. Away from the battlefields. The thought of rolling meadows, of rich farmland, drove him relentlessly. He made the journey again in his mind, as he had so often, searching for familiar landmarks now missing. Nearer he came, and nearer still. There. The familiar town, only different. Something wrong. Very wrong. Home. At last, home. Katherine. Katherine.

"Katherine?"

He awoke, trembling, and sat bolt upright, his hand clutching his gun. The images vanished. The fear and loathing were replaced by a gnawing emptiness. Glancing at the moon, he felt a surge of disappointment. He hadn't made it through the night. There would be hours of darkness to endure before another day. He wiped a hand across his brow. The darkness would be gone soon. Soon. He clung to that thought. Morning would be here shortly, and with it the light that would sweep away the dark shadows from his mind for another day.

Keeping the blanket wrapped around him, he leaned his back against the wagon wheel and struck a match to a cigar.

During the day he could stay busy and keep the thoughts and images from his mind, holding the demons at bay. But at night . . . He blew out a stream of smoke and wearily leaned his head back, feeling the cool air dry the sheen that covered his skin. At night the demons struck, denying him sleep, opening all the wounds.

In the distance a night bird cried, reminding him of a baby's cry. His heart contracted. Stubbing out the cigar, he draped the blanket over his arm and strode naked toward the creek. Once there, he washed and dried himself quickly. The clothes he had earlier washed and spread out on low-lying bushes were completely dry. He dressed, then sat in the tall grass to pull on his boots, wishing he'd brought along his cigar. There would be at least another hour before dawn.

A rustling in the grass nearby caused him to grab for his gun and freeze.

Abby awoke on the hard ground, enveloped in the foul-smelling damp blanket. The fire had died to embers. The rest of her family had retired to the back of the wagon.

Sitting up, she glanced down at the soggy clothes she still wore, then stretched her cramped muscles. Every part of her body ached.

Pulling off her moldy boots, she wiggled her toes, then stood stiffly. Walking to the back of the wagon, she rummaged around for her night shift and a cake of her aunt's bayberry soap. Draping the white muslin gown over her arm, she made her way to the edge of the creek.

The storm that had threatened earlier had blown over, leaving the earth parched, the water calm. A full moon bathed the creek in a pale amber glow. It was that hushed, quiet time between darkness and dawn, when the whole world seemed to hold its breath. Even the occasional chirp of a cricket was muted.

She unbuttoned the scratchy shirt and dropped it in a heap at her feet. Slipping off the oversized britches, she kicked them aside, then untied the ribbons of her white chemise.

Hidden in the tall grass, Rourke was spellbound by the vision who was so close he could reach out and touch her. When she first approached, he expected her to walk past his place of concealment. By the time he realized what she was about to do, it was too late to make her aware of his presence.

Mesmerized, he watched as she removed her clothes. His throat went dry as she stood before him, clad only in a chemise of soft cotton lawn, which barely covered her from torso to hips.

If he had any decency, he told himself sternly, he would stand up now, before this went any further, and walk away. But a woman like Abby Market would be humiliated to be caught undressing. This had already gone too far to stop. The damage was done. He had to stay concealed, for her sake as well as his own.

If he were a saint, he thought, he would avert his gaze and allow her the privacy she sought. He watched as the white chemise dropped to the ground. His breath caught in his throat and he swallowed back the hiss of air that nearly escaped his lips at the sight of her. Though her arms and face had been bronzed by the sun, the rest of her skin was as pale and luminous as the white pebbles that lay at the bottom of a pool, bleached by the rays of a relentless sun. Her legs were long and shapely; her narrow hips softly curved. Her waist was so tiny he was certain his hands could easily span it. Her breasts were small, rounded, and perfectly formed. She lifted her face to the moon. He studied the white column of throat, and found himself wondering what it would be like to press his lips there and feel her pulse throb. Her hair spilled down her back in a tangle of soft waves and he longed to plunge his hands into it and feel its texture.

His hand tightened at his side. He was no saint. There was no way he could turn away from the sight of her. And he hadn't a shred of decency, he admitted. He was glad he was concealed here in the shadows.

She picked up the soap and dipped a toe into the cool water. In the moonlight he saw her draw her foot back for a moment. Then with a laugh, she walked boldly into the swollen creek and dipped below the water. Shaking her head, she splashed and frolicked like a puppy, kicking her feet, then rolling to her back, floating soundless for long silent minutes.

A cloud covered the moon and Rourke cursed the darkness. He strained, seeing only her darkened form, silhouetted against the blackened water. Then the cloud lifted, and he sucked in his breath as she stood in the shallows and began lathering her hair. The scent of bayberry drifted to him, and he inhaled the wonderful fragrance. When her hair was covered with soap, she dipped beneath the water, shaking her hair until she could no longer hold her breath. She came up sputtering and shook her head, sending the fiery mane dancing out before settling down around her like a cloud.

She extended one delicate arm and lathered it, then the other. Moving the soap along her throat, she sighed before stroking it across one breast, then the other, and then across the soft white flesh of her stomach. When she struggled to lather her back, Rourke had to force himself not to go to her and offer his assistance. A smile of pure appreciation lit his features. Then he saw it. The thin dark scar left by her father's whip. His smile fled. He felt a cold, hard fury settle in the pit of his stomach. He hated the man. Loathed him. He could kill him for what he did to her. For as long as that line marred her young flesh, he would hate the man who put it there.

Sitting in the shallow water, she lifted first one leg, then the other, while she lathered and soaped. Reaching for the pile of clothes, she washed them, wrung them out, and tossed them into the grass. Then she turned and settled once more into the water for a final swim.

Following a ribbon of moonlight across the water, Abby glided noiselessly along, feeling a sense of freedom, of exhilaration she rarely enjoyed. She was alone in the universe. In this weightless environment, her muscles no longer ached. The dust and grime that had clogged her throat and burned her eyes along the trail were now forgotten. Her father's vicious temper couldn't reach her here. She wouldn't think about yesterday, and the beautiful mother she missed and the farm that had been her security. There would be no tomorrow, with its torturous trail and endless work and uncertain future. There was only this peace, this tranquillity, this gently flowing water. If she could, she would stay here forever. She glanced at the sky. Already the darkness was growing lighter on the horizon. Dawn would be here soon, and with it reality.

With strong strokes, she swam to shore and pulled herself up the bank. She shivered in the morning air and dried herself quickly, then slipped her white muslin night shift over her head. Slim and straight, it fell nearly to her ankles. Running her mother's tortoiseshell comb through the wet tangles, she tossed her head and her hair settled like a silken veil across her shoulders and down her back. Bending, she picked up her wet clothes and draped them over her arm. Then she turned and gave a last lingering look at the river.

The light of the full moon cast an ethereal glow on the figure on the bank. Her pale gown became opaque, revealing every curve and line of the body beneath it. Rourke came to his knees, wishing he could go to her, touch her. It would be enough. Just to touch her, to feel the warmth of her milky flesh. In that simple white gown she seemed to belong to another world. Clean. Untouched by the terrible war that had devastated this land. Untouched by all the greed and hatred and bitterness. An angel. One touch from her and he would be cleansed.

He clenched his fists tightly and watched as she picked her way through the grass. As she passed, the wonderful scent of bayberry wafted over him.

He waited, willing himself not to move. What he had glimpsed tonight was a special gift. One he would carry with him on the long, tormented nights. But if she were to discover his presence, the vision would be forever shattered. And so he waited, shivering in the morning mist, until he thought she was gone.

The gun he'd continued to hold at his side slipped from his sweating palm and fell to the ground. Startled, Abby turned toward the sound. Under his breath, Rourke swore, then stiffened as she parted the tall grass and stared at him in shock.

"You!"

He saw the stunned look on her face that slowly turned to realization, then anger. "Miss Market, it isn't what you think."

"You scum. You vile, evil monster!" Bearing down on him with her arms filled with wet clothing, she began to beat him about the head and chest.

Rourke was helpless to defend himself against this raging little whirlwind of fury. He couldn't hit a woman, and it was impossible to stop her blows without pinning her to the ground. Backing up to evade her, he stumbled. Instantly she pounced on him, dropping her clothes and pummeling him with her fists.

"You watched me. Without making a sound, you hid yourself here and watched me. You horrible animal. You watched me undress and bathe. You concealed yourself here in the grass to spy on me."

Standing, he caught her fists, easily pinning her. His voice was low and angry. "You've got it all wrong. I came here to retrieve my clothes. You came up on me too suddenly. I had no choice."

"No choice." In her anger, a tear threatened, and she dropped her head to hide it from his view. "A gentleman would have made himself known to me so that I could have fled before"—she hiccuped and swallowed back the sob—"I removed my clothes."

"Miss Market . . . "

"You disgust me, Mr. Rourke. You're lower than a snake." With a shove, she pushed him backward.

Poised on the bank of the river, Rourke struggled to keep his balance. For a moment he seemed to hang suspended, then, unable to stop the momentum, dropped backward into the river. He came up sputtering and swearing.

With her hands on her hips, Abby surveyed the scene with a smirk of satisfaction. "Serves you right, Mr. Rourke. The next time, maybe you'll remember to allow a lady her privacy."

Scooping up her damp clothes, she flounced away without giving him another glance.

Standing in waist-deep water, Rourke let out a string of oaths and watched until her figure disappeared into the darkness. Cursing his luck, he strode from the water and removed his dripping pants. Viciously wringing the water from them, he draped them over his arm. Tomorrow's ride would be twice as uncomfortable in wet clothes. But he had no choice now. Damn the woman. He glanced toward the wagon train through narrowed eyes. What a firebrand. He'd never expected such a temper from that little woman. The same woman who'd allowed her father to whip her. Abby Market was a contradiction. How many other surprises, he wondered, was she keeping hidden?

When the thin, pale light began to streak the sky, he pulled on his boots, retrieved his gun, and made his way back to the train. As he passed the Market wagon, he heard the soft whispers of even breathing. By now she was probably sound asleep. He smelled the faintest scent of bayberry and was stunned by the emotions it evoked. He didn't want to feel anything for Abby Market. Anything except dislike.

Parker was already up and stoking the fire for coffee. Without a word, Rourke rolled his blanket and climbed into the back of the cook wagon. Troubled, he leaned against the canvas and fingered a piece of tattered fabric. The sight of Abby Market's creamy body had brought a rush of desire that left him stunned. In itself, that wasn't so surprising. It had been a long time since he'd held a woman's soft body and lost himself in the delights of the flesh. What disturbed him was the feeling that she was special, different from all the others on this train. She was just a woman, he told himself. No more, no less. And a damned ornery one at that. But what had happened tonight was definitely going to be a problem for him. From now on, whenever he saw her dressed in that shabby man's outfit, he would be able to recall the body underneath.

Dangerous thoughts, he cautioned himself. Next thing, he'd be worrying about her. Hadn't she told him she could take care of herself? Why then did he have this almost overpowering desire to protect her? And why this unreasonable dislike for her father?

There was no room in his life for such feelings. Love, tenderness, concern for others. All were dead. Dead and buried. Buried with those simple pine boxes in a lush green meadow.

Chapter Four

ROURKE AVOIDED THE Market wagon. Each time he saw the slender driver, head bent against the sun, he thought of the scene by the river and felt his blood heat.

If Abby was aware of him, the only indication she gave was a slight lifting of her chin. Even in her father's cast-off clothing, with the scent of horses and sweat clinging to her, she bore herself with regal disdain.

From her perch on the wagon's bone-jarring seat, Abby saw the twisting Oregon Trail like strands of a rope. Leaving Independence, they paralleled the Santa Fe Trail until a simple wooden sign read ROAD TO OREGON. Just west of the Big Blue River the strands of several trails came together into the Platte Valley. Everyone in the wagon train was eager to cross the Platte River, where they would stop for two days to take on supplies at Fort Kearny.

When they were within sight of the river, Abby let the reins go slack in her hands. Ahead of her, shimmering in the afternoon sun, was a body of water two or three miles wide. Though the waters seemed tranquil enough, she felt her throat go dry. How would she ever hold the team on a firm, steady pace for such a great distance?

At the river's edge, the wagons stopped, waiting for direction from Mordecai Stump. As the older man approached on horseback, balancing his cane across the saddle, he called, "Afternoon, Miss Abby. Where's your father?"

"He said he was going hunting with Flint Barrows."

Mordecai frowned. Hunting, was it? More like crawling into the shade of a big rock and draining their jug while the others did their share of the work. He had no use for James Market, but he felt sorry for his three women. If it weren't for this tenacious little creature, they wouldn't have survived the first hundred miles. And as for Flint Barrows . . . Mordecai's frown deepened. He could always smell a trouble-maker, and Barrows reeked of it.

"Will we be crossing soon?" Abby asked, breaking through the older man's reverie.

"Aye. As soon as we round up everyone."

"Look at her," Thompson said, riding up and pointing to the river. "Damned mud flat's too thick to drink, too thin to plow." He squinted through the white glare of the sun.

Seeing Abby's look of concern, Mordecai sought to calm her. "I'm sorry, Miss Abby. It's just the usual lament of a tired man. Dunna' worry about the size of the Platte. Though there are strong currents in places, and pockets of quicksand, the river is only knee deep."

Instead of feeling reassured, she felt the panic tighten her throat. "Quicksand?"

"It is easy enough to spot, if you know what to look for. I'll cross first and find a safe passage. Once done, the other wagons will follow close together. As long as no one strays from the route I lay out, we'll have no problems."

As he and Thompson rode away, she pushed her hat back on her head and passed a hand over her forehead. No problems. Just strong river currents and quicksand. And her father nowhere in sight.

While drivers climbed down from their wagons to stretch stiff muscles, and family members drew together to watch from the shore, Mordecai and Parker began to cross the river in the chow wagon. With her hand shielding the sun from her eyes, Abby watched as the wagon slowly eased across the vast stretch of water.

"The water is quite shallow, it seems," Aunt Vi said, coming up beside her.

"Yes."

"It should prove a simple matter to get across."

"Guess so." There was no sense mentioning her fears to this gentle woman.

"Then I'll let Carrie sleep through it. All that bouncing and jostling gave her a headache."

Abby turned, about to remind Violet that a better way to cure Carrie's headache might be to find her a few chores. Noting her aunt's spotless yellow gown, she felt a smile tug at the corners of her lips. "You look just like a pretty little buttercup, Aunt Vi."

The older woman touched a hand to her throat in a disconcerted gesture Abby had come to recognize. "Why, what a sweet thing to say. Why don't you take some refreshment while we wait to cross?"

Abby nodded. Her throat was parched. Her stomach growled for food.

"Go wash up, child. I'll have something ready in a minute."

While the older woman started a small fire and placed a kettle over the flame, Abby filled a basin with water and scrubbed the dust and grime from her face and neck. Bending her head forward, she ran a comb through the long hair matted with tangles and sweat, then shook her head upward, sending the hair drifting like a fine red veil about her back and shoulders. Glancing up, she was startled to see Rourke standing beside a tree, staring at her. For one breathless moment, their eyes met and held. Then, breaking contact, Abby twisted her hair into a fat knot, smashed the dirty hat onto her head, and pivoted away. Despite the refreshing wash, she felt sweat bead her upper lip. Why did Rourke have to look at her like that? And why did his look affect her so? She would have to steel herself to feel nothing for him. Nothing but contempt.

Abby sipped the scalding tea her aunt handed her, and burned her tongue. She felt almost relieved. It gave her something besides Rourke to think about.

When the call came to line up the wagons for the river crossing, Abby pulled herself up to the wagon's seat and grasped the reins. Following the lead of the other wagons, she spoke softly to her team and urged them into the water. The river was shallow, coming no higher than the lower spokes on the wagon wheels. But the thick muck oozed and sucked at the mules' hooves, forcing them to strain against the harness.

Some of the heavier wagons became mired in mud as wagon wheels were caught and held fast. The Garner wagon, carrying Nancy and Jed Garner and their young son, Timmy, was soon bogged down in muck that resisted all attempts to free it. While the others watched from their position in the long procession, Rourke and Thompson and the scout Brand examined the Garner wagon to find a way to extricate it.

While they waited, Violet climbed up front to sit with Abby.

"What seems to be the problem?" she asked.

"Garner wagon's stuck." Abby wiped her forehead and replaced her hat.

"Oh no."

At her aunt's exclamation, Abby turned. "What's wrong?"

"It must be the piano."

"Piano?"

"Nancy Garner insisted they bring along her family's Spinet. She made Jed promise they would never leave it behind, no matter how heavy a burden it proved to be."

"They're holding up an entire wagon train for a piano?"

Violet's voice held a note of sympathy. "It isn't just a musical instrument, child. It's a piece of her past. Something to prove that her life wasn't always just dust and heat and backbreaking labor."

Abby thought of her aunt's little chest in the back of the wagon, filled with lace and ribbons and bits of fine fabric. She was glad she'd persuaded her father to take it along. To Violet it contained so much more than sewing remnants. It was her aunt's testament to a better way of life, a life of gentle culture, of shade trees and lemonade, of church choirs and Sunday picnics. A life they had left behind and might never see again.

"Nancy Garner is such a lady," Violet sighed.

Abby absentmindedly nodded her head in agreement. Ever since they'd joined the wagon train, Aunt Vi had held the Garners up as the model young family. Jed was hardworking and ambitious. Nancy, always dressed in clean gingham, her long dark hair pinned in a perfect little knot, walked submissively alongside her husband's wagon, keeping an eye on their young son. They were a handsome, cultured family, who had plans for a long and prosperous life in California.

Hearing shouts and crying, Abby stood on the hard seat and watched in horror as the men struggled under the weight of the piano. Pressing their shoulders to the task, they managed to shift it to the edge of the wagon. Without ceremony, they shoved it over into the river. While the young wife let out a wail, her husband drowned out her cries with a shout to the team and a crack of the whip. Relieved of their burden, the team easily pulled the wagon ahead. The young wife watched from the back of the wagon, her eyes streaming with tears, a handkerchief pressed to her mouth to stem her weeping.

One by one the rest of the train followed. As each wagon passed the submerged piano, the passengers stared at the scene, then turned their heads away. Every wagon carried something precious, something that might yet have to be sacrificed to this harsh land.

As their wagon passed the piano, Abby glanced at the mud gurgling over the keys, spilling into the top of the instrument to rust the wires and soak the precious wood, and felt tears sting her eyes. Glancing at her aunt's white face, she averted her gaze. It was only a piano. A piece of one woman's history. Yet for the moment, they shared the pain of her loss. What price would they all be forced to pay before they reached California?

As Violet retreated to the back of the wagon, Abby viciously cracked the whip and cursed the team. It gave her no measure of satisfaction to vent her anger on the silent, plodding beasts.

Fort Kearny, Nebraska, was the first real concentration of people the train had encountered since leaving Independence. A stockade fence surrounded the encampment. Inside, a tall wooden tower afforded a view for miles in every direction. There was a plain wooden barracks for the soldiers, and a series of small wooden houses for the married officers. A little further away from the military complex there were several separate houses, built by settlers who ran the post store and traded with trappers and Indians for pelts and other goods. Homesteaders came from a hundred miles to trade at the fort, to gossip, visit, and refresh themselves with this small vestige of civilization before once more going back to the business of carving out a living in this wilderness.

For the people of the wagon train, this was an opportunity to refill their depleted supplies and to pause in their journey before moving further into the unknown.

After securing their wagons and caring for their stock, most of the men were eager to visit the back room of the trading post, where liquor was served by the bottle or glass. Even the men from the Reverend Coulter's congregation seemed eager to put aside their strict rules for a day or two of unbending.

Rourke sat with his back against the wall and drained the tumbler of whiskey. He waited, then felt the familiar surge of heat. Tonight he was determined to drink a whole damned bottle of whiskey and fall into a stupor beneath the cook wagon. At least for this one night, he would dull the pain and sleep until morning. He saw Mordecai glance his way and gave him a look that was meant to stop him from coming any closer. Tonight he had no intention of being neighborly. Let the men of the wagon train socialize among themselves. All Rourke wanted was to get pleasantly drunk and fall asleep.

James Market and Flint Barrows sat huddled at a corner table, an empty bottle between them. They'd been there when Rourke entered. He'd seen neither of them with the train today and found himself idly wondering whether they'd crossed the river even before the wagon train had started its crossing. Arrogant, lazy bastard, Rourke thought, watching Market through narrowed eyes.

When the two men stood and approached his table, he tightened his grip on the bottle.

"Where'd you learn to handle that gun?" Barrows asked. He was a tall, thin young man, with brown, stringy hair falling nearly to his shoulders and a scraggly growth of facial hair. The gun stuck in the waistband of his buckskins probably cost him a month's pay.

When Rourke didn't answer, James Market sneered. "Too good to speak to us, Rourke?"

"I don't have anything I want to say. And I prefer my own company." With that he poured another drink, lifted it to his lips and drained it, then set the tumbler down, all the while watching their faces. He didn't like what he saw.

Skin flushed. Eyes watery. They were both drunk and itching for trouble. Rourke saw Barrows look down at his gun. His hand twitched. Rourke tensed.

"Mr. Hawkins, who owns this fine establishment, would like you two gentlemen to leave now." Mordecai walked up behind the two men and spoke in low tones that the others in the room couldn't hear. "Asked me to see that you obliged him."

"My money's as good as anyone else's," Market snarled.

"Not tonight. Mr. Hawkins says he's all through serving the two of you." With his hand firmly under Market's elbow, Mordecai eased him toward the door. Behind them, Barrows shot an angry glance at Rourke, hesitated for a moment, then followed. When the door closed behind them, Rourke released his grip on the gun under the table and poured himself another drink. Glancing up, he saw three men from Reverend Coulter's congregation looking his way and mumbling among themselves. He knew that look. A delegation from the good reverend was no doubt planning to invite him to partake of their church service. He didn't think he could stomach another interruption in his well-laid plans. A moment later they started across the room. Swearing under his breath, Rourke picked up the bottle and glass and strode toward the door, completely missing the look of surprise on the faces of the men he'd managed to evade.

As soon as the men drifted toward the post, the women put kettles of water over the fire, and strung blankets from their wagons to nearby tree branches for privacy. Then they got down the tubs and indulged themselves in an orgy of washing. First there were the clothes, that had only been rinsed in rivers since their departure from home. Then came the children. And finally the women immersed themselves in warm, scented bathwater, soaking away the dirt and grime of hundreds of miles.

Abby allowed Carrie and Aunt Vi to go first, knowing how much they'd looked forward to this luxury. When they were finished, Abby stripped off her rough, scratchy clothes and left them soaking in a bucket of lye soap. Later she would rinse them in a kettle of boiling water and hang them over a line to dry.

When she emerged from the tub, Carrie and Aunt Vi were giggling like two children.

"All right. What are you up to?" Abby asked, vigorously rubbing her hair with a towel.

"This," Carrie said, holding up a gown of pale ivory voile.

"Where did you get that?" Abby touched a hand to the soft fabric.

"We've been sewing it while you drive," Aunt Vi said proudly. "It was an old dress of your mama's. I ripped the seams and made it smaller. And Carrie added the smocking across the front and back yoke."

"It's beautiful." Abby hugged the two women, then stepped back, afraid to wrinkle the fabric. "But it's too grand for me to wear. Why don't we save it for you or Carrie."

"Because it's yours. We made it for you, and we want to see you in it." Aunt Vi took the towel from Abby's hands and finished drying her niece's hair. "I hope it fits. I had to guess at your size. You're so thin, Abby."

Abby laughed, choosing to ignore her aunt's veiled fears. "I know it'll be perfect. And so are both of you."

Climbing into the wagon, she dressed quickly, then stepped out for their inspection.

"Oh, Abby. I knew you'd look beautiful in it."
Carrie caught her sister's hand as she began to braid
her hair. "Let me fix your hair, Abby."

With a sigh of resignation, Abby knelt in the grass
and allowed Carrie to brush her hair and pin it back
with two combs. It fell in soft waves down her back.

"Now you look like a lady."

Both sisters laughed.

"Spoken like a true niece of Violet Market," Abby
intoned.

"There's nothing wrong with looking like a lady,"
their aunt said in all seriousness.

"I know, Aunt Vi. But sometimes we just can't help
teasing you."

"Come on," Violet said, putting an arm around
each girl's waist. "Let's go join the other women for a
grand visit."

While the women sat around a campfire in the
circle of wagons, they could hear the sound of men's
voices and raucous laughter emanating from the post.
Occasionally one of the women would smile, hearing
her man's voice above the others. They could easily
forgive such lapses, since their men rarely had the
chance to drink and forget the hard work ahead of
them.

While the women talked, they sewed or quilted,
exchanging recipes and gossip. As the small children
gradually stopped their play and drifted to sleep, they
were tucked into the wagons.

Carrie's head bobbed. "I'm going to bed, Abby,"
she whispered.

"All right. I'll be along in a few minutes." Biting the
end of the thread, Abby studied the face on the rag
doll she'd been repairing for Nancy Garner's little
one. Nancy, her face grim, eyes swollen from crying,
sat a little apart from the circle of women, staring
listlessly into the fire. She would have to get over the
loss of her piano, but Abby knew it would take her

awhile. In the meantime, her small son had been feeling neglected until Abby picked him up and used the old doll to make him laugh.

When his eyes began to droop, she handed him over to his mother to be tucked into bed. Dropping a kiss on her aunt's cheek, Abby bid the others good night and made her way in the darkness toward her wagon.

Flint Barrows leaned against the wagon and listened to the sounds of the women's muffled conversation. He'd left his drinking companion sleeping beneath the chow wagon. Mordecai would see to it that Market made his way back in the morning.

Seeing Carrie approach, his lips curved into a chilling imitation of a smile and he moved deeper into the shadows. As she passed, he slipped silently in step behind her. For tonight, the Market women were fair game. With James out of the way, they had no man around to look out for them.

He watched the sway of her hips and felt the juices begin to flow. She and that crazy old aunt of hers always looked like they were going to a church social. While the other women in the train trudged along beside the wagons, those two rode inside, fanning themselves like queens. They weren't anything special, he thought, feeding the hostility that always manifested itself in desire. They were just women. And Flint Barrows knew what he liked to do with women. All women.

When Carrie stopped beside her wagon, Flint crept closer. If he moved fast, he could cover her mouth before she could scream. There'd be no one around to hear her struggle. With a grin, he snaked out a hand and caught her by the shoulder, jerking her backward against him. As her mouth opened, he clamped his hand over it and caught her around the waist, lifting her up into the back of the wagon. Before she could cry out, he was on top of her. Seeing her eyes widen with fear, he felt a surge of excitement. They were all alike. Young or old, it mattered not to him. Just as long as they knew real terror. The more a woman cried and lost control, the more excited he became. With one vicious tug her dress gave way at the shoulder, revealing pale creamy skin. His mouth covered hers, swallowing her cries.

As she approached the wagon, Abby smoothed down the skirt of her gown. It had been sweet of Aunt Vi and Carrie to make over one of her mother's dresses for her. Now it was going to be even more difficult to have to be the one to tell them that they would have to walk alongside the wagon once the train left Fort Kearny. The journey to California was a long one. The extra weight of two women would have to be eliminated if the team was going to make it. Abby wondered how her fragile aunt would endure the trek. Dear Aunt Vi. If only she could have been spared this ordeal.

Hearing a muffled sob, Abby paused. Was that Carrie crying? Had Pa done something to make her cry?

"Carrie?"

The sound stopped abruptly.

"Carrie, what's . . . " Drawing back the flap of canvas, Abby saw a man struggling with her little sister. Pinned beneath his weight, the girl was sobbing and thrashing.

Abby's voice was a hiss of fury. "Let her go!"

The man looked up, swore, then shoved Abby backward with such force, she was flung against the rough bark of a tree. Crying out, she picked up a broken limb and sprang forward to strike him.

He leaped down from the wagon and advanced on the slender figure brandishing the club.

"So you like to fight, do you? Well let's just see how long you can hold out against me."

In the glow of the firelight, Abby recognized Flint Barrows. His eyes were glazed. He reeked of liquor.

"You animal. How dare you attack a helpless little girl."

"Little girl?" He laughed, and the sound sent shivers along her spine. It was the laugh of a madman. "If she's old enough to bleed, she's old enough to take."

With quick movements, he grasped the end of the tree limb and wrestled it from her hands. "Maybe you'd like to take her place."

As he advanced on Abby, he felt a sharp pain on the side of his head as he was struck from behind by a boulder. He swung around to find Carrie, her dress hanging in shreds, bending down to retrieve another weapon.

"Two little she-cats. Now ain't this going to be fun." Swinging the club, he caught Carrie at the back of the head, sending her sprawling in the dirt. When she didn't move, Abby let out a cry.

"You've killed her." In a frenzy, she bent and picked up a flaming stick from the fire and threw it at her attacker. With a scream of pain, Flint Barrows caught the fiery missile against his chest, setting his shirt on fire.

Rolling around in the grass, he put out the flames, then turned all his fury on the girl who was bent over her younger sister.

"You're going to pay for what you just did, girlie."

As he advanced on Abby, he heard the click of a revolver and felt cold steel pressed against his temple.

A voice as chilling as death said, "You have five seconds to get out of my sight. Or you'll be dead."

Barrows froze, then turned and stared into Rourke's hard slate eyes. As he started to speak, Rourke cut him off.

"I'd relish the chance to kill you, Barrows. Now you've got three seconds."

Without a word, Flint Barrows turned and ran into the darkness beyond the circle of light.

Tears stung Abby's eyes as she bent over her younger sister. "Carrie. Oh Carrie, please be all right."

The girl moaned, and Abby clutched at her, then felt the warm, sticky mass of blood on the back of her head.

Instantly Rourke was at her side. With an efficiency of movement, he lifted the girl in his arms and placed her on a blanket in the back of the wagon. Probing the wound, he said, "Bring me some water and a clean cloth."

As he washed the blood from her head, he felt the swollen mass at the base of her skull. "It's bloody, but nothing serious. She'll have a hell of a pain in her head tomorrow."

Kneeling beside him, Abby took the cloth from his hand. "I'll tend my sister now."

Rourke glanced around the neat wagon. "Where's your father?"

Abby shrugged. "I don't know. I haven't seen him all day. I suppose he's at the post drinking with the men."

Or sleeping it off somewhere, Rourke thought.

As he climbed down from the wagon, Abby followed him. All her earlier anger at this man had disappeared. Extending her hand, she swallowed and said softly, "Thank you, Rourke. For saving Carrie and me."

"You were doing a pretty good job of it yourself." He glanced at the figure of her sister, lying so still.

As she followed the direction of his look, her voice choked with anger. "She's just a little girl."

"That won't matter to a man like Barrows." Rourke thought of some of the men he'd met in the war. Something had snapped inside them. Whatever goodness or decency they'd once had was gone. Now they knew only anger and killing and revenge. "Stay close to her."

Abby nodded. "I won't let her out of my sight." She stared up at his face, half hidden in shadow, and couldn't think of anything more to say.

As she climbed into the wagon, he realized for the

first time that she was wearing a dress instead of her usual men's clothes. He wondered if she knew how small and delicate she looked. Not at all like the kind of woman who drove a team and brandished a club at a man twice her size.

Rourke glanced at the whiskey bottle he had dropped beneath the tree. All he'd wanted tonight was to be left alone, to drink away his memories and find relief in blessed sleep. The last thing he wanted was to get involved in Abby Market's life. Dark clouds scudded across the sky, obscuring the moon. These women were alone. Alone and vulnerable. He let out a string of oaths. With reluctance he bent, picked up the bottle, and corked it. He'd need a clear head if he was going to keep watch on the Market wagon for the rest of the night. Not that he wanted to get involved in their troubles, he told himself. But if James Market wasn't going to look out for these women, someone had to.

Sitting with his back against the rough bark, he checked his gun, then drew out a cigar and bit the end. Might as well be prepared for a long sleepless night. But, he consoled himself, as long as he stayed awake all night, the painful dreams couldn't touch him.

47

Chapter Five

ABBY HELD HER sister in her arms and waited until the latest bout of weeping subsided. So far she had managed to ascertain from Carrie that Flint Barrows had not managed to accomplish what he had set out to do. Abby's intervention had fouled his plans. But he had managed to steal something precious from Carrie this night—her carefree childhood. Would she ever again feel safe? Abby shivered and watched as her sister lapsed into restless sleep. Or would she forever remember a man's cruel hands hurting her?

The men in Abby and Carrie's young lives had not been kind. Until his death, their grandfather had been a harsh, demanding taskmaster, a preacher whose own children had never measured up to his expectations. Their father, aware of his own father's disappointment in him, had become bitter, reclusive, turning to the contents of his jug to smother his feelings of inadequacy. And if Flint Barrows was any indication, Abby thought with growing resentment, the men on this wagon train were no better.

"What's this? What has Carrie done to her dress?" Violet climbed up into the back of the wagon and stared in dismay at the torn fabric.

In a whisper, Abby told her aunt what had happened. In her mind, she had rehearsed the delicate language she would use in order to spare this very proper lady any embarrassment. Her aunt's uncharacteristic response surprised her.

"We must find James and report this incident immediately. Your father will see that Flint Barrows is removed from the wagon train."

Relief flooded through Abby. She had expected tears, pity, even hysteria. What she discovered was a hint of steel beneath the ribbons and lace.

Abby caught her aunt's wrist as she turned to leave. "The men have all been drinking. I wonder if we should wait until morning."

Violet hesitated. What her niece said made sense. It was very late for her brother to be away from the wagon. Perhaps by now Mordecai Stump and Mr. Thompson were asleep. There was no point in waking them and causing a scene.

"All right, dear. But in the morning, your father will go to Mr. Stump and demand that Flint Barrows leave the train."

Abby nodded, then squeezed Violet's hand. A moment later Carrie began to cry. The two women lay on either side of her and stroked her hair, sharing with her their comfort and strength.

Rourke stretched stiff muscles, then stood and holstered his gun. In the morning mist his damp shirt clung. Picking up the bottle, he gave a last glance at the object of his night's watch and strode toward the cook wagon. He didn't want to be caught sitting there when they awoke. Each time Abby Market looked at him, he felt like every kind of fool. After that incident at the river, he'd never again be easy in her presence.

He had observed Violet Market's return, and had heard snatches of a whispered conversation. Though he had stayed awake all night, he hadn't seen James Market return. Damned jackass didn't give a damn about these women. Why should that fact bother him?

Rourke wondered with growing anger. Stowing the bottle in his bedroll, Rourke pulled on a dry shirt and headed toward the fire. What he wanted was strong hot coffee. And enough work to keep his mind off people who weren't any of his damned business.

Abby awoke with a start, feeling guilty that the sun was already up. The long night with Carrie had left her disoriented. She dressed and hurried to feed the team, then started a fire for their morning meal. Her father still had not returned to the wagon, and she felt a growing sense of dread. What if he had fallen in the darkness? What if he were lying somewhere, alone and hurt? Coffee boiled in a blackened kettle over the fire. Chunks of pork snapped and sizzled in a pan. The aroma of biscuits, baked over coals, added an almost festive air to their morning at Fort Kearny. Abby, kneeling by the fire, heard the sound of whispers from the wagon and knew that Carrie and Violet were awake. Glancing up, she saw the figure of her father approaching. With a little cry of relief she leaped up and ran toward him. At the look on his face she stopped.

His skin was pale, his eyes puffy. His mouth was drawn into a tight line of anger.

"I was worried, Pa. Where've you been?"

"Worried, were you? But not worried enough to come looking for me. I spent the night in the wet grass, probably about to catch a fever, and not one of my family even thought to come fetch me home."

Abby touched a hand to his wrist. "Pa, we have to talk."

"Talk? I'm near to death and my lazy, good-for-nothing daughter wants to talk." Snatching his hand away, he headed toward the wagon.

"Pa." Abby's voice instinctively lowered so the people in wagons nearby wouldn't overhear her. "Flint Barrows attacked Carrie last night."

James Market swung around to face her. Behind

him, Carrie and Violet poked their heads through the flap of canvas.

"Attacked her? With what? A gun? A knife?"

"He grabbed her and threw her into the wagon, Pa. He was trying to . . . " Abby saw the look on Carrie's face and stared down at the ground. "He was going to force himself on her."

James ran a tongue over his lips. His mouth tasted like straw. "Well? Did he?"

"I came along in time to stop him. We fought. He knocked Carrie to the ground with a club. I thought she was dead."

James Market swung around and glared at his youngest daughter. "She don't look dead to me."

"I'm all right, Pa," Carrie said softly. "Just got a lump on my head."

"My head hurts too. I'm going to sleep."

"James." As he pushed past them, Violet looked stricken. "Aren't you going to do anything about this?"

"What would you have me do, woman?"

"Talk to Mr. Stump and Mr. Thompson. Have them remove Flint Barrows from the wagon train."

"The man has a wife, big with child. What will they do? Stay on here at the fort while the rest of us go on to California? Are you suggesting that we should do without another pair of strong arms on this train just because he tried to steal a kiss from Carrie?"

"James." Violet lowered her voice, striving for the patience a lady should always display. "What that man did last night was much more than try to steal a kiss."

Abby's voice cut in, louder than she'd intended. "He was forcing himself on Carrie. If I hadn't come along when I did, you know what would have happened to her."

James climbed back down from the wagon and turned to face Abby. In his rage, color returned to his cheeks. "Could it be you're jealous, girlie? Look at you. You're so busy trying to be a man"—he stared pointedly at her shirt and britches—"that you wouldn't know what it feels like to have a man put his hands on you. And you know what, Miss High-and-Mighty? You never will."

For one stunned moment Abby could only stare at her father. How could he be this hateful? How did he always manage to turn things around, until she was somehow to blame for everything that happened? Regaining her speech, she asked, "Does this mean you don't intend to speak to Mordecai Stump about Flint Barrows?"

"That's exactly what I mean. Now leave me alone." Pushing past the startled women, he climbed into the wagon and rolled himself into a blanket.

For long silent minutes the three women stared at each other. Then Abby turned back to the fire. Resentment, fury, fear boiled inside her. What chance did they have in this wilderness with men who considered them little more than servants? A man like Flint Barrows thought he had every right to take a woman too weak or small to fight back. Her father resented having to take care of three helpless women, when his only son had died at birth. And Rourke. Rourke had warned her to watch out for Carrie. But how much could she do? Feeling drained, she poured a cup of coffee.

"Food's ready," she said listlessly.

"I'm not hungry." Turning away, Carrie stared around the enclosed fort, her arms wrapped tightly about herself.

"Eat something, child," Violet urged.

"No." Taking a blanket from the wagon, Carrie wrapped it around her shoulders and sat down beside the fire. Things weren't going to change, she thought. Nothing ever changed. Except the landscape. They had gone from a miserable existence on a hardscrabble farm to a more miserable existence here in the wilderness. She swallowed back the tears that threatened. Abby never cried. Abby endured. Like a mule, Carrie thought angrily, then immediately regretted the thought. If it hadn't been for her sister, Flint Barrows would have . . .

Filling a plate, Abby set it in front of Carrie, then filled a second plate for herself. She ate mechanically, her mind working frantically. Without her father's cooperation, they would never be able to go to Mordecai Stump and have Flint Barrows removed from the train. The men made the decisions around here. The women were forced to live with those decisions.

At least now they knew what sort of animal Flint Barrows was. They would have to become more vigilant. From now on, besides the dangerous trail, the river crossings, the Indians, there would be another danger. But this one was far from unknown. And probably far more dangerous.

The respite at Fort Kearny left everyone in the train except the Markets more cheerful. The women had a chance to wash and sew and take on fresh supplies. The men had time to repair their harnesses and wagons and swap stories around the campfire. But when the wagon train made ready to pull out at dawn on the third day, the Market wagon was nearly left behind.

James had spent the second day of their stopover sleeping off the effects of the liquor. By evening, he was back at the trading post, sharing a bottle with Flint Barrows. When James brought up the subject of his youngest daughter, Flint suggested that she was nothing more than a little temptress.

"Flaunted herself in front of me, James, and asked me to come up in the wagon and help her move something."

Market downed his drink and poured another generous amount. "I thought as much."

"When she threw her arms around my neck, I figured the girl had gone crazy as a loon." Flint leaned forward, giving his friend a conspiratorial wink. "Girls that age get strange notions. Want to test them on any poor fool who comes along."

James nodded. "She and that sister of mine. Always sitting around talking about kings and princes and castles and such. Useless." He made a fist and pounded it on the table, causing several men to glance his way. "I've had enough of all that. From now on those two are going to pull their share. It's time they found out what real life is like."

Flint signaled for another bottle and filled their glasses. "I'd be glad to take your youngest into my wagon. She could be a help to my wife. The baby's due in another month or two."

Market gave him a narrowed look. It was tempting. Especially if Barrows was willing to pay him for Carrie's services. But then he thought about the gossip that would ensue. "I ain't giving away any of mine. She can earn her keep with us. And by God she'll learn what it is to work."

The entire Market family learned to work together the following morning.

Abby had managed to harness the team while Aunt Vi and Carrie prepared breakfast. When James crawled from between the blankets, his head aching, his stomach rolling, they discovered a broken axle. Mordecai Stump was so angry, he threatened to pull out and leave them behind.

"What in God's name have ye been doing for the last two days, man?" Mordecai's burr was thick with fury.

"I didn't think to check the wagon. When I bought it I was told it was sound."

"Aye. 'Tis sound. But nothing survives this journey unless it's well cared for. Ye've been neglecting your duties, James Market. Leaving all the work to a mere slip of a girl. The care of this wagon should be yours."

Stung by the words that had been heard by half the

wagon train, James bent to the task of repairing the axle, while his women were forced to empty the wagon of all supplies. It was late afternoon before the wagon was repaired and the train was able to roll out the gates of the fort. James Market took the reins while the women tramped beside the wagon. At dusk, when the train finally stopped for the night, Carrie and Vi were too exhausted to even consider making a meal. The chore fell to Abby, who started a fire and set strips of rabbit to roast. Checking the game sack, she realized that they had only enough for another day.

Her father, angry and sullen, sat alone beside the wagon, drinking from the jug.

"Pa, we're nearly out of meat."

"What's that to me? Stump says I have to stay with the wagon."

Abby stared at the ground. "Maybe I could barter for one of the men from the train to hunt for our game along with his own."

"And how will you pay him?"

Abby bit her lip. She didn't know. They had no money, and few goods to trade.

"What's wrong with you hunting?" James asked, taking a final pull of whiskey and shoving the cork into the jug.

"Me?" Abby stuck her hands in the pockets of her dirty britches. "I've fired a rifle before. But I've never killed an animal, Pa."

"Then it's time you learned. If I have to stay with the wagon, the least you can do is take care of our food." He stood. "Now where's my dinner? I'm hungry."

As he walked away, Abby watched his retreating back. She'd never killed. And she'd never been alone in the wilderness before. But then, she'd never driven a team before they joined the train. She'd never done a hundred things she now did routinely. And at least she would have an excuse to be out of her father's way for a few hours each day.

Walking to the back of the wagon, she lifted the rifle down and tested its weight. Later, she decided, she would find the wagon master. Mordecai Stump would teach her what she had to know to hunt their food.

Chapter Six

AFTER SUPPER, ABBY picked up the rifle and made her way through the loop of wagons to the cook wagon. When she entered the circle of firelight, she felt suddenly awkward. Five voices abruptly stopped speaking. Five pairs of men's eyes watched as she approached. Following Mordecai's example, each stood and removed his hat.

"Well, Miss Abby, this is a pleasure."

She had hoped to find Mordecai alone. After meals the men usually went about the business of finishing their chores. Tonight Mordecai and Thompson, Brand and Rourke and Parker still hovered by the fire. Casting a glance at the others, she began to explain her presence.

"Since Pa has to stay with the wagon now, I'll be expected to take care of some of his chores. I'll be needing to lay in a supply of game." Holding the rifle out in front of her, Abby said simply, "I was hoping you could show me how to be a better shot." She lifted a shoulder in embarrassment. "And tell me anything I ought to know about this land when I leave the protection of the wagon train."

Mordecai swallowed his smile. She was an altogether unusual young woman. Shy yet bold. Hardworking,

57

while managing to retain an air of fragile vulnerability. Despite the mannish clothes and tough talk, there was no hiding the fact that she was every inch a lady.

He took the weapon from her hand and examined the Sharps breech-loading rifle. "Ever handle this, lass?"

"Once or twice."

"Hit anything?"

She grinned. "Hit a tree one time. Trouble is, I was aiming at a fox in our henhouse."

Mordecai laughed good-naturedly, and the others joined in before he indicated the blanket and saddle beside him. "Here. Sit a spell, Miss Abby, while I take a closer look at this rifle."

When she was seated, the others sat back down near the fire and began to pass the blackened coffee pot around. When it came to Abby, she poured herself a cup and passed the pot to Parker, the cook. Rourke, she noted, chose to sit a little beyond the circle of light so that his face was in shadow. Why did the man always avoid the light, like a man on the run?

"Rifle's in good shape," Mordecai pronounced after a thorough examination. "Shouldn't give you any trouble. But it's a mighty big gun for someone as small as you. Has a kick to it." Handing it back to her, he added, "You'll get used to it. Tomorrow, why don't you ride ahead of the train with Brand here. When he's not scouting, he can give you some pointers on the use of this rifle, as well as signs of trouble you ought to take notice of."

She felt immediately relieved at Mordecai's ready acceptance of her request. She'd half feared she might be an object of ridicule. As for riding with Brand, though she knew little about the scout, and had rarely seen him around the wagons, she valued Mordecai's judgment. If the wagon master thought the man worthy of her trust, she wouldn't question him.

Brand looked up from his coffee. When he spoke,

his words were very precise, the result of a Boston-bred missionary who had taught his family English. "You directed me to ride ahead to Fort Laramie."

Mordecai, reaching for a cup of coffee, paused. "So I did. Rourke, what are you up to tomorrow?"

There was a perceptible pause. The voice in the darkness sounded guarded. "You asked me to find a shallow river crossing before we make camp tomorrow night."

"Good," Mordecai said, pouring, then drinking. "Take Miss Abby along. There ought to be a few times in the day when you can stop to give her a lesson or two." The Scotsman's eyes twinkled. "Should have thought of you in the first place. Nobody handles a gun better'n you."

Abby felt her heart sink. Not Rourke. Anyone but Rourke. How could she endure an entire day in his company? He had to be feeling just as reluctant as she. She'd heard the edge in his voice. She felt her cheeks redden and blamed the heat of the fire. "I don't want to be any trouble. I'd . . ."

"Nonsense. Everybody on the train, man and woman, should be able to handle a rifle. Never know when you'll need it."

Trapped, she thought, wishing there were some place to hide. She was as trapped as a rabbit in a snare.

She glanced in Rourke's direction. Except for the gleam of the tin cup in his hands and the gunbelt at his waist, he was invisible. And yet she knew that he was watching her. She could feel his look, as physical as any touch.

Mordecai leaned back against his saddle and cradled the tin cup in his hands. "I've known a few women in my time who could handle a gun better'n a man. I remember the time a girl no more'n ten or twelve shot my hat clear off my head. What a shot. Parted my hair without drawing a drop of blood. It was back in fifty-eight," he said, his voice warm with the memory. "I was a rider for the Butterfield Overland Mail."

At his tone, Abby unconsciously relaxed, hugging her arms around her drawn-up knees, tilting her head to one side to watch the older man as he reminisced.

In the shadows Rourke studied the slender figure in the dirty men's clothes and found himself remembering the woman he had seen in the river. No matter how he tried, he couldn't forget the milk-white flesh, the soft, womanly curves she tried so hard to hide. Never again would he be able to think of her as simply James Market's daughter. Every time he looked at her he saw the real beauty she tried to disguise. Noting the way the firelight touched her cheeks and put a glow in her eyes, he decided to stop fighting it and just enjoy watching her. It gave him real pleasure. Despite the hat, tiny wisps of fiery hair broke free from the fat braid to kiss her brow. He glanced at the hands locked around her knees. The fingers were long and tapered. Her hands were meant to hold a fragile teacup. Or a cooing baby, he thought, the muscles of his stomach suddenly tightening. Dismissing such alarming thoughts, he forced himself to face the facts. Abby Market's hands were rough and callused from handling the reins of an unruly team. And the only thing she'd hold for the next thousand miles was a rifle and a team of mules.

Rourke forced himself out of his reverie to concentrate on Mordecai's musings.

"That was the year we began twice-weekly runs between the Mississippi River and California. Twenty-eight hundred miles in twenty-five days. I ate so much dust, I figure I got more sand in me than blood."

The others laughed.

"What about the girl?" Abby asked.

"Rode up to my usual stop along the route. A young fellow, his wife, and three little kids were trying to carve a ranch out of some god-awful wilderness. This day, just as I get within sight of the sod shack, a shot rings out. I holler that I dunna' mean anybody any harm. I start up again and a second shot rings out. Takes my hat, parts my hair, and leaves me shaking in my boots. Then this little mite of a lass steps out from behind a tree and says in a squeaky little voice, 'Your name Stump?' When I say yes, she says, 'You ride for the Butterfield Overland Mail?' Again I say yes. She drops the rifle and says, 'My pa said I could trust you. You have to take me with you.' In the house I find her mama, papa, and two younger sisters all dead. Pawnee."

"How did she manage to survive?" Abby had become so caught up in his narrative, she forgot about Rourke.

"That's the most amazing part of it. There had been a party of six. All six lay dead around the house. The little girl admitted that her father managed to kill the first three before he died. But she killed the other three after they'd slit the throats of her mother and little sisters."

"Whatever happened to her?" Abby asked.

"I took her with me as far as St. Louis. I heard she went east to live with her mother's people." Mordecai chuckled. "Lord help the man who expects her to be a docile little wife."

"If he tried something funny with that one, he'd probably find his throat slit or his hands chopped off before he could blink," Parker intoned.

The others chuckled, and Abby realized with a twinge of discomfort that she didn't belong here. These were men, eager to relax with man's talk. For these few minutes, she had felt a companionship she had rarely known. If she could have picked any man in the world to be her father, Abby thought, it would have been Mordecai Stump. He could be as mean and frightening as a rampaging bull with anyone who questioned his authority. Yet in her presence he was always respectful, even gentle. It was comfortable to sit with these men, listening to their easy conversation. It was something she had never shared with her father.

When she stood, Mordecai and the others stood, making her once again feel awkward. They treated her like a lady, but she didn't know how to act like one. She wanted to be one of them, but their private jokes and knowing smiles warned her that she could never completely fit in. Yet they tried to make her feel special. All except Rourke. With him, she simply felt . . . clumsy.

She offered her hand to Mordecai. "Good night, Mr. Stump."

"Night, Miss Abby. Be sure to look for Rourke tomorrow morning."

As she turned away, she couldn't see Rourke's face. It was still hidden in shadow. But from the prickly feeling along her spine, she was certain he was still watching her, as she'd sensed he'd watched her all the while she was there.

Morning dawned dry and hot. No morning mist shrouded the ground. No cooling breezes ruffled the leaves of the poplars. Each footstep brought a cloud of dust that clung like powder to clothing, clogging lungs and throats and eyes.

Abby watched as her aunt carefully wound strips of soft cotton around her arch and instep, then pulled on heavy knit stockings before lacing up her high shoes. Though she never complained, Abby had seen Violet soaking her feet after her first day on the trail. Still, her aunt insisted, walking was good for a body, made the heart pump, the lungs expand. Dear Aunt Vi, Abby thought with a gentle smile. She would always make the best of any situation.

Carrie wasn't nearly as flexible. Though her young body could adapt more easily to the rigors of this trek, she complained loudly at night about the blisters on her feet, until James reminded her that she wasn't too old to have a few blisters inflicted on her backside as well. This morning she maintained a sullen silence as she dressed and ate.

While Abby drained her coffee, she fought to calm the nervous flutters in her stomach. An entire day with the moody, mysterious Rourke. When the train was ready to roll, she saddled her father's horse, lifted the rifle across her lap, and headed toward the lead wagon. As she drew abreast, Mordecai waved a cheery greeting, then called, "Rourke's up ahead, Miss Abby. You can't miss him."

Far ahead, she could see a lone rider. Gritting her teeth, she dug her heels into the sides of the mare and moved out at a faster pace.

Though he heard her approaching, Rourke never slowed his pace or looked back. When her horse galloped up beside him, spewing dust, he angled his head, tipped his hat, and continued at an easy lope. Within minutes her mount altered his gait to keep pace. They rode that way, without speaking, for miles.

At first Abby was tense, waiting for Rourke to grumble about having to put up with a female companion. When he continued to say nothing, she began to relax and take the time to look around her.

Since leaving Independence, the landscape had been gradually changing. But here the changes were abrupt. Thick turf had given way to bunch grasses. The earth's colors had gone from green to brown and tan. Even the sky had gone from deep blue, awash with fluffy clouds, to a blinding white light that made distances deceptive. Could she reach out and touch that boulder, or was it a mile away? And that mountain range. Would they reach it by nightfall? Or would they need several more days to even draw near?

They passed unfamiliar animals. Bison, pronghorn, jackrabbits, prairie dogs.

Without realizing it, Abby began to enjoy the view. When she had been forced to drive the team, she had felt a responsibility for Carrie and Violet and all their worldly goods. There had been no time to watch the passing parade. Now, unhampered by responsibility, she was free to simply enjoy.

"Oh, aren't they magnificent." At the top of a rise, Abby reined in her horse to watch a herd of bison.

Rourke drew up beside her. Lifting his hat, he wiped the sweat from his forehead, then replaced the hat, leaving the upper part of his face in shadow.

"The way they're being slaughtered, there'll soon be none left."

"Oh, Rourke. There must be a hundred of them. It wouldn't be possible to kill all of them."

"Wouldn't it?" His voice was chilling. "You haven't seen some of the kills I've seen. I've watched half a dozen men sit on their horses and bring down an entire herd in a matter of hours."

"How can they butcher that many animals?"

"They don't. They just leave them to rot in the sun."

"But why?" Without thinking, she reached out a hand to his arm and felt his muscles flex at her touch.

Rourke turned to her. Sunlight played across her face, accentuating her high cheekbones, touching her lips with color. He felt a sudden sexual pull that left him dazed.

Abby saw his eyes darken from slate to molten lead. Confused, she withdrew her hand and turned her head away, pretending to watch the herd.

He fought to keep his tone even. "For the thrill of the hunt. There are men like that in this world. Their only concern is their own pleasure, their own sense of power. They give no thought to the beautiful creatures they destroy in the process."

Abby heard the underlying pain in his voice and wondered about it. Was Rourke still talking about the bison? Or had there been something—or someone— else to cause such intense feeling?

The tone of his voice changed. "There should be a

river in about a mile or so. We'll stop there for lunch."
He wheeled his horse.

Abby gave a last look at the magnificent herd, then
turned her horse and followed his lead.

Lunch was dried meat, hard biscuits, and some
precious coffee and chicory boiled over the fire until it
was the consistency of molasses. Abby thought it
tasted better than some of the meals her aunt and
sister had prepared.

While they ate, Rourke pointed out landmarks. A
cluster of rocks. A deformed tree, bent and gnarled
from wind and sand. Ruts worn deeply into the
sandstone from hundreds of wagon wheels.

"Notice where you're heading. Mark where you've
been. Watch the sky for wisps of smoke. They could
be signals from Indian scouts."

"What would the signals tell?"

Rourke pulled his hat lower on his forehead to
block the sun overhead. "In your case they'd tell of a
woman traveling alone. They'd give your location and
probable destination. They'd say if you were on foot
or riding. Carrying a weapon or unarmed. Within safe
distance of a wagon train, or too far away to reach
safety."

Abby shivered despite the heat. "An Indian could
tell all that from smoke?"

"It appears so. If they choose to, they can pretty
much know everything going on in their territory."

She peered around, wondering what might be hidden behind the rocks and trees. "Is this hostile Indian
territory?"

Rourke grinned. "We're the hostiles. They're just
trying to defend what is theirs."

"But we don't mean them any harm."

"Don't we?" Rourke doused the fire, scattering the
ashes, then covering them with dirt until no trace
remained of their presence. "A few bison can feed a
small tribe for an entire winter. How do you think the

Indians feel when they see white men destroying entire herds just for the fun of killing?"

Abby's gaze swept the plain. For the first time she began to see this land as someone's home. To the people who were born here, it was as cozy and familiar as the old springhouse at her family farm. The thought of the farm brought a twinge of homesickness she hadn't felt in days.

Seeing her frown, Rourke paused. "Something wrong?"

"No." She pulled herself into the saddle, then waited until he mounted. "Where are you from, Rourke?"

"Maryland."

"What's it like?"

He flicked the reins, and she moved her mount into position beside him. "Green," he murmured. "Everything so green." His eyes took on a faraway look. All his features relaxed, until she thought he was the handsomest man she'd ever seen. "Gentle rolling hills, clear bubbling streams, and a climate perfect for growing crops."

"Why'd you leave?"

His smile fled. "Beyond those rocks I spotted a deer. Let's see how well you can handle that rifle."

As he urged his horse forward, Abby watched him with a puzzled frown. She wished she hadn't spoiled the moment. Rourke was obviously a man who didn't care to answer too many questions. She'd remember that next time.

At the top of a ridge, he halted and waited for her to reach his side. Climbing down, they left their horses and proceeded on foot. Scrambling through rocks, Rourke suddenly paused and pointed. Standing quietly, his head lifted to the slight breeze, stood a young buck. Watching him, Abby felt her heart hammering against her ribs. How could she kill something so magnificent?

Rourke motioned for her to shoot. Lifting her rifle

to her shoulder, she studied the animal and felt her hands tremble. Taking careful aim, she fired. The rifle's report sent her tumbling backward. As she sat up, she saw the deer begin to run. Her heart fell.

"I missed him."

The animal ran several steps, stumbled, then dropped to the ground.

Pulling her to her feet, Rourke gave her a smile. It was the first real smile she'd ever seen on his lips.

"You did it, Abby. Bagged your first game."

"I did, didn't I?" Her smile was radiant.

"Come on. Let's take a closer look."

Leading the way, Rourke clambered over rocks and loose pebbles, then offered his hand when she paused. As soon as Abby allowed her hand to be engulfed in his, she felt the jolt of his touch. A jolt as shocking as ice water. She told herself it was just a nervous reaction from the kill. But for one stunning moment he stared into her eyes, and she could sense that he'd felt it too. Instantly he released her hand as if he'd been burned.

They stared down at the animal, whose blood oozed from its lifeless corpse and mixed with the earth to form a dark, mottled pool.

"I wish I hadn't killed him." Abby sighed.

"Your family has to eat."

"But he'll never again run across these hills or swim in that river."

"Don't think about that. He was put here as food. Without him, we couldn't survive. There will be others to take his place on the plains."

Abby nodded, knowing that what Rourke said was true, but it still bothered her.

"Now that I've killed him, how do I get him back to the wagon?"

Rourke handed her a knife. "While I search for a river crossing for the train, you can stay here and skin and dress him. Did you bring your game sack?"

"Yes, but . . . "

"Good. I'll bring your horse. You can start a fire."

"Rourke, I . . ."

Seeing the stricken look on her face, he turned away to hide his grin. "Hunting can't be all fun, Abby. Now that you've had the thrill of the hunt, you have to take the responsibility as well."

As he walked away she felt her stomach give a nervous flutter. She couldn't possibly skin this beautiful animal. And it would take her all day to cut up this much meat.

When Rourke returned with their horses, she was gathering dry wood for a fire. When she had a blaze, Rourke made a rack of sticks and boulders. "Roast as much of the meat as you can manage," he told her. "That way, you'll have enough for several weeks."

"Are you going to stay and help?"

"Can't. Have to inspect the river for a spot to cross. But I'll be back before the wagons get here."

As he swung into his saddle, he looked down at the slender figure and felt a wave of sympathy. Abby Market looked as if she'd like to sit down and cry.

"I thought you grew up on a farm. Didn't you have to slaughter animals?"

"Pa and my uncles took care of that."

"But surely you've plucked a few chickens."

She shrugged. "Of course I did. But this isn't like plucking a chicken. I've never skinned anything as beautiful as this."

"Take it slow and easy, Abby. You'll find it isn't so hard once you get started."

Her chin lifted. He would have sworn little sparks shot from those green eyes. "Don't worry about me, Rourke. I can take care of myself."

"Sure." As he wheeled his mount, he called, "Try to cut off the hide in one piece. I'll show you how to cure it when I get back."

Abby clutched the knife so tightly, her knuckles whitened. What she really wanted was to plant it squarely between Rourke's shoulders. Kneeling, she plunged the knife into the hide and felt it bite into still-warm flesh. She ran behind a boulder and retched. Even before Rourke had disappeared over the rise, tears trembled on her lids, then formed little rivers in the dirt that streaked her face.

Chapter Seven

WHEN ROURKE RETURNED, he found Abby up to her elbows in blood. Spatters of blood smeared her face and matted her hair. Chunks of meat were carelessly scorching over the fire, and piles of entrails were lying in the dust.

"What in hell . . . ?"

"Get out of here, Rourke." She snarled like some kind of madwoman. "Just leave me alone. I can take care of myself."

"I can see that. But can you take care of one little deer?" As he dismounted, he bit back the laughter that threatened. "Are you certain you want to feed your family, or just the wolves?"

"What do you mean?"

"Why did you throw all this in the dirt?"

"The guts? What should I do with them?"

Taking the blackened pot from his bedroll, Rourke walked to the river and filled it with water. Then, washing the entrails, he placed them in the pot of water and set it on the fire. "Soup, Abby. The innards make the best soup."

She nearly gagged before going back to her task.

Within an hour, Rourke calmly took charge and managed to put everything in some semblance of order. In no time the rest of the meat had been cut into neat strips for drying, and the hide had been cleaned in preparation for curing.

When the task was completed, Rourke sat back on his heels and took a good look at Abby. "I think, before the wagon train catches up with us, you'd better wash that blood out of your hair and clean yourself up."

Not understanding just how shocking her appearance was, she gave him what she hoped was a withering look. "So you can hide in the bushes and watch again, Rourke?"

He felt a flash of anger. With deadly calm, he said, "I guess I deserved that. But unless you wash yourself, you'll scare the good people on that train. They're not accustomed to seeing a woman smeared in blood from head to toe. Not to mention her ears," he said, taking hold of her earlobe and giving it a tug.

Abby shook his hand off and backed away. "I have no intention of taking off my clothes for your pleasure, Rourke."

His voice lowered, and she felt a tiny tingle of fear. "If I wanted to remove your clothes for my pleasure, I wouldn't ask permission." Turning away, he said through clenched teeth, "I'll clean up the rest of this mess. Get yourself down to the river before the wagons get here. There's soap in my bedroll."

For a minute Abby could only stare at his back. Then, needing the last word, she said, "I'll wash. Downstream. And you see that you don't come within a mile of me, Rourke, or I'll blow your head off."

As she went to his horse, he called, "There's a clean shirt in there too. Might as well use it while yours dries."

She kept her spine stiff, her head high as she walked to a spot hidden by thick brush. Stripping, she stepped into the water. There would be no laughing and splashing, no playful swim. After washing her shirt, she spread it on a low-hanging bush before stepping back into the water. As soon as the blood and grime had been removed from her skin and hair, she stepped from the river and reached for Rourke's shirt. Rubbing it briskly over her flesh, she pulled on her chemise and tied it at the shoulders. Just as she bent to pick up her britches, she heard the telltale warning of a rattler. Looking down, she saw that the snake had coiled itself around the handle of her rifle. Stunned, she dropped the britches and ran screeching across the expanse of ground that separated her from Rourke.

Rourke looked up at the sound of the scream and grabbed his rifle. Abby nearly ran into his arms before coming to a skidding halt.

"Indians?"

She was breathing so hard she could barely speak. "Rattlesnake."

"Did he bite you?" He felt a hard, cold lump of fear in his stomach and, without thinking, gathered her into his arms.

She shook her head, too breathless to say more.

The fear slowly dissolved. "Where is he?"

"Down by the river." She took in a long gulp of air, then added, "curled around my rifle."

Rourke gave a little sigh of relief, then absorbed the first shock of holding her. Water streamed from her flowing hair, soaking his sleeves. Her body was cool from the river while his was quickly heating. He inhaled the clean, fresh woman scent of her. The rifle in his hand dropped to the ground.

He reached a hand to her hair and drew her head back until she was looking into his eyes. She still looked a little bit dazed, a little bit frightened. But he thought he could read something else in her eyes.

"Remind me to thank that old rattler," he murmured as his arm drew her perceptibly closer.

She brought her fists up to his chest, as if to put a barrier between them. He drew her close, ignoring her feeble protest.

"Don't, Rourke."

His lips hovered just above hers. "Don't what?"

She fought to ignore the realization that it was wonderful being held against him. She felt her heart thudding against her rib cage and hoped her voice wouldn't betray her. "Don't do what you're thinking of doing."

Her voice was low and husky. That alone would have driven a man crazy, Rourke thought. But having her in his arms, wearing nothing more than a thin cotton garment that revealed more than it covered had him going around the bend.

"Abby," he breathed, and for the first time in her life, she thought her name sounded beautiful.

He ran a hand up her spine and felt her quiver of response. Then, tangling his fingers in her hair, he drew her head back and stared into her eyes. She was no longer frightened. But some of her defiance still danced like green sparks.

His mouth covered hers. Heat seemed to pour through her veins. If she had felt a jolt at his simple touch, his kiss caused thunder and lightning to rumble through her. Without realizing it, her fists uncurled and her fingers clutched his shirtfront, drawing him even closer.

The swift surge of desire left him stunned. Her lips were soft and warm and slightly parted in surprise. Her breasts were flattened against his chest. She smelled of soap and river water and vaguely of evergreen. He plunged a hand into the tangles of her hair and combed his fingers through the silk. Then, unable to get enough of her, he changed the angle of the kiss and took it deeper, deeper, until she found herself gasping for breath.

Abby tried to pull away, but Rourke's arms kept her firmly locked against him. His gaze swept the wisp of cotton chemise, its ribbons and lace an odd contrast to the clothes she usually wore over it. Without the dirty hat, her hair flowed down her back, more colorful than autumn foliage. Her eyes were no longer cool or resentful. She couldn't hide the warmth. Or the desire that smoldered just below the surface.

He wanted her. If she were another kind of woman, he would take her here, on the warm sand, beneath a blazing sun. But unless he was a bad judge of character, he'd swear Abby Market had never even kissed a man before. That thought left him shaken.

He dropped his hands and took a step back. Abby blinked, swallowed, and wondered if he could read her confusion.

"Stay here," he said, bending to pick up his rifle. "I'll take care of that rattler."

When he walked away, Abby stood rooted to the spot, wondering why the ground didn't seem quite steady.

At the shore of the river, Rourke looked around and found the snake scurrying toward the brush. As he lifted his rifle he realized that his hands were shaking slightly. Damn her. What had she done to him?

When he returned with the dead snake, he avoided her eyes. "Hardly more than a baby. His venom wouldn't have killed you. Probably would have made you pretty sick, though."

Rourke handed her the clothes she had dropped in her panic and tried not to stare as she hastily dressed. It was an odd sensation to see her in his shirt. Odd and somehow pleasant. As she stepped into her britches, he tossed the dead snake in the brush. When he turned, she was rolling up the sleeves of his shirt. Her fingers fumbled.

"Here. I'll do that." His voice was gruff.

Propping his rifle against a tree, he rolled first one sleeve, then the other. All the while, Abby felt the fires he ignited each time his fingers brushed her skin. Why had she let him kiss her? Why hadn't she stopped him? What must he think of her? She'd behaved no better than a scarlet woman. She could feel herself blushing.

74

As Rourke rolled the sleeves, he watched the play of emotions on her face. He should never have allowed her to come with him today. But no one on the train dared to defy Mordecai. Now this damned little woman was going to cause all sorts of problems for him. He resented the feelings she stirred up in him. And he resented the way she was intruding in his life.

Looking up, he shaded his eyes with his hand. Pointing, he said tersely, "Train's coming. First wagon ought to be at the river's edge shortly. Better pull your boots on and check that venison. There'll be a feast at the Market wagon tonight."

"I think the entire train deserves a feast. I want you to help me give a portion to every family."

His eyes narrowed. "I don't think your father will approve of such generosity."

"I'll handle Pa."

"Like you handled him when he whipped you?" The minute the words were out of his mouth, Rourke could have cut out his tongue.

Abby's eyes blazed. So Rourke had witnessed that shameful scene. "You're another man who likes to humiliate me, aren't you, Rourke?"

He spun on his heel, seething with anger. The trouble was, he couldn't figure out who made him angrier. Himself. Or Abby Market.

An occasional cloud scudded across the full moon. A diamond-studded sky looked close enough to touch. Everything in the west, Abby thought, watching the path of a shooting star, seemed larger than life.

She found herself thinking about the people who lived here and called this wilderness home. She found herself thinking about Rourke, and what drove him. She found herself thinking entirely too much, she decided, draining the last of the coffee and getting to her feet.

There was a festive mood tonight on the train. Abby's generous gift had people laughing and talking, and taking the time to visit for a few minutes before turning into their wagons for the night.

James Market leaned against the wagon wheel drinking from his jug, a scowl on his face.

Nancy Garner walked from the shadows and approached Abby. Though the young woman was still smarting over the loss of her piano, she bravely tried to lift herself out of her gloom.

"Good evening, Abby. We're so grateful for the venison." She looked down, embarrassed by the admission. "It was the first meat we've had in a week."

Abby had heard rumors that due to Nancy's depression, Jed Garner had been afraid to leave his wife and young son long enough to hunt.

Nancy took two jars from a basket on her arm. "These are some of my mother's peach preserves. She wanted us to have something of home when we reach California."

Abby was reluctant to accept the cherished sweets, but she knew that to refuse would cause the proud woman more grief.

"Thank you, Nancy. My family will certainly enjoy this."

When the young woman walked away, James gave a snort of disgust. "Feeling like Lady Bountiful, aren't you?"

"Leave her alone, James," Violet said, taking the jars from Abby's hands. "Everyone is so grateful for the meat. Why, the Reverend Coulter's wife Evelyn brought us a tin of biscuits. And Lavinia Winters gave me a basket of dried rose petals for my clothes chest."

"When we run out of meat in a few days, I suppose we can eat your precious rose petals," he hissed, taking another drink.

"We won't run out of meat out here, Pa," Abby said. "You should have seen the animals we spotted today." Turning to her aunt, she said, "Great herds of bison, and wild sheep high up in the rocks. And deer and rabbit."

"And all you manage to bring in is one scrawny deer." James corked the jug and stumbled away in search of more friendly companionship.

"Don't mind him," Violet said, taking the kettle from the fire. "James is just in a huff because Mordecai Stump ordered him to keep his wagon in better repair or we'll be forced to drop to the end of the train. And you know what that would mean."

Abby nodded. They would eat everyone's dust.

Crawling into the back of the wagon, Abby undressed and slipped into her night shift. Outside, she could hear the conversation of her aunt and sister.

Carefully removing her shoes and heavy stockings, Violet slipped her feet into a basin of warm water and gave a little sigh. "You should try this, Carrie. It eases the discomfort."

"Nothing short of amputation will ease this discomfort, Aunt Vi. I swear I walked my feet clear off today."

"But think how much more we can see by not being in the wagon. While we walk we're able to see so much of this strange country. Don't you agree, Carrie?"

The younger girl shrugged. "So far, all I've seen is a lot of dust."

"Yes, it is dry." Violet dabbed cocoa butter on her lips and passed it to her niece. "This will help your cracked skin, dear."

Brushing her hair, Abby wrapped a blanket around her shoulders and climbed down from the back of the wagon to join the others.

Violet glanced up and gave a little gasp. Both girls looked at her in alarm. Composing herself, Violet touched a hand to her throat. "You gave me a start, Abby. With your hair like that, wearing a long flowing gown, I thought for a minute I was seeing Lily."

The girls had grown up hearing all about their father's family. Besides Violet, there had been two younger sisters, Rose and Lily. Their names were a result of their mother's fondness for flowers. Rose and her farmer husband lived in Illinois. Lily, the beautiful, headstrong youngest member of the family, had died during childbirth. According to Violet, her baby had died as well. And Lily had gone to her grave without revealing the name of the father of her child. It had been the family's greatest disgrace. And Abby's grandfather, the stern minister, had borne his dishonor in sullen silence. Like his father, James never forgave his sister her sins. He never allowed her name to be mentioned in his presence.

"Did she have red hair like Abby's?" Carrie asked.

Violet nodded, studying Abby in the glow of the fire. "Beautiful red hair, and skin like alabaster." She grew silent for a moment, and neither girl wanted to intrude on her thoughts. Then, in a softer tone, she continued her reminiscences. "I don't think Father ever forgave Lily for being the cause of our mother's death from complications of Lily's birth. Since I was the oldest, it was up to me to raise her. When she was growing up, Father constantly reviled her beauty, saying that she would cause men to lust in their hearts." Violet gave a deep sigh. "Poor Lily. I always thought she went out looking for the love our own father couldn't give her."

Glancing up, she realized she'd just revealed something scandalous to her nieces. "I don't mean that what Lily did was right. But everyone deserves to be loved."

Abby watched as her aunt dried her feet. "Is that why you never married, Aunt Vi? Because your father made you stay and raise the younger ones?"

Violet's chin lifted. Tossing the water to one side, she dried the basin, then turned back to the girls. "My father didn't have to make me stay. I wanted to help. And then when Lily died, I felt I should stay and give whatever comfort I could to my father." She bent and kissed each niece good night, then climbed into the wagon.

"And now she's stuck taking care of us," Carrie whispered. "Poor Aunt Vi."

After Carrie climbed into the wagon, Abby sat in the darkness, staring at the glowing embers. All her life she'd been made to feel ugly, by her father's and grandfather's rejection, by her own feelings of inadequacy. Yet today Rourke had kissed her, and suddenly she'd felt like a beautiful woman. And tonight Aunt Vi said she was reminded of Lily. Lily, the family outcast. Lily the infamous. Beautiful, fiery Lily.

Climbing into the back of the wagon, Abby crawled between the blankets. Despite the rigors of the day, she knew that sleep would not come easily. There were too many things she wanted to think about, to cling to. For this one precious night, she wanted to savor the feeling of being a woman. A beautiful woman.

Chapter Eight

BECAUSE OF HER success on her first hunt, Abby was invited to accompany the men whenever they hunted. On this hot day, she accompanied Mordecai's partner, Mr. Thompson.

Big Jack Thompson, like Mordecai, had worked for the Butterfield Overland Mail. He claimed to know every watering hole in the west, and handled a horse with the firm assurance of one born in the saddle. Though he stood ramrod straight and had the bearing of a general, he quickly put Abby at ease. He could be very abrupt, yet he was scrupulously polite. And when he corrected her use of her weapon, or warned her of the dangers that lurked in this strange countryside, she knew that he was only looking out for her welfare.

They had spotted the pronghorn nearly two hours earlier. Since that time, they had stalked, searched, and broiled under the relentless sun. Now, huddled behind a column of rocks, they waited for the animal to approach.

"Mordecai used to love this part of the hunt," Thompson said, wiping the sweat from his brow and replacing his hat.

"Then we should have persuaded him to come with us." The minute the words were spoken, Abby regretted them. She had grown so accustomed to seeing Mordecai's cane, she'd stopped noticing it. The limp seemed a natural part of the man. "How stupid of me. His leg."

Thompson nodded, watching for the telltale antlers to appear around an outcropping of rock.

"How did Mordecai injure his leg?"

Thompson's eyes narrowed slightly. Averting his gaze, he said, "Took a bullet in the knee. Shattered the bone. Doctor probed, but never did find the bullet. It's still in there somewhere. At first, we thought he'd never walk again. But Mordecai's tough. A month after doc gave up hope, Mordecai just fashioned himself a walking stick, pushed himself out of bed, and limped to his horse. Been getting around like that ever since."

"He must be in a great deal of pain."

Thompson's eyes watered as he strained to see something in the distance. "That he is. Most of the time he hides it. Sometimes you can see it in his eyes, though."

"Did they ever get the man who shot him?"

Thompson turned to look at her. Abby thought she'd never seen such misery. His voice was raw, as though every word burned his throat. "I used to be a hard-drinking man, Miss Abby. Mordecai and I rode together. One night, in a saloon, I got liquored up and suckered into a gunfight. Mordecai knew that even stone sober I didn't stand a chance against the man. When he tried to reason with me, I shoved him away and headed for the street. Just as we drew our guns, Mordecai stepped between us. He was a few seconds too late. The shot rang out, hitting Mordecai."

"The gunfighter shot Mordecai? How awful." She turned away and brought a hand to her mouth.

"No, Miss Abby," Thompson said so softly she had to turn and look at him. "I shot Mordecai. And if it takes me a lifetime, I'll make it up to him."

Abby felt tears spring to her eyes. She blinked them

away, determined not to let Big Jack see her cry. For long minutes, the silence hung between them. Then Thompson touched her arm and pointed. The pronghorn was standing quietly, studying the rocks above them. Motioning for her to take the shot, Thompson aimed his rifle, prepared to back her up if she missed. Abby swallowed, fired, then watched as the antelope leaped up, scrambled several steps, then toppled.

When they rode back to join the train at the end of the day, the pronghorn, a smaller, antlerless deer, and four jackrabbits were slung over their saddles. For a few more days the wagon train had more than enough food. And Abby had a clearer image of the men she rode with. Her minister grandfather had preached about a life divided into good and evil. But now she found herself wondering about those murky areas between the two extremes. She had no doubt that Violet was everything good. But Thompson, once a drunk and a fighter, was spending a lifetime atoning for his sins. Surely that made him a good man. And Lily, the aunt she'd never known, had been punished all her life for the sin of being beautiful. And so she had come to live out her family's expectations. Did that make her evil? Or had the evil come from those who'd failed her? Abby wrestled with the timeless question. Who really were the good? And who the bad?

The wagon train limped into Fort Laramie with two damaged wagons and a dangerously low supply of water. Morale was also low. Flint Barrows's wife had been in labor for over thirty-six hours. Despite the ministrations of Violet and Evelyn Coulter, the baby had made no progress. And still her cries went on.

"Brand said there would be a doctor at the fort," Violet said, taking a respite from the Barrows wagon to walk with her family. "If he can't do something soon, I fear for both mother and child."

Abby still felt a seething anger whenever she

thought about Flint Barrows. But his pale, timid wife evoked only pity. The woman rarely spoke to anyone on the train, keeping to her wagon. Until she had gone into heavy labor, she had walked alongside the wagon, keeping pace under a scorching sun. Every woman in the train sympathized with her. And shared her prayers for an end to the pain.

"How long will we stay at Fort Laramie?" Carrie asked, staring eagerly toward the cluster of houses.

Though the fort could hardly be called a town, the houses of the traders and military men were a comforting sight.

"Only a day or two," Abby replied. "Unless they can't get the Coulter wagon repaired in time."

"What about Mrs. Barrows?"

Abby heard the shriek of pain and winced. "That baby has to come soon. She can't hold on much longer."

Shielding her eyes, Abby studied the fort. Like all military outposts, there were the familiar barracks, the simple wooden houses for the married officers, and a few other buildings housing a fur trader's, a post store, and a two-story boardinghouse. Unlike many forts, there was no fence or wall. Built on the Wyoming plains, it offered a view for miles in every direction.

Brand had prepared the military for the arrival of the wagon train. After being directed to the far end of the fort, the families set up camp. While the women started fires and prepared supper, the men and children hauled empty buckets and barrels to a community well.

"I'd better get back to the Barrows wagon," Violet said, leaving Abby and Carrie to attend to the chores.

When she was gone, Carrie whispered, "I don't ever want to have a baby. I wouldn't be brave enough to go through all the pain Mrs. Barrows is suffering." She looked up from the fire. "Don't you wonder how women ever have more than one baby?"

Abby grinned. "Ma used to say a woman forgets the pain the moment that little one is placed in her arms."

Carrie made a face. "All babies ever do is wail, eat, and crap in their britches."

"Carrie. You watch your mouth." Abby gave her sister a piercing look.

"It's true. I remember Belinda Moffet's baby brother. After he was born, she couldn't do anything except feed him and change his drawers. And her ma laid in bed for weeks before she died." Carrie's voice lowered. "I saw her once. Her skin was all blotchy, like she had measles or something. Then after she died, Belinda never left the house. Just fed that baby and cleaned up after him."

Abby walked closer and dropped an arm around her younger sister's shoulders. "Did you ever hear Belinda complain?"

Carrie shrugged. "No. But I didn't get to talk to her much."

"I'll bet if you asked her, she'd have told you that little baby was the most precious thing in her life."

Carrie looked up. "You think so?"

Abby nodded and squeezed Carrie's shoulder. "There's something special about a baby. One of these days you'll see."

"Not me," Carrie said dramatically. "I'll leave all that fun for you."

Abby tousled her sister's hair. "Can you finish dinner while I feed the stock?"

"I guess so. But don't be too long. If Pa thinks I made the dinner myself, he'll find something to complain about."

As Abby walked to the team, she heard the mournful sound of Emmaline Barrows's cries above the din of camp. They caused the hair on the back of her neck to prickle. She'd never heard such suffering.

Abby's lids fluttered. Pale, luminous light flickered on the far horizon. For a moment she lay, listening to the hushed silence of dawn. She sat up, straining in the darkened wagon. Something was wrong. It was too quiet. Emmaline had grown silent. That's what it was. There were no cries coming from the Barrows wagon.

She felt her heartbeat quicken. The babe could be sleeping, she thought, fumbling with her clothes. Please God, let the baby be resting contentedly in its mother's arms.

Pulling on her boots, she dropped from the back of the wagon and shivered in the dawn chill. Threading her way through the circle of wagons, she pulled up short at the low murmur of voices. Violet, Evelyn Coulter, and the post doctor huddled in earnest conversation.

"What's happened?"

Violet looked up. "Go back to bed, child. There's nothing anyone can do now."

"What do you mean?" Abby glanced at the slightly opened flap of canvas. Beyond there was only darkness. No lantern burned in the Barrows wagon. It was as still as death. Abby shivered again, feeling a chill that had nothing to do with the weather.

"Emmaline is dead," Violet whispered. "Poor thing suffered the pains of hell. There was nothing we could do for her."

"And the baby?"

"A tiny little girl. No bigger'n a doormouse. But her lungs are healthy enough. She came into the world squalling."

"How will Flint Barrows care for a newborn?"

Violet shook her head sadly. "He doesn't want to have anything to do with her. Said he can't stand to even look at her."

"What will be done with her?"

"Reverend and Mrs. Coulter want to raise her. They've lost three babies in childbirth and feel as if God has given them another chance."

"But how will Mrs. Coulter feed her?"

"Everyone on the train who has a cow will share

with the Coulters. If the infant can't tolerate that, the Fenwicks have goats. They swear the milk is rich enough to rival mother's milk." Violet dropped an arm around her niece. "The little one's in good hands now. I think the Coulters will do just fine. And maybe," she added softly, "it's a godsend that Barrows didn't want his daughter. I shudder to think what her life would have been like with him."

Abby agreed with her aunt's assessment. Kissing her cheek, she said, "You look tired, Aunt Vi. Why don't you come to bed now?"

"In a little while. We want to wash the bloody linens and prepare Emmaline's body for burial. Flint wants his wife buried right after first light. Reverend Coulter has agreed to hold a small service."

"But why so soon?"

"Those are Flint's wishes. The post doctor agrees. He advised us not to wait. With the heat, and the strain of the journey still to come, he thought we should put Emmaline to rest as quickly as possible."

"I'll stay and help."

"No child." Vi lowered her voice so the others wouldn't hear. "Stay close to your pa today. This death will remind him of his own loss. He shouldn't be alone."

Or he'll get drunk, Abby thought, feeling her stomach begin to churn. Aunt Vi didn't need to say it out loud. They both knew. Whenever Pa started talking about his wife and stillborn son, he turned to his jug for comfort. And for days afterward, he would be sullen and abusive.

Hearing her father moving inside the wagon, Abby squared her shoulders and started a fire. She'd see that he had a hearty breakfast. It might be the last food he'd take for a while, if he started drinking. If her pa and Flint Barrows should band together to drown their sorrow, there'd be no living with them.

* * *

Word of the death spread through the train at first light. After breakfast the men fashioned a wooden casket while the women finished cleaning the Barrows wagon. Flint had said that he wanted no trace of his wife's clothes or precious belongings. Though Abby found his request strange, Aunt Vi argued that every man grieved in his own way.

"Maybe the sight of her things would keep opening the wound," Aunt Vi said, folding the few faded and patched dresses that lay in a chest. Except for a few simple undergarments and a shawl that had seen better days, Emmaline Barrows seemed to have few possessions.

"What will you do with these?" Abby asked.

"I thought Evelyn Coulter might like to use them to make some infant clothes. Though Emmaline had a few things ready, they weren't nearly enough." Handing the pile of carefully folded clothes to Abby, Violet climbed down from the Barrows wagon. In a low voice she sighed, "I'm glad to be finished, child. Though Flint seems to have enough money for whiskey and guns, they lived poor. That young woman barely had enough to keep herself warm. I don't know how she planned to care for a baby."

Leading the way, Violet directed Abby to the Coulter wagon, where the sound of a baby's cries could be heard.

When the reverend's wife poked her head from the wagon and saw Abby and Violet, she smiled warmly. Though barely thirty, Evelyn Coulter's hair was already shot with gray. She was as wide as she was tall, and when she hugged Abby, the girl felt herself engulfed in warm, baby-scented flesh. The fine lines around her eyes deepened with her smile. "Come on up and have a look at our little Jenny."

"Is that what Flint named her?" Abby asked.

"It's the name we chose. My mother's name," Evelyn said proudly. Opening the blanket, she cuddled the baby close for a moment, then laid her on her lap to be admired.

The baby was so tiny she reminded Abby of a newly hatched bird. Her skin was red and wrinkled. Her arms were as spindly as little sticks. Her fist curled tightly around Evelyn's finger. Her eyes squinted shut as she bleated in hunger.

Placing a twisted corner of handkerchief dipped in water and sugar into the infant's mouth, Evelyn smiled as the baby's eyes opened.

"Oh, she's so sweet," Abby cooed, watching in fascination as the baby began to suck.

"And hungry," Evelyn added. "Later on today I'll start giving her a little cow's milk diluted with water. If she tolerates it, she'll soon be plump and pink and sleek as a kitten."

Abby had her doubts that this tiny creature could ever look plump and sleek, but she kept her thoughts to herself.

"We've brought you Emmaline Barrows's things," Violet said. "They aren't much, but we thought you ought to have them."

"How nice." Rummaging through the meager pile, Evelyn suddenly smiled. "I know what I'll do with these. I'll make a patchwork quilt out of Emmaline's things to save for Jenny. That way, when she's older, she will have something of the mother she never knew."

Abby felt a lump in her throat. This kind, gentle woman would make the perfect mother for a homeless child.

The men were somber in their Sunday suits or dark vests. The women wore simple dresses, their heads covered, their eyes downcast.

James Market stood beside his spinster sister, who had dragged from the chest her good black funeral dress and hat. Beside her, Abby, wearing a proper dress, clung to Carrie's hand and stared at the casket.

Was it only a month ago that they had stood like this to bury their mother?

Reverend Coulter read from his Bible, and with trembling voice spoke eloquently. "Greater love hath no man than that he lay down his life for another. Our sister, Emmaline Barrows, joins those noble women of history who willingly gave their lives in order to bring new life into this world." The preacher's voice rose and fell over the people like a benediction. "Paul tells us of finishing the race, of fighting the good fight. Our sister Emmaline now enjoys the reward of those who stay the course. Where she is, there is no more pain, only joy." With tears glistening in his eyes, he intoned, "Thank you, Lord, for the child who was the fruit of Emmaline and Flint's love. We could ask for no greater blessing."

Just then the baby cried. Abby chanced a look at Flint Barrows. He kept his gaze fixed on the wooden box. The look in his eyes was thoughtful. Thoughtful and cruel. If he heard the sound of his baby's cry, it didn't show.

When the service ended, the casket was lowered into the hole in the ground. Each mourner stooped and picked up a handful of sand to scatter on the box while Reverend Coulter reminded them that man was dust and unto dust he would return. When Carrie bent to scoop up a handful of dirt, the breeze lifted the hem of her gown, revealing a length of shapely ankle. Abby saw Flint Barrows's eyes glint with amusement. Dropping a protective hand on her sister's shoulders, she shot him a cutting look. The shame of the man. Her heart pounded. Her palms grew damp with the thought. His wife wasn't even cold in the grave.

As Carrie and Abby made their way back to their wagon, Abby thought about how strange life was. It was obvious that Flint Barrows hadn't loved his wife. She had been more a . . . convenience to him. She wondered just what circumstances had brought about their loveless marriage. Had he needed a wife to accompany him west? Or had she, finding herself with child, coerced him into marriage? Or had they simply drifted into marriage and then found themselves bound for life? She sought to dismiss such appalling thoughts from her mind. Maybe once they had loved. She would cling to this one wonderful fact. Emmaline Barrows had died giving life to a tiny baby girl. The baby's own father rejected her. But a loving couple, with no children of their own, would have their lives enriched because of it.

Abby could imagine what life would have been like with the cruel Flint for a father and the dour Emmaline for a mother.

Maybe there was a God, Abby thought. And maybe she had just witnessed His mercy.

Chapter Nine

THE WAGON TRAIN stayed on at Fort Laramie for three days. When the wagons finally rolled on, they were in good repair and stocked with fresh supplies. The people seemed imbued with fresh enthusiasm. And they had added a newcomer to their ranks.

Will Montgomery still wore the tattered shirt of the Confederacy, one sleeve dangling over an empty socket where his left arm used to be. His still-boyish face was dusted by pale blond hair, but his eyes were old, showing the ravages of war and pain. At nineteen, he was thin, withdrawn, and painfully shy. Mordecai had hired him because, despite having only one arm, he could sit a horse and shoot a gun. At least that's what Mordecai told anyone who asked. The wagon master had been warned that several tribes of Plains Indians were fighting among themselves. So far, no white men had been harmed. But the young captain at the fort had hinted that these feuds had a way of spilling over into all-out war.

Still, Mordecai had another reason for hiring the shy young man. The first time he'd seen Will Montgomery, his heart had gone out to him. He knew what it was like to be cut down in his prime. He understood the challenge of learning how to perform simple tasks again, without the use of a limb that had once been taken for granted. Watching Will struggle to shrug into his pants and tighten his belt, Mordecai knew there wouldn't be too many jobs out there waiting for a man with only one arm.

The first thing Will Montgomery noticed when he joined the train was Rourke's faded Union cap. The second thing he noted was the gun at Rourke's hip. It was a Union-issue Spencer eight-shot, which carried seven cartridges in the butt stock, while another was loaded in the chamber. Will and his Confederate buddies used to say, "The Yankees loaded that gun on Sunday and shot all week." Whenever Will saw Rourke coming his way, he turned aside to avoid him. And when, over the fire, he saw Rourke looking at him, he turned his head away, avoiding eye contact. How many of his friends had he buried because they'd come in contact with that gun? He felt the tingle where his arm used to be and wondered whether it had been a Spencer eight-shot that had been the cause of his empty sleeve.

"Here, Will. Make yourself useful," Parker said, handing the young man an empty bucket.

Will took the bucket and headed toward the river. He liked the fat cook. From his first day, Parker treated him like just another member of the train. If there were chores to be done, he expected Will to carry his share. Will liked that in a man. He hated feeling different. The hardest part of all was being made to feel like a cripple.

The sky was a cloudless blue, with a white glare of sun already climbing overhead. Breathing deeply, Will thought how different the air was here in Wyoming. Thin, hot, dry, like needles in the lungs. His cheeks were sunburned, his lips dry and cracked. Even the insides of his nostrils felt parched. This land sucked all the juices out of a body, he thought. How different it was from his lush, green boyhood home of

Louisiana. His smile faded for just a moment as he allowed himself to think about the rich plantation he'd called home. After the war, he returned to find the buildings burned to the ground, the livestock slaughtered, the crops rotting in the fields. His father was a beaten man. The final blow had been seeing his handsome young son standing before him in ragged clothes, the empty sleeve reminding him of all the lost promise. It would take dozens of men in their prime to repair the damage done to this once-fine plantation. And here they were, a tired old man and a war-ravaged boy. With tears streaming down his face, he'd given his only son what money he could and told him to seek his future elsewhere.

Will knelt at the river's edge and filled the bucket. Glancing across the plains, he felt the hope begin to rise in him once more. The land on the horizon was new, untamed. Somewhere in this vast wilderness there was a place for him. He wouldn't lose hope. He'd keep on searching until he found it.

Lifting the bucket, he stood and turned, colliding with a vision in pink. Carrie Market stood perfectly still, absorbing the shock, her mouth dropping open in surprise. The contents of the bucket spilled down the front of her gown, completely soaking it. Will stood there, horrified, watching the water run in little rivers down the skirt and spill onto the toes of her shoes.

"Oh, miss. Oh God, I'm sorry." The bucket dropped from his nerveless fingers and landed in the dirt with a thud. "Here, I . . . " Reaching into his pocket, he withdrew a soiled handkerchief and looked as if he might actually try to swipe at her bosom.

Carrie leaped back as if the thought of his touch repelled her. "It's all right. Please. Don't fuss. It's only water. I'll change. It'll dry."

She was babbling. Carrie knew it, but she couldn't seem to stop. She felt her cheeks redden and brought her hands up to hide the revealing blush.

"I feel awful," Will stammered. "Smashing into a beautiful little thing like you. And that dress is so pretty. I've ruined it."

Carrie had stopped hearing what he was saying. Beautiful? Had he actually called her beautiful?

When she said nothing, Will felt even worse. Here he was, saying all the wrong things to the prettiest girl he'd ever seen, when all she wanted to do was have him get out of her sight. How could he have forgotten what he looked like? The sight of him probably made her sick.

Picking up the bucket, he turned away. "Excuse me, ma'am. I'm sorry about your dress. But I promised the cook I'd fetch some water."

Carrie could only stare at his back while he refilled the bucket. When he stood, he made certain that he stayed far to the right of her as he passed her. Like I'm a leper, she thought.

She watched until he disappeared behind the cook wagon. Then, staring down at her dress, she seemed to realize for the first time just how she looked. The thin cotton clung to her skin, outlining firm young breasts. At the first dash of cold water her nipples had hardened. Just below her waist, the wet fabric indented at her navel. She was mortified to think a man had seen her like this. Lifting her skirts, she ran to the wagon and crawled inside. When she had changed into dry clothes, she hung the wet ones on a line strung across the back of the wagon. All day as she traversed the dust-choked miles, she watched the flutter of pink dress and thought about the intriguing man who had called her beautiful. And then, before she could enjoy the thought, she would remember how silly she'd looked and her head would droop in shame.

Like Rourke, Will Montgomery avoided the people on the wagon train as much as he could. Rourke kept his reasons to himself. But it was obvious that there was an anger seething inside him. An anger that seemed directed at the world.

Will's reason for avoiding people was obvious. His empty shirt sleeve was the first thing to draw a person's gaze. Then, to avoid staring, they would look away, steadfastly refusing to meet his eyes. Out of pity, many women took to looking through him as if he weren't there. Some of the men tried to do things for him, assuming he was no longer capable of a man's work. It was only the children who were willing to deal with Will honestly.

"I'm Jonathon Peel." A six-year-old boy stopped Will as he carried a log toward the cook wagon one night. "You're the new man, aren't you?"

Will nodded. "Will Montgomery."

"Where's your arm?"

Jonathon's mother glanced up from her sewing with a look of horror. The other women, seated around the Peel campfire, looked distinctly uncomfortable. Only Carrie Market stared directly at Will.

"I left it in a field in Richmond," Will said.

"How'd it fall off?"

"A doctor had to cut it off." Will knelt down until his gaze was level with the boy's.

"With an ax?" Jonathon's eyes got as big as saucers.

"A knife and a saw, as far as I can remember," Will said matter-of-factly. "I passed out after the first few minutes."

"Why did you let him? Why didn't you stop that doctor from cutting it off?"

Will was acutely aware of Carrie, watching him across the fire. He wished he could say something that would make him sound brave and noble. But all his life he knew only how to tell the truth. Besides, she couldn't possibly be interested in him. Except as a freak. "He said I'd die unless I let him take off the arm. And I didn't want to die."

The boy stared at the shapeless sleeve. "I think I'd rather die than lose my arm," he said softly.

"Jonathon," Mrs. Peel shrieked. "How could you say such a terrible thing? You apologize to Mr. Montgomery this minute."

"It's all right, ma'am." Will dropped the log and brushed the hair from the boy's brow. In a soft voice he said, "There are times when I've felt that way myself."

"If you could do it over, would you still let him cut it off?" Jonathon stared deeply into Will's eyes, as only a child can. And Will felt he owed him the whole truth.

"Some days I would." He shrugged. "Some days I wish he'd have let me die."

The boy digested this a moment, then nodded, accepting Will's statement without any show of pity. "Guess there'd be days I'd feel that way too." He turned away, then turned back. "See you, Will."

"Yeah. See you, Jonathon." Will wrapped his arm around the log, bringing it to balance against his chest. Struggling to his feet, he avoided looking at the women. Especially Carrie. He wouldn't be able to bear the look he knew would be in her eyes.

As he strode away, Carrie watched him, then turned to glance at the others. Their heads were bent, their gazes riveted to their sewing.

"Poor thing," Lavinia Winters said, biting off a length of thread. "I knew a family in St. Louis whose son came home from the war without a leg. Two weeks later he went to the barn and shot himself. His poor mother was the one who found him."

Carrie's eyes widened.

"I wonder if this boy's family turned him out," Doralyn Peel said. "I suppose a lot of people don't want to see half a son return from the war."

Feeling tears scalding the backs of her eyes, Carrie blinked them away with a fury she couldn't seem to control. With her hands on her hips she stood and faced the others. "He isn't half of anything. He's a person. And just because the war did this to him, don't think he can't still think and feel and do. Don't you think he knows we're talking about him right now? And don't you think he feels your pity?"

The tears she'd been holding back now spilled down her cheeks. She wiped them away with the back of her hand and picked up her sewing. "Excuse me. I—I have to go to bed now."

Feeling ashamed, Carrie ran from the light and hurried to her own wagon. Crawling inside, she lay on her blanket and wondered why she should be crying for a man she hardly knew. Why should it matter to her what Will Montgomery thought? And why should she care how others treated him?

She blew her nose in a delicate lace handkerchief, then, still sniffing, sat up and stared at the stars in the night sky. Aunt Vi said the measure of a man was whether or not he was capable of giving of himself to others, whether it be God, country, or family. A man who was so wrapped up in himself that he didn't have time for others wasn't much of a man, she said.

Carrie found herself wondering about Will. It was obvious he'd served his country. And tonight he was so gentle with Jonathon Peel, treating his questions with respect. Another man might have told the boy to mind his own business. Will Montgomery was a kind man. And, Carrie knew, she was going to find out more about him. But she wasn't sure why.

After their chores were finished for the day, Flint Barrows and James Market had begun spending every evening drinking together. Because Violet refused to allow them to drink in her presence, they retired to the Barrows wagon, away from the scornful eyes of the women. In each, the other had found a kindred soul.

After a couple of drinks James Market would begin his litany of hate. He hated men in positions of authority, insisting that he could do better.

"We pay Stump good money to lead us across the country. Why?" Market said, reaching for the jug.

"Because he makes us think he knows more than anyone about this wilderness. Know what I think?"

Flint Barrows shook his head.

"I think if everyone on this train gave me all that money, I'd find the shortest route to California too."

Barrows chuckled.

Market was just warming up. "Know what else I hate?" Without waiting for Barrows to ask, he said, "Whiny little women who constantly nag and complain. Look at my sister, Vi. What a waste. Dried up old prune. Always telling me how to treat my children. Never had any of her own, and she thinks she knows everything about raising a kid."

Barrows grinned. He made no secret of what he thought of Market's spinster sister.

"And I hate useless women who can't pull their own weight," Market said, slurring his words slightly. "The only thing I think Carrie is good for is . . ." He paused, then laughed, a cruel, harsh laugh. "Can't think of one. That girl is just plain useless."

His companion could think of one. He wisely kept his thoughts to himself. "What about the older one?" Barrows asked.

"Abby?" Market gave a snort of disgust. "She can work like a mule. But she's a bad one. Bad seed. Talks back. Goes her own way. Defiant little bastard."

Barrows squinted at the man seated across from him. He was used to hearing Market badmouth his women. But there was something new, something ugly in his tone.

"What seems to be the problem?"

Market nervously wiped his mouth and stood. "Nothing. I've had enough to drink. I'm going to bed."

"You haven't finished your drink." Flint picked up the cup and held it out to Market.

Market shook his head. "I've had enough. Too much in fact. G'night."

Before Barrows could protest, Market stumbled

away in the darkness. Lifting the cup, Flint drained Market's drink, then finished his own. Climbing into his darkened wagon, he rolled himself into a blanket and stared at the moon. What had set Market off? he wondered. What had his stupid daughter done this time to make the old man so angry? Against his will, his eyes closed. He was too tired to sort things out. But tomorrow he'd poke around. It would be good sport watching James Market and his spirited daughter go a few rounds.

Abby listened to her father's labored breathing as he crawled into the back of the wagon and fell into a deep sleep. She knew he went to drink with Flint Barrows every night. The stench of liquor clung to him, permeating the wagon, their clothing, even their food. She hated it. And there was nothing she could do about it. Except endure.

When she was little, she would lie in her bed and listen to the muffled voices two floors below. Her mother's voice, frightened, timid. Her father's, angry, abusive. Though she couldn't make out the words, she recognized the tone. When had they loved? she wondered. When had they ever managed to love?

Abby remembered her father's joy when her mother announced that there would be another baby. After Carrie's birth, Margaret had lost five children to stillbirth. All sons. Grandfather had said they should accept God's will. James had said he would have a son or die trying. Abby shivered and drew the blanket close. She wouldn't have minded if her father had been forced to pay the price. But things never seemed to work that way. It was her gentle mother who had died trying. Her mother, and the son James had wanted more than life.

James began to snore, and Abby rolled to one side to drown out the sound. Why did people marry? she wondered. Did they love one day and hate the next? Or did they confuse love with something else? Passion? Lust? Could it have been possible that her mother, in her youth, had wanted so badly to sleep with James Market that she was willing to spend a lifetime with him for the privilege?

Abby listened to her aunt's gentle breathing. Dear Aunt Vi would be scandalized at some of the thoughts that flitted through her niece's mind in the darkness. Abby admired her aunt. Though James Market scorned his sister as a dried-up old maid, she could point with pride to a lifetime of service without compromising her individuality.

That was what she wanted, Abby thought, suddenly sitting up in the darkness. She did want to love a man someday. And she wanted him to love her in return. But she wanted him to love her without smothering her. Without taking over her control. Without making her lose her identity. She wanted someone to love her for herself.

Touching callused fingers to her lips, Abby thought about the shabby men's clothes she wore, the harsh chores she was forced to do. A man wanted a gentle beauty, who would wear fine gowns and smell of lilac water. A woman with soft hands and a clever mind. What man could love a woman like her?

With a sigh she lay back and drew the blanket to her chin. Aunt Vi thought she was beautiful, but that didn't count. The thought came into focus so slowly, she wondered just how long it had been hovering on the edges of her mind. Rourke kissed me, she thought. And for as long as I live, I'll remember what it felt like to be held in his arms. For those few brief moments, I felt beautiful.

Smiling, she drifted back to sleep.

Chapter Ten

"Morning, Miss Violet. Miss Carrie." Mordecai got painfully to his feet and removed his hat. The other men seated around the campfire did the same. "My, don't you two ladies look as fresh as an April breeze."

"Why thank you, Mr. Stump," Violet said. Beside her, Carrie said nothing, though she was painfully aware of Will Montgomery standing less than a foot away.

Carrie Market, Will thought. So that was the pretty one's name. Holding his hat awkwardly at his side, he tried not to stare.

"My niece and I have been trying to think of some way to thank you gentlemen for all you do for us and the others on the train."

"No need to thank us, ma'am. We're just doing our jobs."

"No, no," Violet said, holding up her hand. "We'd like to feel useful. And it occurs to us that perhaps you gentlemen would be in need of some sewing."

"Sewing, ma'am?" Mordecai shrugged. "Parker here takes care of our needs."

Violet gave the rotund cook a gentle smile. "And a fine job you do, Mr. Parker. But my niece and I are excellent seamstresses. Actually," Violet said, turning toward Carrie, "I'm afraid my niece is by far the better of the two."

"Aunt Vi," Carrie protested, feeling herself blush. She saw Will turning the hat around and around in his hand while he watched her.

"It's the truth, child. Never belittle your talents." Turning back to Mordecai, Violet added, "It would please us to take care of your mending, Mr. Stump. You and the other men, I mean. Carrie can mend torn fabric in such a way you won't even see the seam. The two of us can shorten, lengthen, or make over. And when we're finished, your clothes will be better than new."

"Well now, ma'am." Mordecai scratched his head, perplexed.

"You see, Mr. Stump," Violet was quick to explain, "my niece Abby is able to work with the men, hunting, felling logs, even helping with the repair of the wagons. So Carrie and I would like to think we do our share. It would mean a great deal to us if you'd let us do this."

"I see." Mordecai glanced over her head at the cook, whose grin nearly split his face in two. Of all the chores Parker handled, sewing was by far the most vexing. "That would be most appreciated, Miss Violet. Miss Carrie. I'll have the men go through their things and send them around to your wagon later."

"That's fine, Mr. Stump." Violet gave all of them the benediction of her smile. "Good day, gentlemen."

Carrie gave what she hoped was a fair imitation of a smile, even though her heart was thumping so loudly in her chest she could swear they all heard it.

Looping her arm through Carrie's, Violet led her away. When they were out of earshot, Violet whispered, "Satisfied?"

Carrie nodded and swallowed down the lump in her throat.

For days she had pondered a way to get Will

Montgomery to notice her. But though she was up at dawn, walking about the encampment, he never seemed to be around. And although until dark she often strolled among the wagons, she never again ran into him. It was almost as if, she thought, he was deliberately avoiding her. And then she had latched onto the idea of sewing for the wagon master and his men. If she were to mend his clothes, Will Montgomery would have to notice her.

It took some smooth talking to convince Aunt Vi. But once Carrie pointed out how much work Abby did, and how important it was for everyone on the train to pull together, Violet had become a convert. Single-handed, she and Carrie would have the men of the cook wagon in proper clothes.

Of course, conceiving the idea and carrying it out were different matters. Until Carrie had actually stood beside a silent, withdrawn Will Montgomery, she had thought it would be a simple task to be introduced to him. From there, she reasoned, they would talk, ask questions, and get to know one another. In fact, she thought now, standing beneath a darkening sky, stirring a pot of rabbit stew, neither of them had had a thing to say to the other. Oh, how was she going to get that man to talk to her?

"Ma'am."

Hearing the low, almost whispered word, Carrie whirled, dropping the wooden spoon. "Oh. Mr. Montgomery. You startled me."

"I'm sorry, ma'am. Seems like I'm always causing accidents around you."

"No. It's nothing. Really." Wiping the spoon in the grass, then on her apron, she glanced at the pile of clothes balanced in Will's hand. "I see you've brought your mending."

"It isn't all mine, ma'am. Just this shirt on top." He looked embarrassed. "Caught it on a tree limb. Tore it clear across the back."

Walking closer, Carrie lifted the shirt from the pile and examined it carefully. "I can have that fixed in no time."

"Really?" She was a little thing, he realized, the top of her head reaching no higher than his chin. "The rest of these things belong to the others. They wanted you and your aunt to know that they weren't in any rush to have them done. Take your time, ma'am."

"Carrie," she said softly.

"Ma'am?" She smelled of biscuit dough and vanilla. And those little wisps of golden hair that tumbled about her cheeks held him fascinated.

"My name is Carrie, not ma'am."

"Yes ma'am." He felt his face grow hot. But when she laughed, a clear, musical sound, he forgot to be embarrassed and laughed with her and asked her to call him Will.

"Here. Why don't I put these in the wagon." Taking the pile of clothes from him, she turned away.

He watched the way her hips moved. When she turned back to him, he brought his gaze upward to meet hers. He thought he'd never seen bluer eyes or a prettier smile.

"Have you had dinner yet, Will?"

"No ma—" He licked his lips and tried again. "Parker was cooking something that smelled good."

"We're having rabbit stew. Would you care to join us?"

"Oh no ma—" He chanced a quick glance and realized she was laughing. He burst out laughing himself. When they were both finished, he said softly, "Carrie. It's a pretty name. It suits you."

She felt her cheeks redden. "Thank you. Will's a nice name too." To fill in the silence, she added, "Carrie is short for Caroline. But all my life I've been Carrie."

"Will's short for William. But I've been called Will all my life too."

They stared at each other, wishing they could think

of something more to say. Wishing the moment wouldn't end.

"Well, I better go. Parker will have supper done."

As he turned away, she said, "I'll mend your shirt tonight, Will."

He hung his head. "You don't have to do it so soon."

"I want to."

He turned. For long moments he only looked at her. Then he cleared his throat. "Good night, Carrie." If he could, he would say her name forever. It was the most beautiful name in the world.

"Good night, Will."

When he was gone, Carrie stirred the stew, staring deeply into its depths as if all of life's mysteries were hidden there. When she heard the sound of her family's voices, she looked up guiltily and began to spoon out their supper.

Flint Barrows pried the floorboard of his wagon loose and reached inside for a jug. When Emmaline had been alive, he'd hidden his liquor here so she wouldn't find it. Spiteful little bitch would have emptied every one of the jugs along the trail if she had found his hiding place. Just because he'd gotten drunk one night and beaten her. Women were like that, he thought, taking a long pull on the jug. Whined and cried when you hit them, then stood up on their hind legs and roared when you least expected it. How was he to know she was pregnant. Damned witch hadn't even told him. Him. The kid's father. He wouldn't have hit her if he'd known. At least he wouldn't have punched her in the stomach. But if he'd known it wasn't going to be a son, he'd have probably beaten her to a pulp. Should have, he thought, taking another long drink. Would have put them all out of their misery a lot sooner. A man had a right to have a son. Especially a man whose brothers were all dead. And a woman had a duty to give him what he wanted.

He smelled the food cooking at the other wagons and frowned. Emmaline had been a good cook when they first got married. After a while she'd stopped trying. He didn't like to eat when he was drinking. Food got in the way. But later, in the middle of the night, he would wake up ravenous and eat everything she had fixed earlier.

Glancing up, he saw Lavinia Winters heading his way with a towel-covered plate. Stopping at the back of the wagon, she lifted the towel. Steam rose, perfumed with the scent of roasted meat.

"Thank you, Mrs. Winters. That was kind of you."

She smelled the liquor and backed away. "Be sure to eat all of it, Mr. Barrows. I don't think you're eating enough lately. I'll send Aaron around for the plate later."

"Yes ma'am. Thank you, ma'am."

When she was gone, a scowling Flint shoved the plate away and took another drink. Damned nosy old biddie. Just wanted to see if he was drunk or sober. Now she'd run back and tell the others about the jug she saw.

Stretching out in a more comfortable position, Flint poured a generous amount of whiskey into a tin cup and sipped. James Market hadn't been around his wagon for over a week. Ever since that night he'd gotten so drunk and rambled on about the damned women in his family. Flint tried to think back to what had been said. He'd complained about the old-maid sister. Then about the lazy young one. And then about the older daughter, Abby. Something about her being a defiant little bastard. Flint chuckled aloud at the look he'd seen on Market's face when the words spilled out. He'd been angry, but embarrassed as well. As if he'd said more than he ought to. Why had James Market suddenly stopped talking? And why was Market avoiding him since?

Sitting up, Flint stared out at the gathering darkness and thought about the Market daughters. Carrie was rounder in all the right places. Flint's teeth gleamed as he smiled. High firm breasts and well-rounded hips. Young. Young and tight. He thought of those prim little dresses, buttoned clear to her throat. It would be fun to take her, he thought, remembering how many times lately she'd passed his wagon without even glancing his way.

Abby. She had a different kind of beauty. Despite those dirty shirts and britches, he'd had glimpses of small, firm breasts and slim narrow hips. And though she tried to hide it, her hair hung past her waist and was the color of fire. Probably smelled like horses, he thought, taking another drink. But what a fight she'd put up. Just thinking about it had his excitement growing. All the younger one knew how to do was cry and thrash around a bit. But the older sister would put up a damned good fight. And when he managed to overpower her, he'd have her purring like a kitten.

Corking his jug, he stepped down from the wagon and began walking. From the shadows he watched as Abby Market brushed the horse, cooing softly to it while she worked. In the light of the campfire, her movements were smooth, sensuous, as she brought the brush over the animal's back, down his flank, along his leg. Flint watched in fascination and felt himself grow hard.

A voice nearby caused him to drop to the ground.

"When you're finished with the team, I want you to help me with the axle."

"Yes, Pa."

Flint turned back to his own wagon. Next time, he told himself, it was going to be Abby Market he took. He'd bide his time and watch, and sooner or later he'd find her alone, without the protection of the others. And when he did, he'd show her what a real man was like.

* * *

Abby wiped her dirty hands on an old rag and tucked it into her back pocket. She and her father had worked on the axle until she'd thought her back would break. Satisfied at last, James crawled into his blanket without a word of thanks.

Abby glanced around the camp. Everyone was asleep by now. She was bone-weary, but too keyed up to sleep. Because she spent so much time with the men, she was privy to information that was often kept from the women. Probably thinking their womenfolk too weak to deal with the harsher facts of the perilous journey, the men foolishly caused them to be ill prepared for what lay ahead.

"I've heard rumors of an Indian uprising," Big Jack had remarked that afternoon as he and Abby stalked a deer.

"I haven't heard a thing about it." Abby studied the surrounding rocks, then swung her gaze back to him. "Are we in any danger?"

"So far they seem to be fighting among themselves. Mordecai thinks it may be confined to a couple of small tribes."

"What would happen if they turned on us?"

Big Jack took a long time examining his gun before replying. "We'd have to take measures to protect the people on this train, Miss Abby."

Now, with the moon just a narrow slice of golden light against a darkened backdrop, Abby walked slowly among the wagons, then climbed a low hill and stared out into the distance, wondering just how many dangers lurked in this strange land.

"It isn't safe to wander away from the camp."

At Rourke's deep voice, Abby whirled. In the darkness, he appeared to be no more than a shadow, until he stepped closer.

"Then why are you out here, Rourke?" She hoped her voice sounded steadier than she felt.

"I couldn't sleep. Thought I'd keep an eye out."

Damn her. Why did she have to come out here tonight? He'd been fighting thoughts of her all evening.

"Are you expecting trouble?" Abby felt a tremble pulse through her. Was it from fear? Or merely the reaction she always seemed to feel whenever she got too close to this man?

"Let's just say I like to be cautious."

"Thompson said there's been some trouble with Indians."

"Indians are just one problem."

"What are some of the others?"

He scratched a match across his boot and held the flame to the tip of a cigar. In the light that flared, she studied his harsh profile. "You mean besides the weather, the mountains, the diseases, and the predators?"

Abby shivered and tried to keep her voice from trembling. "You make it all sound like such fun, Rourke."

"Nobody said it would be easy."

"We made it this far, didn't we?"

He blew out a stream of smoke and watched it dissipate into the night air. "We aren't even halfway there. A lot can happen between here and California."

A stray breeze caught a strand of her hair. He curled his hand into a fist and fought the urge to brush it back from her cheek.

"Thanks for cheering me up, Rourke. I needed this before turning in."

He laughed. "Sorry. I guess I sound pretty morbid." His voice lowered. "The night does that to me."

"Afraid of shadows?"

"Maybe I am." He took a long drag, then tossed the cigar aside. When he caught her roughly by the shoulders, she was so startled she couldn't move. His thumbs caressed the soft flesh of her upper arms as he drew her closer. She couldn't see his eyes in the darkness. But his voice sent a thrill racing along her spine. "There aren't too many things in this world I'm afraid of. But you scare the hell out of me, Abby Market."

Abby stiffened, pressing her palms against his chest. Rourke was a very strong man. Strong and determined. But she knew how to use her voice with authority. She did it with the team. She did it with her younger sister when all else failed.

"Stop it, Rourke."

His lips curled in the darkness, revealing white teeth. "Ever try stopping a stampede?"

She tried to pull back but he was quicker and stronger. His hand cupped the back of her head, holding her still. His other hand glided to her waist, drawing her firmly against him.

She could feel the pressure of every one of his fingers along her spine. He lowered his head and she watched him as if transfixed.

His mouth was surprisingly soft and warm. She absorbed the first tremors and tried not to react. Patiently he rubbed his lips over hers, teasing, nibbling, until he felt her gradual response. Her fingers curled into the front of his shirt. And then, without even realizing it, she wrapped her arms around his neck and plunged her fingers into the dark hair that curled at his collar.

He smelled of soap and leather and that distinct male scent that would always remind her of him. She breathed him in as he drew her closer. And then she was tasting him, dark, mysterious tastes that only Rourke had ever shown her. Her body strained against his, no longer stiff and awkward, but eager.

She heard his quiet moan as his lips left hers to roam her temple, her eyelids, her cheek. He took her earlobe between his teeth and nipped, but before she could gasp her surprise, his tongue darted to her ear.

"Rourke."

His lips covered hers, swallowing her protest. The hands at her hips pulled her closer, tormenting both of them. And then his hands were moving along her sides, until his thumbs encountered the swell of her breasts.

She pulled back, shocked at the contact. Sensing her confusion, he drew her gently to him and kissed the tip of her nose. The gesture was so painfully sweet she could only stare at him. Then, behaving in a way she would have never believed possible, she placed her hands on his arms, lifted herself on tiptoe, and touched her lips to his.

Her offering was his undoing. His arms came around her, pinning her against him. His lips covered hers in a savage kiss as his tongue plundered her mouth.

Abby felt herself tumbling into some wild, dark place that frightened yet exhilarated her. She absorbed the heat of his breath as his mouth roamed her face, then once more covered her lips. Her heart pounded, keeping time with his.

Rourke was stunned by his need for her. Since the day of the hunt, he'd wanted to kiss her again, to feel the rush of desire, to experience the thrill of the challenge. But this. This left him reeling. He knew he had to end it. He knew he had to step away or be consumed by the fire. And yet he allowed himself one more touch, one last taste.

Beneath the rough shirt he felt the incredibly soft body. Beneath the slender frame he felt her indomitable strength. Lifting his head at last, he stepped back.

Abby stood very straight, absorbing the shock. Though her legs trembled, she stood her ground. Taking a deep breath, she sought to fill her lungs and steady her breathing.

Rourke cursed the fact that he'd tossed away his cigar. He needed to do something besides stare at her. He wanted to smoke, but he knew his hand would shake and give him away if he lit another match. Instead, he shoved his hands into his back pockets in an arrogant pose.

"I suddenly realize that not all the dangers are out there." Abby's voice was husky in the darkness.

"That's right. So now that you're warned, stay close to your wagon, and as far away from me as you can."

Abby turned away, keeping her spine stiff. Rourke watched until she disappeared below the hill. Then he lit a fresh cigar. He'd been right to wait until she was gone. His hand was definitely unsteady. He exhaled a stream of smoke, then glanced back at the circle of wagons. He wanted her. God help him, he wanted Abby Market as he'd never wanted any woman.

Chapter Eleven

ROURKE LAY IN his blanket and thought about Abby. He seemed to be doing a lot of that lately—thinking about Abby. Damned little female had gotten under his skin like he'd vowed no woman ever would again.

He admired her spirit. Though he'd seen her hand tremble when she first fired that rifle, she'd refused to back down. And gutting her first deer had been sheer hell. Now she hunted with the men and butchered her kill without a qualm.

She could handle a team better than some of the men on the wagon train. Yet she admitted that she'd never harnessed a mule or driven a wagon before joining the train. Rourke had watched her with the animals. She had a real love for them. And they returned her affection. She was more comfortable with them than she was with some people.

Abby Market was a contradiction. She allowed her bully of a father to treat her worse than a dog. And yet she stood toe to toe with him when he tried to intimidate her aunt or sister. Rourke had watched her share the precious meat with everyone on the wagon train, despite her father's violent objections.

Thinking of James Market always made Rourke

angry. Sitting up, he reached for a cigar. He held a twig to the glowing embers of the campfire and lit the tip of the cigar, then blew out a stream of smoke. Leaning back against the wheel of the cook wagon, he turned his thoughts back to Abby, so soft and warm in his arms. It was obvious that she had no experience with men. When he touched her, she jumped like a jackrabbit. He knew, by the way her cheeks flushed, that she felt awkward and uneasy with him. Somehow that only made her more appealing. He loved the way she reluctantly responded to his touch, his kiss. In time her woman's instincts would show her what to do, and when. It tormented him to think about her callused fingertips caressing his skin.

His thoughts flew to Katherine. Everything about her had been soft. Her skin, her hands, her eyes, her manner of speech. Because of her aristocratic upbringing, she'd never been forced to do anything more complicated than set a fine table. And because she'd been thrown from a horse as a child, she'd never again been astride one. The lingering injury to her hip had kept her from doing anything more physical than climb the stairs. Her hair, her skin, her clothes had smelled of the finest milled soaps and imported perfumes. She'd been a soft, gentle woman who wanted only to love him and make a home for him. He exhaled a cloud of smoke. It wasn't fair to compare Abby to Katherine. Abby could never be to him what Katherine had been. Besides, Katherine had been a lifetime ago.

Abby Market was just someone who happened to be on this wagon train heading west, he told himself. Someone who had caught his attention and was different from any woman he'd ever known before. When they reached California, she and her family would settle in. And he would be back on the trail, searching, seeking.

He crushed out the cigar, checked the gun he kept hidden under the saddle he used as a pillow, and rolled to his side. Closing his eyes, a vision intruded. A vision of a slim, lithe figure walking naked from the river. He felt the need rising and cursed the woman who was causing him such distress. Abby Market was, he thought, the most fascinating creature in the world. And if he wasn't careful, he'd find himself getting caught up in something he'd later regret.

While the rest of her family was still asleep, Carrie rolled from bed and climbed down from the back of the wagon. In the predawn chill she filled a basin with cold water and, ignoring the gooseflesh, gave herself a thorough sponge bath. Liberally sprinkling on her aunt's favorite rosewater, she dressed carefully in a pale blue muslin gown. Aunt Vi had often said that particular color made her eyes seem even bluer. Brushing her hair, she tied it back with blue ribbons, then gathered her shawl about her.

Last night, by the light of the fire, Carrie had mended Will's shirt. With fine, even stitches she had repaired the tear, then added a seam across the entire back of the shirt, so that it looked better than new. Then she had washed it and hung it on a tree limb to dry. Now, folding it carefully over her arm, she made her way to the river.

Will Montgomery sat with his back against the trunk of a gnarled tree. On the eastern horizon an eerie white light was just beginning to roll back the darkness. In the shallows a frog croaked, and nearby on the riverbank a second one answered. Will liked this time of day best. Though man wasn't up and moving yet, nature was already humming. Insects buzzed. A chorus of birds chirped. The horses, in tune with their wild cousins, neighed and nipped one another.

Will thought about his father and the plantation on which he'd grown up. From the time he was a toddler, he'd followed his father about the land, imitating him. By the time he was twelve, Will could plow a furrow straighter than most men. He was big for his age, and strong as a mule. His father had boasted of his son's farming skills. It had always been expected that Will would take over the plantation when he married. When he married. Will tossed a stone into the river and watched the ripples.

He'd seen the look on his father's face when he'd returned from the war. He had known. They had both known that his father couldn't bear to see his only son like this. His father had been shocked by his son's gaunt, haggard appearance and the loss of an arm. What had shocked Will even more was how old his father had grown while he was away at war.

"They've won, Will. I've been beaten," his father had said, counting out the money he'd saved. "And if you stay, I'll be forced to watch you become old before your time too. Make a new life for yourself, son. Someplace with a future. Someplace untouched by this hellish war."

Will often wondered if it was the war and the land that had beaten his father, or the loss of his only son's arm.

Carrie stood a moment, willing her heart to stop its hammering. Just the sight of Will sitting so quietly, staring somberly at the river, caused her pulse to race. He was so handsome. She would have stayed a few moments longer watching him. But he turned his head and noticed her, and she smiled and forced herself into action.

"Good morning. I didn't know if you'd be here this early."

"I'm a light sleeper," Will said, coming to his feet. Especially last night, he thought. He hadn't been able to sleep at all, knowing he was going to meet her in the morning.

"I'm usually a sound sleeper. But I found myself awake at dawn," she lied. The fact was, she'd been awake for hours, anticipating this meeting. "And here's your shirt," she added, holding it out to him. "Just as I promised."

Will examined the seam, then gave her an admiring look. "That's fine sewing, Carrie. I'd never even guess the back of this shirt had been torn clear across. But I wish you hadn't gone to so much trouble."

"It wasn't any trouble. I like to sew."

She stood with her hands behind her back, staring at the ground. Will swallowed. Before she got here, he'd thought of a dozen things to say. Now that she was standing so close, he couldn't think of one.

"I was just sitting, watching the river. Want to sit?" He indicated the flattened grass under the tree.

Carrie sat, smoothing her skirts down around her ankles. Will sat beside her and breathed in the scent of roses that lingered about her.

"Where'd you learn to sew like that?" Will asked.

"My ma. She was . . . sickly. Frail, sort of. She couldn't do a lot of farm chores. So she spent a lot of time sewing, knitting, doing fancy handwork. And I just picked it up from her."

"You lived on a farm?"

When Carrie nodded, Will said, "So did I. Couple hundred acres. Cotton mostly. Some corn and tobacco."

"Ours was just a little farm. My pa wasn't much good at farming."

"Is that why you're heading west?"

Carrie gazed out over the water. "I don't know why we're going. My ma died, and my pa just sold the farm and said we were going. I think he's just running."

Will fell silent. Was that what he was doing too? Running?

"What do you want to do in California, Carrie?"

No one had ever bothered to ask her that before. No one else seemed to care. But she knew. She'd always known.

"I'd like to open my own dress shop."

"You mean, you want to work?"

Carrie turned to study him. "Of course I want to work. Why wouldn't I?"

Will shrugged, embarrassed. "I guess I just thought all girls wanted to do was get married."

She felt her cheeks redden. "I want that too. But I can make simple dresses without even using a pattern. And I know how to add fancy stitches, and lace, and ribbons, to make them special. I know what looks good on a woman, and what doesn't. And if there are going to be fancy ladies in California, I figure I ought to be the one to make their dresses."

Will was astonished. This pretty little thing, who looked like a princess in a once-upon-a-time story book, wouldn't be content to be loved and waited on. She wanted to work. He had never met a girl like this before. In fact, he never would have believed that a girl like this existed.

"What do you want to do when you get to California, Will?"

"All I know is the land. I want to work it. I want to grow things. Different things," he said, watching the mountain peaks in the distance glisten pink and gold in the rising sun.

"What do you mean by different things?"

He turned to her. The little frown line between his eyebrows disappeared. There was a light in his eyes she'd never noticed before. "Fruit maybe. I read a wonderful book called *Life, Adventures and Travels in California* by T. J. Farnum. He says the climate in California is perfect for growing fruit and grains. In fact, he says the fruit will be so heavy it will practically weight the trees right down to the ground. Imagine. Oranges. Grapes. Melons." His voice trembled with excitement. "I've been reading about all the fruit I could grow."

"But who'd want it?"

"People, Carrie. With all the people going west, there are going to be houses built. And houses mean businesses. And businesses mean towns. Think of all the towns that will be built in the west. That means that the people living and working there will need food. They'll need farmers. They'll need my fruit."

Carrie smiled. "And all their women will need my dresses."

They looked at each other and both began laughing. Oh it was so good to have someone to share the dream with. Someone to talk with and laugh with. Someone to be with while the rest of the world slept.

A voice filled with venom sliced through their happiness. "What are you doing down here, girl?"

At James Market's angry tone, Carrie jumped up guiltily. "I brought Will the shirt I mended."

"You could have taken it to the cook wagon. You didn't need to sneak down here for that."

"We weren't sneaking. We were just talking, sir," Will said, scrambling to his feet. He towered over the short, stocky man.

James turned on him. "You do your talking to someone else. I don't want you hanging around my daughter, do you hear?"

"Pa, we were just—"

"You back-talk me again, I'll put you over my knee right here and now."

Carrie looked stricken. She wished the earth would open up and swallow her so she wouldn't have to see the look on Will's face.

"Now you get on back to the wagon and help your sister and aunt with the chores." He gave her a shove that nearly sent her sprawling. Seeing Will's hand dart out to steady her, he whirled. "And you. Don't you ever touch her. You see that you don't come near my daughter again. Or so help me, you won't have a hand left to touch her with."

Will saw Carrie pause and turn. It galled him that a man would talk to him like that. But this man was Carrie's father. And like it or not, he would have to swallow his pride. And his anger.

"Do you understand me, boy?"

119

Will nodded, and saw Carrie swing away. "Yes sir. I understand."

Market's voice lowered to a hiss. "Then be careful you don't cross me, boy. 'Cause I'll make you wish you'd never been born."

Will watched as Market stormed away. When he was out of sight, Will bent and picked up the shirt Carrie had mended. Lifting it to his face, he breathed in the delicate rose fragrance that lingered still. Then he called himself every kind of fool for dreaming about a woman as beautiful as Carrie Market. She'd be crazy to waste herself on a cripple. And her father had just made it plain as day how he felt about him.

Flint Barrows nursed a smoldering hatred for Rourke. From the first moment he had seen Rourke ride up to the wagon train, Flint had known that he would take his time and find a way to get him. And it had been Rourke who had pulled a gun on Flint the night he'd attacked Carrie. And it was Rourke who got to ride ahead of the train, often in the company of Abby Market, while Barrows was stuck driving his lonely wagon, eating the dust of the many wagons in front of him. But more than anything else, Flint hated Rourke because of what he represented. Though he held no title, Rourke had the respect of the people on the train. Though he was a loner who said little, there was about Rourke an air of authority.

During his nightly prowls, looking for a chance to get Abby alone, Flint had begun to observe certain things about the others on the train.

Will Montgomery, Flint noted, avoided all contact with Rourke. Will's Confederate army shirt was in sharp contrast to Rourke's Union cap and gun.

Flint decided it might be fun to prod those two into a confrontation. If he was lucky, it might even erupt into an all-out fight. Nothing excited Flint more than a good fight. Except maybe a woman.

He bided his time, waiting for the perfect moment.

It wouldn't be much fun to goad them into a fight in private. What Flint wanted was as many witnesses as possible. That way he might even be able to divide the entire wagon train into two camps, Yankee and Confederate. And if Rourke was forced to pull his gun, Flint would have the perfect excuse to shoot him.

His opportunity came one Sunday morning.

Reverend Coulter had persuaded Mordecai to allow him to hold a prayer service every Sunday before the wagons started out for the day. Though the wagon master was constantly keeping an eye on the weather, hoping to reach their destination before the winter snows, he realized that these people needed the comfort their religion brought them. One hour on Sunday mornings was set aside for prayer.

When she was alive, Emmaline Barrows had insisted her husband attend these services with her. Since her death Flint hadn't bothered to attend. But this Sunday, seeing the Market women parade past his wagon in their dresses and bonnets, he decided to go just so he could stare at them.

James Market, at his sister's insistence, wore his stiff-collared shirt and dark jacket. It wouldn't occur to him to miss a church service, even though he hated it. It always reminded him of his father, and the stern sermons he'd been given through the years. Even after he'd married, James had had to endure his father's lectures on everything from treasuring his marriage vows to raising his children in the ways of the Lord. But though he hated the service, and resented the father of whom it reminded him, he thought of himself as a righteous man.

Violet carried a hymnal and a book of prayers from the Methodist church back home. Though the Reverend Coulter was a Baptist, many of the hymns were the same. And, she consoled herself, they were all praying to the same God.

She kept an arm around her younger niece. She was worried about Carrie. For days now she had been silent and withdrawn. Though Violet had tried to talk to her, the child had refused to say what was wrong. In fact, she rarely spoke to any of them. Just went about doing her chores, and spending her nights staring into the flames of the fire.

As they walked, Violet felt her niece stiffen. Turning her head, she saw Carrie staring at the young man who had recently joined the wagon train. Will Montgomery. That was his name. He was studying Carrie as if he wanted to memorize every feature. Violet felt a quickening of her own pulse. So that's what was wrong with her niece. Puppy love, she thought with a smile. Poor little Carrie was smitten. And from the looks of him, Will Montgomery was every bit as strung up as Carrie.

Releasing her grip on Carrie's waist, Violet whispered, "I believe I'll just take your father up closer, child, where we can hear Reverend Coulter better. Why don't you and Abby stay back here?"

Carrie shot her aunt a puzzled glance, then gave a shaky laugh. "All right, Aunt Vi. If you insist."

Violet lifted the hymnal to her lips to cover the smile that quivered there. Then, taking James's arm, she nudged him through the crowd before he could look around and see what was happening.

As the crowd began to draw together, Carrie found herself separated from her sister. Feeling someone's hand brush her shoulder, she looked up to find herself standing beside Will. They glanced at each other, then down at the ground. He was so tall, Carrie thought, noting that her head barely reached his shoulder. When the Reverend Coulter called out a song, Carrie turned slightly, offering to share her hymnal with Will. They stood, almost touching, each holding a side of the song book, and lifted their voices to the heavens. For the first time in a week, Carrie felt the heaviness lift from her heart. As long as she could stand beside Will, she felt like singing. She only wished they could go on like this forever.

Abby smiled a greeting as the Garners passed and pressed forward. Though Nancy Garner had washed her little son and dressed him in clean clothes, her own dress appeared rumpled. And her hair, usually pulled into a perfect knot, was disheveled, with little wisps falling into her eyes. Jed's eyes were downcast, and the corners of his lips were tightly drawn. The perfect couple seemed to have developed a few imperfections.

Keeping to the back of the crowd, Abby watched as more families pushed their way toward the Coulter wagon, where Reverend Coulter waited for the hymn to end. Then, lifting his arms heavenward, he began to pray aloud.

Abby's gaze skimmed the crowd until she found Rourke, standing some distance away. She knew he never attended the prayer services and she found herself wondering why. Did he think their prayers foolish? Or had something happened in the past to harden his heart? He was the only man in camp who had never attended the service. All the others, including Brand, made it a point to attend. Even Flint Barrows, she noted, had managed to leave his jug long enough to pray and sing. She saw Flint glance her way and felt a shiver along her spine. The man made her so uncomfortable she took several steps backward, to block her view of him.

Rourke lounged against the tree, trying not to stare at Abby. Whenever she wore a dress, it was hard to imagine her in those men's britches and faded shirt. Yet later today, when she changed back into her workclothes, it would be harder still to picture her in a dress. Since that night on the hill, he'd worked overtime to avoid her. But in a wagon train as small as this, it was impossible not to see her. Worse yet, she was there in his mind. At night, when he tried to sleep, she flitted through his dreams, leaving him half awake and always hungry.

As the crowd broke into another hymn, he felt the

bittersweet pain of remembrance. He would always think of Katherine whenever he heard this hymn. It was the one the congregation had sung at her burial. Without realizing it, his hands curled into fists. His jaw tightened, causing a little muscle to begin working.

As the crowd began to disperse, Flint Barrows called out in a loud voice, "I noticed that our esteemed gunman never bothers to attend prayer service. Could it be he doesn't think he needs to pray? Or maybe it's because he knows he's too much of a sinner to ever be heard."

Heads swiveled to stare at Rourke as families hurried past. Will Montgomery was so caught up in the beautiful girl walking beside him, he failed to even notice Flint's words until they were directed at him.

"I guess I can speak for our Confederate soldier here, as well as myself, when I say I consider anyone who fought on the side of the Yankees to be traitors to this land."

Will felt the stares of the entire crowd directed at him. He looked up and found himself staring into Rourke's narrowed eyes. Glancing uneasily at Carrie, Will said softly, "You'd better get out of here, Carrie."

"Why?"

"Just go. Get on back to your wagon."

"But I . . . "

"Go. Now."

Carrie had a glimpse of the soldier he must have been. There was a hardness, a determination she'd never seen before. With a quick, frightened glance at Rourke, she hurried away. Most of the other women left also, sensing a fight. The men, some merely curious, others watchful, stayed behind. Abby, nearly hidden in the crowd of men, stayed.

Will had gone very still. What Flint said, he had often thought. But now that the words were spoken aloud, he found them lacking in conviction. The truth was, he and Rourke had chosen separate sides in the war. But each of them, he was convinced, thought he was fighting for the good of his country.

He glanced at Rourke. Though he hadn't moved a muscle and was still lounging against the tree, Will had the distinct impression that the man was coiled as tightly as a spring. One move, one wrong word, and Rourke would draw. Will was a good shot. Maybe even an excellent one. But he had no desire to shoot Rourke, even in a fair fight. In fact, he had no stomach for killing. Not ever again.

For his part, Rourke tensed and waited for Will's reaction. He instantly recognized that Flint was itching to start a fight. Since he was too much of a coward to do it himself, he'd decided to sucker this poor kid into doing the job for him. Trouble was, Rourke knew he might be forced to fight Will before he could deal with Flint Barrows. The choice would be up to Will.

"Well, Reb. Are you going to just stand there? Tell him what you think," Flint yelled.

The others shifted uneasily. Everyone in this train had chosen sides in the war. And if this erupted into a fight, they would all be forced to choose again. What most of them wanted was to put the war behind them.

"A traitor?" Will asked. His voice quivered slightly, but it carried far enough to be heard by the crowd. "There were no traitors, only soldiers. No matter which side you died for, you were just as dead. The war is over," Will said softly. "And I'd like it to stay that way."

A low murmur rippled through the crowd. One by one the men began drifting back toward their wagons. Will glanced at Rourke, hoping the man didn't bear a grudge. Rourke didn't move.

Flint's hand hovered over his gun. He was losing the crowd. And with them, the hoped-for fight. In desperation he cried, "Well, I think we should have kicked their asses all the way back to Washington. But at least we gave 'em hell, Reb."

Will stared directly at Rourke. In a soft voice he

said, "These people don't have any idea what the war was really like. They've never been to hell."

Rourke studied the figure before him. No more than a boy really. But the war had changed him into a man. And a damned fine one at that.

Stepping forward, Rourke extended his hand. For a moment Will could only stare at it. Then, extending his own, he let out a long breath.

"We've both been there, Will," Rourke said, accepting the younger man's handshake. "To hell and back."

As the two men walked away, Rourke dropped an arm around Will's shoulders. Maybe Flint Barrows had just done something good. Maybe, after all, an old hatred could end.

Behind them, Abby let her breath out slowly and turned toward her wagon. To her way of thinking, Rourke never needed to attend a single prayer service. She'd just witnessed something better than prayer. There had been some healing today. Some might even call it a miracle.

Chapter Twelve

THE WAGON TRAIN had been following the Oregon Trail from the Missouri River. At South Pass, the route would branch out to follow the California Trail to the Great Salt Lake, then on to the Humboldt River lifeline.

The summer weather was a furnace—dry, with unbelievable blasts of heat that rose up from the dusty plains to choke the breath from straining lungs.

As they passed Plume Rocks, the travelers counted dozens of carcasses of dead oxen and mules. After twelve hundred miles, the people on the wagon train prayed that the worst of the journey was behind them. But the worst had just begun. None of the travelers would be prepared for the sizzling heat of the desert. Or for the freezing cold of the Sierra Nevada yet to come, the last barrier between them and the promised land.

The sky was overcast, with dark clouds far to the west. Everyone prayed for rain. The summer had been unseasonably dry, and the meager supplies of water were being rationed.

As Rourke was pulling out of camp, Mordecai stopped him. "Hold it, Rourke. I promised Miss Abby she could ride along with you today."

Rourke swung his horse around to face the cook wagon. Beside it, Abby sat her horse, her rifle balanced across her lap. Inwardly Rourke groaned. He didn't think he could take another day in her company, playing the role of impersonal guide.

"Maybe she ought to wait for a clearer day." Turning toward Abby, he added, "Nothing personal, Miss Market." Like hell it's nothing personal, he berated himself. It's about as personal as a man can get. One more day of watching her crouch behind rocks, and bend over streams, and he'd do something foolish and find himself on the wrong end of Mordecai's rifle. "But it looks like rain. Maybe tomorrow you could ride out with Brand."

"Brand might be gone for several days," Mordecai called. He turned to the girl. "What do you think, Miss Abby? Want to take your chances with the rain, or wait for another day?"

"We have no meat left," Abby said. She'd heard the edge in Rourke's tone and wished there was someone else she could ride with. But if she waited until tomorrow, her father would be impossible to live with tonight. "I'd better take my chances on the rain holding off."

"All right then." Calling out to Rourke, Mordecai added, "We'll catch up with you before day's end."

Sunset would be too late, Rourke thought. Sweet Jesus, by sundown, he'd be stark raving mad.

He wheeled his mount, leaving Abby in a cloud of dust. The best way to control his feelings for her, he decided, was to be as cold and distant as possible.

Abby let her horse have its head, knowing the mare would do everything short of breaking a leg to keep up with Rourke's stallion. When she rode up beside him, she noted the tight set of his jaw and decided to keep her own counsel. Something was bothering him. Probably the fact that he was stuck with her again. She wished he wasn't so moody. But she'd grown up with a moody father. The best way to handle these spells was to ignore him until he worked it out of his system.

They covered the miles in strained silence. When the lack of communication between them grew uncomfortable, Rourke pushed his horse to the limit. It gave him a perverse pleasure to know that the skinny girl who had cost him so much anguish was forced to keep up the relentless pace.

Dust rose up around them, and eventually Rourke tied his handkerchief across his nose and mouth to keep from choking. Several miles further on, he paused to look back. Abby's mare doggedly followed his route, horse and rider eating a cloud of sand that seemed to engulf them.

His heart went out to Abby. She was ill prepared for what he'd put her through. Though she'd drawn her hat low on her head, she had no handkerchief to ward off the dust. When she drew nearer, he saw the tears that stung her eyes. Damned woman had grit, he admitted grudgingly.

Dismounting, he removed his handkerchief and poured a small amount of water from his canteen. When she slid from the saddle, he walked up and, without a word, pressed the wet cloth to her eyes.

"You'll have to learn to carry a handkerchief for dust," he muttered.

Abby was so startled she was unable to do a thing. Standing very still, she allowed him to continue his ministrations, bathing her eyes, her forehead, her cheeks. The cool water felt heavenly. The touch of his hands on her skin was the sweetest torment she'd ever known. When he pressed the canteen between parched lips, she drank deeply until he lowered it.

"Thanks." She looked away, hoping he hadn't noticed the betraying flush. "I haven't seen any game yet. Think we might come up empty?"

"Game was plentiful on the plains," Rourke muttered. "Here you'll have to work for it. The animals are smarter than men. They know it's too hot to survive. So they take shelter from the sun."

"How about up in those rocks?"

Rourke shrugged and tried not to notice the way her sweat-stained shirt clung to her. The smartest thing he could do would be to stay out of her sight for a few hours. Maybe by then he'd be able to keep his mind on the game they were supposed to be hunting.

"Why don't you try those rocks," Rourke suggested. "And I'll scout ahead." He lifted his rifle. "If I see anything worth hunting, I'll signal with two quick shots. If you need me, you give the same signal."

Abby nodded. She didn't especially like the idea of prowling these rocks alone. But Rourke set the rules. All she could do was follow them.

"All right. Two shots and I'll come running."

"Two shots from you, I'll do the same." He turned away and swung into the saddle. Within a few minutes, the only sign of Rourke was the dust that rose up from his trail.

Flint Barrows sat on the hard seat of his wagon and watched Rourke and Abby ride off. All week he'd been smarting about the way his planned fight had fizzled. What made him even more furious was the friendship that seemed to have developed between Montgomery and Rourke.

Rourke. Flint's eyes narrowed as he watched the horse and rider take off at a fast clip. Behind them, the slower mare and her rider trailed, eating their dust.

What gave that snotty little Market woman the idea that she could hunt as well as a man? He'd like to show her a few things. He'd like to . . . He smiled. A plan began to form in his mind.

Flint glanced around at the people of the train, hustling about getting their wagons ready for another day's trek. If he could get someone to drive his wagon, he could go hunting himself. And maybe, if he was lucky, he could bag something more than game.

Studying the people around him, he dismissed the Market family. James was needed to drive their wagon. And Carrie and her useless aunt wouldn't be capable of handling his team.

He heard the Garner boy cry and swiveled his head to study the wagon behind his. Jed Garner was looking grim these days. Flint's lips curled into a smile as he climbed down from his wagon and walked up to Jed.

"How're things going?" Flint asked.

Jed looked up from his chores. He and Flint had barely exchanged a dozen words since the wagon train left Missouri.

"Fine." Jed tightened the harness.

"Does your wife ever handle the team?" Flint glanced at the young woman who had hardly smiled in a month.

"Sometimes. When I'm needed elsewhere." Jed shot a glance at his wife, then back to the harness.

"I was thinking I'd go hunting today," Flint said casually. "But I can't leave the wagon and team untended."

Jed paused, watching Barrows.

"I was thinking that if your wife could handle your team, you might be willing to handle mine, in exchange for half of what I bag."

The crying of the Garner child increased, and Flint smiled, reading the irritation on the young husband's face. "I realize you'd have to travel alone all day," Flint added slyly, "but I'd be most grateful."

Jed lowered his gaze, hoping Barrows wouldn't notice his enthusiasm for the idea. With his wife still brooding about the loss of her damned piano, he was rarely able to let her out of his sight. Her moods swung from high to low in a matter of minutes. When she wasn't reminding him of his broken promise, she was taking out her frustration on the boy. If he agreed to Barrows's suggestion, he could find some relief.

Not only would Jed have enough meat for a few days, but he would enjoy a day of peace as well.

"I'd say that's a fair enough bargain." Jed extended his hand. "I'd be happy to drive your wagon in exchange for half your catch."

"Done." Flint pumped his hand, then walked to his wagon to untie his horse and retrieve his rifle. Within minutes he was riding ahead of the train. As long as he kept the trail of dust in sight, he was bound to catch up with Abby Market sooner or later. And when he did, he had a surprise in store for her.

As the horse picked its way through the dust, Abby studied the outcropping of rock up ahead. She had to find some game. If she dared to go back empty-handed, her father would start harping once more on the fact that she had given away meat instead of keeping it for their own use. He was still angry about what he considered her foolish generosity. That meat could have been used to barter for guns or whiskey, or even a better position on the train. It would never have occurred to James Market to give away something he could use for a profit.

Turning her head, she saw a blur of movement among the rocks. She blinked and it was gone. Deer? Or dust? Digging in her heels, she urged the mare closer. When she reached the column of rocks, she tied the horse. She could make better time on foot. Clutching her rifle, she began to climb.

From a distance, the rock ledge that jutted from the desert floor had appeared small and easy to explore. Up close, Abby realized it was a series of rocks and cliffs that could easily conceal a small herd of animals. The boulders offered shade from the relentless sun. Though the rocks appeared barren, tufts of bunch grass and an occasional cactus dangled precariously. Her heartbeat accelerated. If it had been a deer she'd seen, there could be more. Enough to feed the entire wagon train.

Scrambling over rocks and boulders, Abby made her way to a shelf of rock overlooking the shadowed cliffs below. Shading her eyes from the glare of sun, she saw a doe just disappearing behind a boulder. And further on, almost invisible against the buff sandstone, stood a buck, his head lifted for any sign of trouble.

Abby thought of the signal Rourke had arranged. Two shots. But if she were to fire now, the deer would scatter. If there really was a herd hidden among these rocks, they would be gone before Rourke could get here. She would be much wiser to stay concealed until she was close enough to kill the buck. She might even get a second shot off at the doe.

As she crawled closer, she wished Rourke was here with her. Together, they could make a real hunt of this. Besides, she thought, grunting with pain as she pulled herself across the sharp, pointed edge of a rock, it would be exciting to share the adventure with Rourke. She liked the way his eyes looked when he did something satisfying. Like the time Will Montgomery had offered his hand to Rourke, and Rourke had accepted. There had been an unusual light in Rourke's gray eyes that had brought a lump to her throat. Since then, she had seen Rourke and Will talking together, sharing a steaming cup of coffee and a smoke. Whatever tension had been between them was gone. They had formed a bond. One that the likes of Flint Barrows would never be able to break.

Abby took refuge behind a boulder and watched as the buck lowered its head to snatch at a clump of dried grass. While he was momentarily distracted, she raised the rifle to her shoulder and took aim. The buck swiveled his head in her direction and wheeled, as if to flee. His action puzzled Abby. He couldn't possibly have seen her. She was completely hidden by the boulder. Maybe it was her scent, although she had made certain to stay downwind of him. Realizing she was about to lose the game she had stalked so carefully, she stood up and without taking the time to aim, fired. As she was about to fire a second time, she was yanked roughly from behind.

The rifle she was holding fell from her hands, clattering to the rocks below. An arm was clamped firmly around her throat, lifting her off her feet. As the grip tightened, she felt the breath being slowly squeezed from her lungs. Though she clawed and fought against the restraint, she couldn't budge it. Within seconds she felt light-headed. Without the strength left to fight, her hands dropped limply to her sides. She heard a strange buzzing in her ears, and spots floated before her eyes. Just as she thought she was losing consciousness, the grip at her throat loosened. As she dropped to her feet, she feared her trembling legs wouldn't be able to support her. She sucked air into her straining lungs. Rough hands caught her by the shoulders and spun her around. And Abby found herself staring into the leering face of Flint Barrows.

"Well, look what I just found. A pretty little peach just ripe for picking."

Abby froze. This wasn't possible. Flint Barrows should be miles from here, driving his wagon.

"Surprised?" Flint's lips curled in a chilling smile. "I told you someday I'd make you pay." His smile grew. "Today's my lucky day."

His grip tightened on her shoulders until she nearly cried out in pain. Then he dragged her against him and brought his mouth to hers.

"Now it's your turn to see what it feels like to kiss a man, Miss High-and-Mighty Market."

She twisted her head, avoiding his kiss. Grabbing her by the hair, he pulled her head back so hard tears sprang to her eyes. Then with a laugh he covered her mouth with his. She gagged at the stench of stale whiskey on his breath.

"That's just the beginning," he said, still clutching

her by the hair so she couldn't pull away. "There's lots more fun to come."

With one hand, he reached for the top button of her shirt. As Abby tried to jerk away, he caught at her neckline and gave a fierce tug, ripping the shirt from her. It fell away, still connected at each cuff. Abby gave a gasp of shock and pushed furiously against his chest, breaking free. When she tried to run, she lost her footing on the slippery rocks and plummeted downward. She landed with a thud on a flat boulder. All the breath was knocked from her. Behind her, she could hear Flint scrambling to catch her. Loose pebbles and the sharp edges of rocks left her bruised and bleeding. Still she struggled to get her footing. As she tumbled forward, she spotted the gleam of her rifle at the bottom of the gorge. She had to reach it. It was her only chance. Sliding, standing, tripping, falling, she struggled to reach the rifle. Her foot wedged between two rocks. Ignoring the stab of pain, she forced herself forward, leaving her boot lodged between the rocks. At last crawling, she reached out a hand and felt the warmth of the rifle butt in her hand. Her fingers closed around it. Pain seared her hand. She stared in disbelief as Flint's booted foot crashed down, smashing the fine bones of her fingers as he pinned her hand to the hard ground.

"So you like to play rough." He kicked the rifle aside, then bent and hauled her to her feet. "Then you and I are going to have ourselves a real good time."

Abby's breath was coming in short gasps. She was unable to stop him as he ripped the remaining ragged cloth from her wrists. Then, pulling her arms painfully behind her back, he held them in a viselike grip with one hand, while with his other he untied the rope at her waist that secured her britches. She kicked him as hard as she could. In return he slapped her across the face, causing her head to snap to one side from the impact. Tears scalded her eyes, and she blinked them back. There was no time for tears. She was fighting for her life.

With a tug, Flint pulled her britches down around her ankles, tripping her. She fell to the rocky ground and Flint fell on top of her, wrestling her clothes from her. When at last she lay, bruised, battered, wearing only a thin white chemise, he straddled her, pinning her arms above her head, and allowed his gaze to burn over her.

"Skinny. Not nearly as round as your little sister. But you're definitely a woman. And a scrapper. I like that in a woman. A good fight gets the blood heated."

Abby heard his words through a haze of pain. Blood oozed from a jagged cut on her shoulder. Her arms and legs were crisscrossed with cuts and scratches, many of them bleeding profusely. Her cheek still bore the imprint of his hand where he'd slapped her. And her ankle throbbed. Waves of pain radiated from her shattered hand being held firmly in his. But none of this pain could erase the overriding fear that had settled in the pit of her stomach.

With a terrible ripping sound, Flint tore the chemise from her and flung it aside. She struggled, but he held her still while he studied the high firm breasts, heaving with unconcealed panic. His gaze moved lower, to the milk-white flesh of her stomach, now spattered with her blood, then lower still.

"Now," Flint said, fumbling to unfasten his pants, "I'm going to show you what you were made for."

"No." With one last burst of strength, Abby brought her knee smashing into his groin.

With a howl of pain, he doubled over. Abby struggled to roll free, but his hand snaked out, catching her roughly by the arm, pulling her back down. His other hand curled into a fist that caught her on the side of her head. Pain crashed through her. She fell back, moaning softly.

"And now Miss Abby Market, the game has just begun."

She closed her eyes, unwilling to face her tormenter. He had already beaten her and rendered her defenseless. The pain and humiliation he had planned for her now would be his ultimate triumph.

"You got that wrong, Barrows. The game is over."

Through the mist that seemed to cloud her mind, Abby recognized Rourke's voice. She knew that in the whole world she'd never heard anything so wonderful. Her eyes fluttered open. He was standing with his feet spread far apart, a gun aimed at Flint Barrows. He looked even taller and stronger than she remembered. Or was her imagination playing tricks on her?

"Rourke." She tried to say his name, but the only sound she made was a croak.

And then she had to fight to hold on to the last thin thread of consciousness.

Chapter Thirteen

As FLINT LEVERED himself above Abby, he felt the cold steel of Rourke's Spencer eight-shot pressed against his temple. The click of the hammer being pulled back seemed to reverberate through his brain. He froze.

Lifting his hands, he said, "You can't shoot an unarmed man."

"Can't I?"

Abby had to blink to be certain it was Rourke's voice. His image swam in front of her. There was an icy thread of steel to his tone she'd never heard before.

As he struggled to pull up his pants, Flint was jerked roughly from her and thrown against a boulder. He swallowed, causing his Adam's apple to bob up and down in his throat.

As Rourke brought the gun up to his chest, Flint's words came out in a rush. "This was all her doing. She called me over here. Said she had something to show me. Then she started kissing me and taking off her clothes." Flint gave a nervous, hysterical laugh. "You know what women are like, Rourke. What's a man supposed to do?"

Rourke's eyes were the color of lead. His voice was

low, seething with barely controlled fury. "And in the heat of passion she inflicted those cuts and bruises on herself too."

Flint fell silent, keeping his gaze riveted on the gun in Rourke's hand. He knew he was beaten. And he knew that Rourke was itching to pull the trigger.

"Scared, Barrows?" Rourke wouldn't allow himself to look at Abby yet. If he did, he'd drop the gun and kill this animal with his bare hands. It would give him the greatest of pleasure to watch the life slowly ebb from Flint Barrows. He would like nothing better than to smash that ugly face into a rock. He pressed the gun to Flint's temple and felt his fury rising.

Abby moaned softly. Rourke turned. God. She was naked and covered with blood.

"Start running, Barrows." His commanding tone sent a shiver of fear along Flint's spine. "And don't ever stop. If you cross my path, you're a dead man."

Without waiting for Flint's reply, Rourke holstered his gun and dropped to his knees beside Abby. Behind him he could hear Barrows scrambling over rocks in his eagerness to put as much distance between himself and them as possible.

Taking off his shirt, Rourke wrapped it around her and gathered her into his arms, drawing her close to him.

"Oh Rourke."

At her breathless words, he felt his heart contract. "Shh. Don't talk yet, Abby."

He felt the trembling that she couldn't stop. Shock. Her skin was as cold as ice. Laying her gently in the warm sand, he went to his horse and removed his bedroll from behind the saddle. Making her a bed in the shade of a rock, he carried her to it and gently wrapped her in his blanket.

"Don't leave me, Rourke."

He heard the edge of panic in her voice. "I won't Abby. Not for one minute."

Her voice seemed to fade. "The train?"

"Don't worry about the wagon train. If they pass us, we'll catch up to them later."

She clung to his hand, and he marveled at her strength. Even after all this, she was able to grip him with the strength of a she-bear. Gradually he felt her fingers go slack. Her breathing slowed. She fell into a disturbed, restless sleep.

The shadows lengthened, and Rourke tossed another branch on the fire. When the water was warm, he dipped his handkerchief into it and began the task of washing the blood from Abby's bruised and battered body.

Caught in a twilight of fear and pain, she fought him, thrashing out, guarding herself from his intimate touch. He understood her confusion and wished he didn't have to be the cause of any more discomfort. In her mind, she was still fighting Flint.

"Hold still, Abby. I have to wash that shoulder. The cut is deep."

Her eyes blinked open, and Abby realized she wasn't dreaming.

"Rourke." Her voice was low, breathless. "It's you. I thought . . . " She ran a tongue over her split lip.

"I know, Abby." He dipped a cloth in the warm water and wrung it out.

"What are you doing?"

"Cleaning you up. This is going to hurt."

The only disinfectant he had was the whiskey. He heard her suck in her breath as he poured a liberal amount on the wound.

"Sorry. I wish I didn't have to hurt you."

She lay very still as he pulled the blanket back over her shoulder. When he touched a finger to her ankle, she let out a hiss of pain.

"It's badly swollen. Might be broken." He looked up. "What happened to your boot?"

She licked dry, cracked lips. "I lost it back in some

boulders. Flint was chasing me. I . . . was trying to get to my rifle."

He felt the tremors she couldn't hide. Instantly he was bending over her, drawing her close against him. "He's gone, Abby. You're safe. And he's never going to come near you again."

Abby lay very still, trying to believe him, trying to absorb some of his strength.

"Here." Rourke held the whiskey to her lips. "Drink."

She shook her head.

"Drink it. It'll help stop the shaking. And it just might ease a little of the pain as well."

Abby felt the first fiery drops of liquid all the way to her toes. She coughed. Tears stung her eyes. Rourke waited, then held the whiskey to her lips again. After several more sips she pushed it away. It was then that he saw her hand. The knuckles were flattened, the fingers bloody and bruised.

"My God. Your hand looks like it's been crushed."

She glanced down. The pain had become a dull, throbbing ache. "It was crushed. Beneath Flint's foot."

Rourke tested the broken bones, then made small splints from a tree branch. Using her torn shirt for strips of cloth, he tied each delicate finger, then the wrist.

"Looks like you won't be holding a rifle for a few weeks."

Abby thought about her family, expecting her to provide for them. She would have to bargain with some of the other men to do their chores in exchange for meat.

Rourke saw the worry etched in her eyes and cursed the men who were the cause of it. Her father, demanding more of her than she was able to give. Flint Barrows, determined to take what he wanted, not caring about the beautiful creature he might destroy in the process.

While Rourke finished bathing her wounds, she lay still, listening to the hiss and snap of the fire. His touch was gentle. Surprisingly gentle. The sky was a cloak of black velvet. The stars looked close enough to touch. But in the east a thick blanket of clouds obscured the sky. Already she could taste the rain in the air.

"How did you find me, Rourke?"

"I heard your shot. When I didn't hear a second one, I got worried and came running."

He didn't bother to tell her about those minutes of panic, when he'd found Flint's horse tethered near hers. Scrambling up rocks, sliding down gulleys, he'd known a moment of sheer terror, thinking he was too late. He believed the shot he'd heard had come from Flint's gun, killing her. And then, seeing Flint over her, he'd felt relief mingled with an almost overpowering urge to kill.

"If you hadn't come . . . " She started to cry, softly at first, embarrassed by the tears that coursed down her cheeks. Once started, the tears flowed faster, until she was racked with sobs.

Rourke held her quietly, letting her cry out all the fear and pain. And when he felt her struggling to still the tears, he wiped them tenderly with his thumbs.

"Looks like you put up a pretty good fight."

"Not good enough." She sniffed, and he handed her his handkerchief.

"It's over, Abby."

She blew her nose. Her horse stomped and whinnied in the night air, and he saw her go rigid with fear.

It wasn't over for her yet, he realized. It may be a long time before it was over for her. He felt a fierce protectiveness well up inside him. Tucking the blanket up around her chin, he brushed a strand of hair from her eyes.

"Sleep now, Abby. I'll keep watch."

He saw her lids flutter, then close. Poor thing. She was exhausted. He glanced at the whiskey and thought about taking a drink. The night air had grown chill, and she was using his only blanket.

Tossing another branch on the fire, he checked his gun and rifle, then leaned back against a boulder. He didn't need the whiskey or the blanket. She was safe. That thought was enough to keep him warm all night.

Pain tore through her shoulder and Abby moaned softly. A hand reached for her and she jerked back, then went rigid. He was back. He'd waited until she was asleep and vulnerable, and then he'd come back to finish what he'd started.

"No." Rolling to one side, she evaded his touch, but still he tried to grab her. Thrashing, twisting, she was determined to fight him to her last breath. As his hand caught at her shoulder she drew her hand back and tried to make a fist. Her fingers wouldn't obey her command. She became aware of awkward splints holding her fingers in a stiff, inflexible position.

"Don't touch me." She sat bolt upright and opened her eyes.

By the light of the fire she studied the shadowy figure kneeling beside her.

"Rourke." He heard the relief in her voice. "I thought . . . "

"I know." He touched a hand to her forehead and saw her flinch. Would she ever again trust a man's touch? "Your fever's broken. I was worried. You've been fighting demons for hours."

At the sound of thunder Abby glanced up at the night sky. "Are we going to join the wagon train?"

"Not until tomorrow. You shouldn't risk riding until you're stronger." As she opened her mouth to protest he added, "Besides, we'd never beat this storm now. We'll sit it out under these rocks."

Abby didn't argue with him. She was too exhausted to think about mounting her horse and riding out of here. She ached everywhere. Her body was one large mass of bruises.

"Hungry?"

Until he asked, Abby hadn't even been aware of the aroma of meat roasting. "Where did you find any food?"

"While you slept, I went in search of your boot and rifle. And guess what I found?"

When she arched an eyebrow, he replied, "A beautiful buck. Brought down with a single shot."

She smiled and he felt his heart nearly stop at the beauty of it. If only he could always make her smile so easily.

"You mean it was my shot that killed him?"

"It was. One more hide to add to your collection." He pointed to the skin draped neatly over a nearby boulder.

While Rourke ladled broth into a tin cup, she said, "He was the reason I didn't use our arranged signal. I knew if I fired, he and the doe I'd tracked would scatter and I'd lose them." She paused, and as he turned toward her she added, "Next time, I'll take my chances on losing the deer and stick to the signals."

"There won't be a next time, Abby." Rourke held the cup to her lips. As she sipped, he said gruffly, "From now on we stay together. I was a fool to turn you loose in these rocks alone. You were my responsibility and I let you down."

Very firmly Abby took the cup from his hands and set it aside. "Don't go blaming yourself for what happened, Rourke. It wasn't your fault that Flint attacked me."

"No." His tone was flat. "But Mordecai expected me to look out for your welfare. And I let him down."

"Rourke." Abby touched a hand to his chin and was surprised at the rough scratch of his beard. In the firelight his eyes were red-rimmed and haunted. How many hours had he sat here, tending her wounds, butchering her kill, seeing to her needs instead of his own? "You didn't let me down. And you didn't let Mordecai down." Her hand moved upward to caress his cheek, also covered with new, scratchy growth. "None of us expected Flint Barrows to do what he did. You saved my life." He heard the smile in her voice. "Now stop fussing over me, and feeding me like I was a baby, and try to get some sleep."

If only she hadn't touched him, he thought. The touch of her hand on his face was his undoing. For hours he'd hovered over her, bathing and binding her wounds, holding her when she cried, soothing her when she moaned in her sleep. And every minute of those hours he'd been aware of the naked woman who lay in his blanket, just a touch away. Through sheer willpower, he'd forced himself to think only of her fears, her needs. And in the process, he'd been able to suppress his own needs.

But now she'd touched him. And in his weariness, he let his guard down.

"I might crawl into that blanket with you. But I doubt if either of us would get any sleep."

She went very still. The hand at his cheek pulled back. He watched her eyes widen as they stared into his.

"Why do you hide your beauty, Abby?"

For a moment she forgot to breathe.

He combed his fingers through her hair. It spilled around the ground like fiery autumn foliage. "I've known women who would kill for hair like this," he murmured.

Abby strove for something clever to say. Something to hide the way her heart was acting. "I bet you've known lots of women."

There was a subtle change in his voice. Low. Gruff. "I've never known one like you." His fingers left her hair to trace the curve of her cheek, the firm line of her chin. "Your skin is so soft, so white." His finger moved lower, to the smooth column of her throat, where her pulse had begun hammering. "It's the kind of skin a man dreams of when he's all alone, under the stars."

He bent closer, until his lips hovered above hers. "The kind of skin that keeps a man awake, thinking, wanting." His gaze followed the trail of his fingertips and she felt herself begin to burn under that searing look. "It's the kind of skin a man has to touch." His fingers moved lower, to follow the ridge of her collar-bone. "To taste."

His lips lightly brushed her temple, then moved lower, to graze her cheek. She felt his breath, warm against her ear, and shivered.

Why didn't Rourke's touch repel her the way Barrows's had? What was it about this man that set him apart from all the others? Abby wondered if anyone's touch had ever been so gentle. For long moments she held her breath, afraid to breathe, afraid to move. Then, ever so slowly, she turned her face until Rourke's lips brushed the corner of her mouth. Still he made her wait while he teased the edge of her lower lip, tracing its fullness with his tongue, nibbling it lightly, until she thought she would go mad wanting his kiss.

At last his mouth covered hers, and she felt a wild sweep of passion. Ever since that night on the hill, she'd dreamed of his kisses, and worried that she had magnified everything in her mind. It couldn't have been as wonderful as she'd remembered. But this. This was better than anything she ever could have imagined.

In an instant, Rourke's weariness vanished. All his senses sharpened and focused on the woman in his arms. She tasted far sweeter than any woman had a right to. He drew her close and felt the blanket slip from her shoulders. His hands sought the warmth of her flesh.

Abby's hands wound around his neck and her fingertips brushed the dark hair at his nape. How could a man be so strong and yet so tender? How could his simplest touch arouse such passion?

146

He took the kiss deeper and all her thoughts shattered into tiny fragments.

Rourke's hands spanned her tiny waist, then traveled across her rib cage to the swell of her breasts. She was small and perfectly formed. His thumb grazed her nipple and she gasped and tried to pull away.

"Rourke, I . . ."

His mouth swallowed her protest and she found herself engulfed in waves of sensation.

"Do you know how long I've thought of you?" He dropped soft kisses on her eyelid, the tip of her nose, her chin. "How long I've dreamed of holding you like this?" He brought his mouth lower, to her throat, where he ran openmouthed kisses across her shoulder, along her collarbone. "How desperately I've wanted you?" His thumbs teased her nipples until they were erect, and then he lowered his mouth to nibble, to suckle.

Abby had never known such needs. Her body had become a mass of nerve endings, eager for his touch.

Lightning tore a jagged slash across the darkened sky, and thunder reverberated across the heavens. But it couldn't match the storm that raged through both of them.

"Tell me you want me, Abby. Tell me," he commanded. His eyes glittered with a fierceness that frightened her.

"Rourke." His name was torn from her depths. How could she deny what she wanted, what they both wanted so desperately? How could she not have known until this moment that Rourke was different from any other? That he was the only man who could ever make her respond like this?

The wind whipped up the dust in little eddies, cooling their heated flesh. And then the heavens seemed to open, sending a torrent of rain pouring down on them.

Rourke swore and drew her against him, vainly

trying to shield her from the rain. Staring up at him, she blinked her eyes, then wiped the dripping strands of hair from his face.

"Maybe this was a blessing in disguise," she whispered.

"The storm? Why?"

"I can't think, Rourke. When you're holding me like this, I'm not able to sort things out. Maybe the rain will bring us both to our senses."

"We don't need to think, only to feel. I want you, Abby. And you want me." He drew her close against him and brought his lips to hers.

"No." She shrank back.

He let out a slow, angry curse. "If I had any sense at all," he muttered against her lips, "I'd take you now, storm or no."

She shivered and wasn't certain whether it was from the cold rain that pelted them or from the intensity of his words.

He swore again, more harshly. "Come on," he said, lifting her, still partially wrapped in the blanket. "We'll be dry beneath these rocks."

He settled her in a patch of dried grass, beneath a shelf of rock. Then, running through the rain, he brought their rifles and other supplies.

Forcing himself not to look at her, he dropped her britches and one of his shirts at her feet.

"Get dressed." His voice was low and commanding.

Keeping her head averted, Abby shrugged into the clothes he offered her, then pulled on her boots. When she turned, Rourke was staring bleakly at the sputtering ashes of their once-roaring fire. Within minutes the rain had extinguished the flame. And within minutes, their passion had returned once more to cool indifference.

Huddling beside him, she wrapped the blanket around herself and peered into the stormy darkness.

"We needed this rain," Abby muttered, to fill the awkward silence.

"Yeah." Maybe more than she knew, Rourke thought. He had nearly taken her here on the cold, hard ground. And if he had, he'd have never known if she truly wanted him, or if she was merely too weak to resist.

They would make love. Of that he was certain. It was no longer a question in his mind. Her reaction to his touch left him convinced of her feelings as well. But when first they came together in passion, he decided, reaching for a cigar, it would be because she wanted it as much as he did. The decision would have to be hers. And once made, there'd be no backing down.

Chapter Fourteen

ABBY AWOKE TO the sound of water trickling past rocks as it slid from higher elevations. She sat up and felt a moment of panic when she saw that Rourke was missing. The moment passed as she spotted him coming toward her from behind towering rocks, buttoning his shirt. Beads of water glistened in his dark hair. Seeing her, his fingers fumbled for a second. He tucked the shirt into the waistband of his pants and bent to pour coffee from a blackened pot.

"How are you feeling?" His voice was slightly muffled. He kept his back to her.

"Fine. A little stiff and sore." She was relieved that he didn't look at her. She felt as awkward and uncomfortable as ever in his presence. Despite those few moments of passion last night, things were the same between them. Maybe worse.

"If you'd like to bathe, there's a rock basin brimming with water. Just behind this boulder." He turned, and she avoided his eyes.

"Thanks." Carefully rolling the blanket, she limped away.

Clear rainwater pooled in the basin. Removing her clothes, Abby enjoyed the luxury of bathing away the remaining blood and grime. Before she again dressed, she examined her cuts and bruises. They would heal. And when they did, she hoped she would be able to put away forever the memory of Flint Barrows. The wind sighed and she found herself casting a furtive glance over her shoulder. True, the wounds would heal. But they would leave scars. Scars no one would ever see.

Rourke tried not to watch as Abby brushed the tangles from her hair and tucked it beneath the old hat. Maybe, he thought, it was better that she dressed in men's clothes and hid her beauty. If other men saw what he saw, she wouldn't be safe anywhere.

Cursing himself for his thoughts, he doused the fire and saddled the horses. After filling their canteens, he secured his bedroll. Before he could assist Abby, she had managed to pull herself into the saddle. He saw her wince and draw her broken hand close to her chest.

"Here." Removing the handkerchief from around his neck, he handed it up to her. "Tie this around your neck and use it for a sling. It'll ease the throbbing."

Abby gave him a grateful smile and kept her silence. She'd been enough trouble. If it killed her, she would resist the temptation to ask his help for the rest of the trip.

As he mounted he saw her struggling to tie the handkerchief around her neck. With one hand out of commission, it was an impossible task.

"Hold still." Bringing his horse close to hers, he reached over and tied the cloth.

As his fingers brushed the back of her neck, Abby felt the familiar jolt. There was no denying the fact that his simple touch tied her in knots.

"Thanks." She stared at a spot just beyond his collar, avoiding his eyes.

"Tell me when it gets too uncomfortable. We'll take a break from the trail." Rourke studied the flush that colored her cheeks, then moved his horse into the lead.

It was an easy matter to catch up to a slow, plodding wagon train that averaged fifteen miles a day. Despite the dry riverbeds and furnacelike heat of the land, despite the slower pace Rourke insisted on because of Abby's injuries, they caught up to the wagons just as they were making camp that evening.

"Rourke." Abby's voice held a note of panic. On a little rise, she reined in her horse, her gaze scanning the wagons below.

He waited, seeing the look of uncertainty on her face.

"If Flint has left the wagon train, I don't see why I should have to tell anyone what he did."

His eyes narrowed. "We've been over all this before. You can't let him get away with it. If you do, he'll just find another helpless woman to attack."

"But they'll all think that I let . . . that I'm . . ."

He saw the pain and forced himself to ignore it. "Sometimes you can't worry about what others will think." Seeing her quick frown, he said more gently, "You don't have to tell everyone on the train. But Mordecai has to know why Barrows can no longer travel with us."

She swallowed. "All right. We'll tell Mordecai. But no one else needs to know."

"What about your family? Don't you think you owe it to them to explain why you're carrying around those cuts and bruises?"

"Yes. Of course I'll tell them. But I'd like to do it alone, in my own way." When he made a move to protest, she said quickly, "I know them better than you, Rourke."

When she avoided his gaze, Rourke grabbed her reins, forcing her to look at him. "What are you really afraid of Abby?" He was fairly certain he knew the answer to that. It was her father who frightened her, almost as much as Flint Barrows. Maybe more.

"I'm not afraid. I just want to handle this in my own way."

She looked close to tears. Rourke felt his determination dissolving. She'd been through enough. If he could ease her through this ordeal, he would. "All right, Abby. We'll do this your way."

He heard her expel a little sigh as they urged their horses forward.

Mordecai was stretched out in front of the cook fire, his leg resting atop his saddle. He looked up over the rim of his cup to watch the two riders approaching. As they drew into the circle of light, he pointed to the swollen game bag hanging from Rourke's saddle. "I see you had some luck."

"Some good." Rourke slid from the saddle, then reached up and helped Abby down. "Some not so good."

When Abby faced Mordecai, his gaze swung to her hand in the sling. "Accident, Miss Abby?"

Rourke glanced around. "Where are the others?"

Mordecai lifted an eyebrow. "Parker and Thompson are attending to some chores. Brand is riding with Flint Barrows to Fort Bridger."

"Did Barrows say why he was leaving?"

Mordecai blew into his coffee and took a drink. "Said he was getting restless since his wife's death. Wanted to hunt and sell the game at the fort."

"Did he say if he was intending to rejoin the wagon train when we reached the fort?"

"Didn't say." Mordecai set down his cup and poured one for Abby and Rourke. "Why the questions, Rourke?"

"I ordered Flint Barrows to leave the train," Rourke said, accepting a cup of steaming coffee from the wagon master.

Abby, wishing there was some place to hide, sat beside the old man and set the tin cup down so they wouldn't notice her hand was shaking.

"I think you'd better explain yourself," Mordecai

said, his Scottish burr thickening in agitation. "I wouldna like to think ye've taken it upon yourself to do my job, Rourke."

"Flint Barrows attacked Abby up in the foothills."

The old man's head swiveled toward her. "Did he . . . hurt you, lass?" He saw the slight trembling of her hand and felt a wave of sympathy. Without thinking he closed his hand over hers. God, she was as cold as ice.

The tenderness in Mordecai's tone was genuine. Abby shook her head, feeling the sudden sting of tears.

"He would have, if Rourke hadn't come along in time."

"I'm surprised you didna kill him," Mordecai said in a voice low with anger.

"I wanted to. Probably should have." Rourke shrugged. "I was more concerned with Abby than I was with Barrows."

The wagon master's eyes narrowed. "I should have wondered about a lazy bastard like Barrows, begging your pardon, Miss Abby," he said, turning toward her, "suddenly getting ambition. We'll tell the commander at the fort. He'll know how to deal with Barrows." Slowly, painfully, Mordecai got to his feet and, leaning heavily on the cane, walked to the back of the cook wagon. When he returned, he handed Abby a small handgun.

"I want you to carry this at all times, lass. Even when you're asleep, keep it with you. Rourke here will teach you what you need to know about the care and use of it."

Abby stared at the gun in his hand. "I can't pay you for it, Mordecai."

"I want no pay. I want you safe, lass. Take it."

Rourke saw her blink back tears as she accepted the gun from the older man's hand.

"We should be at Fort Bridger in a few days. In the

meantime, you have your aunt tend to your injuries. I hope none of them are serious?"

Abby shook her head, too overcome to speak. This man, a stranger until they joined his wagon train, showed more kindness toward her than anyone she'd ever known.

"Her hand's broken, her ankle's badly swollen, and there's a deep gash in her shoulder," Rourke growled.

Mordecai turned to study the man for a moment. Rourke was a man who rarely let his feelings show. Yet he was showing more emotion about this incident than Abby. "You'll want to see her to her wagon, I suppose, and stay while she talks to her family."

"No." Abby bit the word off, wishing she hadn't been so quick to react.

Both men grew uncomfortably silent.

Rourke handed her the reins to her horse. Turning to Mordecai, he said, "Abby would like to talk to her family in private."

Abby shot him a grateful look, then turned away. Without a word, Rourke began tending to his own mount.

Mordecai watched the two of them with a puzzled frown. He wondered whether it was the anxiety of the attack that had left them so shaken. Or had something else happened as well? They both seemed too edgy. And both teetering on the brink of something.

Along with all his other duties, he'd have to remember to keep an eye on them.

As she neared her wagon, Abby felt herself tensing. She dreaded facing her family. She didn't think she could bear any more tears and tender concern without breaking into a fit of crying. And if she were to cry, she would embarrass herself.

Pausing for a moment, Abby felt a wave of emotions engulf her as she watched her aunt and sister. Aunt Violet was stirring something over the fire. Her gown was rumpled and stained with the dirt of the trail. Her hair, always so neatly fashioned into a prim knot, dripped sweaty little tendrils about her cheeks and forehead. Abby saw her aunt mop the sweat from her brow and felt a pang of guilt. While she was gone, the bulk of the chores would have fallen to her sweet, incompetent aunt. On top of that, Violet must have been nearly sick with worry.

Beside the fire, Carrie was sewing a man's shirt. Since Abby didn't recognize the material, she knew it had to belong to one of the men from Mordecai's crew. Maybe even Rourke. She was a goodhearted child, Abby thought, watching as Carrie bit the thread. Despite her ineptness in most things, Abby was glad to have a sister like Carrie.

Taking a deep breath, Abby stepped from the shadows.

"Abby. Oh my sweet Lord. It's Abby."

Aunt Vi dropped the wooden spoon and hurried to embrace her niece. "Oh child, I was so afraid I'd never see you again. Let me look at you. In my imaginings I've had you stolen away by Indians, trampled by wild animals, and shot by crazed gunmen." Her smile faded. "Dear God in heaven, you've been hurt."

"It's just a little thing, Aunt Vi. Really I'm fine."

Carrie dropped her mending and hurried to hug her sister. "Where have you been? We thought you were dead. Oh Abby, we've been crazy with fear."

Abby clung to her sister for a moment, feeling a welling of love and warmth. "Not dead, Carrie. Just knocked off my feet for a moment."

The three women laughed and cried and clung together, their tears mixing with their smiles, their arms threaded about each other's necks. There was no need for explanations. It was enough that they were together again.

* * *

Rourke began to unsaddle his horse, then realized that he still had Abby's game bag. Slinging it across his shoulder, he strode toward her wagon. Coming up in the darkness, he stood off to one side, watching the joyous reunion of the three women. They were so different, these three, he thought. Violet, all soft and dreamy. Carrie, flighty and childish. And Abby. Earlier he would have said she was tough and feisty. But now he'd glimpsed a gentler streak in her. She was tough. But she was also tender. She was obstinate and cocky. And she was sweet and vulnerable. And beneath those shabby clothes and rough demeanor was hidden a beautiful woman who was capable of great passion.

"So. You've come back."

James Market stepped down from the wagon, holding a jug. He made no move to go to his daughter, Rourke noted. And although she started at the sound of his voice, she didn't rush into his arms.

"She's hurt, James. Look at her hand."

He ignored his sister. "A good excuse to come back without any food, I'd say."

"We have game," Abby said stiffly. "I shot a deer."

"Funny. I don't see it." James made a great pretense of looking around, then glowered at her.

"It's . . ." Abby stopped. She had left the game bag with Rourke. "I forgot. It's on Rourke's saddle. I'll get it."

"Good. I'm tired of eating mush that isn't fit for a dog." As Market turned away, he lifted the jug to his lips and took a long pull. "When she brings it, put some meat on the fire, Violet. I'm going to look for some pleasant company for an hour or two."

"Don't you think you'd better find out what kept Abby away from the wagon train all night, James?" Though Violet's words were spoken softly enough, there was an underlying thread of anger.

"If she has something to tell me, let her tell me."

Abby's voice trembled. "I was attacked in the rocks while I was hunting."

James Market whirled to face her. "Attacked? Indians?"

"No." Abby glanced at her younger sister, then away. "Flint Barrows."

James Market's jaw dropped. "What do you mean, Flint Barrows attacked you?"

"He came up on me from behind, Pa, and knocked me to the ground. I managed to get away, but he caught me. When I fought him, he became violent. He tore my clothes from me, and if Rourke hadn't come along when he did, he would have taken me by force. I have no doubt that when he was finished with me he would have killed me."

Market studied his daughter in silence. Then, in a voice tinged with sarcasm he asked, "Is that your story?"

Abby blanched. "My . . . story?"

James Market weaved slightly as he took several steps closer to his daughter. "Flint came to see me before he left the train to go to Fort Bridger. He told me all about you and Rourke and what he'd seen the two of you doing."

"Pa!"

In the darkness, Rourke's hand clenched at his side.

"James, I won't have you speaking this way in front of Carrie." Violet turned toward her younger niece. "Carrie, go to the wagon."

"I won't. I'm old enough to hear what Pa says, especially if he's going to believe a coward like Flint Barrows." Carrie's chin jutted. "What kind of lies did he tell you about me after he attacked me, Pa?"

James Market lifted his hand as if to strike Carrie. She jumped back, her eyes blazing. "And now you're going to take his word over Abby's, aren't you?"

As he moved menacingly closer, Abby stepped between her father and sister. "Don't you lay a hand on her, Pa. This doesn't concern her now. I want you to tell me what Flint said."

"He said he's a lonely man since his wife died. Said you and Carrie flaunt yourselves in front of him." As the two girls gasped, he added, "He said he'd even be willing to marry a tarnished woman like you, Abby, as long as you'd be willing to work hard and give him lots of children."

"Tarnished." Abby advanced on her father and winced at the stench of liquor on his breath. "The only man who tried to tarnish your daughters was Flint Barrows. He's evil, and you know it. Why would you want to believe him over me?"

"Because you're a liar and a cheat. You're nothing better than a slut. Just like your—"

"James!"

At Violet's outburst, he looked up. His glazed eyes seemed to focus for a moment.

"I'm going off to drink with my friends. See that we have meat for supper."

As he began to walk away, he paused, rocked on his heels, then turned back. "You could do a lot worse than marry Flint Barrows. You're getting old, girl. Take a good look at your shriveled-up old aunt and see what you'll look like in a few years. In fact, you ought to take a good look at yourself right now. You're rough and dirty and dried up. You look more like a boy than any woman I know. Even where we're heading, there aren't going to be too many men interested in the likes of you."

"I'd take my chances on the devil before I'd marry the likes of Flint Barrows," Abby hissed.

Her father studied her for long silent moments before spinning away.

When he was gone, Rourke blended deeper into the shadows. Now at least he understood why Abby had wanted to face her family alone. She hadn't wanted anyone else to hear the disgusting things her father would have to say. How long had she been hearing them? he wondered. All her life? Had she grown up thinking she was plain and unwanted? Rourke's fist clenched and unclenched. What man would take the word of a snake like Barrows over his own kin? Market was the cruelest father he'd ever known. He treated his spinster sister like an embarrassment. He treated Carrie like a useless child. But he saved the worst treatment of all for Abby. Almost as if, Rourke thought, she was his enemy instead of his daughter.

As he made his way back to the cook wagon, Rourke was deep in thought. He was glad Mordecai had given Abby a gun. He was going to see to it personally that she learned how to use it. Abby had said she would rather take her chances on the devil. Maybe she already had. And his name was James Market.

Chapter Fifteen

OVER THE LONG miles, Abby's injuries healed. When asked, she explained away her cuts and bruises by saying she had taken a fall during the hunt. Most of the members of the wagon train were too involved in their own survival to question further. And though her hand caused her much pain, she was young and strong, and it healed quickly.

Fort Bridger provided the travelers a last glimpse of civilization before the final thrust to the west. Situated near the border of Wyoming and Utah Territory, it offered a final opportunity for the faint of heart to change their minds. But because they had already invested so much of themselves in this journey, few were willing to turn back.

The fort had become the gathering place for ranchers, trappers, even Indians, who came to barter game and hides for much needed supplies, or for guns and whiskey.

Instead of looking forward to this respite from the long journey, Abby felt her heart grow heavier with each mile that brought them closer to the fort. Here she would have to face her attacker. Once again she would have to relive the nightmare of Flint Barrows's brutal assault.

When the train pulled into Fort Bridger, Mordecai made his way to the camp commander. Abby watched him climb the steps of the command post, then turned away and busied herself with the team to keep herself from thinking. Would Flint deny the attack and spread more lies about her? Would he insinuate to everyone, as he had to her father, that he had actually come upon her and Rourke lying together? At that, Abby's heart began to beat in double time. The thought of lying in Rourke's arms had cost her many a sleepless night.

"Miss Abby."

At the sound of Mordecai's quiet voice, Abby spun around. She waited, a questioning look in her eyes. The time had come to face her attacker.

"Flint Barrows left the fort yesterday. When a rider came with word of our approach, he left without a word."

Relief flooded through Abby. Clinging to the wagon wheel, she was surprised that her legs could still support her.

"He didn't say where he was headed?"

Mordecai shook his head. "He could be anywhere." His voice lowered. "But I don't think he's eager to see any of the members of this train, Miss Abby. I think maybe we're rid of him for good."

Abby swallowed.

With a smile, Mordecai patted her shoulder. "Rest easy, lass. You're done with that devil."

She made a feeble attempt to smile. "Thank you, Mordecai."

As he walked away, she touched a hand to the gun in the pocket of her britches. Barrows might be gone, but as long as he lived, she would never again feel completely safe. She'd grown accustomed to having the little gun with her. It was comforting to know she could take care of herself. And if the devil ever decided to return and finish what he'd

started, she would show him the quickest way to
hell.

As they had at each post, the men of the wagon
train sought solace in the saloons while the women
indulged in an orgy of washing and fancy cooking.
And when the daily chores were completed, and the
men returned to their wagons feeling mellow, the
fiddles were tuned and the company took on a festive
air.

Abby studied her reflection in the chipped looking
glass and groaned. Where her younger sister, Carrie,
had firm, ripening breasts and softly rounded hips,
she seemed to have lost what little feminine shape
she'd once had. Her hips were little more than bony
slopes flaring from a tiny waist. Though high and firm,
her breasts were so small they were easily disguised
beneath a heavy shirt. Even in this dainty gown of
ivory voile, her figure gave only the merest hint of a
woman's curves. As she brushed the tangles from her
hair, she sighed in agitation. With her hair hidden
beneath a cap, wearing her father's cast-off clothing,
she could easily pass as a young boy. And now,
dressed in a lovely gown, she felt like a fraud. Her
father was right, she thought, giving an angry tug at
the tortoiseshell comb. She was plain. Worse, she
didn't know how to flirt like other women. Even if she
knew how, she wouldn't care to. Even in the rugged
west, where women were scarce, there would be few
men standing in line for her hand.

Carrie stepped from the wagon dressed in a gown
that matched the blue of her eyes. Her cornsilk hair
had been brushed until it gleamed like spun gold. She
smelled of Aunt Violet's rosewater.

"Are you coming with me to listen to the fiddlers?"
Abby nodded.

"Here then." Touching her fingers to the vial,
Carrie dabbed the fragrance at her sister's throat.

"You don't want to go around smelling like the mules."

"Don't waste that on me," Abby said with a laugh. "Save the rosewater for yourself. Looking like that, I think there'll be more than a few who'll want to stand close to you tonight."

There was only one man Carrie cared about, but she kept her thoughts to herself. "Maybe we'll even dance," Carrie said aloud, looping her arm through her sister's.

"I'll leave the dancing to you."

Violet joined her two nieces, and the three headed toward the cluster of wagons.

"I've brought some old pieces of fabric along," Violet said, showing the girls the contents of her sack. "Thought I'd start a quilt while I enjoy the music."

On one side of a roaring fire, the women sat in groups of three or four, patching and mending by the firelight. On the other side sat the men, smoking, repairing harnesses, tapping their feet to the tune of the fiddlers. Children darted in and out among the wagons, playing tag, shrieking with laughter.

As Violet settled herself in the company of several ladies, she gave a sigh of satisfaction. "Oh, isn't this lovely? It reminds me of home on a Saturday evening."

The women smiled and nodded, then grew thoughtful and dreamy at the thought of the homes they'd left behind.

Carrie studied the cluster of men, her eyes eager and searching. Suddenly she smiled, and Abby watched as she made her way slowly toward the cook wagon. In the shadows, Abby could make out the tall, slender figure of Will Montgomery. As Carrie approached, Abby saw him whip his hat from his head. They leaned close, in whispered conversation, and Abby knew that Will was probably drowning in the wonderful scent of roses. When Reverend and Mrs.

Coulter appeared, the young couple quickly drew apart. Abby chuckled to herself. Poor Carrie. She had probably dreamed for weeks of this chance to be alone with Will. And now that she had the opportunity, the dear Reverend Coulter and his wife would probably engage them in conversation until the small hours of the morning.

When the fiddles stopped, someone strummed a guitar and sang about sweet Betsy from Pike. Abby strolled among the wagons, nodding and smiling as friends called out. At the Garner wagon, she heard the sound of sobbing. Pausing, she debated about getting involved. It was common knowledge that Nancy and Jed weren't getting along. As Abby began to move on, the sobbing increased. It was soft, high-pitched, more like a child than a woman. She felt a little prickle of alarm.

"Nancy? Is that you?"

The crying continued.

Abby drew back the canvas. "Nancy? Are you in here?"

A tiny, tear-streaked face appeared.

"Timmy." Abby held out her arms, and the child fell into them, burying his face against her shoulder and weeping as if his heart would break.

"Shh. There now, Timmy. Nothing can be as bad as all this. Come on, love. Let's go find your mama and papa."

"No." The child clung to Abby's neck while his tears began anew.

Abby heard the fear in his voice and stroked his head. "All right. Let's just stay here awhile." Standing still, she allowed him to cry until his tears began to subside. Then, drying his tears with her lace handkerchief, she sat down beside the wagon and cradled him in her lap.

When the boy grew quiet, Abby began to rock him gently, crooning the tune the fiddlers had struck up. She felt him slowly relax in her arms.

"Now. What was so bad it made you cry like that?" she whispered.

"Mama doesn't love us anymore."

"Timmy. Don't say such things. Your mama loves you very much."

"No she doesn't. She said so. She told my papa she hated him for taking her so far away from home."

"She's just upset because she lost her piano," Abby whispered, nuzzling the child's forehead. "She doesn't mean what she says."

Fresh tears shimmered in the child's eyes. His lower lip trembled. "She said I'll probably grow up to be just like my papa. Wild, dirty, and uncivilized."

Abby tried to hide her shock. Nancy Garner's unhappiness was taking an ugly turn. "You musn't think about what people say in anger, Timmy. Tomorrow, when she's feeling better, your mama will be sorry, and she'll hug you and tell you how much she loves you and your papa."

One fat tear rolled down his cheek, and he brushed it away. His little face was so solemn, it nearly broke Abby's heart. "I don't believe you, Abby. I don't think my mama will ever again love me and my papa."

"Your parents will always love you, Timmy. That's what parents do best." Thinking about her own father, Abby swallowed back the pain that threatened. There were people, she knew, who were incapable of loving. Her voice lowered to a mere whisper, as if she were talking to herself. "Sometimes, when they're tired or sad, they say things they don't mean. That's when we have to find it within ourselves to love them even more." She forced a note of hopefulness. "But you'll see. Tomorrow, or the day after that, things will work out. They always do."

Abby drew him close to her heart and began humming the tune that played in the background. Though her own heart was heavy, she rocked the little boy until, exhausted, he fell asleep in her arms. Standing

166

up, she cradled the boy against her shoulder. As she came around the Garner wagon, she nearly collided with Rourke. With wide eyes, she touched a finger to her lips, warning him not to wake the boy. Without a word, Rourke took the sleeping child from her arms. He felt a sudden shaft of pain as the boy snuggled close against him. Just as swiftly the pain was gone. And as Rourke placed him in his blankets inside the wagon, he experienced a fresh sense of loss.

Abby felt a great well of tenderness at the sight of a strong man like Rourke tenderly holding the little boy.

Closing the flap of canvas, Rourke turned to her. "That was a nice thing you did."

"I didn't do anything." She felt her cheeks burn, and was grateful for the darkness.

"I didn't mean to pry. But I couldn't help overhearing. You took the time to comfort a frightened, lonely little boy. You were there when he needed you, Abby. And he won't soon forget it." He touched a finger to her cheek, sending heat racing along her spine. "Nor will I."

Abby could think of nothing to say.

Rourke recognized her distress and sought to put her at ease.

"That's a pretty dress."

"Thank you." Oh, how she wished she were taller so she wouldn't have to tip her head so far back to look up at him. And how she yearned for a lush figure as his gaze swept the length of her. "Carrie and Aunt Violet made over one of my ma's old dresses."

"It looks good on you."

She fell silent, wishing she knew how to be clever and charming in the company of a man.

Rourke saw her watching the couples dancing a reel in the circle of light.

"You ought to be dancing, Abby."

She laughed, a low, husky sound that shivered across his nerves. "I don't know how."

"I thought every pretty girl knew how to dance."

Her smile faded. "Then I guess that's why no one ever taught me how to dance. I'm not pretty enough."

Rourke frowned. That was her father speaking, not her. How could she believe such nonsense? Removing his hat, he made a little bow in front of her. "Miss Abby Market, would you do me the honor of this dance?"

She drew back, embarrassed. "I told you. I don't know how."

"Then I'll teach you." Taking her hand, he drew her into the circle of his arms.

Abby felt a rush of feelings. Gathered close to his chest, she felt the rough scratch of his freshly laundered shirt against her cheek. His lips were hovering just inches from her temple. His warm breath feathered across her face. He smelled clean, like soap and water, reminding her of the land after a fresh spring rain. He kept her one small hand in his, and she prayed he couldn't feel the trembling. His other hand was pressed to the small of her back, and she felt a warmth radiating from it that left her nearly weak.

She didn't know what to do with her other arm. At first it hung limply at her side. But slowly, instinctively, it moved along his arm, then curved gently around his neck. As her fingers grazed the spill of dark hair at his collar, she drew her hand away, then ever so slowly brought it back until her fingers were twined in the hair at his nape.

As they moved slowly to the music, he drew her perceptibly closer, until their bodies were touching. Bringing his mouth close to her ear, he murmured, "I thought you said you couldn't dance."

A tiny thrill shot through her. Without realizing it, her hand clutched at his head, drawing it even lower, until his mouth was tantalizingly close to hers.

"I . . . didn't know it was this easy," she said, feeling a dryness in her throat.

"It gets even easier," he whispered. His lips grazed

hers and he saw her eyes widen. "When two people dance together often enough, each learns how the other moves." His fingers began to burn a trail of fire along her spine. Through the soft fabric of her gown she felt each fingertip leave an indelible mark on her flesh. She would know Rourke's intimate touch anywhere, anytime.

She didn't know when they stopped moving. She wasn't even aware that he had gathered her close, or that her own arms had curled around his neck, drawing him to her. In a cocoon of darkness, locked in his embrace, she forgot about the music. The only sound she could hear was the rhythm of her own heartbeat. The people dancing in the circle of light no longer existed. There was only this man, and the warmth of his touch, and the thrill of anticipation as she waited for his lips to cover hers.

Slowly, so slowly she thought she might die of waiting and wanting, his mouth lowered to hers. She felt a shudder race through him seconds before his mouth covered hers in a savage kiss.

He forgot to be tender. He'd intended to be tender. In fact, he'd intended to walk away from her the minute he'd seen her. But seeing her led to the need to hear her voice, that low, sultry whisper that touched him as no other woman's voice ever had. And talking to her had led to the need to touch, to hold, to taste. And now, holding her, kissing her, needs ripped through him, shattering his veneer of cool control.

There was still time to walk away, he told himself as his lips plundered hers. But first he needed to touch her. Touch her in a way he'd never dared before. While her arms twined around his neck, he ran his hands across the slope of her hips, then upward, to span her tiny waist. He'd held his passion too long in check. Now needs broke free, and while her breath trembled in his mouth, he brought his hands higher. She was small and firm in his palm, and his thumbs stroked until he felt her moan and take the kiss deeper. He wanted her, needed her, had to have her, with a need that bordered on desperation.

And then she was pushing away with a fierceness he hadn't expected. He grabbed her roughly by the shoulders and she pushed away again. Above the thundering of his heart, above the sound of his breath, ragged and shallow, he recognized the sound of footsteps drawing nearer. And then Mordecai and Thompson were coming directly toward them on their way to the cook wagon.

"Evening, Miss Abby. Rourke." Mordecai touched the brim of his hat, then cast a sidelong glance at Rourke.

"Evening."

"Enjoying the music?"

"Yes." Even that simple word was difficult to say with her throat gone dry.

Abby and Rourke stood apart, struggling to control their breathing, hoping the darkness hid them enough to cover their confusion.

"Good evening, Miss Abby." Mordecai leaned on his cane and gave the couple a long look. "Rourke."

"Good night."

When they were alone again, Abby turned away, ashamed to face him. "I'd better get back to my wagon. Thank you—for teaching me to dance."

"My pleasure, ma'am." Rourke swallowed back the smile that threatened. There'd be another time. Another place. And many more steps of the dance to be learned.

Carrie stood beside Will, smiling into the faces of Reverend Coulter and his wife. While they talked, she was careful to keep the smile in place. How long, she wondered, could two old people babble on about the weather, the land, and the goodness of the Lord? The evening was quickly rushing by, and she and Will hadn't had a single moment to themselves. The wagon train was pulling out in the morning, and it might be weeks before they would have this much time to themselves again.

". . . said to Evelyn, praise the Lord, I think we're all going to make it safely to the promised land."

"I think you're right, sir," Will said politely. "Mordecai Stump strikes me as a man who knows every trail from here to Sacramento."

"Well said, son. Put your faith in the Lord, and in a few men of good will. And nothing will be denied you."

As the fiddlers started up, Carrie's foot began tapping to the rhythm. Seeing it, Reverend Coulter smiled at his wife. "Here I am going on and on and these young people are itching to dance. Come on, Evelyn, let's join the old married folks."

With a laugh, he and his wife walked away arm in arm. Behind them, Will and Carrie stared at each other, gave a nervous laugh, then grew uncomfortably silent.

Will twisted the brim of his hat between his fingers. "You look awfully pretty, Carrie."

Her smile could have lit up the entire fort. "You look fine too. How did that shirt fit?"

"Fine. Just fine." He found himself staring at her breasts, reddened, then looked up to find her staring directly at him. God, he thought, she had to know what he was looking at. The realization made him blush more.

"Do you dance?" she asked as the music grew livelier.

"No. Well, I used to. But I don't anymore."

"Why?"

The minute she asked the question, she nearly died from embarrassment. "Oh. You mean because of your arm?"

No one had ever come right out and said it before. Will couldn't make up his mind if he was angry or glad. He'd need time to think about it. "I just don't anymore," he said softly.

"That's too bad."

He glanced at her. "You like to dance, Carrie?"

She shrugged. "I don't know. I never tried it."

"You never danced?"

She glanced down at the toes of her shoes.

Will cleared his throat. "Every girl ought to dance, at least once in her life."

"Why?"

He couldn't think of a good reason. "Just because. It feels good to sway to the music."

Without thinking, he held out his hand. Surprised, Carrie accepted it. They began swaying, slowly at first, then vigorously as the tempo of the music increased. Like two shy children, they held hands and swayed, bowed, then swayed again. Will grinned, and Carrie threw back her head and laughed.

Oh, it felt so good to hear her laugh. Will couldn't imagine anything sweeter than the sound of her laughter.

"So this is dancing."

Still holding her hand, Will drew her closer. He stared down into her eyes and wondered if there could be anyone prettier in the whole world than Carrie Market.

"There's a lot more to dancing than this. But I don't think I could handle anything more complicated."

"Why?" Without realizing it, Carrie moved a step closer, until they were almost touching.

Will let go of her hand and touched his knuckles to her cheek. She was so soft, so sweet, she made him ache. She lifted her face to his touch, the way a cat arches its back, and he opened his hand, feeling the fine softness of her skin against his rough callused palm.

"I just couldn't." His voice lowered to a reverent whisper. "I don't have any right."

"To what, Will?" Without realizing it, Carrie touched a hand to his chest and felt the wild thundering of his heart.

172

"To touch you like this." He allowed his fingertips to trace the feathery blond eyebrow, the curve of her cheek. And still she didn't pull away or flinch at his touch. His heart soared until he thought it would fly clear out of his mouth.

"I don't mind." Like Will, Carrie's words became hushed, the whispered conversations of two lovers.

"Your pa does."

"My pa doesn't speak for me."

"He doesn't?"

She shook her head, afraid to move, afraid even to breathe.

"Oh, Carrie." Will cupped her face in his hand and leaned forward, enveloped in the fragrance of roses that would always remind him of her.

Their lips hovered, a fraction apart, and Carrie's parted in a soft sigh of expectation. Will's head dipped lower, until his lips were brushing hers. And then he stiffened.

"Don't let him do it."

At the raspy sound of Nancy Garner's voice, Carrie froze.

"All men want the same thing, Carrie. Let me tell you. The minute they get you, they start to rule your life. First it's your father. Then it's your husband. You'll never be free if you give in to him."

Carrie's eyes widened at the slurred words. Drunk. Nancy Garner was stone drunk.

"Will, go get my sister. She'll know what to do," Carrie whispered.

For a moment, Will could only stare at the weaving woman. Then he nodded and hurried off to find Abby.

"You wanted him to kiss you, didn't you?" Nancy said, her voice high-pitched and wavery.

"People can hear you, Mrs. Garner."

"Mrs. Garner." The voice turned to a whine. "Mrs. Garner. Jed's wife. Timmy's mother. Mr. Vance's little girl. When do I get to be myself? When?"

"Shh." Carrie glanced around, terrified that the

woman's shrill tone would draw a crowd. "Please, Mrs. Garner. Won't you let me take you to your wagon now?"

The woman slapped Carrie's hand away. "Don't touch me. I don't want any of you to touch me."

Carrie breathed a sigh of relief when Will returned, followed by Abby. Without a word, Will then went off in search of Rourke.

Abby took one look at the disheveled appearance of the young wife and came to a halt.

"Nancy. What have you done?"

"Done? Nothing. Nothing more than I should have done as soon as Jed threw away my piano. Right then and there I should have jumped from the wagon into the river and drowned."

Abby kept her tone even. "The Platte was only a few inches deep. You'd have had a hard time drowning in a few inches of muck."

"They drowned my piano," she shrieked.

Abby caught her arm, but the woman pulled roughly away. "Don't touch me, Abby Market. You're on Jed's side."

"I'm not on anyone's side, Nancy. But you have a husband and little boy to think of now. Aren't they more important than a piano?"

"No one, and nothing, is more important than my piano," she moaned, starting to cry. She sat down in the middle of the grass and covered her face with her hands.

When Rourke and Will stepped from the shadows, the young woman was rocking and moaning as Carrie and Abby watched helplessly.

Assessing the scene, Rourke came forward and knelt before Nancy Garner.

"Your husband's been looking all over for you, Mrs. Garner. I told him I'd find you while he stayed with your boy."

"They don't want me," she cried, and covered her face once more.

174

"They do. They're both worried sick. Please let me help you, Mrs. Garner."

The young woman looked up through a mist of tears. Rourke offered a hand and helped her to her feet. With one arm firmly around her shoulders he led her to her wagon and then helped her inside.

Carrie, Abby, and Will trailed along feeling helpless, able to do nothing more than watch.

From inside, they heard the sound of Nancy Garner's crying, and the soft, soothing tones of her frantic husband. Feeling like intruders, they crept away until they could no longer hear the sounds of the Garners' voices.

"Thanks, Rourke," Abby said softly. "I just didn't know what to do for her."

"You were doing just fine. She'll be all right now," he said.

Abby took her sister's hand. "Come on, Carrie. We'd better get back to the wagon before Pa misses us."

Carrie glanced at Will, wishing they could have had those last few moments alone. Reluctantly she allowed herself to be led to the wagon.

Behind them, the two men watched until they were safely inside. Then, lost in their own thoughts, they made their way back to the cook wagon.

The fiddles were silent. The happy couples had turned in, to conserve their strength for the coming journey. By the coals of the campfire, a lone guitar strummed a sad, haunting melody. The dancing and merriment, at least for tonight, had ended. And while many in the camp fell into an exhausted sleep, others lay awake watching the stars and wondering what the fates had in store for them.

Chapter Sixteen

MOST OF THE people on the wagon train had never seen mountains as rugged as the Rockies. Some days, the entire train was moved, one wagon at a time, over jagged peaks. Men and beasts struggled as ropes were tied to wagons and hauled, inch by painful inch. Muscles were strained. Tempers were frayed. Many, like Nancy Garner, teetered on the edge of despair.

By day Abby worked alongside the men, pulling on ropes, driving teams of stubborn mules. When the train made camp for the night, she learned from Thompson and the others how to treat the cracked and bleeding hooves of the mules and oxen by painting them with hot tar. Watching the beasts' eyes glaze with pain, Abby glanced down at her hands, torn and callused from hard labor, and turned away in horror. Had they all sunk to the level of dumb animals, driven to plod onward, ever onward? When would it end? When would they ever find rest?

By evening she assisted her aunt and sister, masking her own fear and uncertainty, encouraging them in their efforts to adapt to this strange, savage environment.

Violet had brought along a copy of *The Emigrants' Guide to Oregon and California,* from which she read aloud each evening. The author, Lansford W. Hastings, promised all necessary information about equipment, supplies, and methods of transportation. He had apparently never crossed the Rockies by mule and wagon. His romantic description of the west made it sound like a Sunday picnic. In addition, Will Montgomery had loaned Carrie his copy of *Life, Adventures and Travels in California.* Whenever Violet read in her carefully cultured voice about the rich, verdant land and its gentle climate, the three women would feel their heartbeats quicken at the promise that beckoned.

"Will says that fruits and vegetables practically jump out of the soil," Carrie said as her aunt finished her nightly reading.

"He makes it sound like the Garden of Eden," Abby muttered dryly.

"And what's wrong with living in paradise? After the hell we've traveled along the way, I'd say we deserve it."

"Carrie. You watch your mouth." Violet nestled the books among the bits of ribbon and fabric in her chest, then closed the lid.

"Reverend Coulter talks about hell all the time, and no one tells him to watch what he says."

"That's different."

"Well, anyway, I can't wait to get to California. I want to bathe in crystal-clear waters, and lie in warm sunshine, and pick fruit right off my own trees."

"What happened to the Indian chief you were going to meet?" Violet asked with a gentle smile.

"She met someone better."

At Abby's words, Carrie flushed and turned away. "I'll go fetch some water from the river."

"You seem to spend a lot of evenings fetching water," Abby said, grinning at her aunt behind Carrie's back.

Violet touched a hand to her niece's shoulder. "Just don't let your pa catch you dawdling down by the river with Will Montgomery. You know what his temper's like."

She may as well have talked to the wind. Carrie tossed her curls and lifted the bucket before flouncing away. When a girl was fifteen, and in love, and all of life was spread out like a banquet, nothing else mattered.

The sun lay low on the horizon. Even as Will watched, it seemed to disappear below the waters of the river, leaving behind a shimmering golden glow.

He turned to study the girl who hurried toward him. Her dress was pure white, reminding him of the cotton fields of home. Her hair fanned out around her shoulders. As she ran the empty bucket slapped against her thigh. Her light, girlish laughter trilled on the breeze.

"You beat me. I thought I'd get here first." She set down the bucket, then took the hand he offered and was pulled behind the tree, where both would be hidden from view.

"I finished my chores early." Will grinned. "I think Mordecai noticed that I was itching to get away."

"Me too. But Aunt Vi was reading from your book. I want to learn all about a farmer's life in California before we get there."

"I thought you were going to be a seamstress."

She smiled a secret, woman's smile. "I am. But something tells me I ought to know all about farming too."

"Carrie . . ."

"Shh." She touched a finger to his lips. Instantly he felt the jolt clear down to his toes. As he started to back away, she laid a hand on his arm. "I think about you, Will. I think about you all the time."

He studied her hand, feeling the warmth of her touch through his shirt, but made no move to touch her. "I think about you too." His voice was low, shaky.

"I knew you did. Oh, I just knew you did." Carrie took a step closer, until their bodies were almost touching. "When you think about me, Will, what do you think about?"

He felt the beginnings of a flush creep along his throat. "It wouldn't be right to tell you."

"If you tell, I'll tell."

He swallowed. "I think about kissing you. About holding you." His voice lowered. "About lying in the grass with you."

Without realizing it, Carrie's fingers tightened at his shirt. "I think about the same things."

Will closed his hand over hers, then drew it away from his chest. Dropping his hand to his side, he said softly, "What we're thinking wouldn't be right."

"Why? I love you, Will."

His voice took on a fierceness, an earnestness she'd heard only once before; on the day he'd confronted Flint Barrows. "It isn't enough to love someone, Carrie. My father loved me. But he had to send me away because he couldn't bear to look at me."

"But I . . ."

"Listen to me." He grasped her arm, holding her away when she tried to move closer. "To me you're a princess, a wonderful, glorious dream. You're the most beautiful creature I've ever seen. But Carrie, you're a sweet, sheltered girl." His voice lowered to a whisper. "I couldn't stand to have you look at me, at my ugly shattered body, and turn away in horror."

"How can you say such things?"

"Don't you understand?" His tone roughened. "I'd rather just live with my dreams of you for the rest of my life than have to watch you face the stark reality of what I am."

Tears glimmered in her lashes, and she blinked them away. "What you are, Will Montgomery, is the man I want to spend the rest of my life with. I don't want just a few stolen kisses by a river. I want to be with you forever. Just like everyone else, you think

179

I'm a child. A spoiled, helpless child. But I intend to prove to you that I'm a woman. And your scars won't make any difference to me."

As she reached her fingers to the buttons of his shirt, Will grabbed them. She was surprised at the strength in his hand. He easily pinned both her hands in his big palm.

"Don't, Carrie. Once you cross this line, you can never go back." His voice was no longer shaky. It was low and firm, the commanding tone of a man who had given orders and taken them.

She tilted her head back, staring into his eyes. She could read the pain there, the hopelessness. And something else. The loneliness. He was as desperately lonely as she. And just as afraid of rejection.

"I don't want to turn back," she whispered.

For long, tense moments their gazes met and held.

"I want to look at you, Will. I want it to be my decision to go or stay."

Still he didn't move. Unblinking, his eyes stared down into hers. Watching her, he allowed his hand to drop to his side. With stiff, nervous movements, she unbuttoned his shirt, and let out a barely audible gasp. A thin, jagged scar crossed from his left shoulder to his right side. With her finger, Carrie traced the scar, feeling his muscles contract as she reached his stomach.

Will didn't speak. He even forgot to breathe. He studied her eyes, waiting to see the shock, the horror.

Bringing her hands to his shoulders, she slid the shirt from him. It floated to the ground and lay unnoticed. Where his left arm used to be, there was now an indentation over which had been pulled a flap of flesh, and a mass of scars twisted like a rope.

Tears sprang to Carrie's eyes. "Oh, Will. How you must have suffered."

He hung his head, waiting for her to turn away from him. Now that she had been given a chance to see for herself just how mutilated his body was, he knew that she would be unable to look at him. How would she react? He knew. With horror. Pity. And then revulsion at what he had become. He had seen it all before. All these emotions, he was certain, would cause her to run and hide.

Tentatively Carrie touched a finger to the scarred flesh that had once been his shoulder. Will flinched and forced himself not to turn away. She had to see it, to touch him, before she walked away from him for good.

"Does it hurt?" she whispered.

"Sometimes." He swallowed. "Sometimes I swear my arm is still there, throbbing like a toothache. Sometimes I have to reach over and feel the empty sleeve to prove to myself that it's really not there."

Most people met that response with complete rejection. How could a man feel an arm that wasn't there?

Still, Carrie didn't question him. She accepted his answer as fact. "And this. This scar. Does this hurt?"

"Not anymore." He felt his flesh quiver beneath her probing fingers, and cursed himself for his weakness. Even now, knowing that she was probably feeling revulsion at the mere touch of him, he was becoming aroused.

"They're wicked scars," she murmured, tracing the pattern of raised flesh that crisscrossed his abdomen and side. "But your body, Will"—she lifted her face to him—"is beautiful. I've never"—she moistened her lips—"touched a man before."

"Don't, Carrie. You don't have to pretend to be brave for my sake."

"Brave?" She took a step back and stared up at him in surprise. "I'm not brave. I'm the biggest coward there is. You're the brave one, Will. I don't know how you managed to go through a war, and the loss of your arm, without dying, or at least wanting to. I would have run away rather than face what you did. I think you're the bravest man I've ever known."

As she moved closer, he dropped his hand to her

shoulder. "Now that you've satisfied your curiosity, I want you to go, Carrie. Walk away. And never look back."

"I can't do that."

His voice roughened with emotion. "Go on now. Save yourself for a real man."

The tears she had been fighting spilled over, coursing down her cheeks. She wiped them away, angry at their betrayal. "I've already found a real man. And I won't settle for any other."

"For God's sake, Carrie." The words were torn from his lips. "I can't even hold you in two good arms."

Carrie wrapped her arms around his waist and pressed her lips to his throat. "One good arm is enough, Will, as long as it's yours. We'll hold each other."

"Oh God." Her words unlocked all the emotions Will had so long been denying.

As he brought his arm around her, they fell to their knees. For long minutes he stared into her eyes, feeling a welling of love he'd never known was possible. Then, slowly, reverently, he lowered his mouth to hers.

Her lips opened for him, and he felt her warm breath mingle with his. She was sweeter, far sweeter than anything he could ever have imagined. She clung to him, thrilling to his strength as he drew her even closer.

As the night crept over the land, they lay nestled together, murmuring the words that lovers have spoken from the beginning of time. And they knew that from this moment on, each would find it impossible to live without the other. Their bodies, their hearts, their souls were one.

Chapter Seventeen

ABBY STIRRED THE ashes and patiently fed kindling to get the morning fire blazing.

Her father had been too drunk last night to notice that Carrie wasn't in her blankets. But if she didn't return before he awoke, he was bound to fly into one of his famous rages.

Where had that girl gone? Abby had lain awake most of the night worrying. And she knew that beside her in the darkness, Aunt Vi had been unable to settle down as well. Carrie had done some foolish things before, but never anything as worrisome as this.

She heard her father moving inside the wagon and felt the first tiny thread of fear skitter along her spine. What could she possibly say or do in Carrie's behalf?

Violet emerged from the far side of the wagon, drying her hands and face as she walked. Though her skin glowed from the vigorous washing, her eyes were still puffy from lack of sleep. Both she and Abby turned at the sound of footsteps.

Carrie and Will approached hand in hand.

Violet took one look at their nervous little smiles, at the way they looked at each other, and knew. Even a spinster lady like herself, unschooled in the ways of the flesh, recognized the look of love.

"Carrie." Abby dropped the wood onto the fire and wiped her hands on the back of her britches. "Where have you been? Pa's going to throw a tantrum when he sees you and Will together. How could you be so foolish?"

"We . . ." Carrie glanced at her aunt, then back at Will. "We want to talk to Pa about . . ."

"About what?" James Market stepped from the wagon and shot his daughter an angry glare.

"About getting married, sir," Will said softly.

"Married! By God, Violet, bring me my rifle."

As James turned, Carrie rushed forward, clutching his sleeve. "Please, Pa. Just listen to what we have to say."

James allowed his gaze to trail her rumpled dress, her uncombed hair streaming down her back. His eyes narrowed, then focused on Will Montgomery.

"I told you once, boy, that if I caught you hanging around my daughter I'd blow your head off. I'm not blind and I'm not stupid. From the looks of her I'd say you've taken liberties no man has a right to, least of all a cripple like you."

"Pa!"

Will's hand clenched into a fist. Carrie ran to Will, gripping his hand as tightly as she could.

Staring around the wide-eyed family members, Will's voice grew thoughtful. "Maybe he's right, Carrie. Maybe a few days from now, when you've had time to think it over, you'll agree with your father."

Her eyes were clear and cold, and hard as ice. "We've been over all this before, Will. My father may not agree with me, but he can't live my life for me." Turning to her father, she said, "We've agreed to marry. Will came to ask your permission to court me."

"Court you." James laughed, a cruel, harsh laugh. "From the looks of the two of you, I'd say the courtship was a short one." He strode closer and grasped Will by the front of his shirt. "Now you listen to me, Montgomery. And listen well. I'm not going to allow my daughter to waste herself on half a man. The next time you come near her, I'll kill you." He gave Will a shove and sneered when he stumbled and fell. "Do you understand me, boy?"

When Carrie tried to go to his aid, James caught her roughly by the shoulder and threw her to the ground. Seeing Will make a move toward her, he stepped between them. "Don't come another inch closer. You're never going to touch my daughter again, boy."

From the dirt Will stared up at the man and felt hot anger roiling inside him. If ever he had wanted to unleash his anger and frustration, it was on this man. In that moment, he felt a hatred building inside him that left him stunned. He had thought such emotions dead. But if Carrie was able to unlock feelings of love, her father was even quicker to bring out a deep hatred.

As he got to his feet, his hand clenched and unclenched at his side. Just inches away, his gun rested in its holster, taunting him. It would be so easy. There was no way James Market could get to the wagon and his rifle in time. Then Will's gaze slid to Carrie, lying in the dust, crying as if her heart would break. If he were to kill her father, he would lose her forever. If he walked away, she would think him a coward. Either way he was bound to lose.

"Get out of here, boy. Quick, before I really lose my temper and show my daughter what a man with two good arms can do to the likes of you."

Will turned and strode away. As he did, the sound of Carrie's sobs followed him.

All day as they ate the dust of the lead wagons and sweated beneath a scorching sun, Abby and Violet tried to reason with Carrie.

"You just have to be patient, Carrie, and give Pa a chance to get used to the idea of you and Will."

"Patient?" Carrie snorted. "Why? So Pa can find

me a man more to his liking? Maybe we can catch up with Flint Barrows and Pa can decide which one of us to give to him."

"Carrie." Violet dropped an arm around her niece's shoulder, but Carrie pulled away.

"Do you really think Pa's ever going to change? Can the two of you really believe things will ever get better?"

Abby and Violet glanced at each other and grew silent.

"I love Will, and I intend to marry him, whether Pa approves or not."

"That's fine, Carrie. But why not give it some time? We'll be in California in another month or two. Why don't you and Will wait until we're settled to make a decision?"

"That's fine for you, Abby," Carrie hissed. "I wouldn't expect you to understand how I feel because you've never been in love. Look at you." Her voice rose in anger. "You're determined to be a dried-up old maid just like Aunt Vi."

Stunned at the vehemence of her sister's words, Abby glanced at their aunt. Violet plodded along the dusty trail, holding her head high as if she hadn't even heard the cruel words just hurled in anger.

Abby bit her lip. Was Carrie right? Would she counsel patience if she were in her sister's place? She knew in her heart that if she truly loved a man, her father's opinion of him wouldn't matter at all. She would probably do what Carrie was doing. If she loved a man. If any man could ever love her. The words echoed in her mind, causing a fresh stab of pain.

Driving the team, James Market studied the three women and cursed the fates that had given him no sons. Women. Silly, useless women. At least he could have two fine strapping sons-in-law. They might not know it yet, but those two daughters of his were going to learn that he was the lord and master of his family.

They would do his bidding, or they would taste the whip. He gave a last contemptuous look at his sister. Frivolous woman. She ate his food, accepted his shelter, and then chose sides against him. But not this time. This time he would make her understand that his word was law. If he had to, he'd kill Will Montgomery before he'd allow his daughter to be touched by him again.

The wagon train barely made twelve miles that day. When they finally stopped for the night, the travelers felt drained. All day they had trudged into the wind. Everything was covered with a fine layer of dust. It was in their clothes, on their food, even in their drinking water. As evening settled over the land, the wind picked up, sending dust clouds that clogged eyes and lodged in throats.

Carrie sat alone, refusing dinner. Her father ignored her. When James had eaten his fill, he picked up his jug and headed for Jed Garner's wagon. Jed had become his latest drinking partner.

Nancy Garner, her clothes dirty and rumpled, her hair wild and unkempt, spent the evenings prowling about the wagons, muttering to anyone who would listen that they were all doomed. The once-perfect wife and mother was clearly teetering on the edge of insanity.

Abby's heart went out to little Timmy Garner, whose parents seemed to be drifting further and further away from him and from each other. Most evenings, she brought him back to her wagon, where she and Violet would bathe him and wash his clothes before taking him back to his own wagon. There she would tuck him into bed and tell him stories. Whenever she made ready to leave, he would cling to her, begging her for one more story, one more song. She understood his fears, and usually relented, sitting with him until he fell into a troubled sleep. Often when she left him, she would see Rourke standing in the shadows, watching her. Once or twice when she was close enough to see his face, she was shocked by the haunted look in his eyes. Almost as if he were seeing a ghost.

This night, when she returned from the Garner wagon, Abby saw Violet sitting beside Carrie, her arm around the young girl's shoulders. Their heads were bent close, their conversation whispered. When she approached, they looked up, then fell silent. Feeling like an intruder, Abby climbed into the back of the wagon, allowing them their privacy. She could hear the low rumble of their voices long into the night. And though she couldn't make out their words, she detected the soothing note in Violet's tone, and gradually began to relax. Aunt Vi was a reasonable, sensible woman. She would calm Carrie's fears and give her good counsel. And in the morning, her father's temper would cool. They would have weathered another storm.

Carrie was gone.

In the eerie gray dawn, Abby moved stealthily about the wagon, searching for her sister's belongings. Everything was gone. Her clothes. Her blanket. Even Will's book.

Leaping from the back of the wagon, Abby began to run, not even realizing that she was heading toward the cook wagon. When she arrived, barefoot and panting, everyone was asleep. Everyone except Rourke, who was calmly pulling on his shirt. Abby tried not to stare at the mat of dark hair that covered his chest.

"Where is Will Montgomery?"

"Will?" He shrugged. "Haven't seen him."

"Is his horse here?"

Rourke glanced toward the tethered animals. Will's was missing.

Abby followed the direction of his gaze, and her shoulders sagged. "He's gone, hasn't he?" Not waiting for his reply, she said softly, "She's gone with him. They've both left the train."

Rourke's eyes narrowed. "Your sister?"

Abby nodded, and felt the first searing pain of separation. They had always been together. From her earliest recollection she had been assigned the task of looking out for her little sister. Through the years they had shared their thoughts, their dreams. She could always count on Carrie's laughter, her sense of humor, to keep her spirits up. Carrie's girlish babbling had been so much a part of Abby's life, she couldn't imagine having to endure life without it.

Rourke saw the pain in her eyes and forced himself not to go to her. It was her life. Her pain. He wanted no part of it. He'd already become too involved in Miss Abby Market's problems. Now he was determined to back off.

"They're not children, Abby. Will's a man. And if your sister chose to go with him, then I'd say she's decided to become a woman."

Abby's voice lowered in anger. "It's so easy for you, isn't it, Rourke? It must feel so good to stand back and watch the rest of us struggle with life. But you wouldn't know about that, would you? Because you don't live like the rest of us mortals. You just stand apart, like some god on a mountaintop, watching us struggle."

His tone was equally angry. "Get as mad as you want. It won't bring your sister back. And all the ranting and raving in the world won't stop them. They made their choice. The rest of you will just have to swallow it."

"And what about my father? Do you have any idea what his temper is like? If he goes after them, he won't stop until he's killed Will. And if he does that, he'll destroy my sister."

"Your father won't catch them. They've been gone for hours."

She whirled on him. "You saw them leave?"

He leaned a hip against the wheel of the wagon and struck a match to his cigar. Watching the stream of smoke through narrowed eyes, he said, "I heard them leave shortly after midnight. As soon as everyone had bedded down for the night." Glancing toward the sky, he said, "I figure they ought to be a good twenty, thirty miles from here by now."

"And you made no move to stop them?"

He flicked ash from the cigar, then met her cold gaze. "Wasn't my place to interfere. When it comes to a man and a woman, they have to make their own decisions. No one has the authority to tell them what's right for them."

"You wouldn't know right from wrong if it hit you in the eye."

He drew on the cigar, then studied her. "You seem to be in a fine temper this morning. You aren't jealous of your little sister, are you, Abby?"

"Go to hell." She spun on her heel and stalked back to her wagon.

Behind her, Rourke watched her stiff spine, her hands swinging furiously at her sides, and felt the beginnings of a grin. Abby Market was one hell of a woman.

Her father's murderous rage was even worse than anything Abby could have imagined. While she bent over the fire, she heard her father moving about the wagon. A moment later he emerged, his eyes blazing.

"Where is she?"

Abby stirred the coals, avoiding his look.

"I asked you where your sister was, woman." He strode toward her with his hand raised as if to strike her.

"She's gone, Pa."

"Gone?" His eyes narrowed. "With that one-armed son of a bitch?"

When Abby didn't respond, he picked up the blackened kettle filled with coffee and tossed it. It landed

190

with a clatter against the side of the wagon, spraying the steaming liquid across the canvas.

Abby flinched and turned away. He caught her by the shoulder and spun her around. "When did they go?"

She avoided his eyes. "I don't know," she lied. "Sometime during the night, I suppose. I woke this morning to find her missing, along with all her belongings."

He hitched up his suspenders and turned toward the wagon. "I'm going after them. And when I find them, she'll have the privilege of watching me kill her lover-boy."

Abby heard him clattering around the wagon, throwing things aside in his haste to find what he was looking for. She had to find a way to stop him. In a black temper like this, he would do what he threatened. In desperation, she ran to the cook wagon.

"Mordecai, please come."

The men looked up from their morning coffee.

"What is it, Miss Abby?"

"My sister Carrie has run off with Will Montgomery. My father is threatening to go after them and kill him."

Mordecai lifted his rifle and without further question followed her.

Rourke, busy saddling his horse, left the cinch unfastened and ambled along behind them. It would never have occurred to him that he was curious. What's more, he would never admit to himself that he cared about Abby Market. He didn't want to get into their fight, he told himself. He just wanted to back up Mordecai in case of trouble.

Just as James Market mounted his horse, Mordecai stepped in front of him, grasping the reins.

"I hear you're going off in search of your daughter." Before James could respond, Mordecai added, "You canna' catch them. They've been gone for hours."

"How would you know that?"

191

"Because I heard them go. Half the camp probably heard them."

"And you didn't bother to wake me?"

Mordecai's voice lowered; the Scottish burr thickened. "I wouldna' do that, Market. You'd have tried to stop them."

"You're goddamned right I would have. She's a child. And she's throwing herself away on a cripple."

Despite the fact that he himself was crippled, Mordecai's tone became calmly reasonable. "I'm sorry you see it that way, man. Whether you care to admit it or not, your daughter has become a woman before your very eyes. And you've been too blind to notice."

James jerked the reins from the wagon master's hand and wheeled his horse. "I'll show you who's blind, Stump. By the time I find them, she'll be so hungry and tired, she'll be only too happy to come back with me."

"I think her husband will see that she's fed and well taken care of."

"Husband!"

Mordecai nodded. "By the time you find them, they'll be properly married. And there will be nought you can do about it."

"I'll show you what I can do. I'll kill that one-armed bastard."

"Market."

At the tone of Mordecai's voice, he drew back on the reins and turned his head.

"I think you should know. Will Montgomery may have lost an arm in the war, but he's one of the fastest gunmen you'll ever come up against. If you go after him, you may be lucky enough to make your daughter a widow. But I'll be betting on Montgomery." Mordecai started to turn away, then paused. Giving the man a cold look, he added, "I consider young Montgomery one of the finest men I've ever met. I'd be proud to have him for a son. Or a son-in-law."

"Then you're a fool."

"No, Market. You're the fool. She's chosen the man she wants to be with. No matter what you do, she'll never be your little girl again. She's a woman now. And she's followed her heart." His voice lowered. "You can try to stop them. You may even kill him. But she'd never forgive you. You'd lose her anyway."

For long, frozen moments, James Market stared at the man, digesting his words. With his right hand gripped tightly around the handle of his whip, Market slid from the saddle and stood, his feet wide apart, his shoulders sagging. On his face was a look of stunned disbelief.

Having heard the sound of angry voices, the people milling about the nearby wagons had paused in their chores to watch and listen. The group of travelers had grown suddenly quiet. The atmosphere was tense and silent.

Watching the defeated man, Mordecai tipped his hat to Abby and Violet and walked away. Seeing Rourke, he muttered, "I think Market has come around. It seems best if we leave him alone now, to work out his sorrow."

"Sorrow?" Rourke glanced at Market, then back at Mordecai. "That isn't sorrow I see, but anger, rage, frustration."

"He'll work it out, man." Clutching his rifle, Mordecai headed toward the cook wagon.

Reluctantly, Rourke followed.

Behind them, Abby turned toward her father. "I made you fresh coffee, Pa." Abby handed him a tin cup.

"I don't want it." Slapping her hand, he sent the cup flying through the air. Hot liquid spilled down her arm, scalding her.

"You fool." His hand raised, as if to strike her.

Feeling the heat of his temper, Abby didn't flinch. "No, Pa. You're the fool. You've lost." Her tone was quietly triumphant. "And Carrie's won. She's finally free of you and your ugly temper forever."

The entire camp heard the crack of the whip as it struck the young woman across the shoulder. Mordecai and Rourke turned and began running in the direction of the Market wagon.

Standing on the fringes of the crowd, Rourke gripped his gun. Remembering the first time he'd seen Abby take a whipping, he felt a shudder ripple through his body. It would be impossible for him to stand by and do nothing this time. Pushing his way through the gaping crowd, he paused at the unexpected sound of Abby's voice lifted in anger.

"Don't you touch me." Leaping at her father, Abby tore the whip from his hand, shrieking, "Don't you dare touch me ever again."

For one long moment, Market could only stare at his daughter in stunned silence. Then, seeing the shocked looks on the faces of the people nearby, he spun on his heel, climbed into the back of the wagon, and pulled the cork from a fresh jug.

Whispering, mumbling, feeling awkward at having witnessed something so intimate, the crowd drifted back to their wagons and resumed their chores.

Mordecai watched as Rourke's hand continued to rest on the gun at his side, his fingers poised, his eyes steely. There would have been no talking him out of it this time, the older man realized. Whether or not Rourke cared to admit it, even to himself, he was becoming deeply involved in Abby Market's life. Maybe, the wagon master thought with a sigh, that wasn't so bad. They were two people very much alone.

Feeling Mordecai's gaze on him, Rourke spun away and stalked toward the cook wagon.

Violet had stood to one side, cowed by her brother's violence, amazed by her niece's unexpected display of strength. As the crowd dispersed, she came forward and embraced Abby.

"You were so brave, dear. I wish I could stand up to James like that."

Abby's eyes misted with pain for a moment. With a weak little half smile, she said, "You would if you had to, Aunt Vi. He just hasn't pushed you far enough yet."

As Violet bathed her niece's wound, she whispered words of endearment. "Lie still, dear. Don't move. This will sting a bit, but I have to disinfect it."

Abby lay still, allowing her aunt to minister to her. All the while, Vi talked in her soft, dreamy voice about Carrie, and how she had managed to elude her father's cruelty. "It will be hard for them, Abby. But with enough love, they can make it."

Would they? Could they? Could a fresh-faced, innocent girl of fifteen and a young man who had been to hell and back really make it on love alone? Abby pushed aside her fears and doubts and spoke the words she knew her aunt needed to hear. "Oh, Aunt Vi. Of course they'll make it. They're going to be fine."

Her aunt gave her a brilliant smile. "They will, won't they? Oh, they'll be so fine. But Abby, I shall miss her terribly." For the first time Violet's voice shook. "I must face the fact that I'll probably die without ever seeing them again. But I'm happy for her. Happy because Carrie knows what she wants, and she's willing to go after it."

The tears Abby had been fighting began to roll down her cheeks unchecked. What had happened to the world she had once known? Where was the security of their green farm, her gentle mother's faith? When had it all gone crazy? Her father's temper was out of control, and he was becoming more violent with each day. Aunt Violet was still living in a world of make-believe, where everything could be solved by love. And the little sister she adored was gone. Like the farm. Like her mother. Like the life she had once known. Gone forever.

Chapter Eighteen

JAMES MARKET STAYED drunk for days. When he wasn't asleep, he was hurling abuse at his remaining two women—two women who struggled to cope with their loss by driving the team, hunting game, providing food and clothing, and hiding his condition from the other members of the wagon train.

One night, when Abby found Violet hunched over her mending, sound asleep, she decided things had gone too far. This poor woman was pushing herself beyond the limits, not only to overcome the loss of Carrie, but also because James Market was unwilling to face reality.

Reality. As Abby helped her aunt into the back of the wagon and covered her with a quilt, she pondered what their lives had become. They were no longer farmers, with roots deep in the soil. Now they were emigrants, crossing an alien wilderness, with no knowledge of what lay ahead.

As a child, she had thought her father and grandfather the two strongest men she had ever known. Her grandfather could do the work of three men as he went about his farm chores each day. Yet, while the others relaxed after their evening meal, he could spend the evening hours preaching the word of the

Lord. And on Sunday mornings, he not only conducted church services for the nearby families, but on Sunday afternoons he went out in his wagon in search of fallen sinners, often bringing them home for supper, where he would lead them in prayers and singing.

Of all his sons, James was the most like him in physical strength. Her father had always been proud of driving himself and every member of his family to the limits of endurance. When the chores were finished, James often went into town to drink or play cards, staying until the sun came up. It was a matter of pride to him that he could return to the fields and work without benefit of sleep. Of course, Abby mused as she stepped from the wagon into the darkness, it wasn't long before their farm had begun to wear the shabby look of neglect. Still, James had seemed to push himself harder than ever, determined to prove to his father and himself that he could succeed.

Had he sold the farm because it reminded him painfully of the wife and babies buried there? Shivering, Abby paused and studied the path of a shooting star. Or was he just tired of trying to pretend he could make it work? She felt a painful contraction around her heart. What had Aunt Vi once said? Maybe everyone heading west was running from something.

What was Rourke running from? Abby glanced toward the cook wagon, then knelt and carefully banked the fire. Standing, she brushed the dirt from her britches and started toward the wagon. Why would a man leave the beautiful, rolling hills of Maryland for this backbreaking journey?

"Evening, Miss Abby."

At Mordecai's greeting, Abby's thoughts scattered.

"Good evening. Is there something I can do for you, Mr. Stump?"

"Mordecai, lass. I'm too young, or you're too old, to be calling me Mr. Stump. I was looking for your father."

"He isn't here." She stared at the toe of her worn boot. "Can I help instead?"

The man's heart went out to this girl. Everyone on the train was whispering about James Market's drinking. Since the youngest girl had run off, he was out of control. It cut Mordecai to the quick to see a determined lass and a delicate spinster trying to hold things together. Much as he hated the embarrassment of a scene, it was time to confront Market with a warning. Unless he was willing to pull his share of the load, he and his family would have to leave the train at the next fort. Of course, Mordecai knew, he would never make good his threat. These two women were too fine to be treated so badly. What he really wanted to do was shake some sense into Market before it was too late. Maybe a good scare was just what he needed.

"No, lass. It's your father I'll be speaking to. Know where he is?"

She shook her head. Lying didn't come easily to her. But she knew that if Mordecai saw her father tonight, before he had time to sleep off the liquor, he would be as mean and surly as a wounded bear.

Mordecai studied her, wishing there were something he could do to make her lot easier. The girl struck a chord in him. She had more heart than most men he knew. But she wouldn't know how to take his sympathy. And she'd be offended by an offer of help.

When she volunteered no further information on the whereabouts of her father, he cleared his throat. "Still practicing with the handgun, lass?"

She nodded and glanced at him, then away. She saw something in his eyes. Not disgust. Not pity. Understanding.

"Good. Maybe some evening when we have time, you can show me what you've learned."

"I will. Good night, Mordecai."

"Night, lass." He turned away.

As she climbed into the back of the wagon, Abby paused to turn and watch him. She hadn't fooled him one bit. The wagon master probably knew everything going on in this train. And he knew that if James Market wasn't in his own wagon, he'd be drinking with a friend. Mordecai was heading in the direction of the Garner wagon.

A shadow moved beside a tree, and Abby saw a light flicker in the darkness. In those brief seconds, she could make out Rourke's strongly chiseled profile. Then the flame died, and the shadow blended into the darkness. Was he looking toward her wagon? Despite the cover of night, she felt a flush warm her cheeks. Did he ever think about her, and about the kisses they'd shared? Apparently not, she thought. He'd made no attempt to speak to her. Closing the canvas, she felt the darkness of the wagon's interior envelop her like a warm, safe cocoon. Since her angry outburst the morning of Carrie's disappearance, Rourke had been avoiding her. Shivering once more, she slipped off her boots and pulled the blanket around her.

The object of her thoughts leaned a hip against the trunk of a tree and drew deeply on his cigar. On a small train like this, rumors spread like fire in dried grass. Most of the people on the train were betting that the two Market women would soon fold under the strain. With the youngest one gone and the old man drunk most of the time, the rigors would soon prove to be too much. These two would be no match for James Market's vicious temper.

Rourke listened to the murmurs and whispers coming from the wagons as people and animals settled down for the night. From the Coulter wagon, the sound of the baby's bleating ended when Evelyn Coulter's soothing lullaby began. A child's laugh was suddenly smothered, and ended up sounding like a hiccup. In the Garner wagon, Nancy's voice, high and whining, began its nightly litany of complaints. Horses blew and stomped. Men snored. And Mordecai, walking slowly beside the staggering figure of

James Market, was speaking in a tone that was low and commanding. Rourke watched as the two figures halted beside the Market wagon. When James started to speak, Mordecai's sharp words cut him off. A moment later, Abby stepped through the parted canvas and caught hold of her father's arm. Steering James into the wagon, she turned to speak softly to Mordecai. Rourke watched as the older man replied, then tipped his hat. Abby stayed where she was, watching until Mordecai was out of sight. Squaring her shoulders, she glanced up to the star-studded sky, then disappeared inside the wagon once more.

Rourke crushed his cigar beneath his heel and made his way toward the cook wagon. The others could say what they wanted about the Market women. He was putting his money on Abby to make it.

As Abby prepared for a day of hunting, she wondered again what Mordecai had said to her father to sober him so quickly. Although she knew James still drank nightly with Jed Garner, he was once again spending his days driving their team, and was shouldering some of his responsibilities. Though he was still surly and abusive, she and Violet were glad for any help he gave them.

The previous night, when she had told Mordecai that their game bag was empty, he had invited her to hunt with one of his men today, and her heart had nearly tripped over itself. Probably, she told herself, because she hoped it wouldn't be Rourke. Or maybe because she hoped it would be.

She loaded the small handgun and placed it in her pocket, then cleaned and loaded the rifle. Filling a canteen with precious water and tying some dried meat to her saddle, she mounted and made her way to the front of the train. With a smile and a tip of his hat, Mordecai waved her ahead. She urged her horse faster, until she'd left the train far behind. As the dust swirled, she tied a handkerchief over her nose and mouth and pulled the brim of her hat lower on her head. Through the dust she could make out the dark horse and its rider. Her pulse leaped. Riding ahead of the wagons was the unmistakable figure of Rourke. As always, her heart began to race, keeping time to the horse's hooves. Why did this man have to affect her like this? Why did she feel this foolish happiness in his company, when he obviously wished he could be anywhere except with her?

"Morning." He turned as she approached, then slowed his mount and gave an approving glance at the protective handkerchief tied across her face. She was learning quickly how to adapt.

"Morning." She carefully schooled her voice to show as little emotion as Rourke. "Where are we headed?"

"Toward those peaks." He pointed. "There's water in those hills. And that means game."

Without another word, he urged his horse into a trot. Abby's horse easily kept stride.

He studied the horizon, trying to focus on something of interest. Something, anything that would keep his mind off the woman beside him. Why did her face have to be young and pretty, with eyes that danced with an inner light? Why did her slim figure, cloaked in those ridiculous men's clothes, cause his insides to ache? Why was it that every time he looked at her he wanted her? Curling his fingers around the leather reins, he kept his face averted.

If she were riding with Thompson, she thought, he would be pointing out a million things of interest, and telling her stories of his youth. If this were Brand beside her, he would be answering her questions in monosyllables and examining the tracks and marks around them. But this was Rourke, and he treated her as he treated everyone on the wagon train. With disinterest. She didn't really mind the silence between them. If Rourke knew of her problems, he chose not to mention them. And though she would have loved to learn more about this mysterious man, she accepted the fact that he was too private a person to ever reveal much about himself. She was content to look, to study, to learn. There were so many new and fascinating things to see as they crossed the rugged west. It was enough to be away from the others, to be riding with Rourke into the unknown.

Abruptly she reined in her mount. "I thought I saw something move behind those rocks. I'll take a look."

As she started to move, he caught her reins. "We stick together, remember?" At her look of surprise, he added, "We'll both take a look."

Abby nodded, and allowed him to lead the way. The truth was, when she was with Rourke, she felt safe. For a moment, just a moment, she had forgotten to be cautious.

When they approached the rocks, she thought she heard a slight shuffling movement.

Rourke circled the rocks. "Nothing."

"Are you sure?" Perplexed, Abby glanced around, and again heard the sound. Nudging her horse, she peered around a second, smaller formation and let out a cry.

"Rourke. Oh, Rourke, hurry."

Slipping from the saddle, Abby stared at the bloody, ragged form of an Indian. His long hair was matted with dirt and dried blood. His torso was crisscrossed with jagged scars and cuts, many of them bleeding profusely.

Abby's first inclination was to run. She had never even seen an Indian before, and she felt a moment of sheer panic at the sight of him. Then, peering closer, she heard his little moan of pain, and all her fears fled. He was badly hurt, maybe even dying.

By the time Rourke had dismounted, she was kneeling beside the youth, touching a hand to his forehead. Black eyes rounded. He drew back from her touch.

"He's burning with fever, Rourke. Bring your canteen."

"My God, Abby. Look out." With lightning speed, Rourke jerked her aside just as the Indian's hand, clutching a dagger, made an arc through the air and fell weakly to his side.

They watched as the knife slipped from his fingers and clattered on the stones.

"He could have killed you."

She shook her head, willing the panic to subside. Despite the trembling that shook her, her voice was firm. "He's too weak. He can barely move. Feel his pulse."

Rourke picked up the knife, then touched a finger to the young man's throat. The heartbeat was faint and uneven.

Rourke walked to his horse and removed the canteen. Taking it from him, Abby held it to the stranger's lips and poured a small amount down his throat. The Indian swallowed, then turned his head away, refusing any more. All the while, Rourke kept his hand on his gun and his gaze swept the rocks above. If there was one Indian, there could be more.

"He's badly hurt. Look." Abby pointed to a pool of blood oozing into the dirt from the young man's shoulder. As she examined him she gasped, "His wrists and ankles are raw. What could have caused that?"

"Rope. Those are rope burns." Rourke knelt beside her, studying the Indian without touching him. He had seen the youth's reaction to a stranger's touch. "Looks like he's been bound, hand and foot."

"But why?"

"Captive, I suspect."

"Who would want to capture him?" She too had seen the Indian's reaction to her touch, and prayed it hadn't been a band of white traders.

As if reading her thoughts, Rourke muttered,

"Could have been whites. There's a lot of fear, and that breeds hatred. Or Indians. Some Indian tribes steal from each other."

"They steal people?" Abby's voice was hushed.

Rourke shrugged. "Maybe they were retaliating for something his tribe did to them. Brand would know better about what goes on."

Abby took her handkerchief from around her neck and poured water onto it. "We've got to stop this bleeding."

"What makes you think that Indian will let you touch him again?"

She stared up at him, then back at the silent figure. "You'll have to see to that. If he fights me, you'll have to hold him still until I'm finished." She knelt down and the youth's dark eyes watched her. "Now, let's get started."

While she worked, Rourke studied Abby with a mixture of surprise and admiration. It was obvious that she was afraid of this strange creature. Yet she was determined to help him. When they rolled the Indian over, they discovered the tip of an arrow still embedded in his shoulder. Apparently he had managed to break off the shaft. The wound was badly infected, yet the youth made no sound when the sharp tip was dug from his flesh with Rourke's knife. Except for a quick hiss of breath, he showed no emotion. When Abby washed the wound and poured whiskey on it before covering it with a strip of cloth, his eyes glazed with pain. Still he made no sound.

"Aunt Vi will have to make one of her balms for these wrists and ankles," Abby muttered as she washed the dirt from his raw flesh.

"Your aunt? You thinking of bringing her way out here?"

Abby gave Rourke a quick look before returning her attention to the Indian's wound.

Rourke's voice lowered. "You aren't planning to take him back to the train, are you?"

"Of course I am. What did you think I was going to do with him? Leave him out here to die?"

"You've taken out the arrow, dressed his wound. These people know how to survive out here. Leave him some water and we'll be on our way."

Abby shot him a dark look. "You can't be serious."

"Abby, I don't think the good people of the wagon train are going to welcome him with open arms."

"He's a human being, Rourke. They couldn't possibly expect us to turn our backs on him."

"You didn't turn away from him. But you're making a mistake if you think you can take him back to camp with you. What'll you do when you want to change his dressings? Tie him up? Hold a gun on him?"

She gave him a withering look. "If I have to."

"Abby."

"I'm taking him to my wagon, Rourke. And when he's strong enough, he'll be free to leave. If you don't agree, you can ride back to the train and warn all those good people. Abby Market is bringing home an Indian."

For long, silent moments Rourke studied her firm chin, her flaring nostrils.

Biting her lip at his silent contemplation, Abby glanced around. "Now, the question is, how will I get him back to the wagon train? He's too weak to ride."

Standing, Rourke gave her a crooked grin. Without a word, he picked up his knife and walked toward a stand of trees.

"Where are you going?"

"To do what I seem to do best for you," he called over his shoulder. "Finish what you start."

"Nobody asked for your help. I'll think of something."

"Yeah. Well, while you're thinking, I'll see what I can come up with."

While Rourke set to work cutting down several tree limbs, Abby studied the Indian. He hadn't moved a muscle. Yet she sensed that he was coiled as tightly as a spring, waiting for his chance to either attack or crawl away. What would drive a person, so near death, to take his chances on the harsh land beyond them rather than stay here with her where he was being offered safety and medicine? Though he seemed not to understand what was said, he had to realize that they were trying to help. The answer came instantly to mind. Home. That wonderful, magical lure of home. Abby felt her throat constrict and, kneeling, touched a hand to the Indian's cheek. He cringed. Wide black eyes focused on her.

"I know you can't understand me," she said in a soothing tone. "But maybe you can understand this." Brushing the dark hair that clung damply to his forehead, she murmured, "I know what it means to be far from home. And alone and afraid." A tear misted her eye and she quickly blinked it away. "Nothing, no one, is going to hurt you. As soon as you're strong enough, we'll find a way to get you home to your family. Trust me."

His expression never changed. Yet something in his eyes seemed different. She found herself looking into the wisest, oldest eyes she'd ever seen. Pouring water from the canteen, she continued bathing his forehead until Rourke returned.

"I was lucky. I found a couple of sturdy saplings," he called, dragging the trees.

"What good are they?"

"I'm going to make a travois," Rourke called, stretching his blanket between the poles. "The Plains Indians use this to carry their sick. Clever people," he muttered, bending to his task.

Abby glanced at the boy. He had turned at the sound of Rourke's voice. He watched in fascination until the job was completed.

Bending, Rourke picked up the Indian, then lifted an eyebrow in surprise. "Don't let his frail appearance fool you, Abby. He may be small. But he has the muscles of a warrior."

Folding the blanket over him, Rourke lashed the Indian to the travois, then mounted his horse. "You ride behind and tell me if he's in any distress."

"Rourke." Abby pulled herself into the saddle and brought her horse alongside his.

He waited, one eyebrow still lifted in a question.

"Thanks."

"For what?" he asked.

She shrugged, feeling awkward as she struggled to find the right words. "For not fighting me on this."

"Maybe I'm just getting smart," he said, the beginning of a grin tugging at his lips. "Looks are deceptive. Like that Indian"—he cocked his head and threw a glance at the travois—"whose frailty masks a strong young brave; maybe the skinny little girl is really a whole lot of woman, with a mind of her own."

"I'm not sure if I've been insulted or paid a compliment." She reined in her horse.

"Maybe both." He threw back his head and laughed as the horse started forward.

Behind him, Abby found herself loving the sound of Rourke's laughter. He ought to laugh more often. It changed him into someone very different from the grim gunfighter she'd first met.

As they began the slow return to the line of wagons, Abby forced herself to keep her gaze firmly fixed on the figure on the travois. The Indian returned her careful scrutiny. But every so often she found herself staring at the broad shoulders of the man on the horse. And when she did, the Indian saw her eyes take on the ageless look of a woman in love.

Chapter Nineteen

IT WAS DUSK when they reached the wagon train. Avoiding the others, Rourke made straight for the cook wagon and sought out the scout.

Mordecai Stump and Parker, the cook, stood to one side while the scout conversed with the Indian.

"Cheyenne," Brand announced. "He is important to his people. He is called the One with Two Shadows. He was taken prisoner by the Kiowa. Now he journeys home."

"Kiowa are hundreds of miles from here." Rourke reacted with surprise. "How could he come so far with such serious wounds?"

Brand spoke rapidly, and the Indian responded.

"He said a true Cheyenne warrior always returns to his people."

Abby listened to the exchange in silence. She had noted the regal way the youth answered Brand's questions while carefully studying Brand's clothing. Except for his long dark hair and mastery of the Indian's language, the scout could have been a white man. Could have been. But wasn't. From what she had learned, Brand's mother had been a member of the Nez Percé tribe, his father a trapper from the Ozarks. The child of their union walked between two cultures, belonging to neither. From his terse responses, the wounded Indian seemed to have little regard for this outcast. He placed as much trust in Brand as he did in a white man.

"Where will you take him?" Brand asked.

"To my wagon," Abby said.

The scout glanced once more at the Indian, who lay as still as death, then at Mordecai. "His wounds are bad."

"I've tended the sick before," Abby said. "And so has my aunt."

"But this is different, Miss Abby." Mordecai glanced at Brand, then at Rourke, hoping they would help him sway her.

"He may"—the scout licked his lips and weighed his words carefully—"shock your delicate sensibilities."

"My aunt and I are hardly delicate."

"You have never tended one of The People."

"The People." Abby glanced at the Indian. "Is that what you call yourselves?"

Brand nodded gravely. "Forgive me, Miss Market, but the others on the train will not like this."

"He's right, Miss Abby," Mordecai said softly.

"What would you have me do? Leave him here to die?"

The scout considered for a moment, then spread his hands. "You will make many enemies."

"And you?" Abby asked, turning to Mordecai. "Do you think the people on this train will object to my caring for a wounded man?"

"A wounded Indian, Miss Abby," Mordecai corrected. He paused, studying the Indian, who watched without emotion. "I think our people will be alarmed. And I suspect that more than a few of them will come to me asking that he be removed."

Abby waited, her heart pounding. They were all against her.

"Your father will probably be the first one in line to

protest. He'll never permit you to keep an Indian in your wagon."

"I'll handle my father." Abby saw the skeptical looks on the men's faces. They had all witnessed her father's rages. And they were all aware of the abuse she had taken at her father's hands. She lowered her voice for emphasis. "I will handle him."

Mordecai shook his head. "It isn't just your father. This lad will need constant watching. If you turn your back on him you could find a knife in it."

"My aunt and I will take turns watching him," Abby said.

"Not good enough." Mordecai gave a glance at Rourke, and was amazed to see the slight nod of Rourke's head. So, he thought, our loner is becoming involved, whether he likes it or not. "I take it, Rourke, you're willing to lend a hand to the Market women?"

"If they want it."

Abby shot him a stunned look of gratitude.

"This lad will need constant care."

"My aunt and I will see to it."

"You're taking a lot for granted, Miss Abby. Seems to me your aunt should have the right to make her own decisions."

Abby flushed. Mordecai was right. She had no authority to speak for Aunt Violet. "He's my responsibility. I'll see to him."

Still Mordecai weighed the issue, hoping to find some way out. They couldn't just leave a wounded man along the trail, even an Indian who resented their care. But the people, already bone-weary and ready to fold, might rise up and refuse to allow him to stay. He'd have to be prepared for anything.

Finally he shrugged. "Take him to the Market wagon."

The scout watched without emotion as the wounded Indian was carried away.

* * *

Abby hadn't been certain just how her aunt would deal with their unexpected guest. Would she fall over in a dead faint at the sight of a live Indian in their wagon? Would she get all pale and flustered, and hold a handkerchief to her nose? Worse, might she refuse to share her quarters with him?

As always, Violet did the unexpected. Since it was evening when Abby and Rourke arrived back at camp, James had taken his jug of whiskey to the Garner wagon. Violet was alone, bent over her sewing. She had bathed away the dust of the trail and had put on a clean dress before dinner. In a pale rose gown more appropriate for Sunday tea, she was a stunning contrast to the trail-weary figures that approached her.

At the sight of Abby, Violet lifted the lid from a heavy pot. The aroma of vegetables, cooked in the last of the meat stock, wafted on the breeze.

"Thank goodness you're back, child. I've been keeping your supper hot."

"I'll eat later, Aunt Vi. Right now, I have to make up a bed for a wounded youth I found on the trail."

"Mercy. A wounded child." Violet was up and heading toward the wagon when she caught sight of the figure in Rourke's arms. "He's . . ." She swallowed, blanched, then tried again. Her voice trembled slightly. "He's . . . badly wounded, I see."

Abby studied her aunt's ashen face. "He's a Cheyenne warrior. His name is Two Shadows."

The older woman hesitated for long moments. Whatever battle she was waging within herself was a mystery to the others. Rolling up the sleeves of her immaculate gown, she said, "I'll make up a bed for him. You eat, child."

Abby watched as her aunt climbed into the back of the wagon and began rummaging around. A few minutes later she motioned for Rourke. When the Indian had been placed between clean linens, Rourke said softly, "We've already removed the arrow's tip from his shoulder, Miss Violet. But the wound will need cleansing daily. And Abby said you'd know a balm for his wrists and ankles."

Violet studied the raw flesh, so dark against the white linens. "Who—did this to him?"

"His captors. Kiowa."

She took a step closer. Despite fatigue, dark eyes watched her. She tried to smile, and her lips trembled. "I'll get him some soup."

"Miss Violet." At Rourke's low tone, she looked up. "Whenever you're going to tend him, come and get me first."

She felt a tiny shaft of fear and swallowed it down. "Why?"

"Because he doesn't like being touched by strangers. Especially white women. He may react violently."

The fear grew and she fought for calm. "He's only a boy, Mr. Rourke."

"He's an Indian warrior, ma'am. Don't ever forget that."

She stared into dark, watchful eyes, then back at Rourke. "Thank you. I won't." She paused. "Will he need watching tonight?"

"He'll need watching all the time," Rourke said patiently. "I'll stay the night."

She gave him a smile of gratitude. "I'll get you some supper, Mr. Rourke."

James Market was tired. And very drunk. He and Jed Garner had emptied the jug. All he wanted, he thought, weaving his way among the wagons, was his bed.

The first thing he noticed was the lantern, still lit. Damned women should have been asleep hours ago, he thought angrily. As he drew closer, he saw the outline of Abby and Violet bent over a figure wrapped in blankets. Dropping the jug, he opened the wagon flap, then stopped. Seated at the far side of the wagon, holding a gun, was Rourke.

"What's he doing here?" James demanded. Despite his fury, his words were slurred. He tried to think where he'd left his rifle, but his mind was slow to respond. "You've got a lot of nerve holding a gun on my women. Get out of my wagon, Rourke."

When the gunman said nothing, Market turned toward Abby. "Goddammit, tell him . . ." His words trailed off as he caught sight of the Indian. "Tell me that isn't what it looks like. A heathen Indian? In my wagon?"

"I found him along the trail. He's been hurt, Pa. Aunt Vi and I are going to tend his wounds."

"Like hell you are. You get that animal out of here."

"This is not an animal, James," Violet said softly. "He's a young man. And he's badly wounded."

"He'll be dead if he isn't out of here now. I'm not sharing my wagon with an Indian."

"I'm sorry you feel that way, James," Violet said, her voice still as soft as velvet. "But if the sight of him offends you, I suggest you sleep outside, under the wagon."

Abby glanced at her aunt, unable for a moment to believe what she'd heard.

Market's eyes widened, then he unleashed his full fury on his sister.

"Don't you ever speak to me like that, woman. All your life I've fed you, clothed you, taken care of you, you dried-up old prune. And now you presume to give me orders. Get out of this wagon. And take that heathen with you."

"No, James." Violet's pale blue eyes frosted over. Her soft voice held a thread of steel. "It's you who has been fed and clothed and taken care of. All that Papa left me from the farm has gone for your needs. And all my life I've taken orders from Papa, and then you. But not this time. I've decided there was only one person in our family who really knew how to deal with you."

When he brought his hand back, as if to slap her, she cut him off with a single word.

213

"Lily."

Abby watched her father pale. His face contorted into a look of pure hatred.

"For Lily's sake, I have suffered the indignities you have chosen to inflict on me. No more, James. Abby and I intend to nurse this young man until he is well enough to return to his people. While he is here, you may share the wagon with us, or sleep outside."

James Market's lips curled into a sneer. "You'll pay for this, woman."

"I have already paid, James. Dearly."

"Are you sleeping here, Pa?"

He glowered at Abby, before hissing, "I wouldn't spend one minute in the same wagon with a damned filthy Indian. The two of you can have him to yourselves."

He grabbed up a blanket and turned away. Outside, they could hear him slamming around beneath the wagon. Inside, no one spoke. While Abby watched, her aunt handed Rourke a blanket.

"Shall we take turns sleeping, Mr. Rourke?"

Rourke studied the older woman with new respect. She'd put the bastard in his place without even losing her ladylike composure for one moment. "You two ladies sleep first. I'll keep watch."

"Thank you, Mr. Rourke." Violet rolled between her blankets and closed her eyes. If she was agitated, she refused to let it show. Within minutes, her breathing was merely a soft sigh on the night air.

Beside her, Abby glanced once at Rourke, then pulled the blankets around her. Closing her eyes, she mentally played back the scene between her aunt and father. The mere mention of Lily's name had left him stunned. Why? Abby wondered. Was it because he had forbidden anyone to ever mention her name in his presence? Or was there something more? His reaction had been so surprising, Abby couldn't figure out if it was due to shock or anger.

214

Aunt Vi was just full of surprises this night. First she had swallowed her fears and prejudices and reacted with a strength of purpose Abby had never seen before. And then she had stood up to her bully of a brother in a manner that had been completely unexpected. Where had sweet, shy Violet come up with such strength? Had she been saving it up all her life for this one confrontation?

Even if Rourke wasn't here in the same wagon with her, so close she could hear his breathing, she wouldn't be able to sleep. Life had become such a puzzle. And there were too many pieces missing.

Rourke leaned his head back and watched the sleeping figures. How had he allowed himself to be talked into playing nursemaid to a couple of women and a half-dead Indian? His gaze roamed slowly across Abby's face, half hidden in shadow. Even asleep, there was a strength, a determination about her that appealed to him. It was there in that strong chin, that upturned nose. She was the most irritating, most abrasive, most—persuasive woman he'd ever met. Against their better judgment, Mordecai, Parker, and even the impassive Brand had caved in. And without even being asked, he had done something he'd promised himself he'd never do again. He'd allowed himself to get involved.

Violet Market had surprised him. It wasn't just the way she'd stoically accepted the presence of an Indian in her wagon. But the way she'd stood up to her brother was completely out of character. There was a lot more to that timid little woman than the rest of the world saw. Beneath the ribbon and lace was steel.

Abby sighed in her sleep and Rourke caught his breath for the space of a heartbeat. Being this close to her, and not being able to touch her, was sheer torture. He studied the way her fingers curled around the edge of the blanket, and thought about those same fingers stroking his skin. A stray wisp of hair had fallen over one eye, and he itched to reach out and brush it aside. Her lashes cast soft shadows across her cheek. In the lantern's glow, he studied her skin, burned and bronzed by the sun. Such lovely skin.

The Indian moaned, and Rourke's hand moved to the gun at his side. He should be glad for the disturbance, he reminded himself sternly. The things he was thinking about Abby Market could only bring trouble.

While Rourke stood guard, Abby changed the dressing on the Indian's shoulder, then rubbed salve over his wrists and ankles. She saw him grit his teeth, and knew that the salve burned the raw flesh. Aunt Vi said she had made it extra strong, because his wounds were so deep. The ropes that bound him must have cut clear to the bone.

When she was finished, she lifted the youth's head and held a cup of broth to his lips. As the liquid entered his mouth, he drew back, then spit it out. It spattered across the front of Abby's shirt, and she was so surprised she dropped the cup, spilling the rest of the hot liquid down her britches.

While Rourke watched, she jumped up, grabbed a cloth, and began furiously mopping up the broth. She glanced down at the Indian and could have sworn that behind his bland look he was laughing at her.

Filling the cup again, she knelt down beside him. "I don't know what you've got against my cooking. It isn't the best in the world, but it's filling. And right now, you need to gain your strength back. So if you know what's good for you, you're going to drink this."

The Indian compressed his lips.

When Abby touched the cup to his lips, he glared at her. She glared back. Behind them, Rourke swallowed back his laugh. If it was a contest of wills, he'd hate to have to pick the winner. Two more stubborn people he'd never seen.

"You have to drink this broth, Two Shadows. It's good for you."

The Indian kept his mouth firmly closed.

"One sip. One tiny sip and I'll go away."

Dark eyes glowered.

Abby set the cup down beside him and gestured, hoping he understood. "I'm going to leave this here. When I come back, I expect to find it empty."

As she turned away, the Indian picked up the tin cup and hurled it through the canvas opening.

Undaunted, Abby filled the cup once more and placed it beside the Indian's blanket. Without waiting to see his reaction, she walked away, leaving him glaring at her back.

An hour later, she returned to find the cup empty. But because she couldn't communicate with Two Shadows, she couldn't be certain whether he drank the broth or dumped it on the ground.

That evening, as soon as they made camp, James Market picked up his jug and headed toward the Garner wagon. He didn't even bother to wait for supper, saying he wouldn't share a meal with a heathen. Abby and Violet felt a wave of relief. At least for a few hours there would be peace.

To stay busy, Rourke mended a tear in the canvas and greased the wagon's wheels. The sound of their creaking for the last ten miles had nearly driven him crazy. When those chores were finished, he sat beside the wagon and took a cigar from his pocket.

Abby tended to the team, then joined her aunt in preparing supper. Venison sizzled in a pan while dumplings thickened in gravy. Rourke held a match to his cigar and wondered why Parker's meals never smelled this good. Content, he leaned back and watched Abby swing a kettle over the fire. The women whispered and laughed, and Rourke saw a side to Abby he'd never seen before. She looked so natural, talking, laughing, working beside her aunt. Natural until she happened to glance his way. He saw her cheeks redden before she gave him a smile. And for some reason he couldn't quite fathom, he felt more lighthearted than he had in years.

Abby prepared a meal for Two Shadows, then, with Rourke beside her, she climbed into the wagon. The Indian's eyes were closed, but Abby knew he was aware of them.

"I've brought you something to eat," she whispered.

The Indian's eyes opened. He showed no recognition.

"Venison," Abby said, kneeling beside him. Cutting the meat into small pieces, she handed him the plate. He stared at it, then back at her.

"Eat," she said. "You need food."

He continued to stare at her. Little wisps of her hair had slipped loose, trailing along her cheeks and neck. He stared in fascination at the fiery strands.

Lifting the first piece of meat to his lips, Abby was stunned when he pushed her hand away, then reached up to touch her hair. For one breathless moment, she sat very still as his fingers explored the silken texture, so different from the women of his tribe.

Beside her, Rourke watched. Though he understood, he felt an unexpected wave of something he'd never before experienced—jealousy.

Pushing the Indian's hand away, Abby firmly brought them all back to the problem at hand. "Watch me," she said, striving for patience. Lifting the meat to her mouth, she chewed, swallowed, then offered a second piece to Two Shadows.

Again he slapped her hand away, this time much harder. Beside her, Rourke's hand tightened on his gun.

Placing the plate beside the Indian, Abby said, "If you're as smart as you look, you'll eat, so you can get strong enough to go home to your people. If you don't eat, you'll just get sicker and never see them again."

Turning, she climbed down from the wagon, with Rourke following.

Violet looked up. "Did he eat?"

"Not a bite." Abby couldn't hide the worry she was feeling. How could they make him understand that he had to eat?

"Don't worry," Violet said. "You two come and eat. And afterward, I'll ask Mr. Brand to speak to Two Shadows. I'm sure he can convince him that our food is safe."

Rourke grinned. This good woman still didn't understand that it wasn't the food that bothered their young Indian. It was the people serving it.

Dinner tasted even better than it smelled. Rourke couldn't remember the last time he'd eaten plump dumplings simmered in gravy. The venison was cooked to perfection. Violet spread wild blackberry jam over biscuits that melted in his mouth. Even the coffee tasted different. Better. While he finished his cigar and sipped a second cup of coffee, Violet went in search of the scout.

"That was a fine meal, Abby."

"Thank you." She tidied up around the wagon, hung the last of the towels and rags to dry, then sat down next to the fire, facing him.

"Did Violet teach you to cook?"

Abby laughed, the low, husky sound Rourke had come to recognize. And love.

"I learned to cook out of necessity. My mother was sickly. She spent a lot of time in bed. So Carrie and I had to learn to do all the chores around the house. With my pa out in the fields with my grandpa, the care of the house and animals fell mostly to me. I kept us in food. With our mother's help, Carrie managed to keep us in clothes." At the mention of her sister's name, Abby fell silent.

"You miss her, don't you?"

Abby nodded, swallowing the lump in her throat.

"It's the first time I can ever remember us being apart."

"She'll be fine, Abby."

"I hope so." She licked her lips. "Oh, I hope so."

Quickly changing the subject, Rourke asked, "What about Violet? Didn't she help you with the chores?"

"She did her best. Aunt Vi sang in the church choir and helped the older ladies of the church. They made bandages for the soldiers off fighting the War Between the States and visited the homes of widows and orphans. She said, with all those brave men out there serving their country, she felt obliged to do her share."

"Sometimes, with all the killing and madness, it was easy to forget that there were still good people going about doing their best." Rourke drew on his cigar and watched the smoke dissipate in the night air.

The killing and madness. This was the first time Rourke had ever volunteered any information about himself and the war. Abby breathed in the scent of tobacco and wondered why it was so easy to sit like this, talking quietly with Rourke. Usually they were so tense with each other. But tonight, the meal, the conversation, seemed as natural as if they'd done it all their lives.

"Why didn't you go home after the war, Rourke?"

"Like a lot of men, I found myself without a home after the war."

"But homes can be rebuilt."

"What about lives, Abby? Can a shattered life be rebuilt?"

She studied him in the firelight and saw the shadow of pain that had probably always been there. But until tonight, she'd never looked. Choosing her words carefully, she said softly, "I don't believe any life can be broken so badly it can't be repaired. If a body tries."

Rourke stared up at the night sky and his voice was gruff. "Only dreamers and fools would believe it was that easy. You didn't strike me as a dreamer, Abby Market."

"And I'm no fool. I didn't say it would be easy. I said it was possible."

"Well, here we are, Mr. Brand." Violet led the way into the circle of light, followed by the scout. "Now maybe you can talk to our young friend."

Abby felt a wave of regret. Just when she and Rourke had begun to open up with each other.

"What would you like to know?" Brand asked.

Violet wondered just how much information they would be able to glean about their strange guest. She decided to take advantage of this opportunity. "We need to know more about him. Who he is. What his family is like."

Brand pursed his lips. These white women did not understand the ways of The People. Crawling into the back of the wagon, the scout spoke rapidly, then listened while the Indian responded.

"He said that he has already told you. He is Cheyenne."

"I want to know more about the Cheyenne."

The two spoke, then Brand turned to Violet. "The One with Two Shadows says that they are the People of the First Man."

Violet's eyes widened. "Adam and Eve?"

Brand studied her a moment. "The People do not give names to the first man."

"No matter. No matter." Her heart was pounding. People of the First Man. What a truly beautiful phrase. Glancing beyond him to Two Shadows, she murmured, "Will he tell me about his family?"

Brand spoke, and the Indian replied. Turning to Violet, the scout said, "The One with Two Shadows said that it is enough that you know that he is Cheyenne. That when he is strong enough, he will return to his people. That is all he will say."

Violet's heart fell. Two Shadows wouldn't even

communicate with one who spoke his language. There was no hope that he would ever attempt to speak to her. Admitting defeat, she said softly, "We want to know why he won't eat. He won't eat or drink anything we give him."

Brand turned and carried on an animated conversation with the Indian. While they spoke Violet climbed down from the back of the wagon. Though the Indian resisted, she was determined to keep trying. Knowledge was the key. If she could learn about this Cheyenne, and he in turn could learn about her, they could become friends.

A few minutes later, Brand emerged from the wagon carrying an empty plate.

"How did you do that?" Violet asked.

Abby and Rourke paused in their conversation to hear his reply.

"He had already emptied the plate before you and I entered the wagon."

"And he ate everything?"

Brand came as close to smiling as he ever had. "He had not eaten it. But he had emptied the plate."

"I don't understand."

"He hid the meat under the blanket."

"Hid it. Why?" Violet's eyes were wide in the firelight.

"His captors often denied him food. He thought you would do the same. So he decided to keep some in reserve in order to keep up his strength."

Violet felt some of the tension evaporate. "Did you explain that we will feed him as often as we feed ourselves?"

"Yes, but I do not think he believes that. The only way you can convince him of your sincerity is to continue to feed him. I think in time he will learn to trust you."

Violet sighed. "At least it isn't our food he dislikes."

"That too," Brand added as he began to walk away.

"He said he has never tasted food cooked in such a manner. But he will happily suffer, as long as he can regain his strength and return to his people."

As he walked away, the scout failed to see the look of consternation on the faces of the two women. Or the grin that lit Rourke's usually dark countenance.

Chapter Twenty

WHILE TWO SHADOWS fought fevers and infections, the other members of the wagon train grew more concerned. At first, they grumbled among themselves and tried to ignore the rantings and ravings of James Market, who seemed to enjoy spreading rumors and misinformation. But as the days passed, and it was whispered that the Indian's wounds were beginning to heal, their fears became panic. What if the boy lying in the Market wagon really was a demented soul whose only intention was to massacre them in their sleep? Convinced that he was a menace to their safety, they sent a delegation to Mordecai to protest.

In order to calm their fears, Mordecai invited the group to the Market wagon, hoping that by facing the object of their fear, they would overcome it.

"Miss Violet. Miss Abby," Mordecai said, removing his hat. "I've asked Reverend Coulter and the others to see for themselves that Two Shadows means them no harm."

"Reverend Coulter?" Violet looked up from her mending and frowned. "I'm surprised that a man of the Lord would object to our desire to tend to one of God's creatures."

The minister looked distinctly uncomfortable as he

yanked the dark hat from his head and stood before them. "I'm sorry, Miss Market. But I have a wife and baby to think about. How do you know that Indian won't slip into our wagons in the night and kill every man, woman, and child on this train?"

"Why should he?" Abby asked indignantly. "Do you think he would kill simply for the sport of it?"

"They're heathens," Jed Garner said, and Abby knew that she was listening to her father's words coming from another man's mouth. "You never know what they'll do just for the fun of it."

"This boy is too weak to even stand yet," Violet said, crossing her arms across her chest. "We still have to help him sit up to eat."

"And what is it he eats?" Lavinia Winters asked. "I've heard they eat human flesh and drink the blood of white men."

"You're being foolish, Lavinia," Violet said, feeling her temper rise. "He eats the same things we do."

If Abby hadn't been so angry, she would have burst out laughing. The truth was, Two Shadows made no secret of the way he felt about their food. He ate what they gave him only because he had no choice.

"And what about our children?" Doralyn Peel asked, thinking about her young son lying this very minute in his blankets, dreaming the innocent dreams of the young. "I've heard they steal white children and make them slaves."

"I've heard that too," Jed Garner said. "It's easy for you two women to ignore the facts. You have no children to worry about. A spinster and a misfit, according to your own kin. But we're parents, and we have a right to fear for our children's safety."

A misfit? Is that how her father described her to others? "If you're so worried about Timmy," Abby snapped, "why don't you and Nancy spend more time with him and less time fighting with each other and drinking my pa's jug dry?"

The moment the words were out, she regretted

them. Glancing at the disoriented stranger that Nancy Garner had become, Abby bit her lip. "I'm sorry. Nancy and Jed, forgive me. I had no right to say such things."

"That's right. You didn't," Nancy hissed. "From now on, you stay away from Timmy. In fact, I think you two should stay away from every decent person on this wagon train."

As heads nodded and voices murmured, Mordecai held up his hands. "Please everyone. This isn't why I brought you here. I had hoped you would see that the lad is too weak to be a threat to anyone on this train."

"Those two are the threat," Lavinia Winters said loudly, jabbing a finger at Abby and Violet. "They had no right to jeopardize the safety of everyone on this wagon train by bringing that Indian here."

The others nodded in agreement.

Rourke leaned against the wagon wheel and lit a cigar. He'd been expecting this. He only wondered why they'd waited so long. It was natural for people to fear the unknown. And in this wilderness, it was necessary for survival. What these two good women didn't understand was the ease with which a mob could turn on anyone who threatened their safety. Not only would these people turn a wounded Indian out, but they would be willing to sacrifice Abby and Violet as well. Hearing the chorus of voices grow, Rourke expelled a stream of smoke and studied the faces in the crowd. How quickly these people were willing to overlook the kindness of these two women. How many times had Abby shared her bounty with the others? When their children were sick, or one of the women took to their beds, it was always Violet and Abby who were the first to offer help. Yet these same people who accepted their kindnesses were the first to turn against them.

He'd have to be more alert, he reminded himself. Especially late at night when fears became magnified. It wouldn't surprise him if someone on the train decided to take matters into his own hands and eliminate the problem of the Indian. Rourke sighed. He wouldn't mind missing a little sleep. Lately his dreams had become more intense. There was no escape for him in sleep.

Crushing out the cigar, he studied Abby, her face flushed, her hands on her hips. He wasn't doing this for her, he told himself. It was just that she and her aunt were women in need of help. And even though he'd argued against taking in the Indian, now that Two Shadows was here, he had a right to protection.

Rourke glanced again at Abby and felt the sexual pull. Who in hell was he kidding? He was beginning to feel things he'd thought he'd never feel again.

While the crowd milled about, staring at the Indian, spewing anger and hate, Two Shadows lay perfectly still, watching and listening.

"All right now," Mordecai said. "You've all had a chance to voice your concerns. I ask that all of you return to your own wagons and think about the lad who is causing you such concern. You can see for yourselves that his presence is no threat to any of you."

The wagon master knew his words were falling on deaf ears. Nothing had changed. He glanced at the silent Rourke and saw that he knew it too. Then he herded the people away from the Market wagon and into the shadowy darkness.

Abby touched her aunt's shoulder. "I'm sorry, Aunt Vi. I had no right to involve you in this. Everyone tried to warn me that taking Two Shadows to my wagon was a mistake. But I wouldn't listen to them."

Violet's voice was low with feeling. "Are you sorry you stopped to help the boy?"

"Of course not," Abby said quickly. "I'm only sorry I involved you in this. Now your friends have turned against you."

"Child, if they choose to turn their backs on me, they weren't friends to begin with. Remember that.

227

You have to live your life according to your own beliefs, not according to what others may think about you." Violet brushed the hair from her niece's cheek, and allowed her fingers to rest there a minute. Peering deeply into her eyes, she murmured, "You did the right thing, Abby. I'm proud of you."

Abby leaned over and kissed her aunt's cheek. "And I'm proud of you, Aunt Vi. You're the finest lady I know."

As she walked away, Violet stood very still, watching the tiny sliver of moon in the blackened sky. What if all those brave words she'd spoken were false? Could it be possible that they had made a mistake taking the Indian in? Were they inviting an attack on the train and all its occupants? Violet shivered and blamed it on the cool breeze from the mountains. She shook her head, as if to dispel any lingering doubts. They were doing the right thing. He was one of God's creatures. If she were capable of overcoming one of her cherished prejudices, she would be a better person for it. She and Abby would stand by their convictions, despite what the others said or did. And if she harbored a few fears, she would just have to live with them.

As she drew a shawl about her shoulders and stirred the fire, two dark eyes watched from the wagon. Ignoring the pain that shot through his shoulder at the movement, Two Shadows shifted in his bed and reached for the knife that had been carelessly left behind from the supper tray. Fumbling beneath the blanket, he slid it between two boards in the floor of the wagon. Checking to be certain it wouldn't fall through the cracks, he replaced the blanket. Then, closing his eyes, he listened to the familiar sounds of the night.

It was nearly dusk when the wagon train stopped to make camp. They were following the trail of the

Humboldt River, which snaked from northeastern Nevada some four hundred miles across the arid flatlands. Lying between mountain ranges of the Great Basin, it was a lifeline that provided water and grass to the travelers heading toward California. Without it, the western crossing would have been impossible.

Rourke saw Brand's riderless mount galloping hard toward the circle of wagons. Instinctively, Rourke checked his gun, then made his way to the cook wagon.

The horse was foaming, his coat thick with dust.

"What do you make of it?" Parker asked, grasping the reins.

"Trouble," Mordecai muttered. "Brand is too smart to ever lose his mount."

"Could be Indians," Rourke said, studying the horse.

"They would have caught his horse to keep from warning us."

"If they could catch it."

Mordecai looked at Rourke, then nodded. "We'll have to ride out and find him."

"I'll go," Rourke said firmly. "That's why you hired me."

The wagon master leaned heavily on his stick and watched as the gunman began saddling his horse. When he swung into the saddle, Rourke called, "Send someone to the Market wagon to watch the Indian." Wheeling his mount, he disappeared into the gathering shadows.

Brand's mount had left a clear trail. From the looks of him, Rourke knew that he had run for miles. What surprised Rourke was that the horse had come from the direction the train had traveled the previous day. Why would the scout follow a trail they had already taken when his job was to scout ahead? He scanned the flat terrain and felt the adrenaline begin to pump. Brand must have seen something suspicious. Something that caused him to circle back on the trail.

It was past midnight when Brand's trail ended just below a small rise. Twice Rourke circled, doubled back, then circled again. Each time he came up with nothing. There was no sign of a struggle. And no sign of the scout. As he had trained himself to do, he began a slow, methodical search for nearly a mile in each direction, then enlarged the area until he had covered every foot of ground for miles.

A quarter moon offered little to light the darkness, and his eyes grew heavy from the effort. Still he continued circling, alert for any sign of trouble.

He had tracked men before. He had taught himself to be patient, watchful. Now it was almost second nature.

He almost passed by. There wasn't anything there really. Just a shadow, slightly darker than the surrounding shadows. Still, on a hunch, Rourke reined in his horse and slid from the saddle.

Brand was lying on his side, one arm flung above his head. His clothes and the ground around him were soaked with his blood. His eyes were wide and sightless, his mouth open as if to scream. His throat had been slit.

Taking a blanket from behind his saddle, Rourke knelt to wrap the body before taking it back to the train. As he rolled the scout's body forward, he spotted the blood-soaked wound in his back. When he examined the flesh, he knew with chilling clarity. Brand hadn't been killed by a lone gunfighter or gang of cutthroats. This was the work of Indians. And they had removed the arrow and then slit his throat to make certain he was dead. Rourke felt his blood run cold. To make certain Brand didn't return and warn the wagon train.

Leaving the body, Rourke pulled himself into the

saddle and urged his horse into a run. Brand had doubled back on the trail because he had spotted the Indians following the train. Ute or Paiute? This was their territory. His eyes narrowed. Kiowa, coming to claim the escaped Cheyenne? Leaning low over the horse's neck, he urged him even faster. Whatever tribe they were, the people on the train were in grave danger. And though he feared for all the people, only one name sprang to his lips. Abby. Dear God, Abby.

Dawn had not yet lightened the horizon. The night sounds had stilled. The morning sounds had not yet begun.

In the wagon, Abby and Violet slept. Beneath the wagon, James Market lay where he had fallen after drinking an entire jug of whiskey. Thompson sat with his back to a tree, a rifle across his lap. He had agreed to keep an eye on the Market wagon until Rourke returned. Though he fought to stay alert, his head bobbed.

Inside the wagon, Two Shadows heard the whistle of a prairie bird and lifted his head. So far from home, that bird, he thought with a smile. Moving his hand slowly to the canvas flap, he peered into the eerie gray light of the predawn. Within a few minutes he saw a figure move from the shadows toward the man at the base of the tree.

Thompson was yanked to his feet. The rifle in his hands went off with a terrible explosion of sound, shattering the stillness before clattering to the ground. The Indian brought his arm around Thompson's throat, cutting off his air.

Instantly the quiet camp erupted into bedlam. Men rolled from their beds, groping for weapons. Women herded the children into small clusters, struggling to still their crying.

Mordecai and Parker leaped from the cook wagon and ran toward the sound of gunfire.

Abby grabbed her rifle and jumped from the wagon only to find herself staring at Thompson, being held in a death grip by an Indian.

A second Indian on horseback motioned for her and the others to throw down their rifles. Seeing Thompson struggling for breath, they did as they were ordered. Behind them, Violet stepped from the wagon. She had wrapped herself in her blanket for modesty.

Beneath the wagon, James Market stirred from his drunken stupor. Befuddled, he tried to stand, fell to one knee, then pulled himself up. Seeing the Indians, he sank back down to his knees, staring in fascination.

As each man came running, he was ordered to throw down his weapon. No one wanted to be the cause of Thompson's death. Soon all the men of the train stood around the Market wagon, feeling helpless.

"We come for the One with Two Shadows," the Indian on horseback said.

"So you can enslave and torture him again?" Abby called out.

The Indian seemed surprised by the woman's voice from the one dressed like a man. "Who would say these things of us?"

"He did. The One with Two Shadows. He said the Kiowa captured him and made him a slave."

"We are not Kiowa," the horseman said. "We are Cheyenne. Where are you holding the son of the chief?"

"The chief?" Stunned, Abby studied the Indian. Hadn't Brand said Two Shadows was important to his people? Were they speaking the truth? Or were they really Kiowa, planning to take him back against his will?

The Indian who was holding Thompson tightened his grip on his throat, causing the man to grunt in pain.

"You will give us the One with Two Shadows," the Indian said. "Or this man will die."

Rourke had never ridden so hard or so fast in his life. Every mile seemed to take forever. While he rode, he studied the shadows, searching for any trace of the Indians who had killed Brand. How far ahead were they? Had they already come upon the wagon train?

A single gunshot shattered the stillness, plunging an icy shaft of fear through his heart. As he crested a hill, he saw the darkened wagons below. Slowing his mount, he peered through the gray light of dawn. Everything appeared normal. There were no cries. He smelled no smoke.

But there had been a gunshot.

Leaving his horse, he made his way down the hill, then crawled toward the wagons. At the scene before him, he froze.

An Indian on horseback was motioning to Abby while the others stood by helplessly. Crawling closer, Rourke could make out her words as she dared to argue with the Indian.

"You. Woman with hair of fire." The Indian on horseback pointed a finger at Abby. "You will hold your tongue or I will have it cut out."

Rourke charged from his hiding place, taking aim at the horseman.

"Rourke." Flinging herself toward him, Abby was caught roughly from behind. She felt the sharp, cold blade of a knife held to her throat.

"You will drop your weapon, or we will kill the woman."

The words, spoken by the Indian on horseback, caused Rourke to freeze. If he could, he would die for Abby. But he couldn't live with himself if he were the cause of her death. Throwing aside his gun, Rourke was struck from behind. The blow left him reeling. Seeing the blurred image of a knife at Abby's throat, he struggled to fight his attacker. Several more Indians, holding the rifles from the wagon train, surrounded him.

The others watched in silence as Rourke was dragged closer, until he was facing Abby and the Indian who held her. Glancing up, they realized they were completely surrounded by armed Indians.

"You will all pay for harming one of The People," the Indian said.

"Kill me," Rourke said. "But let the women and children live."

"All will die." The one in charge began to bark commands.

A voice that Abby didn't recognize shattered the silence. Everyone looked in the direction of the Market wagon.

Speaking rapidly, Two Shadows said something that caused the other Indians to lower their weapons. The Indian holding Thompson suddenly released his grip on his throat. Coughing and sputtering, Thompson fell to the ground, gasping for breath.

"The One with Two Shadows says you are telling the truth. He asks that we spare your lives." The Indian lowered his rifle and stared at Abby. "Because he speaks for his father, we obey."

Two braves came forward to help Two Shadows from the wagon. Though he leaned heavily on them, he stood erect, his head high, his eyes stern. Before he turned away, he fixed Abby and Violet with a look. "You are very brave. You stand up for what you believe even against your own people. You would make good Cheyenne squaws."

"You speak our language!" Violet's eyes were wide with surprise.

"Christian missionaries lived with our people. They taught us your language and customs."

"But why didn't you tell us? Why didn't you ever speak to us?"

"It was not right for a Cheyenne brave to speak to a

lowly white." For the space of a second, Abby thought she detected laughter behind his grave eyes. "It is also a way to learn what a man really thinks." His gaze swept the crowd. His voice grew louder. "My half-brother Black Kettle has counseled The People to never trust a white man. When I return, I will stand with him." Pointing a finger at Abby, he said softly, "But you and this woman will always have safe passage in the land of the Cheyenne. You gave me back my life. I am in your debt, fire woman."

The entire wagon train watched in shocked silence while the Indians gathered up their horses and weapons. When one of them picked up a rifle, Two Shadows spoke sharply. Instantly the rifle was dropped to the ground.

"We do not take what is not ours. In your wagon, beneath the blanket, is a knife. I feared I would need it to protect myself from your people."

"A knife?" Abby blanched. "Why didn't you use it on us?"

The young brave studied her for long minutes. "You saved my life. How could I take yours?"

In a long, majestic procession, the Indians left with the only thing they had come for—the One with Two Shadows, son of their chief.

Chapter Twenty-one

"LORD, RECEIVE THE body of Thy servant." Reverend Coulter stood beside the hastily dug hole in the ground.

They buried Brand beside the banks of the Humboldt River. As the blanket-wrapped body was lowered into the grave, Abby felt hot tears scald her eyelids. She blinked them back and tried to concentrate on the words of Reverend Coulter. But all she could hear was Brand's voice telling her she shouldn't take the Indian to her wagon.

"You will make many enemies."

The words rang in her mind as she studied the faces of the people around her. Angry, accusing faces. She could withstand the wrath of the people on the train. What she dreaded was the knowledge that her involvement with Two Shadows had cost Brand his life. She would have to live with that fact forever.

She glanced at Rourke's grim features. After the Indians had finished with the wagon train, he had stayed only long enough to assure himself that she and the others were safe. Then he had immediately returned to retrieve Brand's body. The long night of tracking had taken its toll. A rough stubble of beard darkened his chin. His eyes were red-rimmed from lack of sleep.

As Parker and Thompson shoveled dirt on the grave, each member of the train scattered a handful, then moved silently away. When it was Abby's turn, she paused and fell to one knee. A few steps away, Rourke watched her in grim silence.

Dropping a wildflower into the grave, she whispered, "I'm sorry, Brand. From the bottom of my heart, I'm sorry. You were right." A tear squeezed from her lid and coursed down her cheek. Ignoring it, she tossed a handful of sand on the body, then took several steps back.

As the others bent to scoop up dirt to toss on the grave, Rourke spun on his heel and headed toward the cook wagon.

He was angry, and he didn't know why. He was angry at Abby, for nearly getting herself killed over an Indian. And yet he knew she had been right to take Two Shadows in and minister to his needs.

He was angry at Brand for not coming to get him before tracking those Indians. And yet Brand knew that Rourke was needed to keep an eye on the Market wagon.

He was angry at the people on the train, for turning their backs on Abby and Violet. And yet he understood their fears.

Maybe the anger was directed at himself, he realized. He had failed Abby. He had left her alone, to face whatever danger might be out there, while he tracked a dead scout. He had failed Abby, just as he had once failed Katherine. Duty. That damned sense of duty that drove him to put the needs of some ahead of the needs of others.

They'd needed him in that ugly War Between the States. But Katherine had needed him more. And he hadn't been there for her. He'd left her alone to face unspeakable horrors. He'd failed her.

Mordecai had hired him to keep the members of this train safe. And while he was looking out for their needs, Abby had needed him more. And he hadn't been there for her. He had failed her. And she was left to bear the burden of guilt.

He should try to comfort her. But what good were empty words? He had no right getting involved in other people's lives. He would only end up letting them down.

Lathering his face, he began to make short, quick strokes across his chin with the straight razor. All the while, thoughts of his failures simmered. With a muttered oath he watched blood ooze up through the soapy foam. Undeterred, he continued shaving, and managed to cut himself three more times. Swearing under his breath, he washed off the blood, dried his face, and pulled on a fresh shirt.

Pulling himself into the saddle, he rode out ahead of the train. He didn't feel like being around people. What he wanted was to be left alone.

By the time the wagon train broke camp, the sun was high overhead. Across the flat, arid land, Mordecai set a brisk pace, hoping to make up for the hours lost. He intended as well to keep the travelers too busy to think about their troubles. Already he'd heard the grumblings of several families, suggesting that the Market women were to blame for Brand's death. The wagon master knew from experience that talk like that could be dangerous. It would become too simple for the travelers to blame all their troubles on someone else.

Mordecai had watched the gradual changes in the people on his train. Jed and Nancy Garner were the perfect examples of what this harsh land did to people. Those two had reached the breaking point. Nancy, once a model wife, was mired in self-pity. She had no energy left for her husband and child. She no longer bothered to wash, or to change her ragged clothes. Her hair was filthy and uncombed. Jed had begun drinking nightly with James Market, completely ignoring the needs of his wife and young son.

On the other hand, Reverend Coulter and his wife were overjoyed with their new little Jenny. For the first time, they felt like a family. But Evelyn had become so overprotective of their baby, fearful of the elements, of Indians, of the unknown, she allowed no one on the train to get close to her. And the reverend, always so outgoing, had begun to pull back from his position of leadership, eager to spend as much time as possible with his wife and baby. The spiritual needs of the travelers were being ignored. And without spiritual leadership, they were bound to falter.

The other families, too, seemed to have drawn a protective ring around their members. Since Abby had brought the Indian into their midst, Doralyn Peel had never once allowed Jonathon out of her sight. The children, cut off from their friends, had become sullen and fearful. Now, with the menace gone, the children were as frisky and unmanageable as new colts.

"Rider approaching."

Parker's call interrupted Mordecai's musings.

As the rider grew closer, they recognized Rourke's dust-covered mount.

"A couple of miles from here the river turns again. Looks like we'll have to cross."

Parker groaned. The meandering river had to be followed. Even though its water had become increasingly salty tasting, it provided the travelers with their only source for drinking. But everyone on the train had begun to hate the repeated crossings, as the sluggish Humboldt crisscrossed the land.

"We'll cross, then make camp," Mordecai called. "I think they've had enough for one day."

Rourke nodded. Glancing along the row of slowly moving wagons, he spotted Abby walking beside her aunt. At that moment she looked up. Their gazes met and held. He lifted his hat, wiped the sweat from his brow with his sleeve, then replaced the hat. She continued to walk, her spine stiff, her head high. Her gaze stayed locked with his.

Wheeling his mount, he took off in a cloud of dust, feeling her gaze boring into his back.

Abby watched Rourke until he and his horse were only a cloud of dust on the horizon.

When he had returned in the early morning with Brand's body, he had made straight for the cook wagon. There had been no chance for them to speak. Immediately after the burial, he had ridden off, probably to take on Brand's duties as scout. But something in his eyes worried her. There was a simmering anger there. An anger that she had noticed when he'd first joined the wagon train. In the last few weeks, she thought some of that anger had disappeared. Or had she only imagined it because she wanted to believe it?

Carrie and Aunt Vi were the dreamers, she told herself firmly. There was no room in her life for anything except harsh reality. He was Rourke. A loner. A gunman hired to protect this train. And whatever softness or kindness she had thought she'd seen in him was the result of a vivid imagination. He did his job well. Too well. She had a sudden image of Rourke in the gray light of dawn, eyes wide, teeth bared, ready to take on an entire company of Indians in order to protect the people on the train. There had been a fierceness, a raging determination in him to fight to the end. She had known a moment of panic, thinking that she was about to witness his death.

"You're too quiet, Abby," Violet said softly.

"I was thinking about . . . Rourke."

"He is a true friend, child. He stuck by us through a most difficult time."

"He was only doing his job, Aunt Vi."

Violet turned her head to study her niece. The deliberate flatness of Abby's tone left her no doubt of her confused feelings. "Mr. Rourke is a very good man. Of that I have no doubt."

240

"He's a gunman, Aunt Vi. He gets paid to protect us."

"No one paid him to stay awake at night so we could sleep safely. No one paid him to mend our wagon wheel, or do the other chores he took on for the past few weeks."

Abby fell silent. It was true that no one paid him to be kind to them. Still, he was avoiding her. She could sense it. And the only reason she could think of was that he already regretted his kindness to her and her aunt.

Crossing the Humboldt should have been an ordinary event. The wagon train had already crossed it four times since first encountering it in Nevada Territory. But the people were weary, their senses dulled by the long journey and the frightening incident with the Cheyennes.

The cook wagon and the two wagons following it crossed without incident. But from then on everything seemed to go wrong.

The Market wagon broke an axle during the crossing. The team was unhitched and led to the far shore. Everything in the wagon had to be unloaded and floated across to shore. When the axle was repaired, the team was led back and hitched up. By the time the wagon was hauled ashore and once again loaded, Abby and Violet were forced to make a hurried meal to satisfy a furious James. While he ate in sullen silence, Abby thought about the meals she and Violet had prepared these past days for Rourke.

It had been so pleasant having a man compliment her on her cooking. She'd known little praise in her life. What's more, Abby thought as the last of the daylight faded into dusk, it had been a wonderful thing to have someone to talk to. Though Rourke revealed little about himself, she had the feeling that he enjoyed those moments as much as she.

While she cleaned up after supper and watched

James and Violet get ready for an early bedtime, she thought about those nights that Rourke had kept watch while she and her aunt slept. It had been the strangest sensation to wake up and see Rourke so near. Several times she'd had the impression that he was studying her while she slept.

A shout from the river ended her pleasant thoughts and caused her to dismiss any idea of getting a night's sleep.

The last of the train was still in the process of crossing the river. From the looks of things, it would take the better part of the night.

The Coulter wagon lost a wheel right in the middle of the river. While water swirled, Evelyn and the baby were carried to the far shore on horseback. Every able-bodied man stood shoulder deep in the water to help repair the wagon wheel. While Rourke strained to lift the wagon, he noticed that Abby worked alongside them, holding the team, murmuring words of encouragement to keep them calm.

Dusk was giving way to darkness, and still all the wagons hadn't managed to cross.

Doralyn Peel and her son Jonathon watched helplessly as their team balked, refusing to enter the river until they were whipped and scolded. Midway across, one of the mules bolted, tearing the frayed harness, tugging Jason Peel from the wagon's seat into the water. The frightened team began to run, sending most of the contents of the wagon sliding into the river. Abby joined the others wading into the swirling river to retrieve them. Further upstream she saw Rourke, his muscles straining as he lifted a heavy chest from the water.

Darkness had settled in when the last of the wagons, the Winters wagon, began its crossing. Amid shouts and curses, the team floundered. The wagon tipped, spilling all its contents into the river.

Men on horseback righted the wagon, then waded

downstream, retrieving food, clothing, and household goods that stayed afloat. Many of the belongings sank beneath the dark, swirling water.

Lavinia Winters stood on shore, terrified to set foot in the river. While her husband coaxed and the others called words of encouragement, she stood rooted to the spot.

"Come on, Lavinia," Abby said gently, wading across the river until she was directly beside the woman. "I'll walk with you. The water isn't deep. Look."

Stepping into the river, Abby held out her hand. "We won't sink. Trust me."

"Trust you?" The woman's voice rose to near hysteria. From the far shore, women stopped to listen. Men on horseback or on wagons paused at the sound of her loud wailing. "Why should I trust you? You nearly cost everyone on the train their lives. If it hadn't been for you, our scout would still be alive, and we'd be miles from here—closer to our destination. This is all your fault."

Abby tried to keep the hurt from her voice, but a note of pain crept through. "I know what you say is true, Lavinia. And I'm truly sorry. But you have to cross the river."

"Why do I have to cross? Who says I can't stay here?" Folding her arms across her chest, she planted her feet firmly. "I don't have to do anything you say."

"It isn't for me. It's for your husband. Your children. Lavinia, you have to keep going. It's the only way to get to California."

As Abby reached for her hand, she drew back. "Get away from me. Don't you touch me. I don't want you to come near me ever again. Do you hear?"

Abby's face was ashen as she felt the stares of the others. Despite the darkness, Abby felt naked and disgraced. People on both sides of the river could hear the shrieks of the frightened woman.

Dropping her hand to her side, she turned away. Just then, Rourke rode up and lifted up the astonished Abby, swinging her in front of him in the saddle.

"Hang on," he muttered.

"But what about Lavinia?"

"Mrs. Winters said she would rather stay here. The choice is hers. When she changes her mind, I'm sure her husband will hold her hand."

Lavinia's mouth dropped open. With a look of fury, she watched as the horse splashed into the water. Rourke and Abby easily spanned the river on his mount.

Instead of stopping when they reached the far shore, Rourke nudged the horse into a run. The evening breeze whipped Abby's hair, flaying it across Rourke's cheeks. He inhaled the clean, rainwater scent of it. The breeze created by the running horse flattened Abby's damp shirt against her breasts. Feeling her shiver, he brought his arms firmly around her, tightening his grip.

At the crest of a ridge, Rourke reined in his horse and slid from the saddle. Roughly pulling her to her feet, he steadied her for a moment, then dropped his hands to his sides.

"What was that all about?" With her hands on her hips, Abby faced him. Her eyes were narrowed in anger.

"You've done enough. How much more are you going to try to prove to those people?"

"I don't know what you mean."

"Don't you?" He glanced down at the lights of the wagon train. People would be eating a hasty supper and settling in for the night. Already several lanterns had been extinguished. "You're as tired as the rest of them. Still you push yourself to the limits. Why, Abby?"

She glared at him. "Because we all have to pull our share if we're going to make it to California."

"But you always seem to do more than your share. I didn't see your father out there in water up to his shoulders. I didn't see the other women wading through the river picking up wet clothes."

"Many of them have children to care for. They don't have the strength I have."

"Or the guilt."

She reacted as if he'd slapped her. Taking a step backward, her eyes blazed. "Guilt?"

"I heard how you responded to Lavinia's attack. We all did. You practically admitted that you were the cause of Brand's death and the Indian attack."

"I was." Her voice lowered, and once again Rourke heard the note of pain. "If I hadn't brought Two Shadows to my wagon, Brand would be alive today. And the Cheyenne would have found the chief's son along the trail instead of in our wagon train."

"And maybe the Cheyenne would have found the son of their chief dead and attacked our train in retaliation. And of course, if Brand hadn't agreed to act as scout for the train, he'd probably be alive today," Rourke growled. "But he knew the risks. We all did. And if anyone is to blame for Brand's death, it's me."

"You!"

"I was hired to see to the safety of everyone on this train. Everyone." She saw the muscle working in his jaw. "But I was so busy enjoying your company, I forgot my duties."

For one brief moment, Abby didn't seem to comprehend what he'd just said. Then she felt her heart soar, and was afraid to speak. Rourke hadn't resented the time he'd spent with her. He'd enjoyed it.

Touching a hand to his arm, she whispered, "It wasn't your fault. And if it wasn't mine, then maybe it wasn't anyone's. Maybe it was just God's will."

He pulled his arm away, and she saw the flash of temper.

"Why are you so angry at me, Rourke?"

"Angry?" He shrugged, avoiding her eyes. "I'm not angry."

"Then why do you look as if you'd like to slap me?"

His gaze lowered until he was staring directly into her eyes. His voice became almost a whisper. "Because if I don't slap you, Abby Market, I'm afraid I might kiss you."

Her throat went dry. Before she could say a word, he pulled her roughly against him. He swore and covered her mouth with his.

She thought about struggling. Thought about it, but didn't. The truth was, she'd wanted the kiss. Wanted it every bit as much as Rourke. A twinge of excitement raced through her as his mouth moved over hers. His thighs were pressed firmly against hers. She felt the power of the arms holding her. He could break her without effort. And yet she could sense that he was holding something back, as if aware of that very strength.

He took the kiss deeper. Instantly he forgot to be gentle. His kisses became more demanding. Abby found herself caught up in something more than she'd expected. This was no ordinary kiss. They were rushing headlong into something neither of them could control.

"God, Abby," he breathed against her mouth. His fingers moved up her back, and she felt splinters of ice along her spine. "I've held a gun in my hands for so long now, I'd forgotten that hands were made to hold a woman."

He drew her even closer, until she could feel the wild rhythm of his heartbeat inside her chest. He nibbled her mouth. Expertly he parted her lips. His tongue explored her mouth then withdrew, inviting her to do the same. Boldly she did, reveling in the dark mysterious taste of him.

His kisses were by turn fierce, then gentle. His mouth was bruising, then soft. Without giving her time to think, he took her on a wild climb, to a high mountain peak, then had her plunging headlong down a canyon, leaving her numbed and breathless. She experienced a wild rush of sensations. All she could do was cling to him and wait until the ground stopped tilting.

"Do you know what torture it was all those nights, watching you while you slept?" He nibbled the corner of her mouth, then, before she could speak, nipped at her earlobe. "I stayed awake by counting the number of ways I could make love with you."

For a moment she went rigid in his arms. Staring deeply into her eyes, he began unbuttoning her damp shirt.

"But you never . . . I had no . . ."

Chuckling at her confusion, he kissed away her words, then ran openmouthed kisses along her jaw, then down the column of her throat.

Abby moved in his arms, loving the feel of his lips on her skin. Arching her neck, she allowed him easier access. With his tongue, he followed the line of her collarbone, then brought his lips to the soft swell of her breast. When he began nibbling, then suckling, she felt her knees buckle. Never had she felt such a surge of passion. No other man would ever be able to touch her like this.

Plunging his hands into her hair, Rourke plundered her mouth with savage kisses. Caught up in a whirlwind, she clutched at his waist and returned his kisses, until she could no longer think, only feel.

"Rourke."

Through a haze of throbbing needs, he lifted his head. "Tell me you want this as much as I do, Abby."

Her head was spinning, her pulse hammering. A part of her was begging for him to go on holding her, kissing her, stroking her. "I'm afraid."

"Of me?" His voice was raw with feeling.

How could she explain? How could she make him understand how terrified she was of losing control? Of being taken over by needs that left her stunned and reeling? She shook her head and took a step backward. "Of me." Her voice was barely a whisper. "It's all happening too fast. I don't know what to do, where to go."

For long seconds, Rourke studied her. How could he have forgotten how sheltered her life had been? She was a woman, and soon enough she would know a woman's needs. But for a little while yet, she was clinging to yesterday, and the girl she had been.

He felt her tremble, and drew her into his arms, holding her tenderly against his chest. Suppressing his needs, he stroked her hair until her trembling stopped.

"Come on, Abby." Turning, he reached for the dangling reins and helped her into the saddle. Handing her the reins, he continued to hold her hand a moment, feeling the delicate bones of her fingers. Lifting them to his lips, he muttered, "Now go to bed."

"Aren't you coming back to camp?"

He shook his head. "I'll walk back. I need to be alone."

Slapping the horse, he watched until the horse and rider blended into the shadows of the wagon train. Then, taking a cigar from his pocket, he held a match to the tip and blew out a stream of smoke.

The sound of a guitar could be heard from one of the wagons. A hint of a smile touched the corner of his mouth. She might not know it yet, but Abby Market had just had another lesson in the dance.

Chapter Twenty-two

THE WAGON TRAIN followed the Humboldt River to its sink. From there, the travelers would be forced to carry enough water to see them to the Sierras. For between the Humboldt and the Sierra Nevada range lay a waterless wasteland known as the Forty-Mile Desert. The members of Mordecai Stump's wagon train were ill-prepared for what was to come.

The heat of the desert was suffocating. What little breeze there was had no cooling effect. The hot wind blew little dust eddies, burning eyes and throats, causing sunburned skin to shrivel and chafe.

The women of the camp were still smarting from the incident with the Cheyenne. Though they visited among themselves in the evening, after supper and chores were finished, they looked the other way whenever Abby or Violet walked by. If either felt the snub, they chose not to mention it. Violet went about her sewing while Abby continued to keep her family in game. Both women held their heads high and pretended that they didn't notice the rift that had grown between them and the others.

It was an uneventful evening. The train had managed almost fifteen miles in the relentless heat. James was busy complaining about the rabbit stew while

Abby and Vi picked at their supper, too hot to even care about eating. Doralyn Peel, who had not spoken to Violet since their confrontation over Two Shadows, came rushing into the circle of firelight, her breath coming in little gasps.

"Violet, would you come look at Jason?"

Vi looked up sharply. "Your husband? What's wrong?"

"He's been sick all day. Couldn't keep a thing on his stomach. He seems to be getting worse."

Violet nodded. "Anything else?"

"At first he was cold. Shaking like a leaf on a tree. Now he's burning up, but I don't know if it's a fever or this heat."

"Let me look through my medicines, Doralyn. I'll be at your wagon in a few minutes."

James sopped up his gravy with a biscuit and glowered at the woman's retreating back. "Let her take care of him herself. I wouldn't give her the time of day."

Violet's tone remained cheerful, despite her brother's frown. "She's asked for my help, James. I can't refuse."

"I'll go with you, Aunt Vi." Abby covered the pot of stew and stood up, dusting off her britches.

As the two women moved through the wagons, they were surprised to hear a woman's cry.

"Now what do you suppose . . . ?"

They halted in front of the Peel wagon. Doralyn Peel was standing with Mordecai and Rourke. Her face was contorted with pain.

"What is it, Doralyn? What's happened?" Violet hurried to her side.

"It's Jason. Mr. Stump says he has cholera."

Violet's eyes widened as she turned toward the wagon master. "How can you be certain?"

"I've seen cholera before, Miss Violet. There's no denying the look. Jason is already becoming dehydrated. He canna' keep as much as a drop of water down. His skin is like clay. I plucked it. It wouldna' even snap back."

Violet put a hand to her throat. Cholera. It was the most dreaded word she knew. More than the elements, more than Indians, the travelers heading west feared cholera.

Placing her hand on Doralyn's shoulder, Violet whispered, "Jason is a fine, strong man. He'll come through this, Doralyn. We'll nurse him. We'll stay with him through his ordeal. You'll see. He'll be just fine."

"I'm sorry, Miss Violet," Mordecai said. "No one except his wife will be able to tend him. Cholera is highly contagious."

"What about my son?" the woman asked, beginning to cry again.

"He'd be better off in one of the other wagons, but I'm afraid he might carry the illness with him. He'll have to stay with you, ma'am."

A low moan came from inside the wagon. Touching her apron to her eyes, Doralyn Peel slowly climbed inside. As she turned to close the flap, her eyes met Violet's. Violet tried to give her a smile, and found that her lips trembled instead. Turning away, she leaned heavily on Abby's arm as they made their way back to their wagon.

"Cholera!" James Market shoved the cork into his jug and set it aside. "Are you sure?"

"Mr. Stump was certain. He said he'd seen it before. He had no doubt that what Jason Peel has is cholera."

"By God!" Lumbering to his feet, James walked away without another word.

"I'm worried about your father."

Abby glanced at her aunt. "Why? He left his jug here."

"That's why I'm so worried." Violet's tone was thoughtful. "What would be more important tonight than his liquor?"

Abby fell silent. Jason Peel's cholera. But what did that have to do with her father?

The answer wasn't long in coming. As the two women worked by the light of the fire, they heard the sound of voices raised in anger.

Dropping her mending, Violet glanced at Abby. "I think I hear James's voice. We'd better see what's happening."

By the time they reached the cook wagon, most of the people from the train were gathered around, listening to James Market.

". . . careful, we'll all be infected. I say, if Jason Peel really has cholera, he and his family should be forced to leave this wagon train immediately. Otherwise, the next one stricken might be me. Or you," he said dramatically, pointing toward Jed Garner.

"I have a wife and baby to think of," Jed shouted. "I don't want to see them die."

"No one wants to see anyone die," Mordecai said, trying to be heard above the crowd.

"People die every day of cholera. The only way to prevent the spread of this disease is to send the Peels away."

"What chance would they have alone in this desert?" Violet called.

"You stay out of this, woman. I'm only trying to look out for your safety."

"Is that what you call it, Market?" Reverend Coulter asked. "I call it running scared."

"And what is that supposed to mean?"

"It means that you're afraid to be around a sick man, so you want to send him away and deny he even exists."

"Oh, he exists, Reverend," James said quickly. "There's no denying he exists. And so does the cholera."

"We can't just send them away," Reverend Coulter retorted.

"I hope that little baby of yours—what's her name? Jenny?—isn't the next one to come down with cholera."

Reverend Coulter's face turned the color of ash. The protest he was about to utter died on his lips.

Pressing his advantage, James Market pointed a finger at Lavinia Winters. "How many children are in your wagon, Mrs. Winters? Three? What chance will they have if this disease spreads?"

Lavinia's lips compressed into a tight line.

"If you want to know what I think, the people on this wagon train have the right to protect themselves. I vote we order the Peel family to leave this train tonight."

"Wait a minute." At the sound of Abby's voice, the crowd turned to study her.

"I understand your fear of cholera. But we have a duty to be humane," Abby said in a pleading voice. "The Peels paid their money, the same as everyone else. They have a right to the protection this train offers. Instead of sending them away, why can't we just ask that they fall behind the others?" Glancing at Mordecai for support, Abby went on quickly, "That way, they won't be able to contaminate the rest of us. But they'll be close enough to fire a shot if they need help."

"That sounds fair to me," Reverend Coulter said. The relief in his voice was evident. He wished he had thought of this solution himself.

"I like that better than sending them away completely," Aaron Winters said. His wife nodded her head in agreement.

"I still say they should be sent away," James Market shouted. "This calls for a vote of the majority."

Mordecai interrupted him. "This is my wagon train, Market. I'll tally the vote. And if there's a tie, I'll cast the deciding one." Glancing over the crowd, the wagon master said, "Miss Abby has suggested that the Peel wagon pull back from the train until the illness is cured. I will add to that, any wagon containing a cholera victim will be asked to do the same." He saw the way the people began reflecting on the possibilities of their own family members becoming ill. When they realized that they could suffer the same fate as the Peels, they were willing to look for more humane treatment. "I ask for a show of hands," Mordecai said.

After counting the hands, he said, "James Market has suggested that the Peel wagon be sent away from the train and left on its own. I will add, any other wagon whose family members become ill with cholera will be forced to do the same." Glancing at the scowl on Market's face, Mordecai said, "I will now see a show of hands for that suggestion."

Only Jed Garner raised his hand. Swearing, James Market went off in search of his jug. Quickly the crowd dispersed. This was not a night to be out. This was a night to draw close around the family and pray that each would be spared the fate of Jason Peel.

Each morning as the travelers broke camp they would turn to look at the Peel wagon, far back but keeping pace. Whenever Abby went out to hunt, she left some of her game along the trail, with a marker, where she knew Doralyn and Jonathon would find it. Her heart went out to the mother and son who valiantly contended not only with illness but with isolation.

The night was unbearably hot and still. The moon was obscured by dark clouds. James had gone off to drink with Jed Garner. Violet lay in the back of the wagon, occasionally dabbing at her face and arms with a damp cloth. Abby walked some distance from the wagons to a dry creek bed. If only there were water, she thought, bending to touch the sun-bleached stones. How she longed to strip off her clothes and swim in cool, refreshing water.

Thoughts of another night drifted into her mind. A night when Rourke had watched while she stripped naked and swam. Just the thought of it brought the heat to her cheeks.

"I thought I'd warned you to stay close to camp."

At Rourke's low voice, she whirled and saw him standing just a foot away.

"And what about you? Why are you out here?"

"It's my job to keep an eye on things. I always check out the territory after the others go to sleep."

Abby hadn't given much thought to what Rourke did. Yet she wasn't surprised. It was like him to see to even the smallest details. Small wonder that people felt safe with Rourke.

"It's too hot to sleep. I was just wishing this creek hadn't dried up."

"We won't find as much as a trickle until we reach the Sierras," he said. "But I sure would enjoy seeing you swim."

She saw the smile light his eyes and was glad for the darkness that hid her blush.

"A gentleman would never bring up a subject that might make a lady uncomfortable."

"I never said I was a gentleman." Rourke threw back his head and laughed. "Damned if you don't sound exactly like your Aunt Violet when you talk like that."

Abby started to turn away, but Rourke caught her by the arm. "What's your hurry?"

"I should get back. They'll start to miss me."

"Your aunt is probably asleep by now. And your father won't head back to his wagon until the jug is dry. By then, he won't be able to see who's in the wagon. Or care."

Abby hung her head at his words. It was true. Everyone knew about her father.

"Abby." With his thumb and finger, Rourke lifted her chin until she met his gaze. "I'm sorry about your pa. But he has nothing to do with you. Nobody blames you for what he does or says. You can't make him behave any more than a breeze can tell the moon when to shine."

"I just wish he was different."

"Wishing won't change anything."

A hint of a smile touched her lips. "Don't tell my Aunt Vi that. She used to tell Carrie and me that all we had to do was wish hard enough and we could have anything."

Brushing a wisp of hair from her cheek, Rourke stared into her eyes. "If you could have just one wish, what would it be?"

Abby found her gaze drawn to his mouth and felt a jolt. What she wanted was to kiss him. To kiss him and never stop. But that wasn't something she could dare to tell him.

"Aunt Vi says if you tell, you won't get your wish."

"Is that so?" His fingers stayed on her cheek, warm and soft, then slowly slid around her neck until he was cupping the back of her head. Slowly he lowered his face, until their lips were almost touching.

Standing on tiptoe, she lifted her face to his. And then, so slowly she thought her heart would break from the waiting, he brushed her lips with his.

It was the gentlest kiss, like the touch of a snowflake to her tongue when she was a child. Such sweet, sweet seduction. Slowly, slowly, the pressure on her mouth grew, until she brought her arms around his neck and pressed herself to him.

She heard his little intake of breath. Instantly his arms were around her, molding her to him. The hands at her back were strong and firm. The lips that touched hers were no longer gentle, but grew demanding. Inside her veins, fire and ice collided, leaving her dazed and clinging.

"Rourke." She sighed, struggling for breath. "I wish . . . oh how I wish . . ."

"You don't have to say it," he murmured against her temple. "Just wish it hard enough. And I'll wish it too. And together we'll have it."

She stepped back. The clouds parted. In the sliver of moonlight, he saw the look in her eyes. Desire. And he knew that now, finally, she could be his.

Moving into his arms, she brought her arms around his neck and drew his head down. Lifting her lips to his, she gave a sigh from deep within, and he felt the little shudder that passed through her slender frame. And then he was lost in the kiss, knowing that no other woman would ever thrill him as she did.

His hands moved along her sides until they found the swell of her breasts. With his rough thumbs, he stroked until she moaned and whispered his name.

They were so caught up in each other that at first they didn't hear the shout that went up from the wagon train. But as the cry grew, they lifted their heads and turned to stare.

"Fire!"

Everyone on the train rolled from their wagons to look at the sky. A bonfire lit the darkness. Even with nearly a mile separating them, the members of the wagon train could smell the acrid odor of burning flesh.

"Oh my God! Rourke, it's the Peel wagon." As tears sprang to her eyes, Abby whispered, "The last thing Mordecai told Doralyn before she pulled back was that when a person dies of cholera, his body and all his belongings have to be burned in order to avoid spreading the contamination."

Rourke tried to draw her close against him, but she pushed away, tears spilling down her cheeks. "Oh, dear God. Poor Doralyn. Jason has died."

"You don't know that, Abby."

"Yes I do. And so do you."

Rourke thought about the men he'd seen, lying in the fields of battle as the life slowly drained from them. How cruel it had been, dying in a strange place, far from home.

"Doralyn and Jonathon will be all alone now. All alone." Abby's voice held a trace of anxiety. "They'll need us. I have to go."

He wanted to comfort her. But there were no words to say. In silence, they began to walk, then broke into a run, side by side until they reached the wagon train. And as they parted, they both found themselves going over the names of the people on the train. Who would be the next victim?

Chapter Twenty-three

THEY DIDN'T HAVE to wait long. By morning, two new wagons had pulled back from the train.

Lavinia Winters, suffering from chills and fever, hid her condition from her family until it was no longer possible to keep quiet. Stricken with a bout of prolonged vomiting, she was forced to admit to her husband that she had been ill for more than two days. While she had been bravely hiding her symptoms, he realized, she had exposed him and their three children as well.

As the wagon turned in preparation to leave the train, the children waved a solemn goodbye to their friends, and Abby noted that the two oldest Winters children were crying. Perhaps the youngest were the luckiest, she thought. They were still too young to know fear.

Reverend Coulter offered a prayer for the Winters family as the wagon train pulled ahead.

Less than an hour later, the reverend passed out, falling into a heap in the dirty trail. A cry went up from Abby, who spotted him. Rourke, hearing her shout, came running.

At first it was thought that Reverend Coulter was merely suffering from heat exhaustion. But soon his wife confirmed that he was indeed suffering from the feared cholera.

While the others watched in stunned silence, Evelyn Coulter climbed up on the wagon seat, with her baby beside her, and turned the team around. As the train continued westward, the Coulter wagon waited until the dust had settled before following at a safe distance.

That evening, over a quiet supper, James Market's face grew purple with rage at the mention of the new victims of cholera.

"Damned fools should have listened to me. The widow Peel and that boy of hers should never have been allowed to rejoin this train."

"James. You aren't suggesting that Doralyn Peel and Jonathon are the cause of this." Violet was appalled at the mere thought.

"'Course they are. You and all those do-gooders who would nurse the sick and bury the dead disgust me, woman. Why, if you'd been allowed inside the Peel wagon, you would have brought that sickness home to us. You'd like that, wouldn't you?"

"Of course not, James. I was simply trying to do the charitable thing."

"Charity be hanged. If the others had listened to me in the first place, we would have been rid of the cholera right away. It was the Peel family that brought it here. They're dirty little devils. She and that grinning boy of hers. They don't deserve any mercy. Now look," he hissed, pointing a knife at the dim lights bobbing in the distance. "The Winters brats will be left without a mother, and Evelyn Coulter is about to become a widow."

"You don't know that, James. Lavinia and the reverend are young and strong. They'll fight this illness."

"You better go wish on a star, woman. Better yet," he scoffed, "go wish for a handsome prince to marry you and take you away from all this." He threw back his head and roared with laughter at his little joke. "You do that, all right. You've got about as much chance of getting one wish as the other."

Trembling with rage, Violet turned her back on his laughter and brewed a cup of tea. Her mother had taught her that a cup of tea could soothe the nerves and calm a rising temper. Besides, having something to do offered a release. Straining the leaves carefully through a linen handkerchief, she tied it and set it aside, to be used again for breakfast. When she turned back, James had picked up his jug and was headed for the Garner wagon.

Seeing the tear that glimmered on her aunt's lashes, Abby placed an arm around her shoulder. "He doesn't mean any harm, Aunt Vi. Pa's just scared. Everybody is scared. Scared they'll be next."

Sniffing, Violet lifted the cup to her lips. "You're wise beyond your years, child. Your father thinks it is unmanly to show fear. So he lashes out instead." Taking another sip, she dabbed at her mouth with a spotless handkerchief. "He's always had a cruel streak." Determined to change the subject, she said, "It would be tragic if we lost Lavinia and Reverend Coulter. I pray the Lord will spare them."

Abby said what they both needed to hear. "They'll be fine." Patting her aunt's hand, Abby went off to attend to her evening chores.

They stopped believing meaningless words meant to comfort.

In the next three days, three more wagons pulled back, leaving only six wagons in the train. Each night, the travelers scanned the horizon, watching for bonfires announcing another death.

Lavinia Winters's body was burned, along with her six-year-old daughter and all their belongings. A simple wooden cross marked the place where their charred remains were buried. When the wagon bearing her husband and two remaining children returned to the wagon train, they wore the haunted looks of those who had stared into the face of death.

Afraid of contamination, the others on the train shunned the Winterses, just as everyone except Abby and Violet continued to avoid Doralyn Peel and her son. Violet, feeling a wave of pity for two motherless children, cooked a pot of hearty stew and took it to the Winterses' wagon. When the children peered through the flap of canvas, she invited them down, where she gave each a fierce hug. Like blossoms opening to the sun, the children were soon talking and clinging to her skirts. While they ate, they told her of their mother's valiant battle with the illness, and about her death and the death of their little sister. By the time she left their wagon to help Abby prepare supper for James, the children had begun to relax, and even smile. They would be fine, she told herself. They would draw together and be a comfort to their father, who was still hurt and bewildered by his sudden loss.

"Fool!" James shouted when he heard what she'd done. "You couldn't leave well enough alone. Like the old busybody you are, you had to run right over to the Winters family and hear all the details, didn't you?"

"James, I wanted to let them know we cared. We're all so afraid of cholera, we're avoiding dear friends. At a time like this, we all need each other."

"Soon there won't be anyone left. You'll have no one but yourself to blame when you come down with the fever," he hissed.

"That's a terrible thing to say." Abby jumped to her aunt's defense.

"Oh, is it? Well, you'll see. She'll be next." Pointing his finger at his sister, he sneered. "And how many of them do you think will come running to your aid, Vi?"

"Stop it." Abby put her hands over her ears. "I can't stand to listen to you anymore, Pa. You sound as if you'd like to see Aunt Vi take sick, just so you could say 'I told you so.'"

"You watch your mouth, girlie, or I'll close it for you."

She frowned as he uncorked the jug. Then she turned away and tended to the team. Still, even from a distance, she could hear the loud mocking voice of her father, taunting her aunt.

Another bonfire lit the night sky, but no one on the train knew who had died. It was only in the morning, when the Coulter wagon approached just as the train was breaking camp, that they knew.

Evelyn drove, with the tiny baby, Jenny, lying on the seat beside her. The look on her haggard face told them all they needed to know.

"Morning, Mrs. Coulter," Mordecai called. "I'm sorry, ma'am. Just as sorry as I can be. Is there anything you need before we move out?"

Evelyn shook her head. "Did Lavinia Winters pull through?"

Mordecai met her steady gaze. "No, ma'am. Aaron and two of the children returned to the train two days ago."

"Only two?" Evelyn was silent for a few moments, fighting the lump that clogged her throat. She and Lavinia had been friends since childhood, growing up on neighboring farms. And after they had married, they remained close. Evelyn had watched Lavinia's children grow, and cherished them as her own. Now she had lost her husband and best friend in a matter of days. And the dreaded cholera was even taking the lives of the very young.

"If Mr. Winters could spare his daughter, it would help if she could ride with me and take care of Jenny. In return, I would be happy to cook their evening meal."

Mordecai nodded. "I'll speak with Aaron right now, ma'am."

Within the hour, the train pulled out. In the Coulter wagon, ten-year-old Mary Winters sat beside Evelyn

Coulter and held the sleeping infant. While eleven-year-old Thaddeus Winters drove his father's team, Aaron Winters went off in search of game. While their wounds were deep and their tears still fresh, the healing had to begin.

By the light of a full moon, James Market staggered among the darkened wagons. Confused, he stared around. Had the damned women moved his wagon since suppertime? Which was his wagon? The half-empty jug dropped from his hand and he bent to retrieve it. Feeling his legs wobble, he sank to his knees in the dirt. Why should he feel so weak? He hadn't had that much to drink. He began to sweat profusely, and passed an arm across his forehead. Something he ate. Violet and Abby were terrible cooks. Margaret was the only one who could ever cook a decent meal. In the morning they'd pay for this. Rotten cooks. Silly do-gooders. Weak, useless women.

A wave of nausea left him trembling. Fighting it, he got to his feet, ignoring the jug. Stumbling forward, he caught hold of a wagon wheel and held on until the nausea passed. Then, his vision blurred, his clothes damp with sweat, he searched among the darkened wagons until he found his own. Just as he started to climb up, he fell back and retched.

Damned cheap whiskey. He swore, then retched again. His skin felt cold, clammy. Trembling violently, he pulled himself into the back of the wagon with great effort. Even after he had wrapped himself in a warm blanket, the chills continued. Within a few minutes he was seized with a fit of vomiting. Leaping from the wagon, he knelt in the dirt, fighting the weakness that had taken over. When it passed, he gathered his strength and climbed back inside the wagon, where even several layers of blankets couldn't relieve the chill. For the rest of the night, he alternately fled from the wagon, retched, then dragged himself back inside. By morning, he was too weak to lift his head.

Abby awoke and lay still, listening to the sounds of morning activity. Somewhere a baby cried. Little Jenny. A few moments later the crying stopped. Abby smiled. As her senses sharpened, the smile turned into a frown. The stench of sweat and vomit permeated the wagon. Sitting up, she glanced at the figure of her father. As she watched, the blanket-clad figure began to tremble. A second later, a moan escaped his lips.

"Pa." Crawling close, Abby touched a hand to his shoulder.

He stirred, moaned, then shook violently.

"Pa." At the anxious tone of her voice, Violet sat up and brushed the hair from her eyes.

"What is it, child?"

"It's Pa. He's sick."

Shrugging from her blanket, Violet crawled beside him and touched a hand to his forehead. "Dear God." Bending close, she whispered, "James, can you hear me?"

His eyes opened but didn't focus on her. They were glazed with pain. "Hot," he croaked. "Too damned hot."

The two women stared at each other for long, silent moments. Then Abby began pulling on her boots. "I'll go tell Mordecai that we're pulling back." She glanced at her aunt's face and read the fear that mirrored her own.

Violet nodded. "I'll tend to James."

"We'll both tend him," Abby said firmly. "I'll hitch the team first, then go to the cook wagon."

The older woman watched as her niece climbed from the wagon. Then she whispered a prayer as she pressed a damp cloth to her brother's burning forehead.

Outside, Abby sucked fresh air into her lungs. Already the inside of the wagon reeked of sickness.

265

Her father had been barely coherent. How long had he kept his illness from them?

Murmuring to the team, she coaxed them into the harness and hitched them to the wagon. Tying the horse to the back of the wagon, she loaded their meager supplies, then went in search of Mordecai.

At the cook wagon she halted when she spotted Rourke.

"Morning, Abby." His smile faded at the look in her eyes.

"Don't come close, Rourke. My pa's got the sickness. My aunt and I will be pulling back now."

"Abby . . ." As he took a step nearer, she backed up.

"Stay away. I may be next." She wondered if the weakness she was feeling was cholera, or the nearness of this man. Probably just a reaction to the knowledge that her strong father had been stricken. Her sensible nature took over. It was just a lack of food. "Tell Mordecai that we'll keep far away from the other wagons."

"How will you manage?" Rourke wanted to go to her, to hold her. But all he could do was stand here and make useless conversation. Frustrated, he clenched his fists at his sides and memorized the slope of her brow, the curve of her cheek.

"We'll be fine." Swallowing the lump that threatened to choke her, Abby swung away.

"Abby."

She half turned.

He couldn't think of a single thing to say that would give her any comfort. He let out a sigh. "Take care."

She tried to smile. He watched her lips curve upward before quivering. Then she strode away.

Behind her, Rourke fought a helpless rage. Swinging into the saddle, he attacked his chores with a vengeance.

*　*　*

Word spread quickly.

As each family passed, they waved or nodded at the slender young woman who sat stiffly in the front of the Market wagon, clutching the reins.

As the Coulter wagon drew abreast, Evelyn called, "Conserve water, Abby. James will be feverish for days." As Abby nodded, Evelyn added, "God give you strength."

Strength. Always, it seemed, her strength was being tested. How much more would they have to endure?

As the dust from the wagon train settled, Abby flicked the reins. The mules plodded slowly along the trail carved by the wheels of hundreds of wagons that had crossed this barren wilderness. How many had died before reaching the promised land? she wondered. How many more had turned back in despair?

All through the day, while Abby drove, the sound of her father's moans could be heard, and then the soft, soothing tones of Violet as she sat beside him. They crossed endless miles of desert before stopping to make camp. While Abby started supper and fed the team, she found herself glancing at the lights of the wagon train in the distance. She hadn't realized how much comfort they offered each other. Out here all alone, she felt abandoned. She missed the cries of babies, the laughter of children, the shouts of men to their teams.

"Abby."

She turned at the sound of her aunt's voice. "Is it Pa? Is he worse?"

Violet shook her head. "He's no better or worse." She sighed, feeling the loneliness close in around them. "I just need to hear the sound of your voice."

Abby nodded her understanding. "I'm heating some broth."

"I doubt he'll be able to keep it down." Violet slumped down in the dirt and Abby felt a wave of pity for her aunt. Her hair had fallen loose from its neat knot and clung damply to her neck. Her once-spotless gown was soiled with signs of her brother's sickness.

"Clean yourself, Aunt Vi. Then rest awhile. I'll see to Pa's needs."

"And what about your own?"

Abby shrugged. "I don't have any. It's Pa who needs tending now."

Taking the warm broth from the fire, Abby made her way to the wagon. Her father's breathing was labored. His skin was the color of clay.

"Here, Pa. I brought you some broth. You need it if you're going to fight this."

Holding the spoon to his lips, she was relieved to see him drink the steaming liquid. This was what he needed to regain his strength. They would not let this illness beat them.

As she fed him a second spoonful, he let out a moan.

"Water."

Instantly, Abby set aside the steaming liquid and lifted a dipper of water to his lips. He drank greedily, then began coughing. Leaning up on one elbow, he covered his face with a rag and retched, then sank back.

When she again tried to feed him, he refused, too weak to even lift his head.

Touching a hand to his forehead, Abby began sponging his face and neck. His skin was so hot. So hot. She felt a moment of panic, then swallowed it back. They weren't going to let this sickness beat them. She was a fighter. And so was her father. Together they would fight this. And they would win.

All night Abby sat with her father, bathing his fevered brow, forcing him to swallow water. Still he grew weaker as the illness raged within him, draining his body's fluids, sapping his strength.

When the wagon train moved out, Abby climbed aboard the seat and flicked the reins. While the mules plodded, her head bobbed, until they hit a rut, shaking her awake. Then she scolded herself for her carelessness, and weakly nodded off until the next bump jolted her into consciousness.

By the time they stopped to make camp, Abby was close to exhaustion. But the sight of her aunt, pale and disheveled, left her no choice but to take over the care of her father for another night.

While Violet dozed in the wagon with her back against a cushion, Abby sat beside her father. He couldn't tolerate even a single drop of water. The hand in hers was too weak to even grasp her finger. His voice, when he spoke, was barely audible.

"I'm dying."

Violet's eyes blinked open. Kneeling up, she made her way to his side and grasped his hand.

Yesterday, Abby would have argued with him. Tonight, she could no longer deny the fact. While she watched, she could feel the life slowly ebb from his frail body.

"Pa," she whispered, bringing her lips close to his ear. "Before you join Ma, give me some sign that you've forgiven Carrie. If I ever see her again, I want to be able to tell her that you sent her your blessing."

"No, damn you. I will never forgive her for defying me." He took a fit of coughing, and Abby stared in horror at the blood that spilled down his shirt.

"James, you're about to meet your Maker. It's time to heal the wounds. Say you forgive Carrie," Violet pleaded.

"Forgive?" He stared at his sister for long moments before rasping, "I forgive no one. Not Carrie. Not Lily. And not you, for foisting her brat on me."

Violet's mouth dropped open at the vehemence of his words. "James! No. You promised."

Beside them, Abby could only stare in silence. What were they arguing about? It made no sense.

"I kept my promise. I raised her like my own. But now it's time for the truth." He was racked with another coughing spell, and as Abby watched, Violet began to cry.

"God forgive me, James, but I pray God will strike you dead before you can inflict any more pain on her. You've done too much to her already."

"You hypocrite," he spat.

"Pa. Stop this."

Turning toward Abby, he said, "Don't call me that. I'm not your pa. It was all a lie. You're Lily's bastard."

Abby's face went white. Staring at him, she felt tears stinging her eyes. "What are you saying?"

His voice rose, sounding for a moment like the old James. "Lily defied me. Just like Carrie. Ran off with a man like a thief in the night. Pa found her in another town and dragged her home just before she gave birth. She died without ever revealing the name of her lover."

Abby turned a stricken face to Violet. "But you said her baby died, Aunt Vi."

"Your aunt's a liar. Your whole life's been a lie. Margaret and Violet insisted I take you in and raise you like my own."

"But why would you agree when you hated Lily so?"

"Because he was the reason she ran away in the first place," Violet sobbed. "His brutality drove her away. Just the way he drove Carrie away."

James wasn't her father. Lily's baby. Abby felt her mind whirling. There were too many things happening too fast. She couldn't seem to take them all in.

"I should have expected this from you, James," Violet said, tears still streaming down her cheeks. Her voice, Abby noticed, had become too soft, too silky. "You enjoy hurting others, don't you?"

She waited until another coughing spasm had quieted, then added, "I think you should know. I was the one who encouraged Carrie to leave with Will."

Abby's mouth opened in silent protest, but her aunt went on, "Just as I encouraged Lily all those years ago.

I couldn't escape you, James, because Father needed me. I was the oldest, and expected to care for him and the younger ones when Mother died. And by the time he died, it was too late for me. But I saw to it that it wouldn't be too late for Lily. I gave her what little money I had. And as for Carrie, I gave her my little chest of ribbons and lace, and sent her away with my blessing."

"You bitch." The words were torn from his lips as he began to retch.

"Lily didn't want your forgiveness. Neither will Carrie. All either of them wanted was to be free of you. Carrie will have a much better life without your cruelty."

"You'll burn in hell, woman."

"I think God is more forgiving than you, James. But if not, I have no doubt you'll be there with me."

James turned to Abby, whose ashen features reflected the shock she was still suffering. "As for you, girl, you should have taken my advice and married Flint Barrows. No decent man will ever have anything to do with a . . . mongrel. You'll end up being a dried-up old maid like this one."

He started to laugh. The sound was abruptly cut off as he clutched at his sides and began to retch. When he lay back, the rag at his mouth was soaked with blood.

"Get away from me," he whispered fiercely. "Both of you. I want to be left alone. It's all I've ever wanted."

Rourke stood on the crest of the hill and stared at the Market wagon outlined against the night sky. He'd been standing here for hours, unable to sleep, unwilling to go back to the train. Pulling a cigar from his pocket, he held a light to the tip and watched as the smoke drifted above his head.

He missed Abby. That thought came as a complete surprise to him. Ever since the Indian had left, taking away his reason for staying with her, Rourke had missed her.

He wondered if she had enough game to last. He wondered if she could manage the team, the meals, the repairs to the wagon, and her father's illness.

Most of all, he wondered if she missed him. Did she think about him as she drifted off to sleep? Did she ever whisper his name as she rolled from her bed at dawn? Had she ever . . .

He saw the flicker of flame coming from the direction of Abby's wagon and strained to see more. A few minutes later, the flame had grown to a bonfire.

There was no doubt of the meaning of the fire. Market was dead. As the knowledge sank in, Rourke felt nothing. No regret that another life had ended, no joy that Abby's tormentor was gone. There was only a numb acceptance of the facts. James Market was dead, and Abby and Violet would be on their own.

The wagon train was nearly across the Forty-Mile Desert. They had left a glowing trail of night bonfires and simple wooden crosses along this barren wasteland to mark the graves of those who didn't make it. James Market was among those who would never see California.

Tossing aside his cigar, Rourke mounted and rode slowly back to the train.

Chapter Twenty-four

ABBY AND VIOLET were welcomed back to the train in the same manner that all the others had been: a brief nod, a quick wave, and a hasty retreat by the survivors, who still feared contamination.

On their first evening back in camp, Mordecai dropped by their wagon and was surprised to find Rourke there as well.

"Good evening, Miss Abby, Miss Violet," the wagon master said, removing his hat.

"Mordecai. Rourke just joined us for coffee." Abby indicated a bench in front of the fire. "Please stay."

"Thank you, ma'am. It smells too good to refuse." With a chuckle he sat on the wooden bench and leaned his back against the wheel of the wagon. "Parker's coffee seems to get worse as the days go by. I wouldn't recommend it for any but the strongest of men."

As the women smiled, he cleared his throat. "I wish to offer my condolences, ladies, on the death of Mr. Market."

"Thank you, Mr. Stump." Violet sipped a cup of tea and Abby found herself studying her aunt, and marveling at the complex woman she had come to know.

The face Violet showed to the world was of a delicate, proper lady. Yet it was she, Abby realized with a swelling of pride, who had encouraged Lily and Carrie to defy the domineering James and follow their hearts. It was Violet who had managed to overcome her fear and prejudice and help care for a wounded Indian. And it was she who had last night counseled Abby to look beyond the sorrows in her own young life and seek the joys.

Abby sipped her coffee, letting her aunt tell Mordecai and Rourke the details of James's death. She did not wish to speak of him. While the conversation droned on around her, Abby thought of her little sister. Was she happy? Were she and Will as deeply in love now as when they had first run off? Had they put down roots? Were they making a life for themselves? Or were they still on the run, afraid of James Market's wrath?

Oh Carrie, she thought, feeling herself close to tears. Be happy.

"You're quiet tonight."

Abby looked up, and realized that she and Rourke were alone.

Seeing the arch of her eyebrow, he explained, "Your aunt and Mordecai are paying a call on Evelyn Coulter. With the help of Aaron Winters and his children, she's been doing just fine."

"I'm glad. It must be hard for a woman like Evelyn to be alone. Reverend Coulter was such a helpmate."

A smile played at the corners of Rourke's lips. It was so good to see her again, to hear her voice. "Maybe that's what you and your aunt ought to be looking for."

Abby burst out laughing. "Aunt Vi and I are going to be dried-up old prunes."

"Who told you that?"

"My p—" She swallowed back the word. He wasn't her father. Had never been. It had all been a lie. And

274

all those years that she had taken his abuse, he had been hating her because she was Lily's daughter. Lily's daughter, she reminded herself, searching for some pride in that title.

Misreading her hesitation, Rourke touched a hand to Abby's shoulder. "It's too soon to talk about him, Abby. Wait until the wound isn't so fresh."

Abby glanced at Rourke's sympathetic look and wished she could tell him. But it was too personal, too painful. It was her secret. Her shame.

"I don't mean to speak ill of the dead," Rourke said, running his hand across her shoulder and lifting her chin until she met his dark gaze. "But your father didn't know what the hell he was talking about. There's nothing old or dried up about Violet. She's quite a woman. And you." He brought his other hand up to cup her face. "You're something very special, Abby Market."

Lowering his face to hers, he kissed her almost reverently, moving his lips slowly over hers until he heard her little sigh of pleasure. Then, plunging his hands into her hair, he drew her head back and kissed her hard, taking her fully into the kiss, until her head was spinning.

Clutching his arms, she stared up at him in surprise. He took a step back, his eyes narrowed. "Very special."

He turned and walked from the circle of firelight into the darkness beyond.

By the time the cholera epidemic had run its course, the only wagon untouched by the dreaded disease was the Garner wagon. That fact should have brought Nancy and Jed even closer together, and made them more protective of their young son. Instead, Nancy had become completely disoriented, going for days without eating or washing. At night, while Jed drank alone, she prowled among the wagons, talking to anyone who would listen about the wrath of the Lord and the coming of the end of the world. She had decided that their family had been spared because she was touched by God. She insisted that she possessed special powers.

When the train left the deep, choking dust and cruel heat of the Forty-Mile Desert behind, Nancy Garner intoned loudly that the Lord had told her there would be refreshing water and even shade trees ahead. The weary travelers, desperate for relief, clung to her predictions as if they had been given by God Himself.

Rourke, returning from a scouting expedition, reported that they were only a few miles from the Carson River, which flowed westerly into the Sierra Nevadas.

In this early autumn setting, the tree-lined Carson River was placid and cool, its winding course marked by giant cottonwoods. Though Mordecai had promised the travelers respite once they crossed the Forty-Mile, some of them, dazed, frightened, began to put more stock in what Nancy Garner said than in the words of their wagon master. There was even talk of appointing her to replace Reverend Coulter as the new minister. Evelyn, hurt and angry that they would pass her by in favor of the unbalanced Nancy Garner, became quiet and withdrawn. On Sunday mornings, while Nancy preached loudly about fire and brimstone, Evelyn and a few of the others, including Abby and Violet, prayed together and sang some of the old familiar hymns.

Mordecai watched with growing concern. Too much divisiveness on a wagon train was dangerous. These people needed to work together if they were to survive. Yet he could see no way to bring them together, short of force.

"Do you think Nancy has been touched by a demon?" Doralyn Peel asked one Sunday morning after their brief prayer service.

"She certainly does her share of talking—to God," one of the men said.

Everyone burst into laughter.

"I think Nancy Garner is a sad, lonely woman who has lost direction," Violet said softly.

Evelyn Coulter nodded. "My husband would have counseled us not to judge, lest we be judged in the same way. I pray for Nancy. And for her son Timmy."

Abby kept her silence. Her heart ached for Timmy Garner. Each night since their return to the train, the little boy crept to their wagon, where she and Aunt Vi fed him, bathed him, and told him stories until he grew sleepy. Then they cautiously returned him to his own wagon and tucked him into bed. Both women were fearful that they might be caught by Jed or Nancy. In their present condition, the Garners might forbid the women to see Timmy. And, Abby knew, she and her aunt were his only source of comfort.

Late at night, Abby found her thoughts confused and distracted. As she drifted into sleep, she saw visions of a beautiful Lily, wearing a gown of spun gold, carrying a baby. The baby had long dark hair, and the face of Two Shadows. As if in a mist, Lily slowly dissolved into a grown-up Abby, and the child she was carrying was Timmy Garner. He was crying and reaching out to her as someone snatched him from her arms. Crying aloud, she woke, and sat up in the darkened wagon.

The dream left her too disturbed to go back to sleep. Taking up a shawl, she pulled open the canvas flap and stepped down from the wagon.

Though the days were still warm, there was a coolness to the nights that was welcome. Wrapping the shawl about her shoulders, Abby walked to a clearing and sat on a smooth, round boulder. The night sounds were different here, in the forests of the Sierras, than they had been on the floor of the desert. Here were insects, birds, the gurgle of water.

The snap of a dried twig.

She turned at the sound. Rourke was standing at the edge of a row of pine trees, studying her.

"Don't you ever sleep?" she asked.

"When I can. Sometimes there's no rest in sleep."

There was a time when she wouldn't have understood what he meant. But because her dream was still so vivid, she merely nodded in silence.

"What about you? Why are you out here?"

She shrugged. "It's so cool and pleasant. I just want to enjoy it."

"Don't let the beauty of this land fool you, Abby. The worst part of our journey is still ahead."

She thought about the miles behind them, the Indians, the cholera, the fear, the suffering, the death. "Nothing could be worse than what we've been through."

"You've heard about the Donner party?"

Abby nodded. "Everyone knows that most of them froze to death in the winter of forty-six and forty-seven." She shuddered. "And that the survivors were forced to turn to cannibalism. But we'll be clear to California before winter sets in."

Rourke put one booted foot on the rock and leaned forward, resting his arms on his knee. "The only thing certain about this part of the country is that there will be snow. Lots of snow. But we never know when it will fall. There have been blizzards here in late summer, which last clear into early spring."

"Are you trying to frighten me?"

He shook his head. "You're not someone who scares easily. But you show common sense."

Ordinarily those words would have made her happy. But she sensed his concern.

"Right now, the only thing Mordecai wants is to get this wagon train across the Sierras as fast as possible."

"Will it be a difficult crossing?"

His tone was ominous. "They're the most awesome mountains I've ever seen. And we've lost four strong men to cholera. I know their widows are doing all they can to carry on, but the labor of four men will be sorely missed."

"We'll endure."

He studied her face in the moonlight, chin jutted defiantly, nostrils flared. "God," he murmured, stroking her cheek. "You're magnificent."

It happened so quickly, she had no time to react. Pulling her roughly to her feet, he crushed her against his chest and savaged her mouth. Her shawl fluttered to the ground and was forgotten.

How could the feel of one man's lips on hers be so devastating? Why was it that every time he held her she lost all ability to think?

On his tongue, she could taste the passion, the desire. It drove him. Drove them both until they were weak and clinging. And still he continued to kiss her, his lips warm and firm, his tongue seeking the endless delights of her mouth.

God, she was so small, so slender. Her bones were so fragile, he could break her with the slightest pressure. Yet there was such strength in her. Such discipline. Such drive. And buried far beneath was a slumbering passion that he was determined to awaken.

Without realizing it, his kiss gentled. It would be so easy to take her too far, too fast. He wanted to taste, to touch, to savor. Trailing his lips across her cheek, he tugged at her earlobe, then darted his tongue until she caught at his head and forced his lips back to hers.

She moaned and whispered his name as he kissed her again, swallowing down her words. He loved the sound of his name on her lips. Their breath mingled, hot, quick breaths that revealed a control that was beginning to slip.

He brought his mouth to her throat and ran kisses along her shoulder. Burying his lips in the little hollow of her throat, he felt the wild hammering of her pulse.

Was this what it had been like for the beautiful Lily? Abby wondered. Had a man made her feel so special, so loved, that she was willing to turn her back on everything, everyone, to be with him? Oh Lily. Mother. How do I know what to do?

Pushing against his chest, she took a step back. Looking up, she saw Rourke's eyes, dark and heavy-lidded with passion. She felt a sudden thrill, knowing that it was she who could bring him to this point. Still, she was afraid. She needed time. Time.

"Rourke." As he reached for her, she resisted. When she took another step back, she heard his hiss of frustration.

"Dammit. This is what we both want. It's right for us."

"Maybe." There was no sense lying to him or to herself any longer. "But I'm afraid. I need time."

Time. The one thing he would never be certain he had.

"Walk me back to my wagon, Rourke," she said, bending to pick up her shawl.

When she turned and took his arm, he found himself grinning. All his anger and frustration evaporated. She might have lived a sheltered life. She might be completely inexperienced. But there was no doubt about it. She was enjoying his attentions. She was making him court her. And though he called himself every kind of a fool, he had to admit he was enjoying it too.

The train had made camp under a stand of giant cottonwoods. The morning sun filtered through a leafy canopy. Lines of brightly colored clothes, washed the night before in the clear mountain stream, danced in the fresh breeze. The air was clear and clean, with just a hint of coolness. The women pulled on shawls and bonnets. The men turned down the sleeves of their shirts as they hitched up their teams.

It was a day made for smiling, a day made for hope. There was no hint of disaster.

Mordecai called out to his team, and the crack of the whip could be heard. Behind him, each team pulled slowly away from the camp and followed in a long, straight line.

The Garner wagon, hitched and ready, pulled out just in front of Abby's team.

"Abby," Timmy Garner called, waving.

Abby waved back, then turned to say something to her aunt. The next thing she heard was a piercing scream. The Garner wagon ground to a halt, and people from neighboring wagons began running.

Dropping the reins, Abby and Violet followed the others. As the crowd parted, Abby could see the body of little Timmy, crushed and bleeding.

"He fell from the wagon," Jed was sobbing as friends gathered around. "It happened so fast, I couldn't stop the team in time. The wagon rolled right over him."

Mordecai and Rourke hurried from the cook wagon and stopped at the sight before them. No one moved. The weary group of travelers seemed numb from the destruction of so many lives. The others had been sick. But this child . . . No one seemed to know how to offer consolation for such a tragedy.

"Oh God. My boy. My Timmy," Jed began shrieking. Tears streamed down his face.

Violet moved forward and drew him into her arms. He clung to her, crying hysterically.

Abby glanced at Nancy Garner. She was standing very still, staring at the battered body of her son. Her eyes seemed glazed, as if seeing nothing. Her face wore no expression.

She turned toward her shattered husband, who wiped his eyes and blew his nose in the handkerchief Violet offered. Her voice was deadly calm. "He is testing us. You of little faith," she said, pointing a finger at Jed, "will be found wanting. But He will not be displeased with me. I will be strong enough for both of us."

The crowd shifted uncomfortably as she moistened a rag and began washing her son's bloody body.

Looking up, she said, "Are you going to just stand there? Dig a hole."

Snatching the boy away from her, Jed growled, "I need time. Time to look at my son. Time to hold him. Time to tell him I'm sorry."

"You both need time," Violet said softly. "Time to grieve."

"He grieves enough for both of us," Nancy said, picking up a shovel. "He had time to be with Timmy. And with me. But he wasted it on liquor. Go away. All of you. I'll bury my son."

"Mrs. Garner," Mordecai said, taking the shovel from her hand firmly. "You go inside the wagon now and lie down for a little while."

"So you can all go on without us? You'd like that, wouldn't you?" She sneered. "That's what you'd hoped to do if we got the cholera. You would dump me like you dumped my piano. But we beat you. All of you," she shouted, turning to glare at the crowd. "And now you think, while we grieve, you can leave us behind."

"We wouldna' do such a thing," Mordecai said in his sternest tone. "When we leave this place, we will leave together. But for now, we will prepare a place for the lad. And after you and Jed have had some time alone, we will have a proper burial."

Relieved, the crowd drifted away.

They buried Timmy Garner beneath a leafy cotton-wood. As sunlight filtering through the leaves formed a kaleidoscope on the fresh earth, Abby felt hot tears sting her eyes and clog her throat.

She had not grieved when she and Violet had laid James Market to rest under the light of a full moon.

She had felt no grief, only a numbness, and afterward, a sense of relief that her life would be in her own hands. Later, those feelings had left her with a sense of guilt.

Timmy. So young. So innocent. He had tried so hard to please. And his parents, caught up in something that was draining all feeling from them, had neglected his needs. And now, even if they awoke from their long sleep and began to care once more, they would find it too late. Too late for Timmy. Too late to give him all the love he deserved.

As Abby and Violet clung together in their grief, Nancy Garner stood alone, dry-eyed, watching as the final shovel of dirt was tamped on the grave. Then she turned and walked back to her wagon, leaving Jed kneeling alone by the mound of earth.

It wasn't really a town. It was no more than a cluster of shacks and a couple of wagons. These were people who had lost the strength to go on. Nestled here in the foothills of the Sierra Nevadas, it housed men who had harbored dreams of California but who had given everything to the desert. This was as close to the promised land as they would ever get.

Ordinarily, Mordecai shied away from this kind of people, preferring to make camp in a safe, protected area. But the day had been hard. The loss of the Garner boy hung heavily on the travelers. All day they had endured the strained conversations, the muffled laughter of frightened, confused children. Maybe the sight of other people would cheer them.

As the wagons pulled into a circle, they saw the faces of the curious peering from shacks. Most of the faces were men, Mordecai noted. In fact, he hadn't seen a single woman yet.

When the aroma of supper wafted from the camp, men began wandering toward the wagons. Every one of them carried a rifle.

"Check your weapons," Mordecai warned as he passed among the wagons.

"You expecting trouble?" Aaron Winters dropped a protective arm around his daughter.

"Just being cautious. I dunna' know what sort of men these be."

Hearing him, Abby checked her handgun and rifle before sitting down to supper with her aunt. Nearby, she could hear the exchange of conversation between the strangers and the wagon master as Parker invited them to share their meal.

"We don't get many visitors," the leader of the group said.

"How long have you been here?" Mordecai asked. He noted that the men ate quickly, stuffing the food in their mouths like starving dogs.

"A year. Some of us longer. Some just stay awhile, to lay in supplies before going on. Most decide to stay on."

"How do you survive?"

"We hunt, mostly. The widow Barlow is trying her hand at farming."

"A widow? There's a woman among you?"

"Two," the leader said proudly. "We hope to have more by next year. With women, we could have a real town out here." He glanced around the wagons. "You seem to have an abundance of women."

Mordecai shifted uneasily.

"We have a saloon," the man said, loudly enough for his voice to be heard by the entire company. "You're welcome to come by for a drink after supper."

As the strangers walked away, Mordecai glanced at Rourke. "We'll be staying with the wagons tonight. I wouldna' trust these men with our women."

Rourke nodded. He'd had the same idea himself.

After supper, several of the men drifted toward the shacks, searching for the saloon. Among them was Jed Garner. His wife Nancy, he said, had refused to make supper, falling asleep almost as soon as they made camp.

"She'll sleep until morning," he told Mordecai as he walked away.

From her position inside the wagon, Abby saw Mordecai, Thompson, Parker, and Rourke with rifles in their hands, patrolling the camp.

"I didn't like the looks of those men from town," Violet said, glancing up from her mending.

"Apparently, neither did Mr. Stump. He and the others have been walking the perimeter of the camp since dusk."

"That makes me feel safer," Aunt Vi said softly. "I believe I'll turn in. You should do the same. This has been a hard day."

"In a little while," Abby said, watching Rourke's silhouette as he leaned against a tree, blending into the shadows.

"Good night, child."

"Night, Aunt Vi."

Abby sat up in the wagon, watching as lanterns went dark around the camp. She found her thoughts drifting to Timmy Garner. *If he had been mine*, she thought, *I would have been free to lavish all the love I have inside me for a child. If only he had been mine.*

"Abby. Abby Market."

Abby glanced up at the sound of Nancy Garner's voice.

"What is it?"

"I just woke up and I can't find Jed."

"He went with some of the men. There's a saloon in town."

"I should have known."

"He ought to be back soon, Nancy. Why don't you go back to sleep?"

"How can I sleep when I know he's drinking? His son fresh in the grave and he's out there getting drunk."

Abby found she was tired of the woman's whining

tone. Lowering the canvas, she said, "It doesn't look like there's much you can do about it. Good night, Nancy."

"Oh, there's something I can do. I'm going into town to find Jed."

Abby turned and lifted the flap of canvas. "Don't go there, Nancy. Mordecai thinks the men of that town may be dangerous."

But her words fell into the empty darkness. Nancy Garner was already hurrying away.

Dear God, what was the woman thinking of? Abby knew she would never be able to sleep worrying about Nancy Garner in that town alone. Grabbing up her rifle, she climbed down from her wagon and began running in the direction Nancy had gone. From the darkness, a hand caught her, stopping her in mid-stride. The breath was knocked from her.

"What the hell are you doing out tonight? You were warned to stay inside." Rourke's voice was deep with anger.

"Nancy Garner has gone off to look for Jed. I couldn't stop her."

"Damned fool. I'll go after her."

"I'm going too," Abby said firmly.

"No. You're staying here."

"It's my fault she went, Rourke. I was the one who told her Jed was there. I have to make certain she's safe."

He studied her a moment, then nodded. "You stay close."

As they approached the shacks, the sound of raised voices could be heard from a lean-to at the end of the row. Walking closer, Abby and Rourke peered inside through a crack in the boards. Seeing Nancy Garner in the center of the room, her hands on her hips, shouting at her husband, they opened the door and stepped inside. The room smelled of cheap whiskey and unwashed bodies. Jed, surrounded by a group of men, ordered his wife to leave. Suddenly, as the crowd parted, Nancy spotted a piano against the back wall. Her voice died in her throat. The words she'd been about to shout faded. Walking slowly across the room, she lifted the lid and ran her fingers across the keys. The piano, warped and dirty, gave out a tinny sound. A smile spread across Nancy's usually dour features. Pulling up a lopsided stool, she spread her dirty skirts and began to play.

No one spoke. No one moved. Bewhiskered men stared in wonder at the woman who could coax music from a few chipped keys. Gradually, gnarled hands began to clap. Feet, encased in heavy, worn boots, began to tap on the earthen floor. An old man grabbed his son and began to dance a jig. The old woman behind the makeshift bar smiled, showing a gaping mouth where teeth should have been.

The crowd moved closer, smiling, nodding, occasionally singing along.

Abby stared at Nancy's rapt expression, then at the look on her husband's face. Jed Garner emptied his glass in one swallow, then turned and stormed from the bar.

Rourke touched Nancy's arm. "Your husband's gone, Mrs. Garner. We'll escort you back to your wagon."

She yanked her arm away. "I'm not going back there."

"It isn't safe for you to stay alone in a place like this, ma'am."

She barely glanced at Rourke or Abby. "This is the first place I've felt at home since I left Independence. I'm staying."

"For how long?" Rourke was already eager to return to the wagon train. He didn't relish having to hang around here for another hour or more.

"I'm staying for good, Mr. Rourke," Nancy said, flexing her fingers before starting another tune. "Don't you see? This piano was put here by God for me to play. I've found my promised land."

As Abby and Rourke stared at each other in consternation, Nancy began playing "Amazing Grace." When they reached the door to the makeshift saloon, an old man was wiping tears from his cheeks with the back of his hand.

Late into the night, as Abby drifted off to sleep, the strains of a tinny piano filtered on the night air.

And in the morning, when the wagon train pulled away, a pleading Jed Garner rode alone in his empty wagon. Nancy Garner stayed behind, to make music on a broken piano, in a town that was hardly more than a row of rough shacks.

Chapter Twenty-five

THE TRAVELERS HAD been lulled by the lush grass and clear sparkling streams that greeted them at the foothills of the Sierras. Now, as the valley narrowed out and they began to climb, they realized for the first time the enormity of the task before them. If they had thought the Rockies difficult, the Sierra Nevadas seemed impenetrable. The abrupt mountain barrier loomed like a fortress. As they inched along, a cleft appeared, a rock-clogged canyon cut through the mountains by eons of ice and snow. Through that narrow pass, they found even more peaks, reaching higher than the clouds and mist that blotted out the sun.

In order to get the wagons across these mountains, it was necessary to unhitch the teams and join them together. At least fourteen mules or oxen were hitched to a wagon, then pulled straight up and over each jagged peak. While this oversized team strained, the men and women pushed from behind, chocking the wheels each time the team slowed.

Most days, the wagon train was lucky to make a mile or two. Though the days remained warm, the nights were growing increasingly cooler. Mordecai kept watch on the sky, fearing anything that even faintly resembled storm clouds. Every wagon master knew the dreaded word *Donner*. It was absolutely essential to get these people across the Sierras before the first snowfall.

By nighttime, most of the travelers were too exhausted to do anything more than eat and tumble into their blankets. Some of the women no longer bothered to cook, but fed their families dried meats and corn meal. There was no energy left over for baking biscuits or simmering pots of stew. Their hands were bloody and blistered, often wrapped with layers of rag to absorb the shock as they pushed and strained against the heavy wagons. Their feet too had to be wrapped, and Violet found herself passing out meager portions of her special balm. Most of the men used axle grease to cover their cracked, bleeding hands.

On the fourth day the last of the wagons was hauled to the top of a ridge overlooking a clear blue lake. It seemed incongruous that such a lake could exist at the very top of a mountain range.

"Tahoe," Mordecai said, staring down at the glistening water, completely surrounded by towering pine. "We'll stop here and rest, and take on supplies. The water is clear and drinkable, and there should be fish. These woods should be teeming with deer and rabbits, if anyone has the energy to hunt."

While the men picked up their rifles and headed toward the forest, the women and children made for the lake.

As Abby turned from the wagon, Rourke stepped forward. Noting the rifle in her hands, he said, "I'll be hunting game for the cook wagon. May as well bag a few for you and Violet while I'm at it."

"That isn't necessary, Rourke. I can . . ."

He pulled her roughly against him and kissed her, hard and quick. Caught off guard, she could only stare at him as the words she was saying were forgotten.

"What was that for?"

He grinned. "It's the best way I know to keep you

from arguing. Now go take a bath, and do whatever it is you women do when we take a break from the trail."

She laughed, and he saw the faint flush that colored her cheeks.

As he started to walk away, he turned. "I wouldn't mind if you'd make some of those biscuits, too. They're just about the best I've ever tasted. And I'll bring the rabbit."

With a light heart, Abby followed her aunt to the river.

By late afternoon, the weary band of travelers could hardly be called festive, but at least their spirits had lifted considerably. The women had bathed tired, aching bodies. Fresh clothes dried in the warm sun. The children had tied string to tree branches, and a bucket of fish was their reward. The men returned with deer and rabbits, and the scent of meat roasting over fires soon permeated the camp.

Violet rummaged through her trunk and donned a pale blue gown that nearly matched the color of her eyes. Her freshly washed hair gleamed silver in the sunlight. She added a bonnet with little blue ribbons, and, adding a drop of lilac water to her balm before rubbing it over her hands and feet, she stepped from the wagon.

At Violet's insistence, Abby was wearing a dress. Pale ivory, it was the perfect background for a cloud of freshly washed hair that spilled down her back in soft waves.

Rourke was leaning against a tree, drawing on a cigar. The rich aroma of tobacco swirled around him, causing Violet to smile. As she glanced at him, she realized that he hadn't yet noticed her. He had eyes only for Abby.

What a picture she made, he thought. The pristine gown suited her. It was buttoned clear to her throat, with only a hint of the soft, womanly curves beneath.

Her hair was the sort women would kill for. And men would die for.

"Oh." She dropped the kettle, sending water hissing among the flames, then lifted her burned hand to her mouth.

Instantly Rourke was at her side. He turned her palm up to examine the burn. "My God. Your hand is raw."

"That isn't from the fire. I did it pushing the wagons."

"You should have wrapped it." Turning, he called, "Violet, do you have some of that ointment?"

She nodded and hurried inside the wagon. A minute later, she emerged with the precious salve.

Rourke rubbed it into the raw, blistered flesh, then gently twisted a clean cloth around her palm, tying it at the wrist. When he was finished, he lifted her bandaged hand to his lips.

Abby felt the jolt as his lips touched her palm. Flustered, she tried to pull her hand away, but he continued holding it.

"You'll stay to supper, won't you, Mr. Rourke?" Violet didn't bother to hide her smile at her niece's confusion.

"He's already invited himself, Aunt Vi."

"Had to," Rourke said easily, still holding Abby's hand. "If I waited for Abby to invite me, I'd starve to death."

"Maybe that's what I had in mind," she said sweetly, pulling away.

"She doesn't mean that," Violet chirped happily, refilling the kettle with a dipper of water. "Abby isn't the kind of girl who could ever see anyone starve."

"Maybe in your case," Abby put in quickly, "I could make an exception."

Rourke winked at Violet as Abby twirled away and lifted a pan of biscuits. "I think you're right, ma'am. I don't think even a hardhearted woman like Abby could stand by and watch me starve."

"Just watch . . ."

Her words faded as Mordecai, accompanied by several strangers, approached their wagon.

"Miss Abby, Miss Violet, Rourke," Mordecai said, pulling his hat from his head. "I'd like you to meet Andrew McClelland. This is his land we're camped on."

Rourke and the stranger shook hands. As the man turned, Abby and Violet found themselves staring at a ruggedly handsome man, whose white hair was in sharp contrast to his deeply tanned face. Well over six and a half feet, he even towered over Rourke.

"These are my three sons, Frank, who is fifteen, Ian, who is seventeen, and Andy Junior, who is eighteen."

The three young men, all as tall as their father, promptly removed their hats and shook hands.

"And this is my daughter, Mary Rose, who is eleven."

Like her brothers, the girl was dressed in buckskins. Taller than Abby, she was nearly eye level with Violet. Pale yellow hair was pulled back beneath a broad-brimmed hat. Her eyes, like those of her father and brothers, were as blue as a summer sky. Her smile was at once shy and sweet. Her face had an open, honest quality about it.

"Mary Rose. What a beautiful name," Violet said, taking the girl's hand. "I had a sister named Rose. And another sister, Abby's mother, named Lily."

Rourke cocked an eyebrow at the surprising statement, then chanced a quick look at Abby. Except for a slight reddening of her cheeks, she gave no sign that Violet had revealed anything unusual. He made a mental note to be patient. Someday, if she trusted him enough, Abby would tell him what Violet meant. He had no right to intrude on her secrets.

"Mr. McClelland and his family have invited all of us to their ranch for supper," Mordecai explained.

"All of us?" Violet's eyes widened. "Mr. McClelland, we are too many to feed."

293

"When I saw the wagon train in the distance," he said casually, "I had the boys slaughter a calf. There's more than enough for everyone."

"Where is your ranch, Mr. McClelland?" Violet asked.

He moved beside her, and she felt dwarfed by his size. Touching her shoulder, he pointed and she followed his gaze. "Just over that ridge, there's a clearing. The ranch house is that first building."

"And the others?"

"Barn, bunkhouse, storage sheds."

Violet wondered if he knew what his touch was doing to her nerves. That big hand, so gentle on her shoulder, was causing the most uncomfortable feelings to stir inside her. She glanced up, and he gave her the most charming smile she had ever seen.

"We would be honored to take supper with you and your beautiful family, Mr. McClelland," Violet said.

"The honor is ours, ma'am." Pulling himself up into the saddle, he beamed at her. "I'll send Andy Junior, back with a wagon to pick you up." Touching a hand to his hat, he rode away, with his children following.

"Well." Violet touched a hand to her throat. "What a lovely surprise."

"We will assemble at the cook wagon," Mordecai said before walking away. "I suggest you be ready as soon as the wagon arrives."

"I believe I'll just freshen up," Violet said, climbing into the back of the wagon.

Seeing her aunt's flushed cheeks, Abby muttered, "I hope Aunt Vi isn't coming down with something."

"Why do you say that?" Rourke asked.

"I thought she looked a bit feverish." Abby glanced up to see Rourke grinning. "Didn't you notice?"

"I did. And I'd say the fever has nothing to do with sickness."

Abby swung away and began to bank the fire. "Sometimes, Rourke, you don't make any sense."

Behind her, Rourke continued to smile as he watched the figure in the back of the wagon running a comb through shining silver hair.

"Welcome to our highland ranch," Andrew McClelland called as the wagon loaded with all the members of the wagon train pulled up to the front door.

Andrew and his sturdy sons helped the women and children from the hay wagon, while his daughter, Mary Rose, invited them inside.

When he reached out his hands for Violet, Andrew lifted her as easily as if she weighed nothing at all. When he set her on her feet, his hands stayed a moment at her waist. "You smell as good as a meadow of fresh flowers, Violet," he whispered.

"Why, thank you, Mr. McClelland."

"Andrew," he corrected.

"Andrew." She tried the word and found she liked it. "You have a beautiful ranch, Andrew."

"Thank you." He waited until everyone had filed inside, then, seeing that they were alone, said, "You're only seeing a small portion of it tonight."

"There is more?"

"This is just our highland home. Before the snows come, we'll herd the cattle down to lower elevations, where the weather stays mild all winter."

"But where do you stay in the lowlands?"

"We have another ranch down there."

"And the land?" Violet glanced around at the towering pines, and far below, the rich, verdant valley. "How much land do you own?"

"All of it." He laughed. "As far as the eye can see in any direction. It's all McClelland land."

Violet couldn't even imagine it. "But how is this possible?"

"If we clear the land and work it, it becomes ours.

And all we have to do to stay here is battle the weather, the Indians, insects, and disease. And the loneliness."

"How could you ever be lonely with such a beautiful family around you?" she whispered.

He stared down into her eyes and read the loneliness there as well. "Mr. Stump told me you have no husband or children. My children fill a lot of lonely hours. But children aren't enough."

"What happened to your wife, Andrew?"

"She died when Mary Rose was born."

"You mean you've raised her all alone?"

He nodded. "The boys and I do our best for her. But the girl needs a woman's touch."

Violet glanced at the young girl who circulated among the guests beyond the open door. "I'd say you and your boys have done a fine job."

He put a hand beneath her elbow and led her up the steps. "Come inside, Violet. I hope you like my home."

Violet stared around at the rough-hewn walls of the log house. Like the man who lived here, the rooms were overlarge, with a huge fireplace made of stone. On the floor were woven Indian rugs. Along the wall were hung the hides of deer and bear. How could one room be so big and yet so cozy?

Several Indian women carried steaming dishes to the dining table, already groaning under the weight of trays of food.

From the kitchen, a small, bearded Chinese man carried a tray nearly as big as himself, laden with a side of beef. While the others watched, the man carved the beef into thick slabs. When he retreated to the kitchen, Andrew said, "Please, everyone. Help yourselves. Dinner is ready."

Needing no further invitation, the hungry guests filled their plates with precious beef, as well as potatoes, vegetables, freshly baked sourdough bread, and a variety of dishes no one had ever tasted before.

As Violet ate, seated beside Andrew, she shook her head in wonder. "I haven't seen this much food since our last Sunday school picnic. Was it really seven or eight months ago?"

Andrew chuckled. "The days blend together when you're on the trail, don't they?"

She nodded, then fell silent, thinking about the family and friends who lay buried, their graves marked only by flimsy wooden crosses.

Sensing her sadness, Andrew said, "We don't have a chance to entertain often, so the boys have asked if they could play for you."

Everyone looked up with interest. A few minutes later, while the travelers drank coffee laced with whiskey and polished off several rum cakes, Frank, Ian, and Andy began playing fiddles. Within minutes, the men and women, and even the children, were up dancing. Rourke hauled Abby to her feet, nearly spilling her coffee.

"Come on, lady. It's time you had another lesson in dancing."

Giggling, Abby held on while he whirled her around the floor.

"Dance with me, Violet," Andrew said, holding out his hand. A minute later, she felt his strong arms encircle her waist as he flawlessly led her in a waltz. Soon the music grew louder, and the dancers moved faster, until they had broken into several squares. Then, bowing and swaying, they began to follow the directions of Mordecai, who appointed himself caller.

"Bow to your partners."

Abby laughed as Rourke made a deep bow at the waist.

"Bow to your corner."

Abby lifted the hem of her gown and curtsied to Aaron Winters.

"Swing your partner."

Abby felt Rourke's strong arms lift her off the floor

as he spun her around and around. Oh, it was so wonderful. If only it could go on forever.

"Let's leave this to the others," Andrew said, mopping his brow before taking Violet's arm. Leading her from the room, he said, "How would you like to see the rest of the house while they're dancing?"

"I'd like that, Andrew."

Taking her hand, he led her to the kitchen. "This is Lee," Andrew said, introducing the Chinese cook. "And this is his wife, Anh."

Noting their shyness, Violet crossed the room and shook their hands. They seemed surprised at her boldness. No white woman had ever touched them before. If Andrew was surprised, he hid it. But he was fascinated with her reaction.

Turning toward the Indian women, who were clearing the table and returning empty serving trays to the kitchen, he said, "This is Wind Sighing in the Trees, and this is Melts the Snow."

Violet blessed the fact that Abby had dared bring an Indian to her wagon. More aware of their customs, she simply nodded and spoke a simple greeting to each.

"Wind Sighing in the Trees and Melts the Snow, I am pleased to meet you."

Both women blinked, nodded, then continued their chores. Andrew watched with obvious interest.

"In the back of the house are the bedrooms," he said, steering her in that direction before she could voice a protest.

It didn't seem proper to Violet to be given a tour of a gentleman's bedroom. But she didn't know quite how to stop it.

"The first room is mine," Andrew said, pausing barely long enough for Violet to inspect it. She had an impression of a huge room, with another stone fireplace, and a huge bed of rough-hewn timbers, covered with an enormous bearskin throw.

"This room is for the boys," Andrew said, indicating a large room with three bunks, also covered with hides.

"And this room belongs to Mary Rose." As Andrew opened the door, the girl looked up with a smile. "She asked me to bring you here before you left."

"She did?" Violet hesitantly entered, glancing around at the room that, though similar to the others, made of rough-sawn timber and with a rock fireplace, had feminine touches. On a table near the bed was a silver brush and comb. "Oh, how lovely," Violet said, running a hand over the pieces.

"They were my mother's," the girl said shyly.

"Then they are treasures. To be passed on to your children someday," Violet said softly.

From the doorway, Andrew watched and listened.

Spotting a book near the bedside, Violet glanced down at the open page. "The Bible. Oh, Mary Rose. Do you read it?"

The girl glanced down at the floor. "I try to. Dad taught me how to read. But sometimes I get stuck on the big words."

Picking up the book, Violet read the passage aloud. "'And the Lord said, "It is not good for man to be alone. I will fashion for him a helpmate."'"

The girl's eyes rounded. "You can read?"

Violet drew her close. "Yes, dear. I love to read."

"Would you read some more to me?"

Violet sat down on the edge of the bed and patted the space beside her. When Andrew finally turned away to see to his guests, two heads were bent in the lamplight, one reading, one listening raptly.

Andrew McClelland and his children stood in a single line at the door, saying good night to their guests. Once outside, they climbed into the big hay wagon, wrapping blankets about their shoulders to ward off the chill.

As Violet extended her hand, Andrew drew her

close. "I'd like to take you back to camp myself," he murmured.

For a moment, Violet thought her heart would leap clear out of her mouth. Not trusting her voice, she merely nodded. He hurried through the rest of the goodbyes, then went off in search of a warm wrap, calling, "Ian, hitch the rig."

From the open doorway, Violet watched as the wagon clattered off in the night. A short time later, Andrew led her to a small carriage and wrapped her in a fur throw.

"If you're not too tired, I'd like to take the long way back to camp," he said.

"I'm not at all tired," she assured him.

He flicked the reins, and the horse trotted off, circling the ranch house and the outbuildings.

"Why did you never marry, Violet? Did some man break your heart?"

She gave a soft sigh. "Nothing quite so romantic as that, I'm afraid. I was needed at home. The younger ones left, and one day I discovered that I was an old spinster."

Old. He was older than her by years, but he never thought of himself as old. "Do you believe in fate?" he asked.

Violet turned to him. "I believe in God," she said simply. "I believe that He directs our paths."

"I believe that too," Andrew said, dropping an arm around her to draw her closer. Letting the reins go slack, he brought his arms around her and turned her to him. "I believe He brought you here so that I could find you."

"Andrew, we've only known each other for a few hours."

"And I want to spend the rest of my life with you if you're willing."

"But you don't know me."

"I know that you are a selfless woman, who gave up a life of her own to care for others. I know that you like children, and even more important, they like you. I've never before seen Mary Rose take to someone the way she's taken to you." As Violet opened her mouth to protest, he added, "I know that you are not afraid of people who are different from you. You treated my Chinese cook and my Indian helpers with the same regard you give everyone else. And most important, I know that the first time I touched you, I felt a blaze of passion that I thought had died many years ago."

"Oh Andrew."

The midnight sky was awash with a million stars that looked so close, Violet wondered if she could reach out and touch one. On a night like this, she realized, nothing was impossible. This man, this wonderful, handsome, rugged man wanted her. And, wonder of wonders, she wanted him.

"Would you be willing to give up your dream of California and marry me?"

She knew she was crying, but she couldn't stop. Burying her face in his neck, she wept as though her heart would break. But it wasn't breaking. Maybe for the first time in her life, her heart was whole.

Alarmed, he drew her away and wiped her tears with his thumbs. "Violet. My sweet, sweet Violet. Have I said something to hurt you?"

"Andrew." She was laughing and crying, and then laughing again. The tears ran unchecked down her cheeks, but she ignored them. No longer would she be the silly, dreamy, useless dried-up old prune. How many years had she lived with those ugly labels?

She touched a finger to his furrowed brow, then traced his firm, strong mouth. He watched her, afraid to breathe, afraid to hope. He had lost her. His beautiful butterfly was about to fly away. Seeing his frown, she touched her lips to his.

"I love you, Andrew. I love you, and your family, and your beautiful land."

He went very still. He hadn't lost her. Yet. "And you'll stay? I know it's a lot to ask."

"Oh Andrew. I'll stay for as long as you want me. Until the end of the world, if it's possible."

"Violet. Oh God, my beautiful, wonderful Violet."

He drew her tightly against his chest and kissed her full on the mouth. For long moments, she held herself rigid, absorbing the shock of his kiss. Then, slowly, slowly, she felt herself opening to him. Bringing her arms around his neck, she allowed her fingers to twine in the thick hair at his nape.

His kiss gentled as he nibbled, then tugged at her lower lip. But as the fire spread, his kiss became more demanding. His hands moved beneath the fur throw, drawing her closer. And as his fingers encountered the warmth of her flesh, he moaned and lowered his mouth to her neck. She was warm. So warm. So soft. And he wanted to be easy and gentle with her.

Violet was a woman who understood life and love, men and women. Hadn't she encouraged her own sister and niece to follow their hearts? But she had never before experienced anything like this. In fact, she had never before experienced anything at all. Needs pulsed, making her by turn weak, then eager. Somewhere deep inside her was an aching sweetness, driving her to a boldness she had never dreamed of.

She sighed his name and cradled his head in her hands, arching her neck as his warm lips explored her throat, her collarbone, the soft swell of her breast. His lips, his fingertips, explored, aroused, until her body was a mass of nerve endings, begging to be touched.

Stepping from the carriage, he lifted her and held her against his chest. She clung to him, her breathing ragged, her heartbeat unsteady. With great tenderness, he spread the fur throw on a nest of soft boughs, then lay beside her. With reverence, he kissed her eyelids, her cheek, her ear, all the while murmuring words of endearment. And when at last they lay, flesh to flesh, he worshiped her body with kisses, with touches that left her breathless and aching for more. And when they came together, it was she who cried his name and drew him to her. They moved in an ageless rhythm, until needs drove them higher, then higher still.

Her lungs filled with the scent of evergreen and the warm, masculine scents that were alien to her until now. And she knew, with an aching sweetness, that she would love this man even beyond death.

He moaned and called her name, and felt her shudder as she reached the crest. And then he followed her, and felt himself filled with the sweetest fragrance of wildflowers. And he knew that for all time, the woman in his arms was his. She had been made for him alone.

He wrapped the fur around them, and they lay, locked in each other's arms, feeling themselves drifting above the earth. Wrapped in a cocoon of love, they slept.

Chapter Twenty-six

ABBY AWOKE AND shifted in her blankets. The morning chill seeped into the wagon, causing her to draw the blanket higher around her shoulders. In the dim light of near dawn, she glanced toward Violet's blanket. It was neatly rolled against the side of the wagon. Rubbing her eyes, Abby sat up quickly. Had she overslept? Was her aunt up already, tending to her morning chores?

Drawing on a shawl, Abby stepped down from the wagon and peered through the mist. No fire crackled. No coffee hissed and bubbled. There was no trace of Aunt Vi.

Alarmed, Abby hurried back inside the wagon and began rummaging about. Her aunt's clothes were all here, her beloved books. Dear God, what had happened to Violet?

Abby's thoughts slipped back to the night before. She had been alarmed when her aunt had agreed to stay on after the others left. But Rourke had found her fears amusing, saying there was nothing wrong with a woman of Violet's impeccable reputation being escorted home by a man like Andrew McClelland.

What if they had had an accident? What if their

carriage had overturned. They could be lying near death along the trail this very minute.

Flinging aside the shawl, Abby pulled on her boots and ran to the cook wagon. Pounding on the side of the wagon, she cried, "Mordecai. Rourke. Someone. Please get up. Something's happened to my aunt."

Rourke's head appeared in the open flap of canvas, his dark hair mussed, a scraggly stubble of beard darkening his chin. "What's wrong?"

"I don't know. My aunt is missing. Something must have happened. Hurry, please. We have to look for her."

Mordecai stepped down, carrying his rifle, and Abby could see a flurry of activity within the wagon. Soon all the men were moving about, saddling horses, checking weapons, and listening to her go over the night's activities while they worked.

". . . and I came back with the rest of you. Aunt Vi said Andrew McClelland would be bringing her home later."

At that, Mordecai looked up, then cast a sideways glance at Rourke. "Did Miss Violet seem uneasy about staying behind?"

"Uneasy?" Abby considered for a moment. "She seemed a bit—agitated. And I noticed high color about her cheeks. You remember, Rourke? I thought she might be coming down with a fever."

Rourke shot Mordecai a knowing look, then said softly, "I still say your aunt was just fine, Abby."

"But she may have taken sick at the McClelland ranch. Oh, dear God," she cried, clapping a hand to her mouth. "The cholera. What if she's . . ."

"Abby. You're making too much of this. I think you should wait until we've taken the time to look into this before giving your aunt up for dead."

"Why else would she stay away?"

The men glanced from one to another without a word. Whatever thoughts they had were kept secret

from the worried young woman who paced impatiently before them.

"I want to go after Aunt Vi now," Abby said firmly.

"Aye, lass," Mordecai said softly. "As soon as you
have your team hitched and ready to go, you and
Rourke can go in search of Miss Violet."

"The team hitched?"

"We've lingered too long here," Mordecai said,
glancing at the sky. "There's no time to waste. We
must get moving if we're to beat the snows. No matter
what, we leave in one hour."

"One hour?" Abby clutched Rourke's arm. "I'll
have the team hitched and ready in half that time.
Will you go with me to find my aunt?"

He nodded, and she spun away, nearly running in
her haste to be ready.

The other members of the wagon train were up and
loading their wagons as she ran through the camp.
Ignoring the need for food, she harnessed the mules
and hitched the team to the wagon. Just as she had
finished loading the wagon, she looked up at the
sound of carriage wheels clattering over the rocky
trail.

Many of the travelers paused in their morning
chores to look up at the approaching carriage. From
the cook wagon, Rourke and the others left their
duties to hurry to the Market wagon.

A wave of relief washed over Abby at the sight of
her aunt, bundled in a robe of fur.

"Aunt Vi. Oh I was so worried. Rourke and I were
just going out to look for you."

"I'm sorry, child, to have caused you even a moment's worry." Abby noted her aunt's high color and
glowing features, as she turned toward Andrew
McClelland. As their gazes met, Violet's eyes seemed
bluer, more intense. Then she turned once more to
her niece. "Andrew and I had hoped to be here the
moment you awoke. But we . . . were detained."

"Were you ill?"

"Ill?" Violet laughed, soft and low in her throat, and Abby was reminded of Carrie's youthful laughter. "Heavens no, child. I've never felt more wonderful, more alive."

Andrew McClelland stepped down from the carriage, then held out his hand for Violet. Flinging aside the fur throw, she allowed him to help her alight. For long moments he held her hand, then slowly released it. Spanning the short distance between them, Violet embraced her niece. Then, holding her a little away, Violet gripped Abby's shoulders and said softly, "Andrew and I have something to tell you."

Abby waited, staring into her aunt's eyes.

"He has asked me to stay here and be his wife."

"Wife? He . . . wants to marry you?" Shocked, Abby glanced beyond her aunt to the tall, handsome man who was hungrily staring at Violet as if she were a beautiful apparition who might at any moment evaporate into thin air.

"And I have agreed."

Abby's mouth dropped open. She was so stunned, no words came out. When at last she found her voice, she stammered, "But you don't know anything about him. He has children. Grown children. How do they feel about this?"

"We just came from his ranch, where we shared our news with them. They were delighted."

Abby's voice nearly broke. "Why, Aunt Vi? Why now? We're almost there. California. Pa's dream. How can you take this unknown stranger and his children; this barren land over Pa's dream?"

Very simply, Violet said, "Because it was never my dream. This was my dream, Abby. I always clung to the hope that someday a man like Andrew would walk into my life. He's everything I've ever wanted. Family. A home of my own." As Abby's mouth opened to protest, Violet said softly, "Child, he loves me. Imagine. Me. To him I'm beautiful, capable. Perfect. That's why I'm staying. I must. And someday, a man will make you forget everyone, everything that's gone before. When he does, Abby, don't let him walk away from you."

Abby shook her head, refusing to listen. "You can't mean this. Come with me, Aunt Vi. To California."

"I cannot. Stay here with me. With us. With Andrew's children. Andrew and I would both like that very much. We'll be a real family at last."

Abby looked stricken. "No. I have to go. The dream."

"It wasn't your dream, Abby. It was James's, after all. And he wasn't even your father."

Not her father? Rourke had a revelation of another piece of the puzzle that was Abby Market. He stowed it away for another time.

"It's my dream now." Abby couldn't even remember when the dream had become hers. At first, she had only come along because she'd been given no choice. But now the dream of California had become her own. She began to cry, softly, the tears running down her cheeks. "If you stay here with Andrew, I'll be alone."

"I've been alone all my life," Violet cried. "Surrounded by people, yet always alone. I never fit in anywhere, until now. With Andrew, I'll never feel alone again."

They were both crying now, and Rourke watched them cling, their tears dampening each other's shoulders. Then, at the wagon master's sharp command to head up the train, they slowly, slowly, peeled apart. He could almost see the blood spilling from their torn hearts.

"Know that I have always loved you, Abby. You seemed as much my child as Lily's."

"I know." Abby wiped her tears on the sleeve of her old shirt. "I love you too, Aunt Vi. I guess more than I loved anyone, except maybe Carrie."

Seeing the shocked, curious stares of the travelers,

Mordecai shouted once more for them to mount up and pull out. Reluctantly, the people moved away. Whips cracked, men swore at their teams, and the sound of wagon wheels crunched over the rocky ground.

When Violet's meager belongings had been removed, Abby climbed aboard the wagon and picked up the reins. "Be happy, Aunt Vi." Looking beyond her, she said very distinctly, "See that she's always happy, Andrew. My aunt deserves to be happy."

"I will, Abby. I love her more than my own life."

Abby straightened her shoulders and lifted her chin. She cracked the whip, and the team lurched forward.

Violet turned into Andrew's shoulder and began sobbing. Abby turned once, then, seeing her aunt's body shaking with sobs, twisted back and faced the trail ahead of her. The tears ran unchecked down her cheeks. She would not look back again. Never. Only forward.

From his position at the rear of the train, Rourke watched the scene play out and felt his own heart ache for Abby. How many people did she have to lose before she felt completely abandoned? How old was she? Seventeen? And on her own. What drove her? he wondered.

Urging his horse into a trot, he kept pace with the wagons. Tonight, he would have to take great pains to find some time to be with her. Especially on this first night. She shouldn't be alone.

All day Abby threw herself into the backbreaking labor of the trail. Whistling up teams, hitching and unhitching them as one wagon after another was hauled up one mountain trail and down another, she worked alongside the men. When they stopped for a meal, she ate without tasting. When someone handed her a cup of coffee, she drank without noticing that it scalded her tongue. And when at last they stopped for the day, having progressed more than four miles, she stared at the fading twilight, waiting for the darkness. Then she would allow the tears to spill, unclogging the lump in her throat. When no one was around to witness her weakness, she would give in to the grief that threatened to strangle her.

Mordecai kept a worried eye on the girl. From the beginning of this trip, she had been special to him. He took a kind of fierce pride in her accomplishments. Like a father watching over a daughter, he admired her independence while still wishing she would bend and accept his help.

It would be so easy to position her wagon directly behind the cook wagon. That way he would be able to keep an eye on her safety and see to it that she had enough to eat. But the girl was too intelligent for that. She would know that he was singling her out, and would resent it.

While he ate one of Parker's hurriedly concocted meals of dried meat and cold beans, he pondered a way to help Abby without hurting her pride. In the end, he decided that there was no clever way around it. He would have to risk offending her by offering his assistance.

Stopping by her wagon, he found her on her hands and knees, viciously scrubbing.

"Housecleaning, lass?"

She looked up and wiped a damp strand of hair from her eyes. "I thought, since it's my wagon now, I ought to begin by cleaning it."

"Aye." He watched for a few minutes, wondering how long she thought she could push herself beyond the limits. Clearing his throat, he said, "I stopped by to offer my help, lass."

Expecting an argument, he was surprised by her response. With a little smile, she said, "Thank you, Mordecai. I'm sure I'll need your help many times along the way. And when I do, it's nice to know I can go to you. But I'd like to make it on my own as much as possible."

"I see you've been giving this some thought, lass."

She nodded. "With no one to talk to, I have a lot of time to think."

"You will come to me when you need help?" Before she could respond, he added, "Do you have enough food?"

"Yes, thank you." Abby thought about the rabbit she had cooked. If she was frugal, there would be enough stew to last the week. If she was careful.

"All right, lass. I'll leave you to your work."

"Good night, Mordecai."

As he walked away, she bent to her scrubbing, ignoring the ache in her back. It was nothing compared with the ache in her heart.

Rourke watched Mordecai walk away and waited a few minutes longer before approaching. Adopting a casual air, he leaned a hip against the wagon wheel and watched while Abby worked.

"Evening, Abby." He liked the way the sweat glistened on her upper lip. In fact, he liked everything about her upper lip. And her lower.

"Evening." She scrubbed at a spot so hard he thought she might scrub clear through the floorboards.

"I did some scouting after supper. The trail looks a little easier tomorrow." God, he wished she wouldn't wiggle her rump around like that while she worked. It was driving him mad.

"That's good." She moved her blanket and scrubbed the corner of the wagon.

"How is your food holding up?" From where he was standing, he could see the shadowy cleft between her breasts. He felt as though a fist had slammed into his gut. He held a match to the tip of a cigar and pretended to study a stream of smoke curling above his head.

"Fine. I cooked a rabbit tonight. Carrie used to love

my rabbit stew." Her words trailed off as she became lost in thought and felt the lump in her throat start to grow.

He swore under his breath. Why had they all abandoned her? "Maybe I'll find time to hunt tomorrow. If I do, I'll bring you something."

She lifted a callused hand to her brow, then bent once more to her scrubbing. "Don't go hunting on my account, Rourke. I'll be just fine."

He felt like shaking her, and didn't know why. "I know you will."

"You don't believe that."

He glanced up sharply. "What do you mean by that?"

"You don't think I'll do fine at all. You and Mordecai and the others. You're all waiting for me to curl up and die, aren't you?"

Rourke ground the cigar under his heel. "What the hell are you talking about?"

"I know what you think." Frustrated, Abby tossed the wet rag and watched it drop in a soggy heap on the far side of the canvas. She jumped down from the wagon. With her hands on her hips she faced him. "You think I was a fool not to stay with my aunt and Andrew McClelland, where I could have lived on his big, fancy ranch. I could have worn pretty dresses and had servants to cook and clean for me. No more trail. No more working until I drop." Her tone grew more strident. "No more hard times." With narrowed eyes, she said, "You think I can't possibly make it on my own."

Rourke's voice was deadly calm. "Is that the argument you've been having with yourself all day?"

She looked thunderstruck. "Of course not." Tossing her head, she clasped her hands, nervously twisting her fingers. "Well, I mean, I thought of it. But I knew it wouldn't be right for me. If that was Aunt Vi's dream, she can have it. But my dream is still to make it to California."

312

"That's a pretty big dream for such a little woman. And if you don't?" he asked softly. "Can you settle for a lesser dream?"

Her eyes flashed. "There you go again. Doubting me. I know you think I'll never make it."

"Lady, you don't have any idea what I'm thinking," he growled.

Abby started to say something, but her lips quivered and the tears brimmed in her eyes before she could stop them. Embarrassed, she tried to turn away, but Rourke caught her and drew her close. The action was so tender, so unexpected, she felt herself crumpling against him. With her arms wound around his neck, she began to cry. Once the tears started, it was as if a floodgate had been opened. With racking sobs, Abby buried her face against his throat and wept until there were no tears left.

Holding her like this was the sweetest torment he'd ever known. While she cried, he was achingly aware of her breasts flattened against his chest, her thighs molded to his. She was so small, so slender. She fit so perfectly in his arms.

Handing her his handkerchief, Rourke waited while she blew her nose and wiped her eyes. Then, before she had a chance to argue, he grabbed her up in his arms, carried her inside her wagon, and deposited her on a nest of blankets.

"What you need is sleep," he said, drawing a blanket around her shoulders. "You've pushed yourself beyond the limits, Abby. By morning, you'll feel better."

"I feel fine." She sniffed.

"Yeah. And you look fine too." Lifting her hand, palm up, he examined the raw flesh. "My God, look at you. You can't keep this up. These hands will never heal unless you give them a chance."

"Stop bullying me." Snatching her hand away, she scowled at him.

He glared back at her, then let out a long stream of

breath. "You want me to stop? All right. I intend to. You want to be left alone? You can have your wish. Right now."

As he turned away, Abby felt a moment of terror and clutched at his sleeve. Turning back, he studied her for long, silent moments.

The tears were very close to the surface, and she was afraid she was going to embarrass herself by crying again. Swallowing down the lump she whispered, "I'll be just fine, Rourke." She licked her lips. "But would you mind very much staying awhile longer? Just until I fall asleep?"

Would he mind? He had to fight the urge to crush her in his arms and love her until the morning sun broke through. If he could, he would kiss away every hurt, every ache, every pain. Instead, he sat down beside her and tucked the blanket up to her chin. A wisp of her hair brushed the back of his hand, sending shock waves through his system. God, she was so damned innocent, so vulnerable.

"I was hoping I wouldn't have to go back to the cook wagon tonight," he said, forcing his voice to remain casual. "Parker snores like a bear."

Her trembling lips curved into a half smile. "Are you sure?"

He nodded. "Yeah. You get some sleep. I'll just sit here and keep watch."

Taking a fresh cigar from his pocket, he struck a match until the tip glowed, then blew it out. He was glad for the darkness. His hand wasn't quite steady. Swearing, he decided that he'd better not look at the shadowy profile of the woman beside him. It would be a whole lot safer to concentrate on the sky, the mountain peaks in the distance, the weather. Anything but Abby.

Beside him, the object of his concern fell into an exhausted sleep.

Chapter Twenty-seven

AS THE GRUELING days wore on, Abby's sense of loss diminished. Thrust into the business of surviving the harshest part of their journey, she found little time for grief.

The Sierras had seemed impenetrable. But mile by painful mile, the determined travelers were making progress. If the snows held off, they were convinced they would soon see California.

Though they prayed for good weather, the lack of snow made it impossible to track game. In this rocky wilderness, blessed with icy water trickling down the mountainsides, they found they had to ration food. The meat and broth from a single rabbit, doled out to each member of the train, proved inadequate to keep up strength. It became necessary to slaughter their first ox.

Evelyn Coulter and Aaron Winters combined their two teams and offered to sacrifice one of their oxen. The meat, apportioned to each wagon, brought no sense of celebration. Instead, the travelers gave in to the nagging fear that this could be the first of many sacrifices. How could they survive without teams to haul their goods?

They would walk, Mordecai assured them, rather than starve to death.

"Your animals must serve whatever purpose is necessary," he said, his burr becoming more pronounced. "And if it is necessary to slaughter them in order to survive, then we willna' hesitate to do so."

Conversation during supper that evening was muted. Even the children seemed strangely subdued.

Feeling the bite in the air, Abby glanced skyward as she went about her evening chores. Please God, she prayed. Not yet. Not until we cross the Sierras.

Pausing, she studied the yellow aspens lining the hills around the camp. Autumn had come while they weren't looking. And behind it would come the howling winds of winter.

Because it was so cold, she kept her boots on and rolled herself into her blankets. Blowing out the lantern, she cradled her head on her hands and willed her muscles to relax.

After that first night, when Rourke had eased her fears and kept watch while she slept, she had forced herself to accept the fact that she would have to learn to live alone. By working until she dropped, she discovered that it was possible to fall asleep instantly. But often she awoke in the middle of the night and was seized by an almost paralyzing fear. Recalling old Bible verses that Aunt Vi had often read aloud, Abby found she was able to hold the fears at bay. Gradually, repeating the comforting words over and over, she would drift back to sleep. It gave her a measure of satisfaction to know that she had faced her demons alone. And though she was certain they would return, she was equally certain that she would find the strength to fight them again and again.

Abby awoke to a dazzling snowfall. As she opened the flap of canvas, the sun's reflection nearly blinded her. For one brief moment, she could only savor the beauty of it. The land looked softer somehow. Lines and ridges were filled and rounded. Trees and rocks wore caps of glistening snow. All of nature's sounds were muted and muffled. The craggy peaks were no longer harsh and forbidding, but softened. The pristine beauty of it made her heart quicken.

Even as she enjoyed the sight, she realized the danger. Wagon wheels would be mired in snow. The mules and oxen would have to work even harder. Walking would be painful. There was the chance of frostbite. But they dared not stop now. The next snowfall could be a blizzard.

"Abby."

She glanced up at the sound of Rourke's voice.

"Mordecai will be hitching double teams to each wagon to make it through the snow. It could be an hour or more before they can get to yours. Would you care to join me in a hunt?"

Her smile was radiant. There was something good about the snow after all. It would be easy to track game.

"I'll just be a minute."

She checked her gun and rifle, then rummaged around for rags to tie about her feet and ankles before pulling on her boots. Slipping on a buckskin jacket and crushing her old hat on her head, she climbed from the wagon and untied her horse.

"Which direction?" she asked.

Rourke pointed to a shelf of rocks that rimmed the canyon. "I spotted tracks heading up there."

He wheeled his horse and led the way while Abby followed.

It felt good to be away from the train. It had been too long, Abby thought. Besides, she was glad to have the chance to be alone with Rourke. Every waking minute lately had been spent pushing and shoving the wagons across these hateful mountains. Some days, the only thing that kept her going was the thought of a lush, green valley, filled with ripe fruit and fat, sleek cattle.

And then what? she wondered. Would Rourke leave and go back to doing whatever it was he did before he joined the train?

She studied his broad shoulders as he paused to gauge the animal's tracks. How strong he was. How safe she felt whenever he held her. Safe and yet —unsafe. He would never harm her. Of that she was certain. But each time she allowed him to touch her, she felt as if she were losing a part of herself. A part of her hard-won independence. Sometimes she was almost overcome with a desire to forget the dream, forget California, forget everything, and just lie in his arms forever. What would it be like, she wondered, to lie together and love? Was it wicked to have such thoughts?

He turned and motioned for her, and her fantasies fled.

"A second set of tracks. Deer. At least two of them. They're heading up there." He pointed, and Abby shielded her eyes from the sun and followed the direction of his hand.

"It could take longer than I thought. Want to go back to camp, or stay with me?"

"I'll stay with you." She hoped her tone didn't sound too eager.

"If this snow gets much deeper up ahead, we may have to leave the horses and proceed on foot."

Without waiting for her response, he nudged his mount forward. Abby followed, absently watching the way the sunlight glistened on his dark hair. He'd been so patient with her, so kind, especially since Aunt Vi left. Maybe that was another reason why she loved him so.

Loved him! Stunned at the direction of her thoughts, she reined in her horse and stared at Rourke's back. When did she fall in love with him? She couldn't remember. Was it the first time she saw him, leaning against that tree beside the stream in

Independence? Was it the day on the plains when he'd shown her the herds of buffalo? Or the night he'd danced with her in the shadows?

She didn't know. She only knew she loved him. Loved him desperately. And in her ignorance, she didn't know how to show him.

Fool, she berated herself. Silly damned fool.

"What's keeping you?"

Abby started at the sound of his voice. Digging in her heels, she urged her horse forward. "Nothing. Just looking around."

"Keep up. I can't afford to lose you up here."

You aren't going to lose me, Rourke, she thought, feeling a well of laughter bubbling up inside. I'm not going to let you lose me. I'm going to let you find me. If I can just figure out how to do it.

They followed the deer tracks higher and higher, until they could see clear across the mountain range.

"Look," Rourke said, pointing to the far horizon. "There's your dream, Abby. That's California."

Her eyes widened and she stared at the point of land barely visible beyond the mountain range.

"So close?"

Rourke nodded. "Five, maybe six days away at the most."

Five or six days. In less than a week, they would reach the promised land.

"That's the Sacramento Valley," Rourke said.

Abby's heart leaped to her throat. Was it possible? Had they really come clear across the country?

"Come on. We'll see it a lot clearer in a few days." He urged his horse along, and Abby followed.

At last reining in his mount, Rourke slid from the saddle. Abby did the same.

"We'll have to go on foot from here," he whispered. "If those deer are in these rocks, we have to stay downwind of them."

Clutching her rifle, Abby scrambled up rocks and slid down ridges, staying as close to Rourke as possible.

"There." He pointed and they both ducked behind a boulder.

Abby watched as Rourke took aim. Beside him, she studied the animals, ready to fire off a shot if he missed. Before he could shoot, they heard a rumble echo across the mountains. Frightened, the deer bolted.

Rourke and Abby stared around in confusion.

"Thunder?" Abby asked.

Rourke's eyes narrowed. "Gunfire."

He began running. Without questioning him, Abby dogged his tracks, until, their lungs straining in the thin air, they came to their horses.

While the horses picked their way among the rocks on the downhill trail, Abby and Rourke strained to see. There was nothing but ridges, and boulders, and cliffs blocking their view.

When at last they came to a clearing, they were stunned at the sight that greeted them. Below, in the camp, black smoke billowed from burning wagons. The acrid odor drifted to them on the breeze. Abby heard a sound and couldn't tell if it was a moan or the sigh of the wind.

Spurring his horse, Rourke cocked his rifle and yelled, "Stay here."

"I'm going with you."

His horse was running, but he managed to turn. "I don't want you hurt."

She hesitated, torn between wanting to do what Rourke asked and wanting to help if she could. These people were her friends. And more. They were all the family she had left. She had to go to their aid. Digging in her heels, she urged her horse into a run.

Holding the reins firmly, Abby forced her mount through the black smoke at the head of the train. It wasn't until she was on the other side of the wagons, past the smoke, that she realized she was face-to-face with a band of Indians. While she looked on helplessly, four of them wrestled Rourke to the ground. When she saw one of the Indians raise a knife as if to plunge it into Rourke's throat, she fired. The Indian slumped to the ground. Instantly two braves leaped at her, hauling her roughly to the ground. Enraged, Rourke leaped into their midst, shielding Abby with his own body. Several more braves attacked them, yanking Abby from his arms. Her buckskin jacket fell to the ground. As she was dragged away, her hat was knocked from her head and her hair tumbled about her face and shoulders.

While three Indians held a kicking, fighting Rourke, pinning him to the ground, the others stared at Abby in amazement. Who was this white woman, with hair like flame, dressed in men's clothes?

One of the braves, shouting to the others, walked up to her and grabbed a handful of her hair. When he tugged on it, she slapped his hand. The others roared with laughter.

Angry, the brave slapped her back, then pulled on her hair again. With tears stinging her eyes, she kicked at him. Immediately he brought an arm around her throat, nearly choking her. As she scratched and bit, he tossed her to a second brave. The second one began making fun of her britches, then tore at the front of her shirt. When she tried to run, he caught her, then tossed her to a third brave, who ripped her shirt from her. She was indeed a woman, they laughed, pointing to her breasts. Wearing only a pale, ivory chemise, trimmed with ribbon and lace, Abby crossed her arms in front of herself and tried to evade their hands as they reached for her and tossed her back and forth in a circle.

Enraged, Rourke struggled with his captors until he felt the cold steel blade of a knife bite into his throat. Then he was forced to endure the agony of watching the woman he loved being tormented by savages.

The woman he loved. Rourke fought an overwhelming sense of despair. Why had he waited so long to admit his feelings? Now, when it was too late to tell her, he could finally admit what he had been fighting from the moment he first saw her. He loved her. Loved her as he had never loved any woman. And his punishment would be to watch as she was brutalized and killed. It was the cruelest irony.

At the loud voice of command, the Indians looked up from their sport. The command was repeated. Immediately the braves holding Abby released her.

Her britches had been cut away, leaving her only the cover afforded by the flimsy cotton chemise. She stood up from the dirt, clutching the torn fabric about her.

"Fire woman."

At the sound of that name, she stared unbelieving at the brave astride the Indian pony. His face was garishly covered with war paint.

She continued to stare in horrified fascination. "Two Shadows?"

He urged his horse closer. At a low tone of command, the Indians holding Rourke released him and moved away. Free, Rourke stood, keeping his gaze firmly on Two Shadows.

"What have you done?" Abby cried, glancing around at the death and destruction.

"Your people brought death to my people," he said simply.

"Death?" She shook her head in weariness. "I don't understand."

"Understand this." He brought his horse nearer, until he could stare down into her face. "The kindness of you and the white-haired woman gave me back my life. The sickness that your people carried was carried back to my people through me."

"Cholera." Abby glanced at Rourke and felt tears spring to her eyes. "Oh, Two Shadows, I never dreamed I would be the cause of all this pain." She spread her hands. "We didn't know we carried that sickness. It killed many of our people too."

"Many more of my people," he said softly. "The sickness killed my father, the chief. I am now chief."

"And you came here to avenge your father's death?"

Two Shadows stared down at her without emotion. He leaned from his pony and caught a handful of her hair, pulling her close. For a moment he inhaled the woman scent of her, mingled with the undeniable scent of fear. "You would make a fine squaw for a Cheyenne chief."

From his position, Rourke stiffened and instinctively reached toward his empty holster.

Two Shadows watched the fiery strands sift through his fingers. "Because of your goodness, you and this man will be spared. But do not pass through Cheyenne territory again. There is no more debt between us."

He spoke rapidly to the others, and Abby and Rourke watched in silence as the braves gathered up their ponies and their dead and rode away.

When the last of the Indians disappeared into the woods, they turned toward the scene of the massacre.

As flames continued to devour wood and canvas, sending black, acrid smoke skyward, Abby and Rourke were left with the overwhelming task of searching among the charred ruins for survivors.

Chapter Twenty-eight

THERE WERE NONE.

Not a single survivor. The Cheyenne had been very thorough. Their revenge was complete.

Evelyn Coulter's body was huddled atop little Jenny's. Both throats had been cut.

Aaron Winters, alongside Evelyn's wagon, died with his arms outstretched. Nearby, looking as if they had been wrenched from his arms, his son and daughter lay in a twisted heap.

Little Jonathon Peel had died holding a rifle nearly as big as he was. Beside him, his mother Doralyn lay face up, her sightless eyes staring at the heavens.

Choking back sobs, Abby followed Rourke from one wagon to the next, from one bloody scene of destruction to one even worse. Jed Garner had died alone, defending his wagon and team. Perhaps, Abby thought as she stared at his blood-soaked body, Nancy had chosen the better part of the bargain by staying with the crazed, desperate people in the foothills of the Sierras.

Beside the cook wagon, Parker lay with a butcher knife still in his hand. Behind the wagon, Mordecai, clutching his walking stick, lay in a pool of his own congealed blood.

"In my mind, he had become my father," Abby whispered between sobs. "I thought it would be so wonderful to have a father like Mordecai Stump. He was all the things I admired in a man."

Lying beside him was Thompson, his rifle still clutched in a death grip.

A sob was wrenched from Abby's lips. "He died defending Mordecai. Oh Rourke, he gave his life for his friend." Kneeling, she whispered, "You finally made it up to him, didn't you, Big Jack?"

Rourke couldn't speak. The rage that he had experienced earlier was replaced with a numbness as he went about cataloging the dead.

Throughout the afternoon, he and Abby dug into the frozen ground with picks and shovels, determined to bury each family in a separate grave. It was what Abby wanted. And though a common grave would have been simpler, he feared that she was near the breaking point. No matter how difficult the job, it was better than letting the grief overwhelm her. As long as she worked, she wouldn't have time to contemplate what had really happened here.

Maybe it was what he needed as well. There had been too much killing, too much death.

By evening, the mounds were marked with crude crosses, made from charred pieces of wagons. In all, there were five family graves, containing thirteen bodies, and separate graves for Mordecai, Thompson, and Parker.

The Indians had not spared the livestock. Twenty-three oxen and eight mules had been slaughtered, along with two milk cows, a brood cow, and calf, and three goats. Even the horses had been killed. To ensure that they wouldn't be eaten, the braves had burned the carcasses. The Indians had taken no chance that the white man's sickness would be allowed to spread.

When darkness cloaked the land, Rourke took a blanket from behind his saddle. Huddled in the shelter of a rock, he built a fire with the charred remains of the wagons. Drawing an exhausted Abby into his arms, he held her until the trembling stopped and she fell into a restless sleep. With his back against the wall of rock, he placed his gun carefully beside his right hand, then, for the first time in hours, allowed himself to rest.

At dawn they left the place of death. Abby wore one of Rourke's shirts and his old Union army pants, tied at her waist with a piece of rope. She'd managed to salvage her torn buckskin jacket and dirty cap from the dirt. Except for Rourke's bedroll and meager supplies which were always tied behind his saddle, they had nothing. Fire had destroyed everything.

A light snow had started during the night. By morning, the snowfall had become thicker, with no break in sight.

Pausing on the crest of a hill, they looked back. Smoke still drifted from several charred wagons. But already the mounds of earth marking the graves were being covered by a blanket of white. If the snow continued for another day, there would be no trace of the carnage.

"All those hopes and dreams," Abby whispered.

Glancing away from the despair in her eyes, Rourke nudged his horse into a trot. "Come on. We're going to have to keep moving if we hope to beat this blizzard."

They rode for hours, hoping to put as many miles as possible between themselves and the snow. Instead, they seemed to be heading deeper into it. The horses, picking their way between rocks and crevices, often lost their footing and slipped. Finally, Rourke and Abby were forced to plod on foot, leading their exhausted mounts.

When the snow became too deep, they took shelter in a cave. While Abby rubbed down their horses, Rourke went in search of firewood. Dragging a small pine through the opening, Rourke chopped it into small pieces and soon had a roaring fire going. Setting his blackened pot over the fire, he melted snow and added some precious coffee. Filling two cups, he turned to offer one to Abby. She was slumped against her saddle, sound asleep.

He covered her with his blanket and knelt beside her for long minutes, watching her while she slept. If it were possible, he would absorb all her pain and suffering. If it were possible, he would spare her all that they had yet to endure. If it were possible . . .

He sat down beside her, with his back against his saddle, and drank the steaming coffee, feeling the warmth envelop him. Though he struggled to stay awake, his body betrayed him. He, too, fell into an exhausted sleep. The fire slowly burned to embers. And outside, the wind howled and the snow continued to fall, covering the Sierras with the first real blizzard of the season.

Sometime in the night, Abby awoke. Confused, she stared around the darkened cave. Except for the red glow of ashes, the cave was completely black. A horse stomped and she jumped in alarm, then turned to stare at the darkened shadows of the two horses at the rear of the cave. As her eyes grew accustomed to the darkness, she could make out the figure of Rourke nearby, lying with his head resting on his saddle.

Outside the wind sighed and moaned and Abby shivered and drew the blanket around her. She noticed that Rourke had hung his saddle blanket over the mouth of the cave to keep the wind from blowing in. Though the ashes from the fire still gave off some warmth, the cave would soon be as cold as the snows that lay outside their door.

Spotting a pile of pine branches, Abby threw several on the ashes and watched as they leaped into flame, casting wild shadows on the walls of the cave.

Somewhere in the darkness a tree split and crashed

to the ground. Hearing it, Abby nervously pulled her saddle beside Rourke's and spread her blanket over both of them. Lying very close to him, she tried to convince herself she wasn't afraid. Even though he was asleep, Rourke was here. He wouldn't let anything happen to her. He sighed in his sleep and rolled over, flinging an arm across her hips. She lay very still, afraid to move, afraid even to breathe. As his slow, steady breathing continued, she began to relax. It wasn't wicked to lie so close beside him. It was necessary for survival. But she was so achingly aware of him. Aware of the strength of the arm that lay, loose and relaxed, across her body. Aware of the faint scent of tobacco on the breath that mingled with her own. Aware of the warmth of his body, and the musky, male scent that was his alone. Lying this close to him, she knew she would never be able to fall back to sleep. But gradually the sighing of the wind and the steady rhythm of his heartbeat lulled her. She drifted into a gentle, dreamless sleep.

As the first streak of gray light pierced the cave, Rourke began to awaken. Despite the wind keening down the mountains, he was warm. His arm encircled a slender waist and his palm was open against warm flesh. He came fully awake and opened his eyes. Abby was asleep in his arms. She was facing him, her eyes closed, her breathing slow and steady. Sometime during the night his hand had found its way under her chemise. The skin of her back was the softest he'd ever felt. He studied the spill of fiery hair across the saddle. She was so incredibly beautiful.

Needs pulsed through him and he toyed with the idea of kissing her awake. She would be warm, and willing. Utterly defenseless.

He had no right. He, of all people, knew better. Cursing himself, he stood and pulled on his boots. Drinking the last of the lukewarm coffee, he threw several logs on the ashes and fanned them until the flame started. Then, picking up his rifle, he led his horse from the cave.

Beneath the warm blanket, Abby yawned and stretched. A log crackled and hissed on the fire, and she sat up, hugging her knees to her chest. The wind shrieked and Abby glanced at the naked entrance to the cave. Except for a few tree branches, it was exposed to the elements. Where was Rourke's saddle blanket?

She stared around. He was gone. And so was his horse. Leaping to her feet, she ran to the mouth of the cave and peered into the swirling snow. There were no footprints. No sign of a horse or rider. How long would it have taken to obliterate his tracks?

She returned to the fire. The logs had burned clear through. How long ago had Rourke placed them on the embers? An hour ago? Two? Long enough to be miles from here. Long enough to put some distance between them so he would no longer have to be responsible for her.

He'd gone. Rourke had left her. Left her just like all the others. Carrie. Aunt Vi. Pa. Even Lily, her real mother, had left her at birth to fend for herself. Everyone on the train was gone. And now Rourke.

She couldn't stop the tears that sprang to her eyes. Viciously she wiped them away with the back of her hand. No more tears. She wouldn't cry for them. Any of them. Especially Rourke. He hadn't wanted to be stuck with her in the first place. And now he was rid of her for good. He didn't deserve her tears. None of them did. But try as she might, she couldn't stop crying. Tears flowed down her cheeks, dampening the collar of her shirt. Rourke's shirt, she thought, causing another stream of tears. It was the only thing of him that she had left. A torn shirt, and ragged pants. And a few memories.

Listlessly she began to saddle her horse. She had two choices. Stay here and starve to death or face the bitter snow and take her chances on freezing to death. She might get turned around in the mountains and go the wrong way. She might slip and fall into a crevice and never be found. But if there was the smallest chance that she could find her way through this maze and reach California, she had to take it.

As she led her horse from the cave, she was blasted by icy needles of snow-laden wind. Drawing her hat low on her head, she pulled herself into the saddle. Wrapping the reins around her wrist, she dug her hands deep into the sleeves of the buckskin. There was no escape from the cold. It wrapped itself around her, whipping her hair into wild tangles, flaying her cheeks until they were numb.

The horse, balking at the deep drifts, had to be whipped to keep going. With every step he stumbled, until at last, too weary to go on, he stood with head bowed, ignoring the whip and the curses hurled at him.

For long minutes Abby sat, buffeted by the snow and ice, until, defeated, she slid from the saddle. The snow reached nearly to her knees, making it impossible to walk. The swirling flakes blinded her. Which direction would Rourke have taken? Which way was she headed? Which way was the cave?

Above the howling wind, a shot rang out. Clutching her horse's neck, Abby shouted at the top of her lungs. But the words were whipped from her mouth and carried away on the wind. With frozen fingers she reached up to the saddle and removed her rifle. Aiming it skyward, she fired. The sound rumbled across the canyons, bouncing off mountain peaks, then disappeared into the wind. She waited, peering through the swirling snow. All she could see was a blinding whiteness. When she could bear it no longer, she fired again, and listened with sinking heart as the reverberations echoed across the mountain.

Her horse lifted his head and whinnied and Abby strained to see what he had heard. A shadowy form appeared in the swirling storm, and Abby, despite her trembling, aimed her rifle.

"Abby? Abby is it you?" A horse and rider emerged from the storm.

"Rourke? Oh, Rourke is that really you?"

Strong arms lifted her, pulling her close against him. Her teeth were chattering so badly she could barely get the words out. "You left me. Why did you leave me?"

He swore, loudly, viciously. Cradling her against his chest, he grabbed the reins of her horse, forcing him to follow. It took them nearly an hour to cross the few hundred yards that separated them from the cave. Once inside Rourke set her down and hurried to throw new logs on the fire. While he worked he unleashed a torrent of rage.

"Damned little fool. Rushing out in a blizzard. You could have gotten yourself killed."

"And what would you care?" she hissed, throwing off the blanket. "You couldn't wait to get rid of me, could you?"

"What the hell are you talking about?" Whirling, he faced her.

"I'm talking about the way you sneaked out of here while I was sleeping." She brought her hands to her hips, looking as fierce as any wildcat. "I woke up and you were gone without a trace."

"I was out hunting," he said, his voice dangerously low.

"You sneaked off, without telling me, and you expect me to believe you were hunting?" Her eyes blazed; her nostrils flared.

Rourke muttered a stream of oaths. "You were sleeping. I didn't want to wake you. I figured I'd be back before you even knew I was gone."

"Stop lying. You were leaving me," she shouted. "Just like all the others. You were going to leave me in this cave all alone."

Like all the others. So that was it. Hearing the pain

331

in her words, Rourke felt his anger drain away. She was afraid. Not angry, just afraid. How many times in her young life had she been abandoned? Attempting to soothe, he said softly, "I'm sorry, Abby. Sometimes I forget you're just a kid. You were scared, weren't you?"

"I wasn't scared. I was mad. And don't call me a kid," she bellowed.

At the sight of her, Rourke threw back his head and began to laugh. It was such a relief to be able to laugh again. "My God, look at you. Little spitfire. I was right. You reacted just like a little brat, running off into the storm before you even took the time to think things through."

"You take that back." In pain and frustration, Abby attacked him, pounding him about the head and chest with her fists.

Catching both her hands easily in one of his, he looked down at her, still laughing. "See what I mean? A little tomboy who can't even admit when she's wrong."

Stung by his words, Abby kicked him in the knee. Shocked, he let go of her hands. She immediately began attacking him again. In defense, he grabbed her hands, twisting them behind her back, then pulled her roughly against him.

"Goddamned little hellion. Settle down before I . . ."

"Before you what?" Her breath was hot against his cheek. "Leave me again?"

"I told you I wasn't leaving you. That deer in the corner ought to convince you."

She swiveled her head. Abby's expression changed from anger to stunned surprise, and then to the sudden knowledge that this had all been a terrible misunderstanding.

"You bagged a deer? You were hunting? You really weren't leaving me?"

Rourke let out a slow hiss of anger. "If you hadn't behaved like such a damned little fool, you could have spared us a lot of trouble."

Trouble? He'd been furious when he'd found her gone. And terrified, if he wanted to be honest. To have come through so much together, and then to lose her. He couldn't bear it. Like a wild man, he'd rushed out into the blinding snow with no idea where to go, how to find her.

But now she was here, frightened, cold, furious, but safe. Back in his arms, where he could reassure himself of her safety.

Though he continued to hold her firmly against him, she felt the slight change in pressure in the hands holding hers.

"I'm sick and tired of having you call me a little fool."

She saw something flicker in his eyes and felt a moment of fear. Then, as he continued holding her, the fear turned to something new, something that exhilarated yet still frightened her.

"If you don't want to be called a fool," he muttered, his voice suddenly low and husky, "don't act like one."

He drew her perceptibly closer, and a little thrill raced along her spine.

"Rourke, I . . ."

"Don't say another word," he murmured, brushing his lips over hers.

Heat, liquid, golden heat flowed through her, leaving her flushed and breathless.

He'd had no other plan than to hold her. There was no passion, no rush of desire. All he wanted was to keep her close, to share his warmth until he felt her flesh heat, her trembling still.

He took the kiss deeper, savoring the sweet, wild taste of her lips, her mouth, her tongue. He couldn't have enough of her taste. There would never be enough of her. Plunging his hands into her hair, he tipped her head back and plundered her mouth, filling himself with her.

As he lifted his lips, he heard her little sigh of pleasure.

"I'm sorry about all this, Abby. I didn't want to wake you this morning. You were sleeping so peaceful-ly. But I should have realized you'd react like a scared little kid if you found me gone."

"Kid." He saw the temper return to her eyes. "There you go again. Stop calling me that. I'm a woman, dammit." Clutching the front of his shirt, she pulled him close. "And I want you to treat me like one."

His eyes narrowed. Staring down at her, he mut-tered, "I don't think you know what you're saying."

"Yes I do," she whispered, bringing her arms around his neck and drawing him even closer. "Oh yes I do."

He took a step backward, staring at her as if he couldn't believe what he'd heard. Touching a hand to her cheek for long moments, he stared down into her eyes, as if trying to read her mind. He had promised himself that she would have to make the first move. But now, as he watched her eyes soften, felt her body press closer into his, he was thunderstruck.

Slowly, slowly, his arms came around her, drawing her close, pinning her to the length of him. His mouth covered hers in a hot, hungry kiss.

He wanted to drown in her kisses. She was sweet. So sweet. Yet there was something new in her kiss. Something bold. There was a giving, a taking, that he had never sensed in her until this moment.

Abby felt as if her very breath was being taken from her. And still he lingered over the kiss, as if worship-ing her mouth. She sighed and felt herself filling with him, his taste, his breath, his tongue, moving with hers, daring her to explore his mouth as he was exploring hers.

Tentatively, she followed his example, and thrilled to the intimacy of his mouth. She heard his sigh of pleasure before he took the kiss deeper, and she felt herself being caught up in feelings she had never known existed.

Her body strained against his, eager, pliant. Running his hands along her sides, he explored the narrow, slender hips, the tiny waist. When he encountered the swell of her breasts, his thumbs began to stroke, until he heard her little sigh of impatience.

Always before, these sensations frightened her. She had feared losing control. But now, hungry for more, she gave in to the pleasure his touch brought.

When his lips abruptly left hers, she felt bereft. But before she could protest, he brought his lips to her throat. He murmured words of endearment as he ran openmouthed kisses along the column of her throat, before dipping lower to the soft swell of her breast.

She gasped and clutched at him when his lips found her breast. Needs pulsed through her, and she felt warmth radiating through her veins, until she thought she would suffocate from the heat.

His fingers found the buttons of her shirt, and he slipped it from her shoulders and bent his lips to the ridge of her collarbone. His lips, his fingertips, followed the lacy edge of her chemise until he untied the ribbons that held it. With the rest of her clothes, it drifted to the floor about her feet.

"Abby, you're so beautiful." Drawing her close, he kissed her eyelid, her cheek, the corner of her mouth, then brought his lips lower to trail her neck, the hollow of her throat, her breast.

She shuddered. Heat seared her. She felt her knees buckle, and before she could fall he swept her up in his arms and carried her to the blanket. When he lay beside her, she reached for the buttons of his shirt. As her awkward fingers fumbled, he helped her, until they lay at last, mouth to mouth, flesh to flesh.

"Do you know how long I've wanted you?" He

buried his face in her hair and inhaled the wonderful fragrance of evergreen and forest that mingled with the woman scent of her.

"Oh, Rourke," she breathed against his neck, sending spasms of pleasure along his spine. "I don't know what to do. I've never loved a man."

"Shh." He touched his lips to hers, stilling her words. "There's nothing to know, Abby," he murmured, rubbing his lips across hers. "We'll take a journey together. We'll explore," he whispered, tracing a finger across her eyebrow, to the curve of her cheek, and then along the sweep of her jaw. "Together."

As his lips followed his fingertips, she relaxed, allowing the pleasure of his touch to soothe, caress. Steeped in pleasure, she felt warm and contented. But as his lips and fingertips moved lower, the warmth became heat.

He nibbled the slope of her shoulder and pressed kisses to the inside of her elbow, her wrist, her palm, until, hungry for his lips on hers, she drew his face back to hers. No longer content with just her lips, he brought his mouth lower, to taste her neck, and feel her pulsebeat at the hollow of her throat. Then his lips moved lower still, to tease and taunt her already erect nipples. Contractions began deep inside her, and she moaned and clutched at him, begging for release. But he had only begun. Moving lower, he explored the smooth flesh of her stomach, then lower still to the softness of her inner thigh. Before she could jerk away he kissed the back of her knee, and she began laughing.

"Oh, you think that's funny?"

"It tickles," she said, and laughed again as he continued kissing her leg, her ankle, the bottom of her foot. "Rourke, it tickles. Stop."

But he didn't stop. He ran his tongue along the sole of her foot until she yanked it away.

"So you want to play." Twisting, she caught his leg and tried to kiss the back of his knee, but he moved and she caught him at mid-thigh instead.

Her laughter died as her fingers began exploring the muscular, hairy leg. She had never before thought of touching a man like this. But he felt good. All of him, she realized, not just his arms, his lips. Explore, he had said. She suddenly realized she wanted to explore him as he had explored her.

Touching a fingertip to his chest, she moved over him and heard his little moan of pleasure. Beneath the nest of rough hair, beneath the warm flesh, she could feel the powerful muscles. "So strong," she murmured, running kisses across his rib cage. "And yet so tender."

"Just weak," he moaned. "You make me weak."

Bending, she brought her lips to the flat plain of his stomach. For the space of a heartbeat, she paused, wondering if she dared to be any bolder. But he had touched her in ways she had never dreamed of, and she longed to know all of him.

Slowly, tentatively, she moved her fingers lower. As her hand found him, he murmured words she couldn't hear. And then he dragged her against him, and his kisses were no longer gentle. Roughly he drew her head back and kissed her until she was breathless.

Needs, savage, driving needs pulsed through them. Gone was the delicious languor that had seeped through them only minutes ago. Now they were eager, agile, seeking.

He had wanted to be slow, to make this first time easy and gentle for her. But needs ripped through the last shred of his control, driving him to the brink of madness, until all he could think of was her.

When he took her, he felt her strong fingers clutch at his shoulders. At her little gasp, he covered her mouth with his. Slowly, fighting to bank his needs, he felt her begin to move, and he moved with her, allowing her to set the pace. He felt the wild rhythm of her heart keeping time to his.

For Abby, all thought ceased. Now there were only feelings. She had never known such feelings. His heartbeat was her own. His sighs, his moans, became her own voice. They moved in an ageless rhythm, and as needs drove her, she discovered a strength she had never known she possessed. She called his name, or thought she did. Clutching his shoulders, she soared higher, then higher still, until she felt as if she had touched the sun, and it had exploded inside her. She felt him follow her into the sunlight, and together they burst into tiny fragments.

He was part of her now. And she was part of him. They had given something precious, something very special to each other. Something they could never take back. And from this moment on, their lives would be forever changed.

Shuddering, she drifted on a cloud of liquid gold. She had left this western trail of pain and was suspended somewhere in the sky. And with her, locked in her arms, was the man she loved. No one else existed for her. No one else mattered now except Rourke.

Damp with sheen, still joined, he continued holding her. Slowly, languorously, he drew the blanket over them, then rolled to his side and cradled her to him.

As he bent to kiss her, he tasted her tears. "Oh, God, I've hurt you."

She smiled through her tears and brushed them away. Rubbing her lips over his, she whispered, "These were happy tears. You could never hurt me."

Drawing her close against him, he buried his face in her hair and fought back the little worries that nagged at the corner of his mind. He could hurt her, in ways she never dreamed. God, what had he done? He had no right to keep her with him. It only endangered her more.

She sighed and drew him closer, and he felt his worries slip away. At least for this night, she was warm, and safe. And loved. God forgive him, though he had no right, he loved her.

Chapter Twenty-nine

ABBY SHIFTED IN the blanket and felt an arm tighten about her waist, holding her close. Her lids flickered open and she found herself staring into Rourke's slate eyes.

How had she ever found his eyes cold? she wondered. They were liquid silver, and she could see herself reflected there.

"Good morning." She knew she would never tire of hearing that rough, scratchy voice in the morning.

She smiled and stretched, then snuggled close beside him. "How long have you been awake?"

"Hours I think. I was watching you sleep. You sleep like a baby. Peaceful. No fears."

She placed a finger over his lips. "I thought you were going to stop calling me a child."

He bit her finger and she laughed and pulled it away. "I haven't forgotten you're a woman. My woman," he growled, pulling her on top of him.

Her hair fanned out around him, drifting about his shoulders, kissing his cheek. Grabbing a handful, he stared at it, then at her. "My brave little fire woman."

Resting her chin on her hands, she stared down into his eyes. As his fingers began tracing the contours of her back, she shivered. "Do you know what your touch does to me?"

"I hope it's the same thing you're doing to me." She felt his hands move along the flare of her hips, then upward, to span her waist. For all time, he had left his fingerprints on her. She would know his touch even in the dark.

She was aware of his arousal, and of the look of desire in his eyes. It was a strange feeling to have such power over a man. Enjoying her newly discovered power, she shifted slightly and heard his little moan.

"You're a witch. You know that, don't you?"

She laughed and ran a hand over his scraggly growth of beard. "And you're a wild man. My wild mountain man."

She was so surprising. Soft when he expected her to be hard. Tough when he thought she'd fall apart. There was so much to learn about her. So much to share. Share. A strange thought to entertain. In his life, there was no room for sharing.

As he continued staring into her eyes, she smiled, a wicked, woman's smile. "Rourke, are you ignoring me?"

With a single fluid motion, he turned and pinned her beneath him. "Is this enough attention for you?"

Framing her face with his hands, he rubbed his lips across hers. Her lips parted for his kiss, but he paused, studying the look in her eyes.

How was it possible that he could want her again so desperately? All night they had loved, then dozed, then loved again, exploring each other's body with an urgency bordering on madness. They should be sated. But even while he'd watched her sleep, he'd been waiting impatiently for her to wake so he could see himself in her eyes once more.

He'd waited so long. Wanted so long. He stifled his needs, wanting to go slowly, to savor. All night, with lips and tongue and fingertips, he'd learned her texture. She was so small, so slender. But not fragile. He felt her strength and thrilled to it. No, this was no shy, shrinking female. She was curious, and bold, and as eager as he.

His mouth moved over hers, and the familiar heat spread through his limbs, leaving him by turns weak and then eager, almost frantic for more.

As the wind and snow raged against the mountains, Rourke and Abby lay in each other's arms, lost in a world of intense pleasure.

The blizzard lasted for nine days.

For Abby, these were the happiest of her life. Thanks to Rourke's cautious forays into the wilderness, they had food, shelter, and heat. And best of all, they had time. Time to explore each other's mind and body. Time to get to know each other slowly, intimately.

Rourke heard about her life on the farm, and her preacher grandfather, and the fragile Margaret, who had meekly tried to give James a son. And she told him about her father's deathbed admission, that she was not really his daughter at all, but Lily's. Abby told him what little she knew about the beautiful, strong-willed Lily, and Rourke realized from where Abby had inherited her indomitable strength.

He revealed little about himself. When Abby pressed, he described his home in Maryland and his loving parents. But hearing the pain in his voice, she decided not to pursue the subject. It obviously held some painful memories for him. And so she talked about her past, and what she hoped would be her future in California.

Rourke loved to listen to her. With that low, husky voice of hers and her youthful enthusiasm, he couldn't help but enjoy her. While she looked for new ways to prepare venison, he tended her torn, blistered hands and was pleased to see them slowly heal.

This was what home meant, Abby thought, as she watched him go about mundane chores. While he made repairs to the saddle and mended a bridle, he shared thoughts about this great country, about the opening of the west. The men in her life had never shared their thoughts before. And like a flower she opened to him, sharing secrets that until then had only been in her heart.

This was what love was, she realized. Not just a joining of two bodies, but two minds as well. They shared little intimacies that bound them ever closer. While they worked around the cave, Abby found herself humming little tunes from her childhood. Rourke would glance over, their gazes would meet, and each seemed to sense what the other was thinking. Their eyes would soften, with a gentle, knowing smile lifting the corners of their lips.

Rourke thought she'd never looked lovelier.

Abby thought he'd never looked so handsome.

And though Rourke never spoke of the war, or of his life in Maryland, she knew it was because the memories were too painful. Someday, she told herself. Someday, he would be able to put aside the pain. On that day, they would be free to share everything, both past and present.

The nights were meant for loving. While the storm continued to rage, and the fire burned to glowing embers, they lay together, warm, loving, content.

And the days. Abby had never before experienced the luxury of doing nothing more demanding than feed the horses and cook a simple meal. Lying beside Rourke, nestled deep in fur throws while morning light came stealing through the cave, was the sweetest of pleasures.

Watching her, Rourke felt a measure of contentment he hadn't known in years. When was the last time he'd lingered in bed, feeling the warmth of a woman's softness? If this was what heaven had in store for him, he'd willingly go to his death. He knew a happiness, a sense of joy he'd never thought would be granted him again in this life.

On the ninth day, Rourke returned from foraging and announced that the sky was once more clear. "The snow has stopped," he said, placing a log on the fire.

Abby felt her heart contract. If she could, she would have stayed here forever. Hoping her voice wouldn't betray her, she asked, "Will we leave tomorrow?"

He nodded his head, sensing her reluctance and sharing it. "It'll be slow going. We'll probably have to lead the horses. But we have to get out of here before the next blizzard or we could be trapped here until spring."

She felt her heart breaking. "That would be fine with me."

He stood, wiping his hands on his shirt. Turning, he saw the look on her face and drew her into his arms. "Don't fret, Abby. We still have tonight."

Tonight. The word echoed in her mind. One night. And then they would be forced to leave this haven and return to a world of pain and suffering. Tonight.

That night, they loved passionately, with a desperation born of the knowledge that in the morning, they would be on the trail once more. They clung together, holding on to this one last night of heaven before facing hell. As the first thin light of morning crept into the cave, they loved again, lingering over each other's lips, each other's bodies, with a kind of reverence. Afterward, they lay together, unwilling to let go.

"If we stay here long enough, those hands might even forget what calluses are," he murmured as he held her close.

"Would you like me better with soft lady hands?"

He lifted his head and studied her by the light of the dawn. Her hair spilled across the blanket like a splash of liquid fire. Her eyes were so green, they glowed like a cat's. Her skin, so pale in the flickering shadows, took his breath away. "There isn't a thing about you I would change, Abby," he breathed, running kisses along her throat. "I want you to remember that for all time. I love you just the way you are."

She went very still, her heart so filled it nearly burst. It was the first time he had said he loved her.

Rourke, too, stiffened. God, he loved her. He had always known he'd wanted her. But this was more than simply wanting. He loved her. Loved her with a passion that left him stunned and reeling.

He had not meant for it to go this far.

As if realizing his admission, Rourke sat up and turned away from her. Sitting up behind him, Abby brought her hands to his shoulders. "What's wrong? What have I done?"

He kept his back to her. His words, when he finally spoke, were low and quiet. "It isn't anything you've done, Abby. It's me."

"Is that all." She sighed, pressing herself close. Drawing her arms around his waist, she murmured, "I can't find a thing wrong with you. You're a perfect specimen."

He pried her hands loose and turned to face her. His features were grim. At the sight of him her smile faded.

When she tried to touch him, he caught her hand. "Abby, there are things about me you don't know."

She saw the look in his eyes and felt a stab of fear. The chilling look was back, giving his eyes the appearance of cold steel.

Don't tell me, her heart cried. Don't tell me anything I don't want to hear.

"I had no right to your love," he said gravely. When she started to protest, he touched a finger to her lips to silence her. "I took it because I was a starving man. But that's no excuse. I had no right to it."

"Why?"

He met her gaze. "I'm a wanted man."

345

"Wanted?" The pain in her heart grew, and she hugged her arms around herself. "What have you done?"

"I'm wanted for killing some men."

Her eyes widened. She waited for his denial. When it didn't come, she panicked. "We'll find a sheriff, or a marshal and explain the mistake. You're no killer."

"There is no mistake, Abby." Exerting rigid control, he didn't touch her. He had no right. "I killed them."

Her panic grew. He was so calm about it. So rational. "But you had to kill them, didn't you? It was self-defense. You had no choice."

His tone was low, patient, as if explaining to a child. "The choice was mine. I could have walked away. I chose to kill them."

She covered her face with her hands, trying to blot out his words. "Stop it, Rourke. Why are you doing this?"

"Because you have a right to know. I'm wanted by the law, Abby, and I had no right to drag you into this. When I see you safely to California, I'll get out of your life."

"I don't want you out of my life."

"You have no choice," he said. "And neither do I. I made my choice a long time ago."

She watched as he pulled on his clothes. Without looking at her, he began saddling the horses. She sat numbly watching him, unable to think, without the energy to move. The idyll had ended. Those days and nights of love were a lie. A pleasant diversion for him. But now, she thought, drawing the blanket around her, she had to face reality. They could have no future together. He was a man on the run.

How could she face the rigors of the trail after experiencing the joy of this place? How could she go back to being the person she'd been? She was changed. Rourke's love had changed her.

"Get dressed, Abby." She was startled by the tone of his voice. Looking up at his grim features, she felt a knife pierce her heart.

Mechanically she dressed and folded the blanket. Within an hour, they had packed their meager belongings behind his saddle. Stepping out into blinding sunshine, they began the tedious trek through the last snow-covered summits of the Sierra Nevadas.

By day they plodded through snow nearly waist high. At night they made camp wherever they could find shelter from the cold. A low hanging shelf of rock, lined with evergreen boughs and warmed by a fire, offered them a view of the night sky ablaze with millions of stars. They clung together, refusing to dwell on the pain of the past, or their fear of the future.

Another night they found the shell of an abandoned wagon. Their lovemaking was slow and gentle, as if they had all the time in the world. Later, while she lay in Rourke's arms and listened to the steady sound of his breathing, she tried to imagine what it would be like if this were their wagon, and they were heading to California to make a life together. Husband and wife. Though it was only a dream, it was one she would treasure.

On their last night Rourke made a lean-to of evergreen boughs against an outcropping of rocks. Inside, the warmth from the horses and the fire made it cozy. They clung together, neither of them willing to sleep. If they could, they would make this night last forever. They said little. Words were no longer needed. All that was needed was love. They had more than enough of that for a lifetime. But time. They both knew they had just run out of that.

They watched the gray light of dawn color the eastern sky. Without a word they dressed and saddled the horses. And wordlessly they began the descent along the narrow pass that led them from the mountain.

It had taken them almost two weeks to travel a scant fifty miles. To the two weary travelers, it had been a lifetime.

"There's your promised land, Abby."

She sat perfectly still in the saddle, staring at the lush valley that seemed to spread out as far as the eye could see.

"California." Why was there no joy in this?

Rourke smiled at the hushed, reverent way she spoke the word.

"I see a town." She pointed to the buildings in the distance.

Rourke had seen it too. She saw the way his eyes narrowed slightly.

"Will you be leaving me now?"

He admired the fact that she was trying so hard to be brave. Her voice had barely trembled.

"I'll go with you as far as the town and see you settled in before I go."

"Where will you go?"

He shrugged. "San Francisco, maybe."

"Why?"

"There are a lot of people there. I'm looking for a man."

"So you can kill him?" Abby wished the words hadn't tumbled out so quickly. But once spoken, they couldn't be taken back. She turned her head away.

Rourke nudged his horse closer and caught her chin between his thumb and finger. Forcing her head up, he met her gaze. "Yes, Abby. So I can kill him."

"Why? Why can't you just let it go? Why do you have to go on killing? When does it stop?"

"When I kill him," he said softly.

"No." She shook her head. "Then someone will want to kill you in return. And it will never end."

"Maybe," he said. "Maybe it won't end until he kills me. But I can't stop until it's done." He spurred his horse forward. "Let's get you to town."

It wasn't much of a town, she realized as they approached. A main street, lined with wooden buildings. A bank, a jail, a mercantile, a saloon, and beside it a hotel. On the far end of the street were the houses, one or two painted white, with fences around them. Most of them were weathered to a dull gray, with curtainless windows. But there were men and women and children, and Abby felt her spirits lifting as she saw the wagons and carts. People. They had returned to the land of the living.

They halted outside the saloon, and Rourke glanced around before dismounting.

"While you see about a room, I'll have a drink. Then we'll find a place where we can buy a real meal."

It warmed him to see Abby's smile.

He accompanied her to the hotel. After talking to the man at the desk, Abby followed him upstairs.

Rourke waited until they disappeared up the stairs, then made his way next door to the saloon. After studying the faces in the bar, Rourke took a seat against the back wall and ordered a whiskey. He drank it quickly, enjoying the rush of heat as the fiery liquid settled low in his stomach. Pouring a second drink, he sipped it slowly. When a cluster of men walked in and gathered around the bar, he set down the nearly full glass and studied each one. Satisfied that he didn't recognize any of them, he picked up the glass and finished his drink.

When Abby entered the saloon, Rourke saw the men turn and watch her. It wasn't just her beauty they were staring at, it was the way she looked in her ragged clothes. The thin fabric of his shirt strained against her rounded breasts. Her tiny waist was emphasized by the rope holding up the heavy blue pants.

Unbound, her hair spilled around her shoulders like a silken cloud. Realizing for the first time how she looked to others, Rourke cursed himself.

"Wait until you see the room, Rourke," Abby exclaimed when she reached the table. "It's a big room overlooking the town. And there's a real bed." She sighed.

"Come on." Rourke stood, hating the way the men were watching her. "We'll find a place to eat."

If she was surprised at his abruptness, she didn't show it. Taking his arm, she said, "The owner of the hotel told me they serve supper every day. It smelled wonderful. He also said there's a new lady in town who does sewing. But I'll have to find work first so I can afford to have a dress made. He said he knows of only one place that would hire me, but he didn't say what it was."

"I'll just bet he does," Rourke said through clenched teeth. Leading her through the doors of the saloon, he failed to notice the man standing alone at the far end of the bar. But the man watched him with keen interest.

Rourke turned toward the hotel. "Let's get that meal."

"Why are you so angry?" she asked as they took a seat in the hotel dining room.

"I am not angry."

"Then why are you scowling at me?"

"I am not scowling."

She touched a finger to the little furrow between his eyes. "That's a funny-looking smile."

"I just don't think you should go around dressed like that."

The hotel owner's wife ladled hot beef and gravy on each plate, then set a plate of warm bread on the table. When she walked away, Abby asked, "Like what?"

"Like that." He leaned across the table and hissed, "Wearing my old shirt and Union pants. You can

350

practically see through them they're so old and faded."

"It's all I have," she said logically.

"I know it, dammit, but you can't walk around town dressed like that."

"And I don't have any money to pay a dressmaker."

"I do." He handed her a wad of money. When she refused to take it, he dropped it on the table in front of her.

She eyed him suspiciously. "Where did you get the money?"

"I earned it," he said through clenched teeth. "Go on. Take it. I didn't steal it. I'm not a thief."

"I didn't say you were. Why are you giving it to me?"

"Because I want you to look as good as the other women of the town."

"You're ashamed of me." She pushed away from the table just as the lady returned with cups of coffee.

Both Abby and Rourke fell silent until the lady returned to the kitchen.

"I am not ashamed of you. But I want you to take this money."

"So you won't feel guilty when you leave me?"

Rourke flinched. Pushing back his chair, he said gravely, "Yes. I want you to take my money so I won't feel so rotten when I ride out of town. I want you to be dressed like a lady so every man in this town won't think you're cheap and desperate."

"Well you can take your damned money and . . ."

As they glanced toward the door, several men entered. One of them was wearing a badge.

"Is your name Daniel Rourke?" the man with the badge asked.

With a feeling of shock, Abby saw Rourke's hand go toward his gun. The sheriff took a step closer and pressed his gun against Rourke's chest.

"I wouldn't, if I were you. The men behind me have

orders to shoot you if you resist arrest. Now answer me."

"I'm Rourke."

Taking the gun from Rourke's holster, the sheriff said, "Daniel Rourke, you're under arrest for shooting down a band of men in Arizona Territory a year ago. Since Judge Feeny will be in town tomorrow, you'll stand trial immediately for your crime."

"How did you know me?" Rourke asked.

"A good citizen saw you in the saloon and recognized you from your poster. Fellow by the name of Flint Barrows."

The cluster of men parted and Abby and Rourke found themselves face-to-face with her old tormentor.

"Yes sir," Flint said nervously. "That's the man."

Abby glanced at Rourke's face and saw the repressed fury in his eyes. It was the first time she realized just how dangerous he could be. If he could, she had no doubt Rourke would kill Flint with his bare hands.

As Rourke lunged forward, three men grabbed him, pinning his arms stiffly at his sides.

"And this little lady's father asked me to look out for her. It was Rourke here who sullied her, so to speak," Barrows said, his eyes glittering.

"That's a lie," Abby shouted.

"And look at her now," Flint continued.

The men turned to study Abby.

"He's turned her into his harlot. No lady would allow herself to be seen like this."

Despite the men holding him, Rourke managed to break free long enough to grab the front of Flint's shirt and pull him close. Three men lunged and pinned his hands behind him. With his face just inches from Flint's, Rourke hissed, "You keep looking over your shoulder, Barrows. If there's any way on this earth to get free, I'll kill you for this."

While Abby watched in horror, the men dragged

Rourke back while the sheriff pressed a gun to his temple.

"Move along, Rourke," the sheriff said.

As if in a daze, Abby watched the group of men follow Rourke and the sheriff out the door.

Behind their backs, Flint shouted, "And don't you worry about Miss Abby Market, Rourke. I'll see that she's well taken care of."

"I'll take care of myself." Seeing the gleam in his eye, she snatched up the money from the table and rushed after the sheriff and his men. At the jail, she waited until Rourke was placed in a cell. Then, turning to the sheriff, she said, "May I visit with Rourke for a few minutes?"

The older man shrugged. He'd seen so many refugees from wagon trains passing through his town. Only the strong survived. And this young woman, though frightened and confused, displayed a rare inner strength.

"I'll give you five minutes, miss. No more."

She stood on one side of the bars. Rourke stood on the other.

"I want you to ride out of here," he said softly so the others wouldn't hear. "Take the money I gave you, and the horses, and ride. You can sell my horse in another town. It'll give you a stake."

"And what will you do for a horse?"

He gave a dry laugh. "When the trial is over, I won't be needing a horse."

Abby's heart stopped beating. Her features were ashen. "You think they'll hang you?"

"You can count on it. It will be the most exciting thing this little town has seen in years."

"Rourke." She grabbed his fingers through the bars, and the sheriff began walking toward them. Instantly she dropped her hands to her sides. "I can't leave you. There has to be a way to save you."

"You listen to me, Abby." His voice was hard.

"Flint Barrows won't rest until he sees us both dead. I don't mind dying. I've been half dead for years. But I can't stand knowing he's out there waiting to hurt you. You know what he has in mind. You know what he's already tried before. Now you get on your horse and ride out of here. And don't ever look back."

Don't look back. The words echoed in Abby's mind. Hadn't she promised herself she would never again look back, only forward?

"Time's up, miss," the sheriff said, walking closer.

Rourke studied Abby's grim features and wondered if she had listened to a single word he'd said.

She gave him one last glance, then turned and walked from the room.

Behind her, Rourke gripped the bars until his knuckles were white. Why had he spoiled their last hour together with that silly, useless argument over clothes? Why hadn't he told her the only thing that mattered? That he loved her. More than life itself.

Chapter Thirty

ROURKE HAD BEEN right about one thing. This trial was the most excitement this little town had seen in years. The courthouse was packed to the rafters with the good citizens, eager for the spectacle of a tough territorial judge and a cold-blooded killer.

Abby pushed her way through the crowd and took a seat on a wooden bench in the front row. Still dressed in Rourke's old shirt and Union pants, she caused heads to turn. She was oblivious to the curious stares. She had eyes only for the man who was led, hand-cuffed, into the room.

He glanced up and their gazes met and held. She smiled weakly and swallowed back the tears she felt at the sight of him.

Rourke knew he ought to be furious with her for staying. But he felt a wave of relief that she had survived the night. The only thing he cared about now was Abby's safety. His own life was now in the hands of others. And he could sense their lust for blood.

While the bailiff read the charges against Rourke, Abby glanced around the room. Every bench was filled, and people stood in aisles and corners. Those who couldn't fit inside the building stood outside near windows, eager to hear everything that was said.

Abby saw Flint Barrows and felt a little shudder pass through her. Last night the hotel owner had told her someone was asking for her. He had given the man her room number. She knew it was Flint, and she knew what he planned to do. To evade him, she spent the night in the stable with the horses. The hay was clean and dry, and she had covered herself with Rourke's blanket. Somehow, she felt closer to him there. And she had no doubt that the stable was infinitely safer than the hotel.

She turned to study the judge and jury, and missed seeing the tall, thin young man who stood at the back of the courtroom. But he had seen her. Thunderstruck, he hurried away to share his news.

"Daniel Rourke." Abby glanced toward the gray-haired judge who was speaking. "You have been charged with deliberately following and killing four men in Arizona Territory one year ago. These men, a jury of your peers, will determine your fate. The bailiff will now hear your oath to speak only the truth in this court of law."

Abby leaned forward as Rourke was led before the judge, where he swore to tell the truth. When he was seated facing the jury, the packed courtroom fell silent.

"You served in the Union army, sir?" the judge asked.

"I did." Rourke's voice was firm and strong.

"In what capacity?"

"I was a captain."

"Captain? How did you come by that rank?"

Abby glanced around at the faces of those nearby. All were watching and listening intently.

"I took my training at West Point."

"West Point?" The judge studied Rourke for long, silent minutes. "Are you related to General John Edward Rourke?"

"He was my father."

The crowd gasped. He had been a decorated war

356

hero, who, because of his brilliance and fair treatment, was admired by both sides in the war.

"Were you honorably discharged from the army, sir?"

Rourke nodded. "I was."

The judge's eyes narrowed slightly. "And yet a man from a fine military family, educated at West Point, who served his country honorably, has deliberately trailed and murdered four men in cold blood?"

Rourke remained silent, staring straight ahead.

"I see no remorse in you, Captain Rourke. And so I must probe further." The judge cleared his throat. "From the documents before me, I see that you are married."

"I was."

Abby's mouth opened, then closed. Why had it never occurred to her that Rourke could have a wife? She felt a cold ribbon of fear around her heart.

"Was." The judge paused a moment. "Your wife is dead?"

"She is."

"Do you have children, Captain Rourke?"

"I had one son. He is dead also."

Abby thought of the tenderness Rourke had shown Timmy Garner, and she swallowed back the cry that sprang to her lips. Dear God. A wife and son. Both dead. And he had never been able to bring himself to tell her.

"How did your wife and son die, Captain Rourke?"

Along with the crowd, Abby strained to hear his response.

"They were brutalized and murdered." His voice nearly broke. He clenched his hands together tightly, fighting for control.

The crowd began murmuring. Abby's heart ached for him. There was nothing she could do to make this easier. He was being forced to bare his pain in front of a mob of strangers.

Banging his gavel, the judge glared at the spectators,

then turned toward Rourke. "Continue, Captain. Tell us in your own words what happened."

Except for a narrowing of his eyes, Rourke showed no further emotion. His hands were grasped firmly together, the knuckles white. In a clear voice he said, "I returned from the war to find my buildings and crops burned to the ground, my livestock stolen. And down by the creek, I found the bodies of my wife and infant son. Their bodies had been"—he swallowed and the word came out in a whisper—"mutilated."

The crowd gasped.

"Did you know who did these things, Captain?"

"I knew. I had been trailing them for weeks. They left a trail of death and destruction wherever they passed."

"And who were these men?"

"The Borders brothers, James and Jarold, who had deserted the army, and three other men who joined them along the trail whose names I never learned."

"Was it your job to find these men and return them to the army?"

"No, it was not."

"But you were trailing them. Why?"

"I was heading home. I came across the first grisly murder on my way. They and I seemed to be heading in the same direction."

"But you continued trailing them. I ask you again, Captain. Why?"

Rourke's voice lowered. "Because I was sick of the killing. There had been enough of it, too much of it in the war. It had to end."

"Did you know they were heading toward your home?"

Rourke hesitated. "I didn't know. I feared they might be. But though I rode all night, I didn't manage to overtake them."

"And so you found the destruction of your land and the . . . remains of your family?"

Rourke nodded.

"After you discovered the bodies of your wife and son, did you feel you had a right to track down these men without being given that authority by the law?"

Rourke glanced at the judge. His eyes were cold. "I needed no one to tell me I had that right. I swore when I found them I would kill them."

A murmur went up through the crowd. Angrily the judge slammed the gavel down on his desk.

"How do you know that the men you killed were the ones who killed your wife and son?"

"They left a very distinctive trail. Two of the horses, belonging to the Borders brothers, had nail heads that formed a little cross. That made it possible to trail them to the ends of the earth if necessary. Besides their horses' tracks, they left another trail."

"And what was that?"

"They enjoyed killing, especially women and children. Though I was only miles behind them, they managed to kill six more times before I caught up with them."

"Where did you finally catch them, Captain?"

The rapt audience strained to hear every word.

"In Arizona Territory. They were holed up in a shack. When I burst in on them, they had a young Indian girl. No more than ten or twelve." Rourke glanced down at his hands, and for a moment the crowd shuffled uneasily. "I shot the Borders before they knew what hit them. One of the others grabbed the girl and held a knife to her throat. I shot him where he stood. A fourth attacked me with a club. We scuffled. He wrenched my gun from me and shot me. I retrieved my gun. I managed to drop him on the third shot."

"What about the fifth man?" the judge asked.

"He got away while I was fighting with the others. I never saw his face. But I can still identify him."

"And how is that?" the judge asked.

"He had his clothes off when I first came through the door. He was"—Rourke glanced toward the judge, then away—"abusing the Indian girl. He has a dark, wine-colored birthmark on his back, shaped like a diamond."

The crowd erupted into a loud chorus of voices. Glancing around sharply, Judge Feeny rapped the gavel.

"Are you still trailing this man?" the judge asked.

"I've never stopped." Rourke said simply.

"You realize that you have no authority to track a criminal. You are neither sheriff, marshal, nor bounty hunter."

Rourke remained silent.

"What happened to the Indian girl?"

Rourke swallowed. "She begged me to kill her. Said her tribe would never take her back. The Borderses had carved her face with a knife when she resisted them."

The crowd went deathly silent.

"Did you comply with her wish, Captain?"

Rourke let out a long stream of breath. "I wish I could have. I'll never know what happened to her. But I couldn't bring myself to kill an innocent."

"What did you do with the bodies of the men you killed?" the judge asked.

"I left them in the shack. There was no time to return them to the authorities. I wanted to stay on the trail of the man who escaped."

"Did you notify the authorities that you had killed the Borders brothers and the other two men?"

Rourke shook his head. "I did not."

"Why not?" the judge asked.

The room was so still, a child's laughter could be heard filtering through the open window. It sounded strangely out of place in this tense courtroom.

"Because I was not working for the authorities. I was seeking revenge for the murder of my wife and child. I figured the proper authorities would know soon enough about the Borderses' death when the killing stopped."

"And has the killing stopped?" Judge Feeny asked. Rourke shook his head.

"Do you have anything more to say on your behalf, Captain Rourke?"

Rourke glanced around the courtroom until his gaze came to rest on Abby. Though she showed little emotion, her eyes were red-rimmed. What a terrible way for her to learn the truth about him, he thought, hating himself.

"I killed four of the men who tortured my wife and baby. And if I ever get the chance to kill the fifth, I will. I have no remorse. If I had to do it again, I would."

The men who formed the jury had sat impassively, listening to Rourke's narrative. Even now, when his testimony was completed, they tried to hide their true feelings. But to Abby and other spectators it was obvious. Many of them had lost sons to the war. Many had returned from the war to find their own families scattered, their land lost. And many of them had witnessed or heard about the brutality of some of the deserters. The infamous Quantrills had made the war an excuse for looting and killing. More than one man in the jury brushed a tear from his eye.

As Rourke stepped down from the chair and returned to the rough table to await his sentence, a man rushed from the crowd and grasped Rourke's hand.

"I fought under you at Antietam, Captain Rourke. Avery's my name. I saw my comrades fall, and I saw you take both bullet and bayonette. But you fought bravely, sir. And you inspired all of us."

"Order." The judge pounded the gavel. "Bailiff, remove that man from the room."

The man went willingly. But the spectators who remained had heard his glowing words. The men of the jury had heard him as well and were touched by the tribute. As they clustered around, talking, arguing, Abby kept her gaze fixed on Rourke. How he had suffered. And he had kept all this pain locked inside.

If possible, she loved him even more, now that she knew of his private hell. She longed to go to him, to put her arms around his neck and rock him, to whisper that she loved him more than ever now that she knew the truth about him.

But all she could do was sit quietly, watching the back of his head, and pray.

When the jury nodded to the judge, he banged his gavel. The murmuring of the crowd died. Even the people outside the room strained at the windows.

"How have you decided?" the judge asked the jury foreman.

The owner of the mercantile stood. "We've decided that the murder of the band of killers was justifiable. Any one of us would have done the same. We find Captain Daniel Rourke not guilty."

Most of the crowd broke into applause. Some hooted and whistled, until the judge banged his gavel and called for silence or he would clear the courtroom.

In his sternest voice, he said, "Captain Rourke, you have been found not guilty by a jury of your peers. I concur with their decision. But I must warn you. Revenge is a poison that can choke the life of the man who continues to nurture it. I sympathize with your loss. But you must let go of this vendetta. Or it will color all your life."

Rourke stepped forward and shook the judge's hand. Then, seeing the crowd rushing forward to shake his hand and pat him on the back, he pushed his way through and caught Abby in a bear hug.

"I'm free, Abby. Free."

As he held her, she felt the band around her heart break loose. She began to sob, great gulping sobs that tore at his heart. She didn't bother to check the tears. She had never known such blessed joy in her life. She pushed aside the little fear that nagged at the corner of her mind. How could he be truly free as long as one of the men who had killed his wife and child was still out there, taunting his dreams, tearing at his heart?

"Yes, you're free," she whispered. "Free to go home to Maryland at last."

His eyes narrowed. "I no longer have a home in Maryland. I can never go back. The trail has become my home."

Abby felt a fresh wave of tears. How she longed to make a home for him. How she wished she could make up for all the pain and suffering.

"I want to leave this town now," he said, leading her toward the door. "Before I have to see that scum, Barrows. Or they'll be forced to hold another trial for me."

"Abby!"

At the sound of that familiar voice, Abby could only stare in stunned silence. Standing in the middle of the crowd was a beloved figure from her past.

"Will said you were here. I couldn't believe it. I had to see for myself."

"Carrie?"

Rourke stood aside as Abby flung herself into her sister's arms. While the two tearfully embraced, Rourke and Will shook hands.

"Looks like marriage agrees with you," Rourke said, taking Will's measure. The boy seemed to have grown even taller, though he hadn't put on any weight.

"She's a good enough cook," Will said shyly. "And the best seamstress in California."

"You're the new seamstress?" Abby hugged her sister, then stood back to study her.

There was a fullness to Carrie that hadn't been there before. And a soft inner beauty.

"You look beautiful, Carrie."

"Thank you." The younger girl wrapped an arm around Will's waist, and he casually dropped his arm across her shoulders. "Maybe it's the baby."

"A baby?" For some unknown reason, Abby was weeping again. She didn't seem able to stop herself. "You and Will are having a baby?"

The young couple smiled at each other, and Abby thought she'd never seen a happier pair.

"Oh, Carrie. Will. That's just wonderful." She hugged them both, then glanced shyly at Rourke. "We were going to leave, but now that I've just found you again, I have to stay long enough to see where you live. There's so much to catch up on."

Seeing the question in her eyes, Rourke nodded. "I'll go to the stable and get our horses." Turning to Will, he said, "Just tell me where you live. I'll bring the horses around when I'm ready."

"We're the last house in the row," Will said, pointing to a neatly whitewashed house at the end of the street.

Carrie and Abby, arm in arm, were already strolling along the street. Rourke watched as Will walked along behind them. Turning, he made his way to the stable.

Watching from a hotel room, a lone figure waited until Rourke had gone inside the stable. Then the figure turned and picked up a shirt. Sunlight streaming through the window glinted on a wine-colored birthmark, shaped like a diamond. Pulling on the shirt, the figure picked up a gunbelt and checked his guns carefully. Then he slipped out the door and headed toward the stable.

Chapter Thirty-one

PULLING OPEN THE stable door, Rourke shouted for the owner. There was no reply. Probably at the courthouse, Rourke thought. Practically everyone in town was there. After the trial the citizens had continued to mill about, gossiping, visiting. Many of them would probably neglect their chores for the rest of the day.

Walking the length of the barn, he found the horses and began saddling Abby's mount first.

He should be feeling as if the worries of a lifetime had just been lifted from him. Wasn't he free at last? Why then this nagging feeling that nothing had changed? Because, he realized with sudden clarity, he couldn't let go of the past yet. There was still a man out there who had raped and brutalized his beautiful, helpless Katherine. A man who could toss a helpless infant into a stream as easily as if he were a rag doll. A man who was nothing more than an animal. A crazed animal who had to be put to death.

Recalling the judge's words of warning, Rourke paused in his work. The judge was right. Revenge was a terrible poison. But he couldn't stop himself. It wouldn't be put to rest until the last man was found and punished. Only then would the dreams stop tormenting him.

He tightened the cinch, then lifted the saddle to his own mount. Deep in thought, he didn't hear the door to the stable open. It wasn't until he felt the cold steel of the pistol against his temple that he realized his mistake.

"Oh, Carrie, it's beautiful." Abby sighed as she followed her sister about the rooms of the little house. "I can't believe it yet. Your very own place. With room to sew dresses for all the ladies in town."

They stood in the middle of the parlor, which Carrie had turned into a sewing room. There were baskets of fabric and lace, and tables covered with patterns. In the corner was Aunt Vi's little chest, containing her treasure of ribbons and scraps of fabric.

"We love this town. Will sees a real future for us here. He's been scouting the fertile valleys nearby where they claim a man can own as much as he can clear and harvest. And with Will out in the fields all day, it gives me something to do. Aunt Vi knew how much I loved to sew. I'm so glad she urged me to follow my heart."

At Abby's nod of approval, Carrie said, "This is the dress all the ladies in town have been dying to buy." She proudly lifted a green gown from a wooden peg.

"Oh." Abby touched a hand to the lush green satin trimmed with delicate roses and pale green leaves about the softly draped neckline and gathered skirt. "Carrie, I think it's just about the most beautiful gown I've ever seen."

"I made it for you."

Abby could only stare at her sister. "How could that be? You didn't even know you'd ever see me again."

"I knew," Carrie said softly. "I always knew I'd see you again. And when I did, I wanted to have this dress ready for you. It's the gown I'd always pictured you wearing." She laughed, that clear, childish laugh that

Abby had always loved. "You ought to be married in this, you know."

"Who'd marry me?" Abby scoffed. But her heart had already leaped at the thought.

"Rourke. His feelings are there in his eyes every time he looks at you."

Abby blushed, making Carrie laugh even more. "You can't hide a thing like that from me. It's in your eyes too."

The two girls fell into each other's arms again, and then Carrie steered her sister toward the bedroom. "Come on. You're going to wash off the grime of the trail and try on the gown I made for you. And while you do, you're going to tell me all about Pa and Aunt Vi and everyone else from the train."

Abby went very still, wondering how to tell her little sister. She started with the good news about Aunt Vi, then ended with the cholera and their father's death. By the time Abby had told Carrie about the massacre in the Sierras, and about her father's admission that she was really Lily's daughter, she and Carrie had shed a hundred tears.

"But we've found each other again," she whispered, clinging to Carrie as she wept. "And you and Will are happy. It's all I ever wanted for you."

When Will entered, the two girls looked up.

"You mean Rourke hasn't come with the horses?" he asked.

Alarmed, Abby said, "We were so busy talking we forgot the time."

"I'll go find him," Will offered.

"No." Abby touched his arm. "You stay with Carrie. I'll go to the stable."

"Hurry back," Carrie called as her sister ran to the door. "I'll have supper ready."

Proudly wearing her new gown, Abby paraded past the shops and stores, feeling the stares of the people of the town. When she passed the hotel, she peered inside. The men from the jury were having supper, along with most of the men from town. There was a festive air, as people celebrated the end of an exciting trial.

When she came to the stable, she was surprised to find the door closed and bolted from the inside.

Pounding on the door, Abby shouted. "Rourke. Are you in there? Rourke, it's me. Open up."

She felt a tiny thread of fear. What if he'd left without telling her? Her heart denied it immediately. He wouldn't do such a thing. He wouldn't.

"Rourke."

Just as she lifted her fist to pound again, the door was thrown open and she was yanked inside. The door slammed shut and she heard the bolt shoved into position. As her eyes adjusted to the dim light, she realized that she was staring at a gun pointed at her head. And the man holding the gun was Flint Barrows.

"Flint." She saw the evil grin on his face and felt her heart plummet. "Where is Rourke?"

"Your handsome lover is over here," he said, jerking her roughly by the arm.

As they rounded a stall, she came to an abrupt halt. Her heart nearly stopped beating.

Rourke was sitting astride his horse, his arms tied behind him, a noose, tied to a wooden beam, around his neck. His handkerchief had been stuffed into his mouth to keep him from warning her.

"Now isn't this cozy?" Flint said. "We have the man who killed my brothers and the lady he loves."

"Your . . . brothers?" Abby felt her head spinning. What was happening here. None of this made any sense.

"The two men traveling with the Borders brothers happened to be my brothers, Ben and Carl."

"The Borderses," Abby muttered, stalling for time, "and the Barrowses?"

"That's right. The famous Barrows brothers."

"But there were three men traveling with them."

Flint laughed, and Abby felt her nerves tighten. "My two brothers and me."

"You"—she moistened lips gone suddenly dry—"were with them when they killed Rourke's wife and baby?"

"Now aren't you the smart one? You figured that out all by yourself." Flint laughed again, and Abby found herself staring into the eyes of a madman.

Flint slapped at Rourke's mount, causing the horse to sidestep. The noose around Rourke's neck tightened, forcing him to sit higher to keep from being strangled.

"Let him go, Flint," Abby pleaded.

"Now why should I do that? It would spoil all the fun." His voice lifted to a screech. "I've had a long time to plan this. I used to lie awake nights thinking how I'd get even with the man who killed my brothers. Course," he added with a sly smile, "I didn't know the gunman on our wagon train was the man I was looking for. I was busy with a little Indian kid when he burst in on us. All I saw was a blue uniform and the flash of a gun. But when I saw that wanted poster with Captain Daniel Rourke's name on it, I managed to put it all together. And his testimony at the trial filled in the last gaps. Now that I know who he is, I intend to have my revenge."

Her mind raced. She had to get Rourke down from there before Flint carried out his threat to hang him. She forced her voice not to waver. Attempting to sound seductive, she said, "Let him go and I'll give you anything you want."

Flint threw back his head and roared. "Honey, I'm going to have what I want anyway. You don't have to give. I'll just take. Hell, taking's half the fun."

Glancing up at Rourke, he gave him a satanic grin. "Now I'm going to show you what I did to your wife before I killed her. Cause I want you to suffer a long time before you die." Pressing the gun to Abby's throat, he said, "Take off that pretty dress, Miss Abby Market."

"No."

Still grinning, Flint slapped at Rourke's mount again, causing the horse to back away. The noose around Rourke's neck tightened.

Flint's smile vanished. "Now you strip, lady, or your lover's going to swing."

With trembling fingers Abby unbuttoned the gown and slipped it from her shoulders.

From his position on the horse, Rourke watched with a feeling of helpless rage. It wasn't enough that he had been forced to endure visions of Katherine all these nights. Now he would have to spend a lifetime seeing Abby's face as well. For the rest of his life he would hear her cries while this madman had his way.

As Abby slid the gown from her shoulders, Flint moved closer. "You're even prettier than I expected. It's going to be fun watching that creamy skin melt at my touch." He turned toward the man on the horse. "I'll take it slow and easy so you get plenty of time to watch, Rourke."

With his head turned, Flint didn't see the movement as Abby slid her hand into the pocket of her gown and withdrew the little handgun. When Flint turned toward her, his eyes widened in shock and surprise.

"Why you little . . ."

As he lunged she fired. He fell against her and she fired again, then leaped to one side as his body crashed to the floor.

For long moments she stared down at the figure slumped on the floor of the stable. Then she stared at the gun in her hands.

"You once told me to keep it with me at all times." She gave a shaky little laugh, and Rourke feared she might become hysterical. "I'm a fast learner. And once I learn something, I never forget."

Stepping around the body on the floor, she stared up at Rourke. Then, in a tight, little voice, she said, "Now I'm a killer too, Rourke. As much a killer as you."

Lowering his head, he moaned softly. What had he done? Dear God, what had he done to Abby?

With trembling fingers she cut Rourke's hands free, and then the noose.

Before he could even comfort her they heard footsteps running toward the stable and the sound of voices raised. When Rourke opened the door, and the sheriff and a crowd from the town rushed in, Abby was standing in the middle of the room, one trembling hand holding the front of her gown closed, the other still holding the gun.

Rourke longed to go to her and just hold her. But half the town was standing there, staring at her as if she were mad.

At Rourke's insistence, Abby was escorted back to her sister's while he went to the jail to give the sheriff an account of the incident. Dazed, Abby allowed herself to be led away.

Out of habit, Rourke sat at the rear table of the saloon. He downed the whiskey in one swallow, then poured another.

What had he done to Abby? He tipped his head back and drank. Made a killer of her, that's what he'd done. Hadn't she said as much?

Several of the townspeople glanced his way but, seeing the dark scowl on his face, decided to leave him to his own company. Rourke wasn't the kind of man you pushed.

Seeing her in that goddamned gown had only made it harder to bear. There she was, looking like some kind of a dream, and he had to watch her being tormented by scum like Barrows. Helpless. He'd been completely helpless. All he could do was watch. Watch her defend herself. Watch her kill Flint Barrows. And then watch her endure the stares of the townspeople.

She deserved so much better.

He poured another drink, drank it, then corked the bottle and stood. He'd take the rest with him for the trail.

Stowing the bottle in his gear, he mounted and rode to Carrie and Will's little house. As he walked to the front door, he steeled himself. He would make it quick and final.

Abby opened the door at his first knock.

"Come in."

He shook his head. "What I have to say is better said out here."

Puzzled, Abby stepped onto the porch and pulled the door shut behind her.

Rourke studied her in the glow from the windows. He felt his throat go dry. For a moment the air rushed from his lungs, leaving him speechless. How had he ever thought her skinny? How could she have ever considered herself plain? She was stunning. A riot of fiery curls spilled about her cheeks and danced on her shoulders. She was wearing the new gown, which nearly matched her eyes. Embroidered roses and little velvet leaves competed with the creamy skin of her throat and bare shoulders. It showed off her tiny waist and displayed enough rounded flesh at the bosom to make his heart pump a little faster. No man could ever dismiss her beauty. A man could kill for her. Or fall to his knees and beg. If, he thought with a pang, the man had a right. She deserved a man who could offer her everything. A home. Family. A future.

"Will and Carrie are waiting for you inside."

"I'm not staying."

"We're going? Tonight?"

He fought to keep his tone even. "I'm going. You're staying here."

"Staying? Why?"

"Because this is where you belong, Abby. You've made it to California. You've found your sister. Family. That's important to you."

"You're important to me," she said, feeling the panic rise. This couldn't be happening. He wouldn't leave her after all they'd been through.

"You think I'm important, because you're grateful that I brought you here. But this is what's really important to a woman like you, Abby. Home, family. Look at you." His voice rose and he cursed himself. This was no time to get emotional.

"What's wrong with me?"

"Nothing. That's just the point. You look so perfect, wearing a grand dress, standing on a porch. This is what you need. A home. A family. A white picket fence. With me, all you'll ever get is moving on, looking for a better place. All I can ever give you is a hard trail and a cold meal."

"I'll settle for that."

"No. Dammit, listen to me. You deserve the best. You deserve better than I can ever give you. That's why I'm leaving. And that's why you're staying here. You deserve a whole man, Abby. One who isn't haunted by the past. One who can give you a bright future. I'm only half a man. And I don't think I'll ever be whole again."

"Rourke, I . . ."

He turned his back on her, cutting her off. He couldn't bear to hear her speak words of love. It was like cutting out his heart to leave her. But it was for her own good. If he really loved her, he had to let her go. She would find a good steady man in this town and live like her sister. Like a lady. It was all he could give her.

Pulling himself into the saddle, he kept his face averted. He couldn't bear to look at her. It would hurt too much.

Abby watched as horse and rider started along the street. She'd once told him she could take care of herself. And so she would, she thought, as tears threatened to cloud her vision.

Behind her the door opened. Carrie and Will, listening at the door, had heard everything.

It was Carrie who broke the silence.

"Are those tears?"

Angrily, Abby wiped at her eyes. "Of course they are. When I'm hurt I cry. What do you think I am, a mule?"

"I used to think you were," her little sister admitted. "I used to think you and Pa were cut from the same cloth. But now I realize you're a woman. A woman in love. Now what do you intend to do about it?"

"What can I do?" Abby moaned. "He's left me because he thinks he's only half a man."

Carrie and Will shared a knowing look.

"I fell in love with a man who thought he was only half a man too," Carrie said softly. "And I had to prove to him that I loved him so much, his missing arm made no difference."

"And with Carrie's love," Will added, "I realized I was whole again."

"I don't see what that has to do with Rourke."

"Don't you?" Carrie smiled at her sister. "Maybe his heart is broken because you hold the other half. And if you're the woman I think you are, you ought to be able to convince Rourke that he's never going to be whole again without you."

"But how?"

"That's up to you," Carrie said, kissing her sister's cheek. "You'll think of something."

Abby watched as the shadowy figure of man and

horse moved further along the street. Soon they would be leaving the town behind.

Grabbing up the hem of her skirt, Abby started running, and cursed her clumsiness. What she needed were her old britches and shirt and a sturdy pair of boots.

She shouted Rourke's name, but he never stopped, never slowed down. Running faster, she passed the stable, the mercantile, the hotel, the saloon. As she passed the jail, she found herself running out of breath. Soon, very soon now, he'd leave her in his dust.

"Rourke." She shouted at the top of her lungs, but the figure on horseback continued at a steady pace.

"Damn you, Rourke," she shrieked.

Pulling the gun from her pocket, she aimed and fired, sending his hat flying.

Stunned, he wheeled his horse and drew his gun.

Everyone in the saloon came running into the street to watch the gunfight. From the jail, the sheriff came running, carrying a shotgun.

Seeing Abby, Rourke's eyes narrowed. "What the hell's the matter with you, woman?"

"It's about time you called me a woman," she said.

"You nearly killed me."

"If I'd wanted you dead, you'd be lying on the ground right now. Next time, I'll part your hair so neat you'll never have to comb it again."

Rourke thought about Mordecai's story around the campfire and felt the beginnings of a smile.

"All right, what is this about?" the sheriff called, running between them.

"Rourke says he's leaving without me. I say he isn't."

"What do you intend to do about it," Rourke asked, "hold me here against my will?"

"No. You're taking me with you."

"Why should I?"

"Because I love you. Because Aunt Vi said that when I found a man I loved, I should never let him get away. And because you love me too, Rourke. You're just too dumb yet to know it."

Everyone in the crowd began laughing.

Rourke's eyes narrowed. Moving closer, he reached down and dragged her roughly into his arms. "Why would I love a woman with a hair-trigger temper who goes around shooting at me?"

"And why would I love a man who may never settle down? Who can't offer me anything better than a cold meal and a rough trail?"

"Why?" he asked, drawing her closer.

"Because we're both too dumb to know better," she murmured, shoving the gun deep into her pocket.

"Looks like I'm stuck with you."

"Stuck." She wrapped her arms around his neck. "Hell, Captain Daniel Rourke. We make a good team and you know it."

He swallowed back the smile that threatened. "I know one thing. If you ever call me Daniel again, I'll put you over my knee. The name's Rourke." He threw back his head and roared. "Just plain Rourke. And we're changing your name to Abby Rourke just as fast as we can find a preacher. Then it'll be too late for you to change your mind."

Abby brought her lips close to his, feeling the familiar tingle that always began when he touched her. "I don't care where we go, or what we do, Rourke, as long as we're together. I'm never going to change my mind about that."

His mouth came down on hers, hard, bruising. Everything he felt, all the love, all the longing, all the passion, were conveyed in that kiss.

The sheriff and townspeople watched as the two figures rode off into the darkness.

From their porch, two young people smiled, and

watched until the figures disappeared. Then, arm in arm, they walked inside their little house.

Home, Abby thought, clinging tightly to Rourke, as the night wind tousled her hair. Home was just another name for love. And the three Market women had found enough for a lifetime.